Powerfully moving, revealing of world politics, in this first novel of a series, Coleen W. Cain describes the pitfalls and agonies faced by young women and their men in World War II.

Wrapped in her dreams of an exalted place in the art and political worlds, Paula Ann Roncourt still considers having a family as her instinctive right. She believes that as the family fares, so fares the nation.

Death and sacrifice are absolutes in the overwhelming effort to save America. Influenced by President Franklin D. Roosevelt, Paula drops out of the University of Texas, where she studies Art. She takes a job as secretary to the Commanding Officer at Goodfellow Air Corps Base in San Angelo, her hometown. She won't marry until after the war.

Paula's bosom friend, Adele Turner, is betrayed by a northern serviceman who passes off as white. Paula saves the day, but is grieved at the loss of her friend, who moves to Dallas with her family.

Strong in her convictions that a family must have a father, a crash at Goodfellow causes Paula to change her mind and marry 2nd Lt. Garner Cameron, pilot, even though she knows that half of the combat pilots are killed.

Garner is shot down and ditches over the English Channel. He recovers in the hospital, but is later reported Missing in Action. With the help of the Dutch underground, he finds the U.S. Army and is given a Home Leave. Against Paula's wishes, he volunteers for B-29 training and the Pacific Theater. It is for this reason he denies her the privilege of becoming 'fragrant.' She is left alone to face the treacherous future.

Wild Blue

Also by Coleen W. Cain

Fiction

115 Jet Stories For Your Briefcase

Nonfiction

Beth Bauer's Enjoy China More
90 Minute Audio Cassette, Enjoy China More,
voiced by the author, includes Glossary

Wild Blue

World War II Novel
First of a Series

Coleen W. Cain

FirstPublish
A Division of the Brekel Group, Inc.
control your own destiny

Copyright © 2002 by Coleen W. Cain
All rights reserved. Printed in the United States of America.
No part of this publication may be reproduced, stored in
a retrieval system, or transmitted, in any form or by any
means, electronic, mechanical, photocopying, recording,
or otherwise, without the prior written permission of the author.

ISBN
1-931743-02-9

10 9 8 7 6 5 4 3 2 1

Library of Congress Cataloging in Publication Data
2001095636

Coleen W. Cain
Wild Blue

FIRSTPUBLISH
A Division of the Brekel Group, Inc.
300 Sunport Lane
Orlando, FL 32809
407-240-1414
www.firstpublish.com

Dedication

For my son and his peers, the Baby Boomers.

Acknowledgments

My heartfelt thanks go to each member of the Writer's Critique Group at the Mercer Island Community Center under the leadership of Judy Boynton. This novel could not have been written without their help.

Typical of their generosity were the comments made by Jan Gill, who taught me to infuse emotion, and Gail Haines, who exemplified precision. The male perspective, which was critical in the development of the novel, was also given by Jack Evans, Peter Kahle, Ray Cox and Joe Bice.

Special enlightenment has also come from my friend, Ward Carter, former World War II pilot who flew over the hump of Burma into China. His critique and comments have made all the difference, bringing details to perfection. I'm forever grateful, Ward.

PART ONE

PAULA AND GARNER

Chapter One

Outraged and sorrowful, the souls of one hundred thirty million Americans shivered in shock.

On this Sunday afternoon at three o'clock, December 7, 1941, Paula Ann Roncourt, studying at the small desk in her women's dormitory room, paused at the interruption of music turned low on the radio over NBC.

> WE INTERRUPT THIS PROGRAM FOR THE FOLLOWING BULLETIN. IN A SNEAK ATTACK, JAPANESE WAR PLANES HAVE BOMBED OUR NAVAL FLEET AT PEARL HARBOR IN HONOLULU. MOST OF OUR SHIPS ARE SUNK AND MANY OF OUR FINEST MEN LOST. WE REPEAT: THE JAPANESE HAVE ATTACKED THE U.S. NAVAL FLEET AT PEARL HARBOR. STAND BY FOR FURTHER ANNOUNCEMENTS.

Aghast, Paula turned to her roommate, Adele Turner. "Did you hear that?"

Adele was stretched out on the bed reading The *Saturday Evening Post*. "What? Sorry. I was reading."

"The Japanese have attacked Pearl Harbor. A sneak attack! our ships are sunk! Do you realize that means they're waging war against the United States of America?"

"Ridiculous! Where's Pearl Harbor, anyway?"

But the girls, along with their fellow students in Austin at the University of Texas, soon found the Japanese threat to be valid. They remembered their parents talking about World War I. As bastions of God's will, the young people of the previous generation had fought to save freedom in the world. Without being told, these university students and their peers surmised that theirs was the burden to save America all over again, only this time under more drastic circumstances. Their own territory was threatened. For God and country they would give their lives.

Two days later, Paula had a date with Don O'Grady to listen to Roosevelt's fireside chat. Now I've got two problems, she thought, the war and Don. But what about my art?

The dimensions of her life had expanded with the shrinking. Her sights had been transformed from the self-centered passion for her painting to a vision of her particular part in the all encompassing war effort. As for Don, she hadn't exactly made up her mind about him. She had a feeling that she should decline his invitation to spend the Christmas holidays with his family in Kilgore. That was getting too close to an engagement and Paula couldn't see Don staying out of the military. The country needed its tall Texans to win this double-headed, monstrous war. On the other hand, her art would have to be set aside, a shrinking that would distort her soul.

But she should have seen it coming. She recalled that time a year ago last April, in her Art 403 class when Prof. Sheldon Brown had come in late. He appeared in an impeccable black suit, white shirt and checked blue tie that gave his dark looks authority. Lithe, agitated, he took jerky steps over to the lectern and laid down his briefcase. He ran his fingers through his black hair, then paced back and forth, turned, and paced back and forth again, thin mouth set, jaw clenched.

He stopped as if on signal, and gazed at his students, eyes flashing. "I've made a decision," he declared. "It's a decision that will affect us all and you, especially, Miss Roncourt."

Paula stiffened. Her painting! He wouldn't be going to Paris to sell his paintings, nor to show hers, either. She was losing the chance of a lifetime. She crumpled inside while maintaining an erect dignity in appearance. She had been so proud that her pastel artwork had won the competition from among all the students in the Art Department.

Her winning painting was a silky still life. The professor, her friend and mentor, had said, "This painting bears originality. Who has ever painted in such glowing color, flowers on a table with an open button box in the foreground, needle and thread beside the vase? All the elements of an engaging painting are here, the beauty of color, the emotion of pleasure, and the feeling for the subject. The composition shows this as well, for the button box, with its intriguing contents, is central to the whole. The flowers indicate the feminine grace and beauty of a woman, and we feel her intended needlework."

His praise had sent Paula on a flight of aspiration to become a world famous artist. In 1940 there were few women painters of renown in the world, but she was determined to become one.

Now all was lost. The war in Europe had escalated. In the depths of her heart, she knew what Professor Brown was going to say.

He quieted down and took his place behind the lectern. "I've decided that I cannot go into Paris next week for the spring showing on the Left Bank," he said. "I expect you've heard that Norway and Denmark have fallen. France will be next. I only hope the Louvre will not be destroyed and the European masterpieces of her great painters with it. I'm afraid there's little hope for saving this marvelous culture of the free world. The Nazis will no doubt confiscate the treasures and there's no telling where they'll end up. Perhaps destroyed in the bombing of Germany!"

At the shock of this imminent rape, the students sucked in their breath, making an audible sound. The professor became thoughtful, then he spoke again.

"It will affect you and me. As artists, we'll virtually disappear. The art world will disappear in favor of armaments and the military. It will be much worse than World War I. You men will taste battle, so arm yourselves now with your own decisions as to what part you'll play in this all-out war."

He straightened up and scanned his students. With pride in his voice, he spoke again.

"I know we can depend upon you young men and women to do what needs to be done to save our country. Make no mistake about it. Hitler intends to rule the world. He is abetted by Mussolini, enriched by the countries he has already conquered. It will be a long fight. Brace yourselves and make intelligent decisions. I'm going to dismiss class. Go home and think about your future. Is there a place for artists during war? Perhaps there is. Perhaps some of you may wish to be at the front, accompanying a war correspondent to sketch scenes of the action, or to stay back home and become illustrators for war propaganda or publications here. Think seriously.

"As for myself, I'll shift." He gave a wry grin. "We'll all shift if we don't want to be shiftless." His tone changed. "I think I'll try the National Gallery of Art in Washington City. And of course, there's always New York. Anyway, I'll be safe so long as the University keeps me on salary."

The students responded with grins at his spunk. He nodded at Paula. "I'd like to see you for a moment. Class dismissed."

Paula went forward while the students filed out, some expressing their sympathy as they passed by their teacher. Only forty years old, he was at the peak of his worldwide reputation, showing and selling his paintings every spring in Paris. He shook his head at Paula.

"I'm so sorry, Miss Roncourt. I know how much it meant to you to be shown on the Left Bank."

She could not speak. Her enormous blue eyes welled with tears. She blinked, then brightened and lifted her chin.

"You know," she said, "I'm prepared for anything. During the Depression, I took typing and shorthand in high school. I can do my part if we go to war."

"Oh, we'll go. I want you to keep up your art after you graduate. Yours is a talent that must not be wasted. We'll see this thing through together."

Hearkening back to that day in 1940, she thought it seemed that Professor Brown had a premonition of this new threat from Japan. With prescience of mind, he had asked his students to pause, to think seriously about how they wanted to serve their country in time of war.

Their beloved Pres. Franklin Delano Roosevelt, in his third term, would surely lead them safely through this crisis. He had saved them during the Great Depression. And over a year ago, he managed to send help to Great Britain under the Lend Lease program, although there was much opposition in Congress. Also, there was a strong America First Movement headed by the hero, Charles A. Lindbergh. Maybe it was America's reluctance to go to war that made the Japanese so overconfident and feisty. Did they actually think Americans would lie down and roll over after a few licks?

❧ �֎ ☙

A call came from the monitor down the hall. "Paula Roncourt! There's a young man, name of O'Grady, here to see you. He's waiting in the parlor."

Paula hastily fastened the belt to her red dress. She had changed for the occasion on this Tuesday evening of December 9 to hear the President's message about the war. "Coming!" she answered, then said good-bye to Adele as she picked up her coat and purse. Maybe she should quit dating Don, but all the girls considered him the number one catch on campus and he was not the kind to take no for an answer.

O'Grady, popular left guard for the Longhorns football team and well-to-do in Texas oil, had fallen for this attractive young lady the first time he saw her in their Political Science class. But she was tied to her art, eating, sleeping, and dreaming color and beauty. He knew he wasn't handsome and at times, his blood chilled when common sense told him that Paula didn't return his ardor.

But he could give her the security of an envious social position and freedom to pursue her painting in bright, sunny days, while at the same time, she could be an asset to his ambitions in the oil business. They were both staunch Democrats and that was a strong tie. Besides, Paula was loyal to the uncle for whom she was named, State Senator Paul J. Roncourt. With his support, they could work together to get strategic legislation passed.

Don was no dummy. If football had built up his physical strength, it had also taught him maneuvers in offsetting the opponent to attain his goal.

Unable to sit in the parlor and wait any longer, he went to the foot of the stairway and stood watching for her. His skin prickled with pleasure when he saw her.

She stepped down in black and white spectator pumps, wearing a soft jersey dress, red as a rose, clinging to her slender body, black coat and purse over her right arm. The oval face, framed by her black, medium pageboy, shimmered above a double strand of faceted jet beads. Her great blue eyes, shaded by long, curly lashes, signalled a welcome. He was seized by an urge to place his hands around her tiny waist and lift her up to heaven in pure gratitude and joy.

Instead, he controlled himself and burst out singing in his baritone voice, "Oh, the lady in red. The fellows are crazy for the lady in red!"

She responded with an open smile at his elation. She knew boys liked red, but without realizing it, she had chosen this dress to attract Don, her date, and to lift her own spirits on this historic occasion. When she approached him, she held out her coat and he helped her into it.

He noticed her stenographic notebook. "This isn't class, you know."

"I know. But I'm going to take down every word that President Roosevelt says."

He took her elbow and guided her down the passageway toward the portico, where he had parked his car.

"That'll be impossible," he assured her, "but you could get some of the highlights."

"Don't worry. I'll get every word. My Gregg will assist me."

He performed a quick snap, pivoting around, looking everywhere. "Who's Greg? I don't see 'im! Don't tell me you've been dating him, too! I'm jealous!"

Paula broke into peals of laughter. "You know I mean Gregg Shorthand, silly!" He grinned with a mischievous glance. Then all at once, she halted and gave him a stern look. "How can you make fun at a time of crisis like this?"

He sobered. "Baloney! If we lose our sense of humor, we'll lose our lives!"

She gazed at him, seeing him in a new light, a depth that was contrary to his blunt physiognomy. She had always thought of him as a late Neanderthal Man with his strong, jutting jaw and his big boned, muscular body. The deep set, blue eyes and pug nose of an

Irish washerwoman in his square face were not exactly ugly, but his dark curly hair was cut short like a cap on a round head. Hairs grew across the bridge of his nose, giving a shaggy brow aspect. Yet, the burnt orange sweater with the large, white lettering, TEXAS, across his broad chest was attractive and complimentary of his feats on the football field.

"I expect you're right," she said thoughtfully.

Don was exultant. He took her elbow again and escorted her to his green, four-door Chevrolet. They soon arrived at the Lone Star Cafe and found a parking space. Don got his portable radio out of the back seat, then he opened the front door for Paula.

The cafe was almost like two restaurants. It was one of the student hangouts near the campus and the smell of coffee and fried hamburgers greeted them when they entered.

Off to their right was a counter with bright orange stools for individual customers. A few inviting booths in orange formica and white woodwork lined up against the front windows. In addition, there were four extra small tables-for-two with oak tops in front of the counter. The whole interior was cheerful in University colors, the orange more of the hot sun than the authentic burnt orange. Through a wide doorway on the left they could see a crowd of students in the dining room.

It teemed with the voluble vehemence of their chatter.

Paula listened, hearing snatches of their talk. He's gonna declare war! Do you think we'll let those little ol' polliwogs scare us? We'll squash 'em! Yeah, they're too skinny to eat. Oh don't you know it! The Japs'll be dancin' like lizards in a skillet.

"Over there," Don said, diverting her attention. He nodded toward an alcove in the rear, one step up, which was shielded by a lattice of English ivy. "Our gang is there at the Sigma Chi corner."

Five men and two girls greeted them and Jim Wallace introduced everyone around the table.

"Curly," Jim asked, "did you bring your radio? I don't think we'd hear a thing with this wild crowd, even if the owner tried to accommodate us."

"Here you are," Don replied. He pulled out the sixteen inch long radio from under his arm, which he'd been holding like a football, and set it down in the middle of the table. "I want you guys and gals, too, to be quiet once Roosevelt begins to talk. Paula's goin' to take it all down in shorthand."

There were murmurs of approval. Then one mentioned that the school paper, The Texas Daily, had an article on salient excerpts from yesterday's Message to Congress.

The waitress came and Don asked Paula, "What'll you have?"

"I'd like a Coca Cola float," she replied.

He grinned at her and said, "I'll float along with you."

The other orders varied from banana cream pie and coffee to chocolate sundaes. Their attention on the food was short lived. After the waitress left, Irene Maddux asked if anyone had seen the paper. "I have it right here," Bill Pettijohn said. The group was instantly quiet and he began to read quotes from President Roosevelt's message:

YESTERDAY, DECEMBER 7, 1941 -- A DATE WHICH WILL LIVE IN INFAMY—THE UNITED STATES OF AMERICA WAS SUDDENLY AND DELIBERATELY ATTACKED BY NAVAL AND AIR FORCES OF THE EMPIRE OF JAPAN. THE UNITED STATES WAS AT PEACE WITH THAT NATION AND, AT THE SOLICITATION OF JAPAN, WAS STILL IN CONVERSATION WITH ITS GOVERNMENT AND ITS EMPEROR, LOOKING TOWARD THE MAINTENANCE OF PEACE IN THE PACIFIC. INDEED, ONE HOUR AFTER JAPANESE AIR SQUADRONS HAD COMMENCED BOMBING IN OAHU, THE JAPANESE AMBASSADOR TO THE UNITED STATES AND HIS COLLEAGUES DELIVERED TO THE SECRETARY OF STATE A FORMAL REPLY TO A RECENT AMERICAN MESSAGE. WHILE THIS REPLY STATED THAT IT SEEMED USELESS TO CONTINUE THE EXISTING DIPLOMATIC NEGOTIATIONS, IT CONTAINED NO THREAT OR HINT OF WAR OR ARMED ATTACK. ALWAYS WILL WE REMEMBER THE CHARACTER OF THE ONSLAUGHT AGAINST US. NO MATTER HOW LONG IT MAY TAKE US TO OVERCOME THIS PREMEDITATED INVASION, THE AMERICAN PEOPLE,

IN THEIR RIGHTEOUS MIGHT, WILL WIN THROUGH TO ABSOLUTE VICTORY.

WITH CONFIDENCE IN OUR ARMED FORCES—WITH THE UNBOUNDED DETERMINATION OF OUR PEOPLE—WE WILL GAIN THE INEVITABLE TRIUMPH—SO HELP US GOD.

"And here's the kicker," Bill said, looking about. Then he read again:

I ASK THAT THE CONGRESS DECLARE THAT SINCE THE UNPROVOKED AND DASTARDLY ATTACK BY JAPAN ON SUNDAY, DECEMBER 7, A STATE OF WAR HAS EXISTED BETWEEN THE UNITED STATES AND THE JAPANESE EMPIRE.

All were quiet. The waitress came and served their refreshments. They began to eat, heads down, spooked eyes unseeing, tastebuds unknowing, swallowing automatic. They had known, yet they had not known.

Here it was quoted from the President's own mouth. Here it was in their own school paper. They were at war! The burden for victory had judiciously been laid upon their shoulders, a wreath of thanksgiving and death, theirs to do or die. For God and country they would sacrifice to attain victory.

They raised their heads and messages of proud acceptance of this responsibility traveled from face to face around the table. Paula opened her notebook, pencil ready. She had joined the whole population waiting together as one great family across the country, small and large gatherings suspended, ears cocked to hear the guiding wisdom of their fatherly President.

Don looked at his watch, breaking the spell. "It's time for Roosevelt's Fireside Chat. Let's see what he wants to tell us." He turned on the radio and soon had NBC. "Just in time."

LADIES AND GENTLEMEN, THE PRESIDENT OF THE UNITED STATES: GOOD EVENING, MY FELLOW AMERICANS.

It was the President himself, in his charming Ivy League accent and mellow bass-baritone.

> THE SUDDEN CRIMINAL ATTACKS PERPETRATED BY THE JAPANESE IN THE PACIFIC PROVIDE THE CLIMAX OF A DECADE OF INTERNATIONAL IMMORALITY. POWERFUL AND RESOURCEFUL GANGSTERS HAVE BANDED TOGETHER TO MAKE WAR UPON THE WHOLE HUMAN RACE. THEIR CHALLENGE HAS NOW BEEN FLUNG AT THE UNITED STATES OF AMERICA. THE JAPANESE HAVE TREACHEROUSLY VIOLATED THE LONG STANDING PEACE BETWEEN US. MANY AMERICAN SOLDIERS AND SAILORS HAVE BEEN KILLED BY ENEMY ACTION. AMERICAN SHIPS HAVE BEEN SUNK. AMERICAN AIRPLANES HAVE BEEN DESTROYED.

Paula's pencil flew as she rushed to keep up.

> THE CONGRESS AND THE PEOPLE OF THE UNITED STATES HAVE ACCEPTED THAT CHALLENGE. TOGETHER WITH OTHER FREE PEOPLES, WE ARE NOW FIGHTING TO MAINTAIN OUR RIGHT TO LIVE AMONG OUR WORLD NEIGHBORS IN FREEDOM AND IN COMMON DECENCY, WITHOUT FEAR OF ASSAULT.
> WE ARE NOW IN THIS WAR. WE ARE ALL IN IT—ALL THE WAY. EVERY SINGLE MAN, WOMAN, AND CHILD IS A PARTNER IN THE MOST TREMENDOUS UNDERTAKING OF OUR AMERICAN HISTORY. WE MUST SHARE TOGETHER THE BAD NEWS AND THE GOOD NEWS, THE DEFEATS AND THE VICTORIES—THE CHANGING FORTUNES OF WAR.

Paula pressed too hard. The lead point broke, leaving her stymied. "Help! Now I've done it!"

One of the girls gave her a pencil and Paula resumed her shorthand, sorry she'd missed out on the whole speech.

....I REPEAT THAT THE UNITED STATES CAN ACCEPT NO RESULT SAVE VICTORY, FINAL AND COMPLETE. NOT ONLY MUST THE SHAME OF JAPANESE TREACHERY BE WIPED OUT, BUT THE SOURCES OF INTERNATIONAL BRUTALITY, WHEREVER THEY EXIST, MUST BE ABSOLUTELY AND FINALLY BROKEN....

WE ARE NOW IN THE MIDST OF A WAR, NOT FOR CONQUEST, NOT FOR VENGEANCE, BUT FOR A WORLD IN WHICH THIS NATION AND ALL THAT THIS NATION REPRESENTS WILL BE SAFE FOR OUR CHILDREN. WE EXPECT TO ELIMINATE THE DANGER FROM JAPAN, BUT IT WOULD SERVE US ILL IF WE ACCOMPLISHED THAT AND FOUND THAT THE REST OF THE WORLD WAS DOMINATED BY HITLER AND MUSSOLINI.

WE ARE GOING TO WIN THE WAR, AND WE ARE GOING TO WIN THE PEACE THAT FOLLOWS.

LADIES AND GENTLEMEN, YOU HAVE JUST HEARD....

Don clicked off the radio. Paula closed her notebook and returned the pencil to her friend. For a moment, there was silence. Bill Pettijohn folded The Texas Daily, creasing it hard. "We're in the midst of war," he said, echoing the President's words. His voice was low and strained. "We've been giving lend lease to Britain for a year now. What he's telling us is that we'll be fighting on two fronts."

The others, faces pale, gazed at him, taking in his words, and their meaning for themselves. Paula grabbed her stenographic notebook and held it up. "I've got it down, right here! He said every one of us must fulfill our obligation, man, woman and child. We've got to put everything aside. We'll have to give up our dreams for the present. Let's remember that America is the bastion of God's will in human lives and we must not let this greater dream die. We must conquer! America depends upon us!" Her gaze luminous, she rose and shouted, "Remember the Alamo!" As one, they all stood with her and chanted, "Remember Pearl Harbor!"

Chapter Two

Touch and Glow. That was what it was all about. Paula carefully smoothed Revlon's Misty Rose liquid makeup under her large blue eyes, muril in dreamy contemplation.

She'd never been to a Sunday afternoon tea dance in the Sigma Chi House before. It was almost like going to a cathedral among the saints. There in the ballroom, she'd dance with the elite young gentlemen, not only of the University of Texas campus, but of the whole State of Texas. Her curiosity curled about those Houston and Dallas city fellows. She wanted to make a good impression on them. The light touch of gaiety and the glow of natural charm would do. She mustn't be nervous.

She wondered about the architecture and appointments of that great colonial mansion. Would she find some beautiful paintings on those walls?

But Don was her immediate problem. Touch and glow, or touch and go?

Her elbow was jostled.

"Watch out!" she warned.

Adele laughed at her. "Scooch over! I need more of this mirror. Do you think I should wear this cream taffeta or the brown satin?" She held up the two dinner gowns and Paula gave her consideration.

"I like the creamy color on you. It brightens you up. Of course, I have only one dinner gown, so I don't have your trouble."

The taffeta three-quarters length gown, with its peplum about the waist, helped to diminish Adele's tall stature and it also enhanced her golden brown hair and ivory skin. From her height of five feet, eleven inches, she smiled down at Paula, seated at the dressing table.

"Don't worry," she said. "It doesn't matter what you wear. All the guys'll see is you. Your black velveteen is so chic, anyway, with its gold buttons down the front."

Adele looked appraisingly at her friend, approving of her transparent white skin, the high cheek bones in the oval face. Young fellows made a double take when they first saw her, attracted by those gorgeous blue eyes. It was a face befitting an artist, even showing God's mark by the delicate widow's peak in the smooth forehead. She caught a glimpse of herself beside Paula in the mirror. Not all was lost. One could say her features gave the tony effect of a patrician with her deep set hazel eyes, curved brow and long, thin British nose. Her best feature was her beautiful smile and she made the most of it.

When the Roncourts could not pay the expense of their daughter's social standing that membership in a sorority would entail, Adele had chosen to stay with Paula in the women's dormitory, ignoring the sororities. As the only child of a prominent family in her home town, her social position was assured. Her father owned the largest insurance company in San Angelo and had plenty of money. She and Paula had been bosom friends since grade school. The girls had happy times double dating together in high school and naturally continued this custom throughout their college years.

Now, nearing mid-term of their senior year, they were aware that this time together on such a special occasion would be one of their last such pleasures. They were in high spirits. Paula smiled to herself over Don's astute planning. If he hadn't included Adele, she might have turned him down.

"Paula," Adele said, fluffing her bangs, "I know what you're thinking. But what's the harm of enjoying the Christmas holidays in luxury?"

"I'm afraid he'll want to pin me," Paula said. "He's really a nice guy and I'd hate to have to refuse him."

"A fraternity pin isn't a wedding ring, you know, or even an engagement ring," Adele replied.

"I know, but it's the next thing to it." Paula turned to her. "Did you know I received a letter from Burl yesterday?" Burl Stein was the rancher back home who desperately wished to marry her. "He's gone by to see my folks again."

"They're not sick or anything?"

"No. It's just that he says everything has come to a stop. At least for real estate. He says that the ranchers are hanging on to their land and the same goes for houses in town. All of which means that Dad's not doing much business."

Adele was sympathetic. "Slim pickin's, huh?" Then she said with a wicked smile, "But I don't see what you can do about it. Or do I?"

Paula gave her a gliff. "I don't think that's what Don had in mind."

There came a knock at the door and Adele opened it.

"Special delivery, girls!" A young sophomore with a huge Texas section grin on her face, stood holding two boxed corsages in her hands.

Adele took them in her long fingers and peeked through the cellophane covers. "Oooohl They're beautifull! Thanks!"

"Roses!" Paula exclaimed.

The cards from the florist had simple messages, the red roses, 'For Paula from Don,' and the tea roses, 'For Adele from Bill.'

Paula held the deep red roses to her nose and inhaled their heady fragrance. "How gorgeous! They're just right for my black velveteen, and yours are perfect, too."

Adele followed suit, sniffing with zest the lighter scent of the tea roses. "I tell you, that Don doesn't miss a trick."

"It wasn't all Don," Paula assured her. "Bill really likes you. He told Don he's danced with you several times."

"Yeah, but he's never asked me for a date before."

"That's because he's taking Law and they just don't have the time."

Adele gave a small smile. She knew Paula. Always the optimist, seeing things in the most favorable light and always trying to make herself and others feel good. She was a politician, all right, but thank goodness, not a Pollyanna. "Hold still and I'll pin your corsage on for you," she said.

Like a sister, Paula returned the favor and the girls were ready when Don and Bill arrived.

Paula felt at ease in the company of Adele and Bill, along with Don. A group always lessened the vulnerability of any individual person. She was simply out to dance the light fantastic. Anyway, probably all she needed to do when the time came, was to look Don in his blunt face and it would be a cinch to say no. He was nice though, and smart enough for a Business major. She'd have to wing it.

It was dark outside except for shafts of light shining from dormitory windows on the lawn and overhead light from bare bulbs under the portico. The young gentlemen looked like proud swains in their dark suits, white shirts and red ties. Don had reserved a parking space right in front of the Sigma Chi House, hoping to make a good impression on Paula.

Down a lane from West Street near the campus, the great colonial home was surrounded by a spacious lawn. When the couples drove near, they saw its imposing presence, white columns illumined by the soft blue lights decorating a large pine tree in fullsome glory. Strings of blue lights outlined its frame across the width of the veranda and around the dormer windows and roof line above. All was in blue, an ethereal promise of the peace of Christmas, heaven come down to earth.

Paula entered the parlor to the left on Don's arm, walking on air. Here was the beauty she had expected, only more so, the silver and blue decor enhanced by the Christmas decorations of evergreen loops across the high ceiling of the spacious room. An added delight was the beautiful spruce tree decorated in red, green, orange, and blue lights, twinkling on and off. It stood beside the windows just inside the ballroom beyond the parlor. She stifled a gasp at the size of the ballroom, its indirect lighting in the ceiling, the lovely blue and silver wallpaper shimmering with the reflection of the colorful lights.

Here was beauty and comfort combined. The polished floor of the ballroom was inviting, and an alcove with a raised platform just beyond the Christmas tree, afforded a place for the orchestra.

"How lovely!" she exclaimed.

Taking her coat, Don replied, "I'm glad you like it. We did all the decorations, ourselves."

While he hung up the coat in the closet, Paula glanced down at her corsage to see if the flowers had been crushed. She had tried to be careful and was relieved when she saw no harm was done.

Don returned and she thanked him again, saying the red rose was what she would have chosen herself.

"In the language of flowers, the red rose means love," he said, bending down to sniff them. He brushed his lips lingeringly against her ear. "They're what I purposely chose, too."

Paula stood motionless, accepting his sentiment. Then she called his attention to the college orchestra, the White Torrent, gathering in the ballroom. Five student musicians comprised the jazz orchestra. They sported white jackets, silver bow ties, and blue trousers. The name, WHITE TORRENT, was proclaimed in a ribbon of glitter against a blue background on the fronts. The five pieces consisted of a piano, saxaphonist who sometimes substituted on the clarinet, trumpet, base horn, and drum.

Adele and Bill joined Paula and Don and Paula said, "Yess dance, chillun!"

The orchestra struck up "Moonglow," one of Paula's favorites, and she wondered if Don had requested it. She found him to be a smooth dancer and a strong leader and gave herself over to the pleasure of the melody and rhythm. This was followed by "Sophisticated Lady," and "Serenade In Blue."

Neither spoke while dancing and Paula appreciated this courtesy from Don, assuming that conversation was a ploy for those who didn't dance well, or for those trying to become acquainted. Don was only aware of her soft body, her thighs matching his in close touch while following him in perfect step. He rejoiced that she wasn't afraid of this contact and wished it could go on forever.

They were both sorry when the band gave its hoot, meaning it was time for a break.

With Adele and Bill, they moved off toward the dining room, which was to the right of the staircase. Don introduced Paula to Mother Henderson, a middle aged lady with soft brown hair coiffed in waves about her round face. She sat at the far end of the table in white satin, silver tea service before her. Paula accepted tea with lemon.

The table was spread in artistic displays of cheeses, platters of fruit, including pineapple chunks, grapes, melon and orange slices, and various breads and cherry tarts. Paula helped herself to the fruit and a cherry tart but avoided the cheese. To her mind, cheese was surely milk gone wrong and really rotten. She was a bit embarrassed about it, but Don thought it was funny.

"Being an artist, I knew you were probably very sensitive," he said, grinning. "But I didn't know it went so far as to what you would eat or not eat."

"I just simply don't eat cheese," she replied smartly. "Nor will I ever touch beer."

"That so?"

"Otherwise, I eat everything—well, almost. I really don't like oysters."

"Too bad." He laughed with a hearty chuckle. "You know what they say about oysters, don't you?"

She smiled back at him, walking ahead to find a place to sit in the parlor. "I really don't care what they say. It's all a joke, anyway." Who needed an aphrodisiac? From what she'd heard, dormitories put saltpeter in the food.

Adele and Bill joined them and they reverted to the underlying concern thus far avoided in their eagerness to have a good time.

"I've been busy working on a masterpiece," Paula said to Bill. "Any more news about the war?"

"The draft has started," he said, "but I think I'll enter Officers Candidate School, the OCS, after graduation."

Don leaned toward him. "You mean, 'Greetings?' Well, I don't need that kind of pages, either." He grinned at Paula. "You turn my pages."

And put lead in your pencil? But a lady didn't say such things in mixed company. She giggled at his humor, mouth closed, the low vibration becoming almost a purr in her throat, when with a tinge of nostalgia, she recalled the evening she and Adele had sat around on the bed in their next door neighbor's room at the dorm telling innocent jokes. Lucy May had brought out a jug of peach brandy hidden in the bottom of her trunk and passed a flask around during their bull session. They kept an eye out at the door, because liquor was forbidden and if they were caught, they could be expelled. They laughed hilariously like high schoolers, dredging up jokes about the Depression.

"Do you know what the old maid does on Sunday morning," Lucy May asked.

"No, what?"

"She goes to church with hope in her soul."

Paula giggled all the more at this memory. Then another.

"What does the priest do the first thing in the morning?"

"Well, what?"

"He shakes hands with the unemployed."

Then she caught the others looking at her. Don was swelled up with her obvious appreciation of his wit, which brought her back to the present.

"How about you, Don? Will you be turning more pages at OCS after graduation, like Bill?" she asked.

"No doubt about it," he responded. "We're both in the ROTC, the Reserve Officers Training Corps, and it'll only take ninety days for us to become Lieutenants."

"Yeah," Bill said, "we'll become ninety day wonders running the show."

Adele spoke up. "That's what I'd do if I were in your place. It's a good thing you can get in right away to become officers."

The band struck up the music again and they heard the insistent tones of "Night And Day," a compelling song.

They jumped to their feet. Bill and Don returned their plates to the dining room and they were soon swaying to the music. "Night and day, you are the one .... only you be-neath the moon and un-der the sun."

No one tagged.

The haunting words and melody brought premonition of the burning yearning for their darlings and home soon to be borne in execrating battle, the cursed demands of marching, sniping, killing, facing the enemy, destroying to hell and gone.

The song ended and the company applauded, then grew silent, waiting for the next number. The clarinet lead with its soul stirring rendition of "Temptation." The orchestra crooner sang; "You came. I was alone. I should have known. You were temptation."

Don hugged Paula close, his whole being infused with the beat and permeating message of the tortuous torture, an anguish he could only express in his dancing.

Paula, incandescent with sensate empathy, molded herself to his feverish body, hot with desire. This she could do for him and no more. It would be a matter of deception if she should accept his invitation to meet his parents and spend the Christmas holidays with his family. She saw it clearly. She should go home. She could drop out of school at the end of this semester. Her folks needed her. Her country needed her. She should get a job as a secretary out at Goodfellow Field, and the sooner the quicker.

Burl had written, I sure do miss you. What do you plan to do after you graduate? Come back to San Angelo where you belong, I hope.

The music ended and Don broke her revery with, "That was marvelous! You're such a marvelous dancer!"

"You're quite smooth, yourself!"

He took her arm and guided her off the floor to a chair against the wall. "We'll keep on dancin' like this over Christmas. We'll have an open house and there'll be dancin' and bowls of eggnog and plenty to eat. You'll love it."

"Oh, I'm sorry, Don!" She faced him with regret in her gaze. "You remember, I said I'm working on a masterpiece? I just have to stay here and keep at it." Her eyes widened. "I've decided to drop out of school at the end of this semester and go back home to get a job out at Goodfellow."

"Goodfellow! You?" Don was nonplussed at such a scheme. "You're an artist! You've got to get your degree! You can't just drop everything!"

"I've just now decided. You'll be going off to OCS and to war."

"But not for another semester. We'd have lots of fun," he protested. Then he became serious. "It's all the more important that we take as much time as we can to have fun now. It may be now or never."

"I know," she said. "That's why I'm leaving after finals. President Roosevelt said he needs every man, woman, and child and he meant right away. We've got to get prepared and we've got to defend our country, too. Goodfellow is a Basic Training airfield for pilots. I can help. The sooner I apply for a job, the better job I'll get."

Don was silent, trying to swallow his disappointment, thinking of all the pleasures he had planned, now disconsolate.

Paula touched his arm and said in a gentle voice, "Besides, I'm trying to make this painting a real masterpiece in the hope that Professor Brown will take it with his paintings to be sold in Washington City."

"I see," Don said. With grace, he added, "I hope your plans work out."

"I'm sorry, Don."

He brightened and grinned at her. "I hope you won't be painting at night. How about a movie Wednesday night?"

"I'd like that," she said.

❧ ✳ ☙

A couple of days after the Tea Dance, it occurred to Paula that Don hadn't even asked what her masterpiece was all about. It was just as well, since it was an ephemeral subject she was trying to do in a realistic-abstract treatment, if there was such a thing. In other words, she was trying to do the impossible, something she'd dreamed up, and she was too shy about her creation to discuss it with anyone. Maybe Don had sensed this reluctance. Now she wondered at her bravado in bragging that she hoped Professor Brown would include it in his offering to the National Gallery of Art.

But he had said they were in this thing together. He wanted her to keep up her art and said he would coach her even after graduation.

She had stretched the canvas, herself, a piece thirty-eight by forty-eight inches, the size any museum would be proud to display. She covered it with a white cloth and stashed it away in the storeroom adjacent to the art studio. Art students were sensitive to one another's feelings and never touched any work except their own.

The newspapers were full of the changes brought about by the war. All of a sudden, books of coupons for the rationing of coffee, sugar, and meat were being prepared. Rents were frozen. The Japanese on the West Coast were sent to detention camps. Students by the hundreds dropped out of school to enlist. Typewriters with margin releases were confiscated by the government, including portables. Everything must go toward the war effort. Factories of domestic goods were transformed into manufacturers of armaments and munitions, and building was confined to construction of materiel plants. No more houses were built, nor commercial buildings.

Where did art fit into this scheme, Paula asked herself. There must be some solution, some way she could make her art count even during the war. Her painting! Would it inspire those who viewed it? It was a mystic glimpse of heaven come down to earth in the form of a curved stairway leading up to paradise with pink and blue fairies floating up and down the celestial stairs in artful flutter. This was a recurring dream she'd had as a small child and to her it was real, but the evanescence was difficult to catch on a flat surface. It taxed her ability and imagination. What was the matrix from which the stairway had sprung?

These questions nagged at her so that, although shy and timid about letting anyone know of this attempted scene, she decided to trust Professor Brown with her most delicate and intimate rendition of the beckoning fairies. She would have to tell him of her decision to drop out of the University, anyway, and this would be an appropriate time to seek his advice.

She sought him after class one afternoon when he was alone, bringing the half finished painting and setting, it up on a desk in front.

He came around the lectern and stood expectant, a smile on his face. "I was wondering when I'd get to see the creation you've been working on."

She was still hesitant. In his presence, she suddenly felt like a four year old. "Promise you won't ask, 'What is it?'" she pleaded.

"I promise," he said, meaning it. "I understand it's far from finished."

She drew the cover up and turned it back over the top, revealing the cloudy effervescent background in blues and whites with rosy shadows and thin, white lines curving up and twisting, off to the left. It was certainly impressionistic, the composition intriguing, seeming to ask a question. Not only that, but he noticed the intrinsic beauty of technique and color that characterized Paula's work. So fine!

He nodded. "It bears your taste and technique, Paula. Your work is always beautiful and I find this quite intriguing. I'll be happy to wait and see it when it's finished. Then, if I must, I'll ask you what it is."

He was teasing her but she was happy with his complimentary remarks. Now was the time to tell him.

"I've decided to make this my masterpiece before I leave school at the end of this semester," she said with deceptive calm.

He left the contemplation of the artwork and his gaze fell upon her face in surprise. "Leave at the end of this semester?"

"Yes, sir. I've decided to go home to join in the war effort out at Goodfellow Field. I'm pretty sure I can get a good job as a secretary on base. It's a permanent Air Corps base, where they train pilots. I can help, and that's where I belong. My parents and my sister live there."

"But your oils! And you're so close to graduating! You mustn't give up your degree just like that!" He snapped his fingers.

"I can come back after the war and get my degree. I'm really lucky that I don't have to be drafted like so many."

"You don't have to quit school, either," he said.

"No, but I'd feel guilty if I hung back when my country needs every hand."

"I know how you feel. I expect I'll be exempt unless things get truly drastic. I'm forty years old and have a family. It'll be lonesome around here."

"Yes, I know. I've decided to keep up my art, as you suggested. I think I'll teach drawing to young women, Professor Brown. Do you realize there are few women artists of renown? At least, I don't read of many."

"No, there aren't," he agreed. "That's a wonderful idea. And while you're helping them, you'll be helping yourself, too."

She gave him a smile. "I'd thought of that. That's a sort of spiritual law, isn't it? Those who help others, help themselves."

"Yes, that's what makes the world go 'round," the professor said.

"I appreciate your help and maybe some day you'll still take one of my paintings with you to sell along with yours."

He liked her confidence. "What's the title of this new painting?" he asked.

"The Fairy Dance."

Impressed, he nodded. "I'll buy that."

This was practically a promise and Paula was elated.

Later that evening after dinner, when she and Adele had retired to their room to study, Paula presented the chair at the desk for her friend.

"Here," she said. "Have a seat. I have something to tell you."

Adele sank into the chair, while Paula climbed up onto the bed and sat cross legged. "I've decided to drop out after finals. "

Adele's jaw fell open. "Drop out! You don't mean to give up your sheepskin!"

"Temporarily."

"Temporarily! You know better than that. Whatever gave you such a crazy idea? You know Skeet Jones and many others who've said they'd be back. But they never made it. It just isn't in the cards, Paula. Once you leave here, you'll get tied up and you'll never come back. It just isn't in the cards!"

"The fellows are also quitting and I can't do any less."

"That's nuts! They have to go to war. But you don't. I'll bet your folks won't hear of it. Have you told them? I know my father would never let me leave without my degree. That would be just plain stupid."

Adele's father spoiled her, but he also held his will over her head, giving her little freedom. The mother was ineffective in trying to nullify Mr. Turner's overbearing authority. Paula felt sorry for Adele and rejoiced that her own parents were so trusting with her sister, Bonnie, and herself. Freedom! That was her mother personified and for the most part, her parents saw eye to eye. The girls were always expected to make their own decisions. One time when she was twelve, Paula earnestly wished that just once her mother would tell her what to do. But no! She never did. If she told her folks that she wanted to drop out of college without her degree, they'd want to know why and would discuss it with her. But the decision would be hers.

"I've already told Professor Brown," Paula said. "I'll call Mom and Dad tomorrow. They'll understand when I explain it to them, that I need to serve and give my all for my country. Stop and think, Adele. If we do these two things, give more and do more than is expected of us, we'll be devoted and save our country." She paused, thinking of her conversation with her Art professor. "We'll become more of an individual, too."

"What do you mean?" Adele wanted to know. "Each of us is a unique individual. We can't be more unique! You're you and I'm me and nothing can change that."

"That's true. But how much of you is truly developed? That's the thing! Christians strengthen themselves so they can give more and do more. It's our responsibility to develop ourselves. No one else can do it."

"I'm surprised and disappointed in you, Paula. Frankly, I thought your art was your passion. Now you're giving it all up. "

"Oh no! I can come back any time and pick up that last semester." Then Paula spoke with marked enthusiasm. "I've got a marvelous plan, Adele. I'm going to get a job out at Goodfellow but I'm also going to set up Art classes for young women and teach in the evenings. That way, I'll keep up my own painting and help others, especially the girls."

Adele drew her brows together in disbelief. "When will you ever have time to do all that? I think you're crazy. Do you realize you'll just turn into an old maid? I wouldn't give up my degree in Music for anything. Besides, my father wouldn't allow it."

Paula pressed her lips together. "I was really hoping you'd come with me and work out at Goodfellow, too." She paused, then said with resignation, "But I understand."

"You won't catch me being so foolish. I'll need my degree if I'm ever going to give private piano lessons."

"I know, honey. As usual, we're on two sides of the same fence. That must be what holds us together."

Delighted, they laughed into one another's eyes. The fence would hold so long as they stayed in touch. It may be a long fence all the way from Austin to San Angelo, but they were confident it would hold.

⁓ ✳ ⁓

The next afternoon at two o'clock, Paula called home. Her mother answered the phone and she told of her plans to drop out of school.

"What's wrong, Paula? Are you ill?"

There was silence.

"Or did you let that O'Grady fellow get too close and you're ....."

"No, Mother! It's nothing like that."

Paula explained that it wasn't fair for just the boys to drop everything to defend the country. The nation needed its women, too, to win this terrible double-headed monstrous war. She figured she was just as much an American citizen as any man. Then she explained about her art.

Her mother was mollified and said it was all right with her and probably Dad, too, if she'd thought it all out.

"We'd love to have you back home, Paula," she said, "but I might as well warn you. A degree is something valuable, and it won't be easy for you to return to the University and pick up where you left off. You may never get your Bachelor's in Art. "

Paula admitted to herself that she was a bit shaken by this final warning, yet if this were the cost of her patriotism, it was nothing compared to the sacrifices many would have to make. What was a lost semester compared to life? She had made her decision and in her lexicon that was tantamount to its having been performed.

The remaining days and nights passed swiftly in feverish painting, dating with Don, corresponding with her folks and Burl Stein, and taking exams.

She was thrilled when Professor Brown approved of "The Fairy Dance" oil and asked her to leave it with him so he could try to place it, either in a museum or with a private buyer.

"It is truly beautiful, Paula," he said, "and people need beauty more than ever these days."

She promised to write and send more work when she thought any piece was good enough.

She also promised to write to Don and of course, nearly every day to Adele. At times such as these, a feeling of regret at saying good-bye to them and to her college days constricted her throat with a swelling that nearly burst her heart. But then she turned her thoughts to San Angelo, back home, and got excited about being with Bonnie and her folks again. And about breathing the sun washed air of the high plateau, dry and crackly, the sky glorious with rayed sunsets and huge orange moonrises.

Don and Adele took her to the bus station and helped her with her bags. She kissed them good-bye and found a seat next to the window. When the bags were loaded and everyone seated, the bus driver placed himself behind the wheel and closed the door, starting to roll.

Paula waved good-bye till her friends were out of sight. She was off for the cattle ranching country, eager to mount Old Red, her favorite cow pony out at the Lazy S. Ranch and to see Burl.

Chapter Three

The yellow sunlight warmed Paula's inner promise of freedom with the boundless sky singing a wildness caught in the taunting wind of San Angelo. She was birthed anew. Chadbourne Street, wide, flat, level, open, running with Appaloosa horses or Brahma and Longhorn bulls, spirits unhampered, unfettered by greenery or boulders or rivers of water. Only the blue sky, the wind of sage and mesquite, the sun and moon and stars, companions of consonant eternity, space irradicable, secure in visionary distance, yet intimate in cell porous awareness. This blue and gold bowl dominant, swayed the mind and mission of the yellow, dusty earth and its sentient lives of animals, two or four legged, breathing free exaltation.

Paula's eagerness, suspended in responsive memories and future hopes, delighted in the welcome given by her mother and father, a dinner at home in the white bungalow on East Beauregard, with Burl Stein as guest and Bonnie, her younger sister, present.

Bonnie had excused herself from college. Enamored of her fiance, Ralph Byrnes, she thought it wise to stay at home to be near him. The wedding date had not been set and she could take no chances. To her, he was the catch of the whole territory. Ralph was a serious young man rising in his father's business at the San Angelo Jewelry Store. Bonnie resembled her father, Floyd, with her blonde good looks, round face and round body to match. She was also cheerful and jolly, like Floyd.

Paula and Bonnie were close and were glad to be reunited, to have one another with whom they could share their deepest thoughts and secrets. On the other hand, Paula could look at her mother, Esther Roncourt, and see herself reflected there in her quiet Irish coloring and slender face. It was good to be home.

Burl was the same as ever, tawny, masculine and lean. She'd forgotten how he towered nearly six inches above her five foot ten inch father. He was a capable rancher, well off in his own right, and jubilant over Paula's return.

He held the chair for her at the dining table and said, "I brought you a quart of dill pickles, Paula. I made them from my mother's famous recipe. It's out in the kitchen."

"How nice!" she said. "We all miss your mother."

Mrs. Stein had died of heart failure only a year earlier.

"I opened it and put a serving on the table," Mrs. Roncourt said. "They surely do look appetizing."

She picked up the pickle dish and helped herself, then passed it along, the cue for everyone to start the dinner of fried chicken, whipped potatoes, string beans, tossed salad and carrots. Paula preferred sweet pickles, but took the smallest dill pickle she could find without seeming discourteous. One-half would have been enough for anyone, but she understood that Burl was proud of his large dill pickles.

He speared a big one and turned to Paula, seated next to him. "What are your plans, Paula?"

"I thought I told you. I plan to work out at Goodfellow as a secretary. Bonnie and I are both staying here with Mom and Dad till we get settled on our own. I'll have to get a paycheck before I can rent an apartment or room and board somewhere."

"No room and board, Paula," her father spoke up. "You both can stay with us as long as you'd like. Bonnie's got a good job with the telephone company and she's paying for her board. You could do the same thing."

"Housing is scarce," Esther joined in. "Do you know that we not only have Air Corps men coming in by the hundreds, but many of their wives are coming, too. I don't know what they're thinking of."

Burl gave her a lopsided grin and said, "I'll bet I do." Floyd chuckled at that, while Bonnie and Paula exchanged glances.

"But coming for only nine weeks is quite impractical, if not hysterical," Esther countered.

"What about you, Bonnie?" Paula asked. "Is Ralph going to volunteer? Has he received word from the Draft Board?"

"No, not yet. I don't know. I do know I want to get married before he goes, if he has to. But we haven't set a date."

"I wouldn't want to get married until after the war."

Bonnie looked at her sister. "Ralph did mention the Navy."

Paula nodded slowly. "The Navy's a good service, but it surely would take him a long way away."

"Yes," Bonnie agreed. "That's why if he does join, I'll insist we get married before he leaves." She paused and took a bite of the spiffy pickle. "And I want to get pregnant, too."

"What?" Paula was startled.

"Of course!" Bonnie exclaimed. "Everyone's doing it. But that's not my real reason. What if Ralph got killed or something. I wouldn't have anything of him unless I had his baby."

"I could never do that," Paula said.

"You're just not in love. I guess you never have been. When a girl falls in love, she wants to have her man's baby. Isn't that true, Mother?"

"Yes, that's a sign of true love, I'd say," her mother answered.

"But you're not thinking," Paula said. "A child needs his or her father. Besides trying to support yourself and your baby, there's no family without a father. That's why I could never consider getting married until the war's over."

Burl chewed on a chicken leg. "It cain't be too long, anyway," he said. "My cousin, Bob, has signed up for the Navy. I went down with him, but gol darn! They wouldn't look at me for the service! They said I'm essential as a cattle rancher. So here I am! Look at me, Paula. I'm essential!" He crinkled at her. "And I'm probably here to stay. Just your type!"

Everyone laughed, but she knew he was serious. Her idea of waiting out the war was to be somewhat essential herself.

⋄ ✻ ⋄

Paula's thoughts jumped from one promontory to another, the high points of goals she had set for herself, which must be accomplished without slipping. Or falling. Careful planning and skill would be required to establish an art class for young girls, while at the same time, she must secure a worthy position at Goodfellow, inexperienced as she was.

It was Wednesday, the middle of the week in early February, three days since her return, when Burl called. He insisted that she come out to the ranch for a day of riding on Old Red.

"I don't think you know you're home," he protested when she hesitated.

"Oh yes, I know," she countered. "But I have to get a job and I'm still involved with my art. How about next weekend? I can't manage right away. But I do want to come out and I'm tickled to be back home."

"I'm glad to hear it," Burl said. "Let's make it Saturday week, then. I'll fix a picnic lunch for us. How about ten-thirty?"

"That'll be fine."

"I'll come after you in my trusty pickup. It still runs."

"And being a rancher and a Texan, you've got gas," Paula said with a laugh. This part of the world had not yet been hit by gas rationing, nor was it likely to be much affected.

She had a fleeting thought of Don O'Grady who was keeping the oil flowing, then glanced at her watch. It was 9:25 a.m. If she hurried, she could catch the ten o'clock bus out to the field. She changed into her black twill, woolen suit and black and white spectator pumps, put the last minute touches on her makeup, and dashed out for Chadbourne Street.

She climbed aboard the small, worn green bus with hard springs, and spoke to the thin old cowboy driver who sported a tan, beat-up cowboy hat, and put her quarter in the till. He took off like the wind was after him or an imaginary dogie was about to get away, headed south and soon rumbled across the bridge. Paula hung on. Somehow the bus kept to the road through the driver's flashy wheeling and they arrived at the Air Base ten minutes early.

Paula straightened up and smiled her thanks for the ride, while the old cowboy grinned mightily at her.

She stepped down, then up to the smooth, cement sidewalk, looking around, pleased with the immaculate grounds and the newly painted cream colored barracks buildings. She'd never been here before. A couple of trainer planes buzzed overhead in the clear, blue sky and she saw several cadets in olive drab uniform walking in lively cadence to their appointed places. She wondered where Headquarters was. That was where she must go to apply for a job. Aware of the fresh green scent of cut grass, she walked straight ahead.

Then she saw the stars and stripes waving in the breeze high above a building off to the right. The flag! Filled with emotion, she stopped and stood gazing at the red, white and blue, proudly waving, proclaiming America's freedom. *My flag!* Her throat constricted and hot tears welled up. She was bound with her countrymen in spirit and body to keep Old Glory flying, Old Glory that had been so viciously desecrated at Pearl Harbor! Lives were taken, lives were given, and more lives would be given and taken, but the stars and stripes would fly forever.

She wiped her eyes and resumed walking, her pace quickened. Here was Headquarters, Building One.

Paula entered and soon faced the Commanding Officer's private secretary. She was greeted by the young woman and explained that she wished to apply for a secretarial position.

"Have you had any experience?"

"I have good typing and shorthand, and of course, good English, spelling and grammar."

Without a pause, the young, woman replied, "How would you like to be secretary to Colonel McIntyre?"

Wondering what was wrong with him, or if this were a joke, Paula hid her skepticism with a smooth question. "The C.O.?"

"Yes." The young woman nodded, then gave a broad smile of reassurance. "I think you came at just the right time. Who told you about this opening?"

"I came of my own accord."

"Well, I'm glad, because I like you. I only this morning gave my notice to the colonel. You see, I'm a little bit too pregnant to work any longer."

Paula's eyes widened at this revelation. Then she asked, "May I have an application form?"

When she filled out the form, she was wise enough to claim her typing speed at only sixty words per minute, although she customarily typed at eighty. She'd been told that sixty was considered very good and clerk-typists need only type at a speed of forty. But she did state her shorthand speed at one hundred words per minute, which was adequate and better than average. The ranking for the position was GS III, at one hundred forty-three dollars per month, generous sick leave, and a pension plan. This was next to the top for a civilian secretarial position. Paula found herself condensed, her enthusiasm congealed into solid gelatinous calm such as she affected when she was about to make a grand slam in bridge.

She had turned in the papers to the secretary, when the Colonel walked in. After he was settled at his desk, Paula was introduced to him. He took her application and said, "Have a seat."

She sat down in an oak chair beside his desk, facing him, and waited for him to digest herself while she analyzed his personality. He seemed harmless enough, not like a tyrant at all. He was of medium height and build, had medium, blondish coloring, and was about forty, which was getting up there for the Air Corps. Bland was the word. *I could work for him.*

He looked up as if he had heard her say that. And she saw an intelligence in his light blue eyes that pleased her.

"I see you attended the University of Texas," he said.

"Yes, majoring in Art," she said. "After Pearl Harbor, I quit to come home and work at Goodfellow. I would have graduated this June."

He rocked back in his chair, swept away at the news. "You actually quit so you could come to work here?"

"Yes. President Roosevelt said that every man, woman and child is needed to keep our freedom and to save the world." He nodded gravely, putting the application down. "How would you like to be my secretary? You're permanent?"

Paula gave him a frank smile, showing her eagerness. "I'd like it very much. And yes, I'm permanent. I'm not going to get married till after the war."

Colonel McIntyre smiled with satisfaction. "When can you start?"

"Monday?" she asked.

"We'll have to get a security clearance for you...but I'd say you could start a week from Monday."

"There shouldn't be any trouble," Paula said, then added, "but I've never worked for the government before, so I've never had a security clearance."

"You'll need it here because we handle Secret and Confidential regulations of the War Department and Central Flying Training Command. You'll be privy to all these papers. Yours will be a position of absolute trust."

She simply nodded.

"I have your telephone number and will give you a call when the security clearance comes through."

From the FBI, she wondered, but merely said, "Thank you, Sir. The number is in my father's name in the San Angelo directory, if you should need to check."

Colonel McIntyre stood and bade her good-bye, saying, "I'll give you a call when the clearance is in, Miss Roncourt."

She thanked his secretary on her way out, elated over the propitious timing of her interview with Colonel McIntyre, the Commanding Officer, and that he hired her without even considering other applicants. What a prestigious position and at a magnificent salary! She had never dreamed of such good fortune.

Bonnie and her parents rejoiced with her that evening and Paula hoped her luck would hold out for the art class she wished to organize. After much consideration, she decided that the best prospects were in the Methodist Youth Fellowship at her church, the downtown First Methodist Church.

She was permitted to meet with them the following Sunday evening in a small room that mimicked a basement area, but which was on ground level with the sanctuary above. There were no windows, only a blackboard, podium, a studio piano and bench to one side. Wooden folding chairs were placed in three rows facing the podium.

Ten young people assembled at six-thirty o'clock, the girls in the majority. They ranged in age from twelve to fifteen. Paula noticed how the older girls tried to get an elegant fourteen year old's attention. He was self-effacing, yet noticeable for his handsome blond looks with regular features, a deep cleft in his chin, and wavy blond hair. The three other boys hung in together but this taller, slender young man seated himself off in the back row on the edge, where he could make an early escape.

Verna Oldham, the thirty-five year old leader, came in carrying a load of red Sunday School hymnals. Paula saw the resemblance to the popular boy and knew she was his mother. She helped Mrs. Oldham distribute the hymnals and the meeting opened with the singing of "I Walked In The Garden With Him."

Mrs. Oldham rose from the piano bench and introduced Paula, saying she was here to bring a new opportunity to the group. She would let Miss Roncourt explain.

Paula rose, stood at the podium, and smiled at each youth. They responded with smiles for her and she felt encouraged.

"I'm an artist," she said. "I'm looking for other artists to teach. How many of you like to draw?"

The tall, blond youth immediately raised his hand and three of the girls timidly volunteered. "Fine!" Paula said. She brought up her winning painting, "The Button Box," and held it up for them to see. "This is my painting that won the competition in the Art Department at the University." They all looked with wide eyes, impressed. "I'm just showing it to you so you'll know more about me and also to show what you'll be able to do some day with your art." She was glad now that Professor Brown had decided to take only her large masterpiece and had left this painting with her. It stood in good place for her credentials.

"How many of you have ever visited a cattle ranch?" she then asked.

Surprised, most of the youths raised their hands.

"I'm planning a picnic this Saturday," Paula continued, "but I can only take those who want to attend art classes. This will be our first class out at the Lazy S Ranch. We'll meet here at the church at ten o'clock. Our classes will be held every Saturday morning here at ten o'clock for one hour. The fee is five dollars, half that for piano lessons. If you wish to give your regular attendance, I'll teach you to draw and from there we'll advance to painting."

She remained standing but gave them time to discuss this with one another. One girl raised her hand and asked, "How long will these classes go on? Will we have the summer off?"

"Yes, if that's what the class wants," Paula answered.

There was more discussion among the girls, while the blond youth sat quietly alone. Paula was disturbed. She'd meant the art class only for girls, yet she hadn't specified that. Now was the time to explain this, but it would seem as if the Oldham boy was not welcome. Should she include him in a girl's class? She looked over at him and he gave her a big smile. He's truly interested! I'll just have to let him join if he wants to.

Having made that decision, she asked if there were any more questions. "You'll furnish your own sketching pad and you'll also need to bring charcoal sticks for our fun next Saturday. And bring your lunch, too. We can't expect Mr. Stein to feed us."

They all laughed and shook their heads at that.

"Please raise your hand if you plan to take this art class," Paula said. Three girls and the Oldham boy raised their hands and she passed out a green flyer that gave class instructions. "Here is the information you'll need and be sure to show it to your folks. My telephone number is listed and I'll be happy to talk with them."

She picked up her painting and was leaving, when one girl asked, "Miss Roncourt, what will we do out at the ranch?"

"We'll sketch!" she answered, her gaze full of enthusiasm.

*

When Paula called Burl and asked if she could bring four of her art students with her for the picnic, his first reaction was one of disappointment. It was to be a special day with everything planned for just the two of them—riding, eating, and no telling what else. He'd waited a long time. But it would never do to cross Paula if he wanted to make time with her, and here was a chance to prove that he liked children and would make a good father. He quickly assumed the deep voice of paternal and brotherly inclusiveness essential to her plans.

Upon hearing his generous reassurance over the telephone, she could scarcely admit to herself that part of the reason for taking the children was to avoid being alone with Burl. There was safety in numbers. But the main reasons, she insisted to herself, were two-fold. First of all, she wanted to give the youths a good time, a happy time that would make them look upon the art class as a new adventure. And second, she wanted to give herself an opportunity to sort them out according to their abilities.

The handsome lad was Verna Oldham's son and his first name was Thomas. Tom Oldham. Then there were Alice Jones, 13; Doris Main, 12; and Reva Kelly, 15. She wondered if age meant anything in this instance. Probably not. She was thrilled to make this start with a congenial group, though limited in number, and looked forward to having a good time herself.

Burl arrived at the church on schedule and he helped the girls up into the box of his blue Chevy pickup. He had supplied one of his mother's handmade, downfilled comforters for them to sit on. Tom hoisted himself up with no trouble. One by one, Paula handed him four of the wooden, slatted folding chairs, which he carefully put down out of the way near the cab.

Paula checked for lunches, sketching pads, charcoal sticks and pencils, and to see that everyone was seated. Burl helped her into the cab and they rolled off down Beauregard Street headed west. The Lazy S Ranch was situated twenty miles southwest of San Angelo. It would take about thirty minutes to get there, but Paula, hearing the laughter and singing at her back, had no worries about her students. She and the youths were dressed for the ranch with cowboy boots and hats and warm jackets. The sun was shining and Paula bubbled with anticipation as bright as the day.

She loved the ranch and being with Burl, her childhood neighbor and buddy, and the youths of clear conscience, altogether peeled away the years, leaving her a child once more. She told Burl of her scheme to have the young people sit in the truck and sketch the rail fence of the corral from there. That would be the first thing, then he could give them a tour of the barn and stable before lunch. After lunch, maybe they could take turns riding out on the range. Say, for an hour?

"Yeah," Burl approved. "But what're you goin' to do all that time?"

"I'm going to ride with you on Old Red while my *artistes amateur* sketch on their own for half an hour. Then I'll evaluate their work and talk with each one. It won't take long. I'd say at about eleven-fifteen or eleven-thirty, you can give them the tour."

Burl lifted a straight brow. "I can hardly wait to get there. The horses are already saddled, the drinks are in the cooler, and the cole slaw and potato salad just waitin'."

"I know! You want to see if I still have an appetite after a hard ride, or if I can still ride at all. Anyway, we won't starve. The kids all brought their own lunches, but I'm sure they can eat more."

The land stretched away, tan with splotches of grey-green sage, pear cactus, and mesquite. Paula imagined herself up on Old Red, the wind in her face, the roan's eager warmth transmitted through his flanks and rollicking gallop. She sniffed the familiar air of the semi-desert plants and the sun washed dust, where clouds never darkened and rain seldom blew. Home! Like Burl, she could hardly wait.

Off to the left, they saw a leaping deer, but no cattle. They made good time, noticing a few buzzards hanging in the sky. After awhile, they turned in and drove under the Stein gateway, a great arc of black wrought iron letters proclaiming: LAZY S RANCH. The gravelled road was wide enough for trucks to pass, and they soon saw the large red barn not far from the white rambler shaded by a tall pecan tree. It was a frame building behind native grey stone pillars and a gracious veranda. The barn and windmill stood off to the right, across the driveway from the house.

Burl put on the brakes and came to an easy stop near the gate to the corral, where Old Red and a companion Appaloosa mare were tied to a fencepost. Several herefords stood off in an adjoining pen near a water trough and bales of hay.

Paula helped herself down from the truck and slammed the door with a bang in her hurry to get to the students. She got their attention and explained the day's program.

Alice, the thirteen year old who was small for her age, looked shunted, her mouth turned down. "You want us to sketch a crummy ol' fence? What's fun about that?"

The other girls joined in her complaint, vowing there was nothing interesting about an ol' rail fence and a cowboy fence at that. It was for boys. They began to leave the truck, but Paula stood stock still before them.

"This is your first assignment," she said. "I'll admit it may be different to sketch the fence from this angle as you sit in the truck bed. You'll be above it. It will test your abilities in some ways you've never thought of. Can you draw a straight line? Can you make the fence rail? I'll give you half an hour, then I'll be back to evaluate your sketches."

"Are you going to give us a grade?" Doris asked.

"Don't worry about that," Paula said. "You'll be grading yourselves. I expect you to do the best you can."

Reva appealed to her leniency. "Miss Roncourt, if we do the fence, can we sketch the barn or something else we want to afterwards?"

Paula beamed at her. "Of course, Reva! You all can sketch or draw anything you like after you've finished your assignment."

Satisfied then, the girls arranged their chairs so each person had a view of the fence, sat down, and placed their pads on their laps. Tom showed Reva how to hold hers up with her left hand, leaving her right hand free to work. Paula was confident they could handle things themselves. Without another word, she left for that invigorating ride with Burl.

Old Red whinnied at her approach, tossing his head, pulling on his reins to get to her. She laughed, overjoyed that he recognized her. She patted his neck, murmuring into his ear, "How are you, Old Red? Is my cow pony ready for a gallop with his favorite girl?"

His large brown eye gazed at her and she threw her arms around his neck and kissed him. Then, while he obediently stood still, she mounted into the saddle. Burl took the mare and they rode out onto the range, breaking into a trot. They soon sped up into a friendly race. For ten minutes, free as the wind, they galloped across the plain. Then they slowed down, turned around, and took a walking pace while they talked. Paula told Burl about her new job at Goodfellow and he told her about his plans for the ranch.

When they returned to the corral, Paula went to help her students, while Burl took care of the horses.

Tom held out his sketch for her judgment, but Paula still wished to give the girls priority. She began with small Alice. There was no perspective and the fence was an attempt at straight lines, smeared in places. The rails had been filled in so they were solid and one could tell that it was a fence.

"This is good, Alice," Paula said. "I'm pleased that you finished your assignment. Next week we'll take up forms and I know you'll like that. I can tell from your sketch."

Alice was tickled with this praise and gave a triumphant look at twelve year old Doris. Paula saw that Doris had a sense of perspective. In addition, her lines were clear and done in confident sweeps.

She smiled at the budding artist with approval. "I see you have good, clean lines and a sense of perspective, Doris. I like your sketch. Your assignment next week will be more interesting."

Reva, fifteen, was attractive with small features in a square face, although her brown hair was fine and hung in straight strands. She sat looking down, heart pumping with apprehension. Reva had plenty of criticism at home and could expect nothing else. Yet there was something about this teacher that made her glance up with courage.

"Reva! How nice!" Paula exclaimed. "Do you know your fence is smiling?" Reva looked at the sketch and giggled. She hadn't intended for the gate to open like that, but it was true. One could imagine it looked like a smile. "It's saying, Welcome," Paula said. "You've done a good job and I know you'll learn quickly."

Reva thanked her and Paula moved over toward Tom.

The youth appealed to her sense of beauty in color and human form, but beyond this, his elegance sprang more from his sensitivity in a superior intelligence than from his handsome appearance. Paula warned herself that she must not become partial to this lad. Her girls deserved as much attention as he. She recognized that she must not favor any one of them, either. Impartiality was a strong concept for her folks as parents and she should follow the same principle with her students. To be successful, she should not only be impartial, but she must also give her pupils freedom of expression.

Paula stifled a sigh and took Tom's pad in her hands. She held it up and looked.

Amazing!

There was the Stein rail fence floating free in the sky. Far below, the earth was delineated in a realistic manner with prickly pear cactus, sage brush, and even a cottontail rabbit hiding in the shade. The fence crazily zig-zagged off to the right, growing smaller and smaller, till it disappeared. Paula looked at Tom and saw his brilliant excitement glowing in anticipation of her reaction.

"Flying Corral Fence," she said, giving it a title.

He grinned.

"Whatever gave you this idea?"

"My mother told me the Bible says, 'That which is bound on earth shall be bound in heaven.'"

"Fences are certainly binding," Paula agreed, "but the quotation holds a spiritual meaning."

"Then it means that there are fences in heaven," Tom told her.

"The Bible also says that whatever you loose on earth shall be loosed in heaven," Paula replied. "You could be right."

"Everything matters," Tom said with certainty.

"Everything matters," Paula agreed. "Your sketch is now loosed in heaven. It is spirit and matter combined. I congratulate you!"

Tom asked eagerly, "You like it?"

"I should say! It's excellent and you have an unusual imagination and hand for one your age. You're a natural artist!" She returned the sketch pad to him and he hugged it close to his chest.

Paula looked up and saw Burl sauntering toward them. "It's time for your tour," he called. "If you want any lunch."

Chapter Four

The spacious blue skies of Texas buzzed with the propellers of the North American BT-9 Yale and the Vultee BT-13 Valiant planes.

San Angelo, high on the Edwards Plateau, where the wind blew consistently for take-offs and landings, but where no 'weather' interfered, was home to Goodfellow and the more recently established San Angelo Army Air Corps Base out west of town. These were only two of the sixteen Air Corps fields dotting the land of the largest state in the union.

Bombardiers and Navigators were schooled at the SAAC Base. The majority of these young men had applied for pilot training, but their intelligence test scores had not come up to par. They were granted entry into the bombardier/navigator or gunner positions instead, happy to be accepted in the U.S. Army Air Corps, which they considered above any other military command. Instinct told them that victory would in large part depend upon their own acuity, an accuracy that would derive from ninety percent courage and confidence under fire.

The Air Corps was glamorous. A pilot had to depend upon the precision of his crew. They would work hand in hand. The glamour came from the danger in the skies. They were eager to take the risk, a heady elixir to be absorbed in support of their intrepid pilots and co-pilots. Besides, the Air Corps enjoyed top rations and superior quarters. Flying above, they would cover for the ground troops. Those poor ground grunts! Better to fall like an American eagle than to be mired in the dirt and misery of cannon and hand grenade.

Paula had never visited the SAAC and she didn't know anyone out there, but she saw far more of those troops in town than cadets from Goodfellow. Bonnie was distraut these days and this troubled Paula, although she was happy in her job. And her art students were doing well. She had begun to let them draw with pencils, copying still life forms, sometimes cheating with ovals, circles, rectangles, and triangles, which she thought was more cartoonish than real art. But these were juniors and it wouldn't hurt to let them have this fun for awhile before they took up light and shadow and perspective. Bonnie's problem was that Ralph was talking of joining up. And he hadn't mentioned a wedding date before that fatal time.

One Friday evening when Paula came home from work and went into their bedroom, she found Bonnie yawed on the bed, sobbing her heart out.

Paula flung her purse down on a chair beside the dresser. "Bonnie! What's wrong?" She rushed to her sister and smoothed her hair in a loving caress. "It can't be that bad!"

Bonnie sat up, her face woeful, eyes swollen, snuffling, trying to wipe the tears away, which kept flowing against her will. "Ralph doesn't want to join the Air Corps! He says he's not smart enough to be a cadet at Goodfellow and he's not going out to that second rate San Angelo Air Corps Base. He's going to join the Navy!"

"The Navy! I know you're disappointed, but he has mentioned this before. The Navy is a good service."

Bonnie stopped crying, wiped her eyes with a Kleenex, and blew her nose. "But he could be here right at home!"

"You're not thinking. In the Air Corps he'd be sent off somewhere and probably be in more danger than on a ship. Don't you realize that?"

Bonnie looked into her sister's intelligent eyes, a gaze that held a familiar admonition to think. Pause and think. But how could she, when Ralph hadn't even said he wanted to marry her before he left?

Paula flared up. "He hasn't said you should get married before he shoves off?"

Mute and miserable, Bonnie shook her head.

"We'll fix that! You invite him to dinner Sunday and you'll announce the wedding, inviting us all to come. After all, you've been engaged for two years."

Bonnie brightened, wondering at the sly scheme with a mixture of hope and fear.

"Of course you can do it," Paula encouraged. "We'll all be with you and it's quite a normal thing, you know. It's what we all expect. And Ralph, too, truth to tell."

The wedding was held in the church sanctuary, virtually empty except for the officiating minister and the few members of the immediate families. The date was March 10th, only five days before Ralph left for San Diego in 1942.

Bonnie was now a married woman. It seemed like a dream, something she had imagined so many times, but never without a husband to have and to hold after the ceremony. The dreamlike experience suddenly took on a joyous reality when Bonnie's doctor verified that she was 'fragrant.' Her dearest wish had come true.

The Byrnes expected Bonnie to live with them, but Paula persuaded her to stay with her till June, when she could quit her job and Adele would return from Austin. The girls were happy to pay board to their parents and have enough money left over for savings. It was a beneficial arrangement for all concerned.

⁂

In June, Adele returned home, proudly bearing her Bachelor of Arts degree, looking forward to becoming an independent piano teacher. She was aware that only fifteen percent of the young people in the country attended college. This was a statement her Education professor often gave to impress upon his students how fortunate they were and to take their studies seriously. She was well qualified to teach and expected to hold classes at various levels of accomplishment.

Paula was tickled to have the companionship of her bosom friend again and especially since Bonnie had moved out. But Adele didn't seem to understand that she only had Saturdays and Sundays off. She expected her to come see her almost every day.

One Saturday morning Paula agreed to meet Adele at the Concho Cafe for lunch after her art class. They scooted in at a comfy booth against the wall and gave their orders for barbecued ribs, hash browns, and pinto beans, a hearty meal. Adele sat, spreading her long fingers flat on the table, showing the large, blue sapphire her father had given her. It was the September birthstone and she often posed her hands this way, admiring the ring and her hands as if ready to play the piano.

This proud gesture, egotistical in nature, amused Paula. "I like your sapphire, too," she said. "Too bad I can't flourish my gaudy paint brushes."

Adele quickly withdrew her hands. "I'm just glad my wrists are still strong. Brenda Ford ruined hers. I don't know whether she'll ever be able to play again or not."

Paula sobered. "I'm glad you're strong, too. Have you had any response to your ads for piano students?"

Adele's beautiful mouth formed a grimace. "You know I haven't." She pouted with envy at Paula's obvious success in spite of her having no degree and no courses in Education. But she wouldn't follow in her footsteps and seek support from church members. That was beneath her.

The waitress brought their plates of food and also served hot cornbread and butter, asking what they'd like to drink.

"Iced tea," Adele said, and Paula nodded.

She felt bad that Adele's plans hadn't worked out. "Maybe later, Adele," she said. "Rhonda Humboldt has been San Angelo's piano teacher, not to say the only teacher, for ages. She has a reputation that's hard to challenge. Why don't you spread the word personally, and then you can advertise later. In the meantime, I've asked about a clerical job for you out at Goodfellow. I'm sorry, but they don't have any openings just now. I'm really disappointed, because I wanted us to work together."

"That means I'm still stymied."

Paula buttered some cornbread and took a bite. "I've heard there are openings out at SAAC. I'll bet you could get on as a clerk-typist. Why not try it?"

"I guess that'd be better than a lowly file jerk."

"Think of all the fellows you'd meet. Besides, you'd be working for the Air Corps, helping us win the war."

"I presume you're still dating Burl," Adele said, changing the subject.

"Oh yes. I see him once in awhile." The plain food, especially the pinto beans seasoned with chili, reminded Paula of the ranch and Burl. He was tall, strong, hard working, an honest Texan worthy of respect. He had pampered her since childhood and she had come to depend upon him. Burl would always be there with his crinkly eyes, capable hands, and solid feet on terra firma, ready to take care of her. As stable as the earth, he was, a mainstay for life. She could call up his love any time she wished.

Adele gave her a challenging smile.

"You know, Paula, Burl has been absolutely devoted to you for years. But he just might have a change of heart some day and get tired of the way you treat him."

Paula swallowed that along with a bite of potatoes. "Well, he's free to do as he pleases. I'm just not thinking of marriage right now. Times are too fraught with danger."

Adele burst out laughing.

Paula was taken aback. "What's so funny?"

"That's no excuse. Burl's exempt! And look at Bonnie. She got married without any qualms like all the hundreds of others!"

"Can I help it if my ideas are different?"

Adele quieted down. "No, I guess not." She looked at her friend with an understanding smile. "I think I'll take your suggestion and try for a job at the SAAC."

"They're hiring right now. You'll like it out there and I know you'll feel much better with a regular salary to call your own."

Adele grinned at her. "I'm going to save for my trousseau."

Paula was startled.

Adele didn't have any boyfriends. Could be, she was thinking of Burl?

∗ ✻ ∗

Adele sat at her Singer sewing machine, alone in the sewing room behind the front bedroom of the Turner home. Miniature slants of sunlight from the venitian blinds afforded sufficient light without glare on the busy perforating needle, while Adele guided the straight seam of the skirt for a green cotton pique dress. Her hands moved steadily forward, pushing the material at a smooth rate, eyes alert, foot engaged at the electric pedal concomitant with the desired speed. She reached the armhole and let up on the pedal, bringing the needle up out of the fabric. Satisfied, she lifted the lever and released the silvery, forked foot that held the material in place. Then she pulled the dress away, stretching out the green thread, and cut it off.

The dress was freed. Finished! All she need do was to put in the hem. She held the dress up and shook it out. It was just right. Simple, form fitting in the waist with a gathered skirt and an inch-wide belt and side placket zipper. Really elegant with its jewel neckline and short sleeves. She could wear it anywhere.

Adele was a fine seamstress. It was her button box that Paula had painted for the art competition. Her summer days had been spent planning a new wardrobe. Designing skirts, blouses, jackets, and dresses had made her forget everything else, including the hot weather. This dress of dark bottle-green was the last on her list. She turned on the radio and listened to the Sons Of The Pioneers singing, "Cool, Clear, Water," while she quickly hemmed the dress by hand. She loved that song. She loved it so much that she knew the words, so expressive, the Pioneers singing as one voice with marvelous harmony. She sang along with them and continued singing while dashing upstairs to put the dress away.

She opened the door to her bedroom walk-in closet and stood a moment, feasting on her beautiful clothing. From the high rod on the left hung her evening gowns and coats. The rod facing her was seven feet long, running the width of the closet. Here, arranged in perfect order were her jackets, skirts, blouses and dresses according to color. The greens shaded into the blues, then the violets and purples, merging into browns and yellows, paling into ivories and finally, whites.

Her wardrobe was complete.

It's late September, she reminded herself. There's no putting off any longer. It's time to put this wardrobe to use.

As Paula had suggested, she must go out to the SAAC and apply for a job as file clerk or clerk-typist. It was not an exciting prospect. Her typing was strictly hunt and peck. Would she have the nerve to claim she was a clerk-typist?

On the other hand, she mused, I'd hate to spend my days filing, getting painful paper cuts on my precious fingers. But I do have superior dexterity, and if I try, my typing should improve. Maybe as time goes on, I'll get to do more and more typing.

She drew in her breath and gave attention to her clothes again. What should she wear for her interview? The men were all used to olive drab, so that was out. It should be something businesslike, yet attractive. The green of the new dress would clash too much with the O.D. Why not some sort of yellow or cream? That should lighten the mood, but be serious enough.

Adele wore a pastel yellow skirt and jacket with a white blouse, which brightened her spirit and gave her confidence for the interview. It wasn't so bad, after all. The young men were helpful and courteous and she was hired into Supplies to begin the first of October. Staff Sgt. Richard Weaver, a regular army man, would be her supervisor. He welcomed her aboard and she was glad to have someone like him who knew the ropes.

The job gave Adele a new perspective on life. While she worked nearly alone in the office, which held a rank of ten four-drawer filing cabinets, she was doing a deceptively simple task that could make or break efficiency. Hers was the outer office, where another sergeant and a private first class came and went. The stock room lined with shelves of office and classroom supplies, such as notebooks, manila envelopes, pencils, and erasers, including typewriter erasers with their green brushes, was flanked by two offices. The one on the other side was smaller and it was Sergeant Weaver's private office. Adele was glad she wasn't responsible for supplies. The job of filing and typing requisitions was enough to keep her busy. Sergeant Weaver typed his own letters and she seldom saw him.

One morning she was filing a sheaf of papers, her back to the door, when she heard the rapid footsteps of a man approaching. She turned and saw a tall, handsome Second Lieutenant who was new to her. He was in a hurry. He looked around, and upon seeing no one else, quickly honed in on her.

She released a folder and gave him her attention. "Can I help you, Sir?"

"I'm looking for a requisition that Major Sanderson is interested in."

"Do you have the number? I can look it up for you."

He paused. "I think it's a CN Dash Three something. Supposed to be dated 19 September."

"Oh yes. Classroom Notebook 3-142. Just a moment, please." She moved to the cabinet on the right and pulled out the top drawer, glad she was wearing a rubber finger. It made her work easier and faster. Somehow, she wanted to please this young man and not simply because of his rank.

She found the CN-3 series and sorted through the numbers. Within a few moments, she located the 142 dated 19 September and pulled it out. "Here it is." She handed it to him.

He quickly scanned it, saying, "That was quick." Then he looked at her and the joy of discovery dawned in his hazel eyes. He grinned with surprised interest. "Are you single or plural?"

Adele grinned back. "Single."

Their gazes held for a long moment. Something extraordinary was happening. "And you?" she asked.

His whole being nodded assent, although he didn't move. Then in a low baritone, his voice full of intimacy, he said, "Now we're double."

Adele's psyche made an adjustment, an irrevocable change. It was true. In this instant, she had found her soul mate and he had made the same wondrous affirmation.

"We're twins!" she announced.

He laughed. "North and South do make a union."

She sobered. "Where are you from?"

"Chicago."

That explained his clipped speech, rapid and funny. She liked it. "That's where the gangsters rule," she said wisely.

"And this yere, ma'am, is where the cowboys fool."

They laughed together.

"By the way," Adele said, "we don't let any requisitions out of this office."

He waved it at her.

"I'll just take it to show to the Major. Then I'll bring it right back. He wants to verify that it was made, that's all."

"No, you may not do that. I'll make out a copy for you to take." She closed the file drawer.

"But what about the number?"

"I'll just have to cross out the..... Oh, that's what Sergeant Weaver meant about the blank forms if I ever needed to fill one out."

"That doesn't seem right," the lieutenant objected.

Adele stopped at her typewriter. "What is your name, Lieutenant? I've never seen you before. Why didn't Major Sanderson come to check on this requisition himself?"

"I apologize, Miss. I'm Fred Thomas from the Major's office. He's tied up right now and I thought I could be of assistance."

She sat down and fed the requisition form into the typewriter. "He can come see for himself, but we can't let the original out of the master file."

"I understand. I'm sure you know the proper procedure."

She typed up a copy for him, inserting the 142 number.

"I'm sorry to be so much trouble, Miss...Miss..."

"Adele Turner."

"Miss Turner. I really owe you a dinner for all your trouble. How about dinner and a movie tonight?"

She hesitated too long for comfort.

"I'd hate for us to get off on the wrong foot," he said.

She smiled at him. "Do you prefer to drive your limousine into the city, or shall we take our leisure right here?"

It was a charmed evening, the beginning of a whirlwind courtship. Their friends said they never saw a more ideal couple, often remarking they were so alike that they could be taken for brother and sister. They had similar honey blonde coloring, the same tall, graceful physique, and most important, the same sense of humor.

Paula was happy for Adele, but it was as though her friend had died. It seemed she was gone all the time. Paula realized this was only natural and to be expected. She became more and more absorbed in her own job, teaching her students, and with occasional outings at the Lazy S. She and Burl were both Democrats and interested in politics. Paula also kept an eye on what was going on in the community and when a group of local women got together to organize a San Angelo USO, she attended their first meeting. Through her support, they secured a large room adjoining the First

Methodist Church that could be adapted with the installation of a small kitchen.

One Sunday afternoon in early March, Adele called. Her voice was muffled and teary. "My father says he doesn't want to catch me going out with the Lieutenant at the SAAC again. I was just trying to tell him we're going to get married when he went into a rage."

Paula wondered why all the histrionics. Surely Mr. Turner knew his daughter would get married some day.

"Why don't you soft pedal the marriage bit and just announce your engagement?"

Adele calmed down at the suggestion. "But I can't do that! He's forbidden me to even see Fred again!"

"That's pretty ridiculous. You're a grown woman and he's got to realize that."

"Paula, could you come over and talk to him?"

"What about your mother?"

"Mom just sits there making herself invisible. She tried at first, but Dad didn't even hear her. Why don't you come over for supper tonight and with us all at the table, he'll have to at least be decent and listen."

"That's a good idea. Your Mom is on your side?"

"Oh yes. She just feels helpless, but she'd be tickled to have you come for supper. The two of you could surely get some common sense into my father."

"Okay! I'm willing to try. Don't worry. He'll have to come around."

※

The Turner home, a two-story frame house with a large front porch, was situated on the west side of City Park in a nice neighborhood. It was a mile and a half walk for Paula.

Mrs. Roberta Turner gave Paula a warm welcome, saying she was so glad she could come. The tall, buxom woman was the socialite of the town and she held herself proudly erect. Her dark brown eyes and sleek black hair cut in a short bob contrasted with Adele's lighter coloring, but there was a resemblance in the prominent nose and shape of the mouth.

Paula glimpsed Mr. Turner, a heavy set figure of a man, seated in a tan leather chair by the radio. He rose and greeted Paula, showing his sincere approval. If anyone could, this young lady could set his daughter aright.

"We haven't been seeing enough of you lately," he said, his face and voice smiling with pleasure. "I'm looking forward to hearing all about your activities."

"Yes, I've been pretty busy," Paula responded. "It takes a lot of work and caring for our men, too, to keep the home fires burning."

They escorted her through the dining room to the kitchen and breakfast nook, where Adele was busy making waffles.

"A waffle supper!" Paula exclaimed. She breathed in the wonderful fragrance of maple syrup and the combination of coffee and spicy link sausages. "My favorite! My walk worked up an appetite, so I hope you have plenty, Adele."

Fruit dishes holding peeled sections of pink Texas Grapefruit were already served at the place settings. A large bowl of white grapes and ruby cheeked Jonathans graced the center of the table, adding to the attractiveness of the tangarine placemats and bone china.

"What a beautiful table! Paula exclaimed.

"It's just an informal supper," Mrs. Turner said, hiding her pleasure at the compliment.

"I'm sure Adele is learning from you," Paula said. "She'll make a good housewife some day." She glanced over at her and caught a flash of alarm.

"Here, Paula. Have a seat and a waffle," Adele said. She forked up a golden brown, steaming waffle and put it on the plate for her guest. "You too, Mom and Dad. We have plenty to start now."

The conversation became lively with Paula and Adele telling of their experiences out at the airfields.

"Isn't that how you met the lieutenant you've been dating?" Paula asked Adele.

"Yeah. He came in for a requisition and it was love at first sight."

Mr. Turner made a bumbling, churning noise as he cleared his throat. "There's no such thing as falling in love at first sight."

"Oh yes there is," Adele countered. "I know, because that's what happened to me."

"It hasn't happened to you yet, has it, Paula?" Mr. Turner asked.

"No, sir. But I've heard of it and everyone knows it happens. You and Fred have been dating for quite awhile, haven't you?" Paula asked Adele.

"Nearly six months," she answered.

Mr. Turner scowled at her. "Against my wishes."

Mrs. Turner broke in. "What's wrong with her dating and having a good time, Ed?"

"There's nothing wrong with having a good time with one of your own kind. But we don't know a cotton pickin' thing about this man. And he's regular army. Doesn't that tell you something? Do you want our daughter married into that low class?"

There was silence around the table.

Mr. Turner put his fork down. "This fellow's from up North. You two don't have anything in common. What do you think you'd do or where would you live, being married to a damn Yankee? I tell you it's all wrong! There's plenty of time for you to find the right kind of man to marry." He appealed to Adele's common sense, pumping assurance into her.

"I can't live without him!" she wailed.

Mr. Turner was touched.

He lowered his voice to a modulated calm. "I say you're going at this too fast, Adele. I'll let you continue to date him for six more months. Then we'll see. Maybe some other young man will take your fancy and you'll forget all about this Fred."

"Oh no!" Adele said. "But maybe I could stand being engaged to him for another six months."

"That sounds reasonable," Paula said. "What do you think, Mrs. Turner?"

"I think a six-month engagement is a fine idea," she replied.

With this support, Adele grew bolder.

"And anyway," she said, "Fred isn't such a foreign Northerner. He's told me that his family came up North from the South."

Alabama or Kentucky, Mr. Turner wondered. But he cast that thought aside and gave his blessing for a six-month engagement period. "After that, we'll see," he said.

Adele took this conditional assent to be as good as a permission. In view of this turn of events, why wait for six months? They could marry right away in secret. She and Fred schemed to exchange their wedding vows with the SAAC Chaplain officiating. Once married, her father could have no further objections.

Adele confided in Paula, but in none of her other friends.

She asked Paula to be a witness to the marriage. It was with reluctance that she agreed to this willful act of concealment. Yet Adele was her best friend and she could not deny her.

Adele and Fred were like a couple of children on a prank. There was much kissing and hugging and maneuvering, but it was no prank, when a few weeks later, Adele discovered she was pregnant, 'fragrant' like Bonnie.

Paula shared in their joy at the news and was particularly happy that Fred had an apartment in officers quarters where they could live.

"The secret will eventually come out," she told Adele, "but I'm thrilled for you. You can count on me. I promise to be the godmother for your child." Then she laughed. "Do you realize that you and Bonnie will have your babies on about the same day in November? That means I'll be a new godmother twice over!"

Chapter Five

It was disappointing and outlandish.

Except for Tom Oldham, Paula's students didn't take to art very seriously. Spring passed into summer. Tom and Reva stayed with her through August, then when school began and they were busy with practicing for the exciting spelling bee, and in gleeclub and basketball, even they fell away.

The outlandish thing was that Tom, with all his artistic ability and in spite of Paula's efforts, had turned to cartooning. She thought his sketches were gross with heavy strokes of indication, leaving too much to the imagination. He was 'way out in left field so far as her own artistic beliefs were concerned. She could not help him nor approve, but did admit he might make a living at it some day. However, she told him if he ever wanted to take up painting, she'd be happy to coach him.

Typical of her enterprising spirit, she lost no time in complaining about the failure of her educational dream, nor feared an emptiness that could result. On the one hand, she joined the San Angelo Business Women's Club, and on the other hand, she immediately sought and found a tiny, one-room garage apartment and a roommate, Mary Nesbit, the Baptist minister's daughter. These were good moves, since Bonnie and Adele were both preoccupied with their coming motherhood, serene and contented in their growing fullness.

Paula made up her mind to continue her art on her own, and if necessary, she could teach after the war. Things were too disjointed now.

The program speaker for the September luncheon meeting of the business club was a woman with a challenge. She'd been meeting with a group of women on the mezzanine floor of the St. Angeles Hotel, where they knitted woolen socks for servicemen and discussed establishing a USO for the boys in San Angelo. She appealed for help in this worthy cause, explaining that if they could find a place, her group would furnish it. One woman had already promised to donate a piano. Others said they'd help pay for the appliances for a pullman kitchen.

Paula instantly thought of the small vacant building between the First Methodist Church and the telephone company. It was an ideal location, just off Chadbourne on Beauregard Street. She volunteered to inquire about leasing it at a reasonable rate. Her father knew the owner and found that he would be happy to lease it at a nominal rental for the cause.

The deal was closed and the women went into high gear, determined to open by October first. Paula solicited carpenters who donated their labor and built a counter for the kitchen. Contributions of an old gas range, a refrigerator, card tables and chairs, two overstuffed couches, chinaware, glasses, flatware, pans and an iron grill for hamburgers, and even a good carpet poured in. Word got around and some Air Corps men assisted in moving the furnishings, making it more their own home away from home.

Paula found herself spending time there evenings and on weekends, often serving behind the kitchen counter. She wasn't seeing much of Burl these days.

❃ ✳ ❧

This morning, November 16, 1943, Paula's fingers flew over the manual Remington's keys deft as a pianist's, making a cheerful rat-a-tat-tat music of their own. Sunlight beamed on her raven pageboy, which fell around her face in enticing contrast to the white shimmer of her smooth brow. Her blue-eyed gaze concentrated on her work through gold rimmed glasses.

This was the monthly day set aside for cadets to come and complain to their C.O. about anything at all that bothered them. Most of the cadets had come straight from high school and had never been away from home before. At the moment, Col. William P. McIntyre, the Commanding Officer, was acting as a surrogate father to one cadet upset over what he thought to be an unjust rating. Complaining usually did no good, Paula mused, but at least they could get it off their chest to someone in authority. There remained hope of a sort.

Her phone rang. "Colonel McIntyre's office," she sang in her low, melodious voice.

"Hello, Paula!"

Burl! He knew better than to call her at the office.

"Yes," she intoned, maintaining her pleasant manner.

"I'm sorry to bother you, but I've got a chance to run into Abilene and look over a herd of steers at a real good price. First come, first served. Wanta go with me?"

"Burl, you know I can't leave town right now. Bonnie's expecting her baby any minute, and Adele, too. They're counting on me."

"I know, but they're their babies, not yours."

Paula grew angry. "And it's your cattle. I'm sure the babies are more important than any herd of hoofs!"

There was a pause, then Burl spoke again, a plaintive note in his quiet bass. "When am I goin' to see you?" Paula remained silent. Finally, he blurted out, "I suppose I'll have to wait until after the blessed events."

"I expect so," she answered. "And you know I don't like to be called at the office."

"Okay. Next time, I'll send a wire." He hung up, leaving her disturbed.

It wasn't her fault she had no phone at the apartment. She had applied for one, but it took time. She'd have to make up her mind for good about Burl. And soon. There was nothing wrong with him, or not much anyway. That was the trouble.

Paula had known Burl since she was little, when her father bought a chicken ranch on the land adjacent to the Lazy S. The Roncourt and Stein families had been neighbors and friends for years. Now Burl was stuck out at the ranch, while his cousins and friends had gone into the military service. It was hard on him and Paula sympathized. When they were teenagers, Bonnie had had a crush on Burl, but he was cow-eyed over Paula. Bonnie had realized it was hopeless and later, she fell in love with Ralph, now in the Navy fighting in the South Pacific.

Most fellows found Paula attractive and they desired her company. Hers was a sparkling personality bubbling with unquenchable optimism that they found uplifting. But she didn't care to date any Air Corps men. She was a bit older than most cadets and had more education. At the University she had studied French and she still dreamed of becoming an artist famous for her paintings of the broad land and spacious skies on the high plateau, fabulous expressions of fearless freedom and wonder. Some day her paintings would be shown on the Left Bank in Paris and she'd become world renowned. Before this could be realized, though, she must develop an original style or mode of expression. Within her inner core, she asserted that if she kept the faith with her talent, her dreams would come true. Anything was possible. Bolstering her confidence, she recalled what Professor Brown had told her during their last conversation.

"I've learned that art is the very fabric of life," he had said. "The artist is its interpreter and master. Without art there is no culture, no civilization. The artist is worth more, far more than his or her weight in gold. The artist is the priceless human gold."

I am an artist. I am the priceless human gold.

Even as she typed with her own concerns racing about in her mind, Paula wondered how she was going to manage her career in art and if she would ever get married and have a family. Bonnie and Adele were both ahead of her there. But Mary Nesbit, her roommate, was worse off than any of them. Mary was unattractive. She didn't even have a boyfriend. These days with the war going on, it wasn't easy to marry the right person, but Mary surely had a good chance with all these servicemen flooding in for training at Goodfellow and the SAAC. Still, they were here for only nine weeks and gone again, except for the permanent military personnel who were considered undesirable. A girl scarcely had time to say hello and good-bye to the best ones. Paula knew she was lucky to have Burl, but marriage was a serious matter and she wasn't certain about him. Her heart didn't yearn for him as it did for the singular beauty of the surrounding plains.

It was the ranch she loved. If she could have that without Burl.... But even with him and a true passion, that might not be enough. Something in her wanted more. Intuition told her there must be added fulfillment in her brushes and colors, perhaps as far away as other continents. She should settle down in her art and as a woman. Every famous painter became known for his or her own metier, an avant garde affluence, sometimes as shocking as pungent lemon, or at other times fertile in inimical beauty. She would begin here at home. Hers would be different western scenes, not at all like those cowboy and Indian paintings of Ross. Hers would be sky—the sun, moon, and stars! Could she ever paint the ineffable splendor of the heavens?

She typed the final line and carefully took out the eight pages and seven sheets of Carter's Mid-nite carbon paper. Pleased with the clean copies, she quickly separated them. The first cadet had left and someone else entered, bringing to her ears the loud roar of training planes circling for a landing. She looked up.

A tall, dark young man in olive green cadet uniform closed the hall door behind him, then with confidence, he turned and stepped with fluid ease toward Colonel McIntyre's desk, by-passing her own. Stalwart, yet slender, he walked with purpose, his erect posture declaring an assumed authority. In a swift glance, Paula took in this young cadet and his noble features, the high forehead and wide black brows above large, deepset brown eyes. In profile, his nose was perfectly straight. A surge of emotion gripped her, an overwhelming exclamation in soulful recognition.

Confused by this unexpected revelation, she became flustered. Unseeing, she looked down at the chart on her desk, hoping no one had noticed her reaction. This memo wasn't Confidential. *I must get a hold of myself!* It wasn't Secret, either. That was a relief. Otherwise, she'd have to cross the room to place the copies in the safe beside the colonel's desk. Ducking, she picked up a green pencil and colored in a new triangle on an empty square of her chart. Red was for Secret, yellow for Confidential, blue for Restricted, and green for General Distribution. She placed CFTC memo copies in their respective out-baskets, then busied herself, pretending to consult the memo chart while she watched and listened to the two men.

The cadet, at ease with his cap in the crook of his right arm, stood facing his C.O. "But Sir," he was saying, his voice resonating a golden bass, "it would mean a *B* on my record!"

"Would that be so monumental?"

"I was shocked, Sir, when I saw it. I've never had a *B* before."

"A *B* isn't anything to be ashamed of," the colonel responded. "That's a good grade."

"It may be good, Sir, but it isn't excellent. I was too woozy from the flu and that slowed me down. I left out one whole problem. What I'd like to request is that you speak to my instructor and ask him if he would give me another test, a harder one, a make-up. And if I got an *A* on that, he would eliminate the *B* from my record."

Paula, having regained her composure, lifted her head to observe the colonel's reaction. He was nodding, faintly smiling as he looked over the cadet's file. She detected a sense of pride in his manner, the pride a mentor holds in his best student.

A former Flight Instructor in the U.S. Army Air Corps from New York, her boss was still rather astounded to have been appointed full colonel and assigned Commanding Officer of Goodfellow Field, a permanent U.S. Army Air Corps station for Basic Flying Training. Approaching middle age, he was the father figure, the "Old Man," having a slightly pocked face from adolescent scars and a few grey hairs to show he was nearing forty. But he could fly. His was an assured command.

Paula found the C.O. to be fair, not only with her, but also with the officers under him. Her desk stood at right angles to his and she'd seen him deal with both officers and lower ranks of cadets. Having heard horror stories about C.O.s at other bases, she felt lucky to have such a good boss.

"All right, Cameron," he said. I'll make the suggestion to your instructor. But I will say this, you'd better cram for what he'll throw at you. Good luck!"

Paula took off her glasses, picked up her purse from the bottom desk drawer, and quietly left. It was noon and she walked out into the bright sunshine. Her black twilled suit of light wool was comfortable and attractive with a light blue tailored blouse, but her black and white spectator pumps were looking more and more tacky. She almost wished she'd bought another pair before the war instead of those records of Bing Crosby, the Andrews Sisters, and Spike Jones. Yet the music was essential to keep up her morale. It was Praise the Lord and Pass the Ammunition time. Every evening she and Mary listened to the war news over the radio. It was excruciating to hear of the horrible battle on Tarawa Atoll, where one thousand Americans were killed and two thousand wounded. And thousands more Japanese. The war in the gruesome jungles of the South Pacific made her fear for Bonnie's Ralph. But no word of this was breathed to her sister.

And she had become tense again, when raunchy General Patton took his stand against General Rommel in North Africa. At last, the Italian campaign was over. The Allies could concentrate on bombing Germany to hell as if that were the whole battleground. All around the world more and more fine young men were dying for America and to save the world, her Air Corps boys among them. At such times of sorrowful thought, Paula snapped off the radio and played her records.

On many evenings at six o'clock, she absorbed a sustaining hope wafting in the air from the lilting baritone of Kaltenborn's encouraging newscast. No matter how bad the casualties, Kaltenborn always began with, "THERE'S GOOD NEWS TONIGHT!" Then he would tell of some heroic deed and soften the misery. He kept them all going when things were really rough. Paula was thinking about Kaltenborn and that she and her friends would die without him, when she heard someone call her name.

"Miss Roncourt!"

As if by magic, the divine cadet was beside her, speaking her name in a charming manner. She shot a glance at him, but kept going. Her heart raced in time with her quickened step.

He persisted.

"Do you think Colonel McIntyre will talk to my instructor for me?"

"If he said he would, he will."

"I'd be pleased if you'd let me take you to lunch," he said. You headed for the cafeteria?"

"Why yes."

"I thought we could talk it over."

"What over?" She glanced up at him.

"You know. My problem." He was sobersides.

Unable to keep the amusement out of her gaze, she stopped and faced him, as much as to say, This guy is really something!

"You see," he said, trying to get on her good side, "I've wanted to meet you ever since I saw you at the USO, but you were always too busy."

With lifted brows, she gave him a skeptical look. "So you made up this story for Colonel McIntyre just to meet me?"

"Don't get me wrong. Everything I said is perfectly true. But I do think you've got the hang of it." His frank grin showed a row of white, even teeth.

She smiled in return and they resumed walking. I should be flattered, but servicemen are always trying to date me, at least several in each new batch. I'd better stick to my rule and ignore them. They're all strangers from remote places across the country and once they leave Goodfellow, they're expendable. There's simply little future, if any. I don't want to jump off the roof like so many young women. *Caution is the word in wartime. And caution is certainly the better part of marriage.*

"I'm Garner Cameron," he said.

With reluctance Paula introduced herself. Then, as if agreed upon, they remained silent walking down the broad, cement sidewalk toward the cafeteria, which was located half a mile away. Paula became oblivious of her tall companion.

She gazed about and breathed deeply of the fresh air, relieved to be away from her typewriter. It was good to be working on a campus right here at home. Goodfellow is so attractive with its well kept, cream colored barracks, she mused, the green lawns and sweeping air of high purpose.

They passed a platoon of men performing calisthenics in washed out fatigues and she wondered how they could understand the loud barks of the P.E. sergeant. Face down, they did full length push-ups in perfect unity, so there must be some secret male code of communication.

Cadet Cameron guided her across K Street, then later, across B Street to the sidewalk leading straight to the cafeteria. When they arrived, he held the door for her and they entered the familiar dining hall, another barracks building. They fell into place in the serving line and soon chose a vacant table off to one side.

Once seated opposite one another, Paula glanced at their humble lunch of chicken a la king on toast, cole slaw, and chocolate pudding, knowing the young man was giving up a fine meal, probably of beefsteak, potatoes, salad and other vegetables and pie. Air Corps men were well fed, their rations the best in the U.S. Army.

"I'm lucky to be stationed here at Goodfellow," Cameron said. Careful not to come on too strong, he explained, "It's a good base, the girls are pretty, and the Texans are friendly." He soared in a state of euphoria, gazing at this gorgeous girl with her exquisite face and coloring, her heavenly blue eyes. One look at her every morning and he'd be charged for the rest of his life. And having found her, he could never let her go.

He pulled away to take a bite, then looked up again. "Of course, nobody's friendlier than an Arkansawyer."

"You're from Arkansas?"

"Yeah. Pretty close to the Ozarks. And I take it you're a Texan. From San Angelo?"

Paula nodded.

Cameron decided delicacy was the name of the game. He'd heard how the C.O.'s secretary didn't date any servicemen. She seemed friendly enough, but somehow cool, though outstanding in every way. Some even claimed her the most beautiful girl in all of Texas. Plenty must have fallen for her.

"I'm a West Texan," she elaborated.

Drawn to her smile, he sank into those deep blue pools fringed with black lashes. The shapely, full lips quieted. Her eyes changed and he perceived that she was reading his mind. He shifted, beginning to eat again. "Oh, a rancher's daughter. I don't know much about cattle, myself. We have farms where I grew up in the northwest part of the state."

"Near Bob Burns and his bazooka that sounds like a stove pipe?" Paula asked, chuckling over the man's funny radio show. Then she quickly added, "Actually, I have a lot in common with your Bob Burns. I grew up on a chicken ranch. But I'm no comedian."

"That makes two of us. And I see we have something else in common. I'm not from Van Buren, but I used to gather the eggs every day for my mother. I grew up in a stone quarry, though." She lifted her brows in surprise, then covered her curiosity by taking a sip of coffee before she spoke again.

"Sounds like a hard life. What kind of stone? Did you ever do sculpture?"

He took the last bite of his creamed chicken and chewed in a deliberate way, mulling her suggestion over. "That's a new thought. We do have marble in Arkansas, but our stone was not of that high quality. However, it was a good white building stone. I'm really a fly boy. All fly boys tend to be poets, but I try to be as solid as stone. I'm sort of an engineer." Then he smiled into her eyes. "As for you, I think you're a bit of the Irish."

She braced herself against his handsome charm. "I am Irish, and I have a mind of my own."

He sobered. The enigma, a deep hurt perhaps? He must not push. He softened almost imperceptibly. "Do I detect a bit of Scottish blood in your blue veins? A stubborn streak?"

She laughed at his discernment. "You do! My mother's father was a Reid and he played the bagpipes."

He joined in her laughter. "That takes some sort of stubbornness and a strong wind to boot. I'm here to tell you I'm Scottish myself and I've got both. I knew right away we were two of a kind."

Paula's heart quickened at his intimate gaze and for a long moment, they held in mutual wonderment. Then at length, she slowly inhaled. "I'm a painter," she confided. "A fine artist."

"As opposed to commercial?" Cameron responded. "It shows in your face. Your paintings must be beautiful," he murmured in his rich voice. Then with a sardonic look, he swung about in his chair. "But I don't see much beauty around here compared to the hills of Arkansas."

"It's the sky," Paula said, her voice hushed. "The sky dominates the land day and night. It's magnificent."

What an idea! Cameron was surprised at her intense feeling. "How can you paint the sky?" he burst out. "There's nothing there!"

Paula fell back against her chair, chagrinned. "So it seems. But that's only superficial. It's the depth I must catch. It's a difficult task I've set for myself."

"You're not the only one," Cameron said with a meaningful look. Then he brightened. "I tell you what you do. Invent some clouds to make it interesting and give the picture a focus."

Paula smiled. "That could do it. You've got a good eye, I see. But I don't need to bother you with my problems. I've got to remember that I'm Colonel McIntyre's secretary and I'd better get back to the office."

She rose and Cameron followed her out of the cafeteria onto the field, where once again, they heard small aircraft over the airstrip and saw other cadets hurrying to class.

"I have to study for that extra exam," he said, "but I can get a weekend pass. How about a movie Saturday night?"

Paula warned herself to let this be it. "I'm sorry," she said. "I have to work at the USO that night."

She was being unapproachable again. There was something final in her attitude. Intuition told Cameron not to press further. "I'm sorry, too," he said.

He escorted her to Headquarters and after they said good-bye, she watched him as he moved briskly off to his Meterology class, his broad shoulders swaying in rhythm with his quick pace.

That afternoon passed in a haze for Paula. Her mind was filled with Garner Cameron, that handsome cadet, that self-assured Arkansas fly boy. How could she get his voice, his presence, her yen for him out of her system? Colonel McIntyre approached her desk. With a sly smile, he handed her some file folders and asked that she go over them to correct any typos or miscalculations of dates.

"Looks like Cadet Cameron is one young man who knows what he wants," he remarked.

Paula flushed when she saw his file on top and was embarrassed, but the colonel had turned away. He immediately left the office for a conference with the Air Inspector and she felt relieved, free to examine Garner's file in privacy. Of course it was Confidential, but she handled all of the poop anyway, and that didn't make any difference.

She opened the folder, telling herself that she was foolish to make so much of the history of a young man she'd only just met. Nevertheless, she scrutinized each page, looking for errors and also for an insight into Cadet Cameron.

He was born on Armistice Day, November 11, 1921, in Dorsett, Arkansas. Father deceased. Mother's residence in Dorsett. Valedictorian of his high school class. Certificate from Fort Smith Business College. Occupation before entering service: Cabinet maker at the Fort Smith Furniture Mfg. Co. Excellent health. Six foot one, weight 160 pounds. Top marks in aptitude tests and courses with the U.S. Army Air Corps. He probably did not attend college because he had to help support his mother.

He rang true. But what were his prospects? At best, he would become a pilot in the war and half of them were killed in battle, others maimed or casualties of some sort. Even if he did come back, what then?

I could never leave Texas. Texas is in my blood to stay. The free and easy people, the wide blue sky, the clean sweep of land and wind. My big hearted, big, big Texas! Then she laughed at herself. No one was asking her to give up her precious Texas. He is just twenty-two and I'll be twenty-three in April. Besides, he didn't even ask me for another date after my first turn-down and that's just what I wanted.

Is it? Not really. It's what I've decided. I'm trying to fool myself. I'm scared to death 'cause my feelings are so strong. I've never felt like this about any man before. But I've never known anyone else like Cadet Garner Cameron, either. I'll put him out of my mind. Remember, Out of sight, Out of mind. I'll concentrate on my painting, my job, and serving at the USO. The truth is, that should be enough for any young lady. And speaking of truth, my art is the most important of the three. I'll cling to my own philosophy. *Beauty is Truth.*

Paula sighed and closed the folder.

A small voice niggled at her: *What if Love is another kind of Truth?*

It will just have to wait, she answered.

Chapter Six

The streetlights along Cactus Street shed pools of shallow beams in the thick dark and the stillness of early morning. Paula's garage apartment snuggled behind a white bungalow. November filled the chilly void. There was no breath, no sound. People in their beds lay silent, as well as their dogs and cats nearby. No barking or caterwauling interrupted the calm. No creature sounds could be heard. Far above in mute glory, the stars twinkled down their messages of eternity.

It was nearly two o'clock on Thursday morning, the second day since Paula had met Cadet Cameron. She lay gently sleeping beside her roommate in their double bed. Gently, because Paula was a light sleeper and every now and then warm remembrances of Garner added pleasure to the night.

In her dreaming, she heard the faint ring of a telephone. Mary turned over, mumbling something. Paula awakened with the realization that it was their own phone ringing at this ungodly hour. They had connected the phone only yesterday. She wanted to jump out of bed to stop its ghastly ringing, but was careful not to disturb Mary. She slithered out, scarcely moving the covers, her slender feet landing on the cold linoleum. She caught the intruder on its third ring and answered in a low voice.

"Hello! Hello!" A high twang accosted her ear and she recognized Adele's mother, full of stress. "Paula! Something dreadful has happened," Mrs. Turner gasped, trying to control herself. "It's simply dreadful. Oh Paula! I need you here at the hospital." Tears watered her wail.

Alarmed, Paula made an effort to seem calm. "The baby? Did she have the baby?"

"Yes. The baby's all right and Adele, too, only..." Mrs. Turner burst into wrenching sobs.

"Complications? Don't worry, Mrs. Turner. I'll be right over."

"It's not what you think," the older woman managed, her voice fading to a desperation. *"No one must know."*

This was no time for more questions. Adele and Mrs. Turner needed her now. With a brief reassurance that she would soon be there, Paula hung up, then she quickly called for a taxi. It could be there within five minutes. Mary remained asleep. Paula quickly dressed in the alcove bathroom, applying only lipstick, not caring that her white skin would appear pale without makeup. What terrible thing could have happened to Adele? The birth had obviously gone well, so why the secrecy? Was the baby deformed? A cretin ... what? Paula reminded herself that this was a new grandmother and she could be overwrought, imagining things.

Soon, she was tapping on the door of Room 302 in the San Angelo Hospital. As Mrs. Turner opened the door to the private room, Paula stepped inside and immediately smelled the cinnamon pungence of pink carnations standing in a tall vase on a small table between the bed and the window. There was also a service table at the head of the bed, which held a glass of water and a lamp, giving the only light in the room. Two oak chairs stood together opposite the hospital bed.

Paula looked at Mrs. Turner, the town's queenly matron, shocked to see the wild fear and anxiety in the older woman's glance. Her face was furrowed in a deep frown between dark brown eyes, the lines about her mouth compressed, making her long nose prominent like a beak. Under such scrutiny, Mrs. Turner quietly shut the door and turned away from Paula, who moved toward the stark bed.

Placid, eyes closed, Adele lay recumbent on her back, scarcely causing a mound under the white sheet. With apprehension, Paula bent down and peered into her face. Adele's golden brown curls were soft around her lovely cheeks. Relaxed, in repose, her breathing came in the natural rhythm of a deep sleep.

Paula straightened up and said softly, "Adele is fine, Mrs. Turner. She's sound asleep."

But the woman became even more agitated. She stood rooted to the floor, wringing her hands. Icy fear glinted from her roving gaze as if she were seeking a miraculous escape. Paula quickly crossed over to her and took her hands in the steady warmth of her own, trying to calm her.

"She's sedated," Mrs. Turner wailed, her voice spiraling upward. "She's in shock." Paula tightened her grip in empathy, holding on to impart a good grasp of sanity, to alleviate the crazed woman.

"When did the baby come?"

"I don't know...I don't know." Mrs. Turner was on the verge of breaking down. "An hour ago, I guess."

"Well then. What's wrong?"

"The baby! The baby!" Mrs. Turner's eyes rolled wild. "Oh Paula!" She sucked in her breath in a convulsive attempt to stop a cascade of wracking sobs. "I don't know what to do! My husband must never know!"

"Mr. Turner? *Your husband?*" Paula was startled, greatly alarmed. "But why?" Her intense blue gaze fastened on Mrs. Turner, demanding an answer.

"No one must ever know." Mrs. Turner's anxiety drilled into Paula. "That's why I need your help."

"All right! All right! I'll do what I can. But you've got to tell me what this is all about." Mrs. Turner snuffled uncontrollably, then she tremulously took the plunge.

"The baby....it's a darky....*a negro baby girl!*"

The offending words had been said outloud.

"What?"

The two women stared at one another, horrified, disbelieving that such a monstrous thing could happen to Adele. Certainly, it could not be happening to one of the finest families in West Texas. Lt. Fred Thomas was a handsome, upright, intelligent USAAC officer from Chicago. He was Adele's dream-come-true, her knight on a white horse, her attentive, courteous lover. Her husband.

Paula dismissed the charge. "There must be some mistake."

The older woman gave a vigorous shake of the head. "No."

"Sometimes babies do get mixed up, you know," Paula assured her. "There're so many..."

"No, Paula," Mrs. Turner interrupted. "I've been here all along and I know that this is Adele's baby. Besides, there have been no other births for the past two days." Paula's eyes widened. "We have to face it," the mother continued, her mouth grim, "but I can't let this get out. Adele would absolutely be ruined. She'd have no future. There isn't any decent white man who would marry a girl who had given birth to such a baby. She'd be ruined forever. The family tainted. We'd never live it down."

During this rush of words, Paula let go of Mrs. Turner and backed away, trying to think. She was stunned. Adele suffering so! Dark betrayal! This was worse than death. They must act quickly. They'd have to do everything possible to avoid Adele's having a nervous breakdown, weakened as she was from the birth, already subject to post partum depression.

Mrs. Turner fell into a chair, shaking in a nervous rigor. She whimpered in distress. Paula rushed to her and hugged her until she stopped shaking, telling her over and over again that everything could be worked out and Adele would be protected, she'd see to that. She sat down in the other chair.

"Let's be calm," she said. "Let's talk this over. How long will the sedative be effective?"

As though their roles were reversed, Mrs. Turner obeyed Paula, her expression showing relief. "About six more hours," she said.

"We'll have to act today," Paula said. "I'll take the day off and attend to it myself."

Her thoughts tumbled in a vortex. The doctor must be consulted as soon as possible, the nurses made to swear to secrecy, and then Fred had to be dealt with. But she would have to wait until eleven o'clock when the doctor would come for his hospital rounds.

"Where's Fred?" she asked.

"I can't look at him," Mrs. Turner said vehemently. "The doctor said he's one of those who pass off as white."

"What does Fred think?"

"I have no idea." The mother couldn't bear to discuss it. Then scowling, she explained that he may still be in the waiting room. He had been shown the baby shortly after its delivery, while Adele was still under the effects of the anesthetic. Then later, she herself was with Adele when the nurse brought the baby in to her and Adele went into hysterics. She cried and laughed and raved and said she never wanted to see Fred or that baby again. Never! Never!

As she told this story, Mrs. Turner became more agitated, trembling all over. Paula took her hands in a firm grip.

"All right, all right! I'll go talk to him."

Mrs. Turner pulled her hands away and dabbed at her eyes with a white linen handkerchief, blew her nose and nodded with relief. "I knew I could trust you to think of everything. You're so much like your Uncle Paul, the good senator. You have a natural way of taking charge and handling people. I'm so grateful to you, Paula."

"I'll go see Fred now," she responded. "He's probably wondering how Adele is." She heaved a deep sigh.

She was acquainted with Fred and liked him, but now he was a threat to Adele, her sanity, everything she held dear. How could he do such a thing? How could he pass off as white in society, to the military, and to the woman he loved, with no qualms about having a black baby, a throwback unacceptable to white society, bringing a lifetime of misery upon his own child and disaster to the one he was supposed to love? Such betrayal was monstrous. Paula's fury welled up in bitterness toward Lt. Fred Thomas. He knew what he was doing. He was intelligent. He deliberately chose to pretend he was white and live a life of deception. Devious from the word go!

She took the elevator down to the first floor and paused after entering the small waiting room next to Admissions. No one was there. An occasional table to the right held a bouquet of tea roses, their fragrance permeating the air. A coke machine stood in the corner. Several chairs of fruit wood with soft cushions in brown plaid were arranged around the walls, while two sofas in dark green stood back to back in the middle of the room. Lieutenant Thomas was not at the lighted coke machine, nor was he seated anywhere. Then she saw him, his back to her as he stood staring out the window.

Darkness outside, darkness inside, Paula thought. There is nothing but darkness. She hesitated, bracing herself for the encounter. As she did so, she glimpsed a bank of lights at the hospital entrance giving off a dim glow to help the distressed find this haven. No haven now.

What can I say, she asked herself. No one wants your baby. Especially not its mother, your wife, your betrayed wife-no-longer-your-wife. *And you did this!*

No! I must not accuse him. I'll have to be calm, objective, frank, yes, best to be frank about the whole thing, and speak in a reasonable manner.

He did not hear her when she crossed the room on the Westminster carpet.

She spoke, her voice dull, lifeless, like a murmur in a funeral parlor. "Lieutenant Thomas?" She corrected herself and said in a normal tone when he turned to her, "I've come to see you."

At the sight of this disguised monster, Paula twinged with shock and nearly lost her nerve. He was so good looking! With his fine, regular features and dark blond coloring, he looked like any neighbor down the street. A flicker of glad hope and welcome flashed in his hazel eyes, but he remained silent.

"Adele has been given a sedative and she'll sleep for six hours." A flush of agony suffused the air about him and her anger dissolved into pity. "Let's sit down here on the sofa where we can talk."

She let him sit down first, then left enough space for another person between them, turning halfway toward him while she seated herself. It came over her what an impressive figure he made in his army officer's uniform and how well he carried the authority of his rank.

"About the baby..." she started.

Fred crumpled.

He tucked in his elbows, covering his face with his slender hands, fingernails digging into his forehead in a frenzy of grief. His whole body shook uncontrollably, tears flowing, leaking through his long fingers, running down his hands, "Oh God! Oh God!" he moaned. "The worst has happened. I'm struck down. My baby and my wife, too. Adele! Adele! What can I do? Can she ever forgive me?"

Paula remained silent, waiting for the storm to pass.

At length, Fred gave a great shudder. He slowly straightened up. In deep despair, he mumbled, "I know what to do. I'll simply eliminate myself."

Eliminate! That's what the Germans and Japs are doing to us.

Paula grabbed his wrist. "No you won't! We're already losing too many good men to our enemies. We need you. And we're not your enemies, in case you think we are. It's just that we're all caught up in an impossible situation. But you will have to give up Adele."

He hung his head, dejected, sniffling, wiping his nose.

"You probably knew from the beginning that what you did was wrong. You were only hoping somehow, you wouldn't get caught."

He was quiet, taking his beating.

"You know that sooner or later every one of us has to pay for our deceptions and wrong doings."

At that, he lifted his head and looked her in the eye. "I know, but what are *you* going to do? I'll lose my commission, be kicked out of the Air Corps, given a Dishonorable Discharge, carry a black eye for the rest of my life. I'd rather be dead." He hung his head, becoming inert.

Paula relaxed her hold and folded her hands in her lap. "No such thing! Why would we want to do a thing like that? You're a good officer and I meant it when I said we need you. Our country needs you. Don't go back on us now!"

Vacantly staring, Fred's glazed eyes reflected the polish on his dark brown shoes. Paula wondered if he were man enough to disappear from Adele's life and carry on. In that instant, a plan formed in her mind.

"Fred," she said. But he turned on her in a vicious, accusatory glare.

"What are you going to do with my baby?"

"I don't know," she answered, taken aback. "I thought you might have a plan..."

"I don't want to lose my baby."

"But how.... what can you do? You're in the service. I think someone, a nice negro family here in San Angelo would like to have her." She ran her forefinger back and forth across her thumbnail as though trying to smooth things over. No, that would never do. Adele should not have her negro child living in the same town. That would be excruciating for her. Panic rose in Paula's breast. She saw that Fred was rightfully possessive, blazingly fearful and defiant.

"I'll not let you take my baby away! No one will take her away from me!"

She shook her head, trying to mollify him.

"My mother will want her and she'll take care of her for me. She lives up in South Chicago. Is that far enough away for you?"

Paula tasted the gall of his bitterness but was secretly relieved. "Yes," she said. "That's the thing to do. I'm sure Adele would agree. She'd want the best for the baby. That way, the child will have a grandmother to love her."

"And a father," Fred said, his manner strident.

"Yes, a father is most important."

Then, as if she had not spoken, he said abruptly, "I want to see Adele."

At this, tears threatened Paula. She swallowed them down, trying to keep her throat clear, her voice even.

"I'm afraid you can't see her ever again. We're afraid....we're trying to take care of her so she won't have a nervous breakdown. Her mother is with her now."

Fred gave her a long, settling look, eyes narrowed, his head in vibrating spasm as deep attachment warred with the need to cooperate.

"A clean break is easiest," Paula said softly, her eyes brimming. Then she noticed a light of triumph rise in his gaze.

Alarm twisted her heart. "No! You can't expect to see her ever again, either here in town or out at the San Angelo Air Corps Base. I think it would be best for Adele, and you too, if you asked for a transfer. In order to protect Adele and the Turners, Dr. Anderson can report on the birth certificate that the baby was stillborn, dead at birth. That way, no one will ever know what happened. You and the baby will be gone and Adele will have a chance to begin her life all over again."

"So it will be a coverup," Fred said harshly.

"Maybe that's because there was a coverup in the first place." Paula's serious gaze pierced him and he bowed his head again.

After some delicate persuasion, Fred agreed to her plan. He would ask for a transfer and a short leave so he could take his baby girl to his mother, the colored woman who had warned him in his youth that he would come to no good in passing off as white. But she was good hearted and generous. They were both satisfied that she would be a loving grandmother to the child.

"None of this is easy, Fred," Paula said, her round eyes full of understanding. "You'll need to see about the leave and transfer right away. Mrs. Turner and I will see the doctor later this morning, when he comes to the hospital. We'll discuss the divorce before you go."

"Divorce! Adele's my *wife*!" He jumped up, clenched his fists and hung over her, ready to spring in vicious attack.

Paula crouched away, stunned, scared.

Then she stiffened and rose to face him. "Adele has had such a colossal shock and disappointment, her love for you was killed in one stroke!"

Fred paled. His mouth worked as he clenched and unclenched his fists. "You'd think I'd committed a crime!"

It was all she could do not to flinch. This was the moment she had dreaded. The force of her own personality was pitted against this man. For Adele's sake, she must stand staunch and stony strong.

She stared him down.

A look of fatal resignation crept into his eyes.

Shaking her head, Paula laved him in sympathetic tones. "No one wants a divorce, Fred, but at times it becomes a necessity. I think you realize that. Do I have your permission to tell Adele that you won't protest a divorce action on her part?"

Overcome by an invisible enemy, Fred's gaze fell before her. Unable to speak, he slowly nodded.

Greatly relieved, Paula asked him to meet her the next day at Ma's Cafeteria for a final consultation.

Later that morning, she and Mrs. Turner visited Dr. Anderson, Adele's obstetrician. He was most cooperative and understanding. He agreed to a death certificate for the baby in Tom Green County, but said he would make out a birth certificate for her in Cook County, Illinois, using the father's name and a fictitious name for the mother. With compassion, he assured them that the nurses in the hospital could be trusted. They would not breathe a word.

The women gave their heartfelt thanks, thinking how fortunate they were to have such a trustworthy, caring physician to depend upon. He had not only saved Adele and the Turner family, but he had also given the baby her rightful parent and a place in society.

Paula promised Mrs. Turner that she herself would never confide in her parents, Bonnie, or Mary or anyone else, ever. She would never say a word about it as long as she lived. But she thought Mr. Turner should be told the truth.

Mrs. Turner's eyes bugged out. "I couldn't! He'd eat her alive. He was so against Adele's hasty marriage."

"But he'll want to protect her all the more," Paula urged. "And you'll both need him to lean on now."

Mrs. Turner's face became distorted with anxiety. She trembled, shaking her head. "I don't know. I'm afraid he'd be all the harder on her."

"Not if you tell him how broken hearted she is and how much she needs her father," Paula persuaded. "It would draw you all closer together."

As she earnestly gazed into Paula's eyes, the older woman's anxiety slowly changed to a questioning, finally giving way to relief, while Paula nodded encouragement. "I'll tell him. It's true. It would make things so much easier for us all." She paused, then murmured,"We've never had anything come between us before. Till this marriage, anyway." Then she brightened and spoke with confidence. "I'm sure you're right, Paula. Adele must know that we stand firmly together to support her with all our love." She smiled with satisfaction. "I'm sure Ed will understand. He'd want to know."

Instead of seeking relief for her own distress through similar confidences, Paula asked for another day off from work and spent the hospital's visiting hours at Adele's bedside. Once she explained to Fred how shocked Adele was at his betrayal, at the impossibility of her ever loving him again, he was cooperative and made himself scarce. Due to his good military record and sympathetic at the loss of his first born, Fred's commanding officer granted him a thirty-day leave and a transfer. As planned, he took his newborn infant to Chicago, never to return to San Angelo. He would go to his new assignment from his mother's home. The divorce would be granted on the grounds of incompatibility. In the event the bereaved mother ever had a sudden change of heart, Paula, for fear she might slip up and tell Adele, made sure that she was not informed of Fred's whereabouts. It was an appalling situation. Paula felt it imperative to not only protect her friend, but herself as well.

Adele remained hospitalized, sedated for shock. She curled up into the fetal position at first, ignoring anyone who approached. Yet Paula visited her every day.

Seated at Adele's bedside, Paula was filled with the sorrow of being insinuated into the blood and visceral stream of emotion to her other self, her bereaved, lifelong friend. The days of visiting in the hospital, searching Adele's wan face for some life, tolled bands of lost times about her chest, making it hard to breathe. Motionless, the new mother's eyes were usually closed, but when open, unseeing, veiled in hidden pain. One time her wide open eyes came to in a startled awakening. Then Paula, elated, suffered quick rejection as she watched Adele flip over, her back a shield, a wedge between them.

Adele's denial and this pitiful rejection wore away at Paula's inner strength.

Still, she visited every day in spite of the gnawing at her spirit, the misery of contemplating this fallen young woman's future. Despair engulfed her. This unspeakable tragedy became her own. She shrank from the desert of loneliness contemplated, aware that only death itself could give release. It was then that Adele's denial became transformed in Paula's psyche, her grief relegated to the subconscious.

Paula never failed to be cheerful in her duties at work in the office and at home with Mary. But at times the conditions of society surfaced to her inquiring mind and thoughts of politics entered, crashing through the protective Plexiglas of her walled off subconscious.

She thought of Fred and wondered how he was getting along. The African people had first been betrayed by their own kind when sold to the British for the slave trade. Considered little better than apes, they were to be used, for even their kindred in England had been taken as indentured servants, not really human beings with intelligence and feelings like them, the British.

It was true that peoples around the world had had slaves down through the centuries, but America gave a shining new start in a pristine land. In spite of this, superiority was so ingrained that many settlers thought of the native Indians as fearful savages. They were too fierce to serve as slaves. Yet the Puritans, Quakers, and other Christians of America did not wish to enslave them. Rather, they wanted to convert them and assimilate these different tribes into their own culture.

It had been seventy-eight years since the Civil War ended, two and one-half generations. In the beginning, when the colored folks were invited to join the white people in their churches and organizations, they wanted their own churches, their own schools, and their own clubs. This was only natural. They wanted to be with their own kind and keep their own culture. But this separation had gone too far. Without wanting to, it had become a vicious segregation, the separation pounced upon by the jackals of the Deep South, who organized the white hooded Ku Klux Klan to keep the former slaves in their place. They had fought and died to keep them there. The Ku Klux Klan was a veritable extension of the Civil War.

Gone too far! In the South, whites were not even allowed to call a colored person by the title of Mr. or Miss or Mrs., but only by his or her first name. No such respect allowed! Paula knew that in this society, she had done the right thing to protect the new, dark faced baby girl and her innocent mother.

It was strange about man, she mused. Given an idea and utter belief in that certain idea, no matter how wrong or evil, man acted on his belief. Paula had visited an African Methodist Church service once and there she met a lovely woman and her two children, finding them not so much different from herself. But these people in San Angelo were not allowed to enter a department store downtown, nor a restaurant or cafe. Troubled, she had wondered at the time just how they managed to live. It came down to man's long history of man cursing man in the commerce of control and command.

Now, day following day, with Adele no better, Paula kept these thoughts to herself. Adele needs me, she told herself, and I am strong. Nothing can shake my devotion. A healing is bound to come.

※

On a Saturday near noon, Paula walked in with a cold chocolate malted milk. Adele lay with her back to her, but Paula cheerfully announced, "I'll share this deliriously delicious malted milk with you if you'll be good."

Adele turned over and looked at her, a faint smile on her face. Paula took a draw of the thick mix of whipped vanilla ice cream, malt, chocolate syrup and whole milk, reveling in the sweet, rich smell and flavor at the same time, eyes closed in ecstasy, till Adele could bear it no longer. She was hungry.

"That's mine!" She grabbed it and sucked hard on the straw, paying no attention to Paula's howling objections to her idea of sharing, guzzling down the nourishing treat without let-up. When the carton was nearly empty, she kept on, making a rackety-bubbly noise, outrageously impolite, trying to get the last yummy drop.

Paula laughed at her and Adele smiled, handing the empty carton back. Then, without murmuring a word, she rolled over and fell asleep.

Paula slipped away, pleased, but when she walked down the hall, weakened by her menses, legs aching, she almost collapsed. She was oh, so weary. Lonely. Eviscerated. All strength gone, on the brink of succumbing to a grief, a desolation more than she could bear, she wavered, stumbling along. Tears streaming down her face, she forced herself to go on, to continue as she had been doing for days. These evil days! No one else was in the elevator when she entered to go down to the first floor. Empty like herself. All the more dejected, quietly weeping, she leaned against the wall till the elevator came to a stop. When the door opened, there stood Burl Stein.

With a cry, she fell into his arms, bursting into sobs. He kissed her hair, her forehead, her eyes. "I'm so sorry, honey! I've been busy with the steers. I've only just heard about Adele's baby. But she's all right. I want you to take it easy now. You've got to think of yourself."

He pressed his lips to hers and she was grateful for his caring, his comforting, being there when she was at the end of her tether. After he'd let her go, she realized that the kiss had meant no more than that. He was a good friend, like a brother to her, but she was not in love with him. She wondered if her affection could grow into love after marriage. At least, she knew that Burl was German, probably one hundred percent. The worst that could be in him would be some Indian blood, and many Texans had that mixture with seemingly no dire results.

She smiled up at him and observed his tawny good looks, the bright blue eyes and wealth of curly hair. She was glad of these attributes and at more than these, his reliability.

"Thanks, Burl. I really needed someone just now. I think Adele has turned the corner. She was on the verge of a nervous breakdown, but she has just taken a malted milk and that's a good sign."

The next morning, Bonnie's baby, a husky boy named Douglas Ronald Byrnes, was born. Mother and infant were doing well, another good sign for which Paula was grateful.

❧ ✻ ☙

Within the week, Adele returned home from the hospital. To ease his daughter's terrible grief, her affliction and bereavement, Mr. Turner made arrangements to take the family away from San Angelo and move to Dallas, where he had obtained a position in his insurance company's headquarters office.

After work on Thursday afternoon, Paula visited Adele to help with her packing. The moving van was to come the next day. Upstairs in Adele's bedroom, they sorted out books, games, jigsaw puzzles, pictures, old shoes and clothing and anything else she wanted to discard.

"I'd like to take these old games and books and things to the USO," Paula said. "Let's make a pile for the Salvation Army and another one for the USO."

Adele held up a fringed, ranchero shirt. "How about this? I'll never need it in the city. Maybe you could wear it."

Paula looked at the long sleeves and its length. "No, I'm too short waisted and it's too long sleeved, anyway."

They were interrupted by Mrs. Turner's nasal voice.

"Paula," she called from the bottom of the stairs, "can you come down here to the kitchen and help me? I need to get some things down from the top shelf."

"I'll be right back," Paula told Adele. "Don't go away."

Adele made a face at her. "That's exactly what I'm planning to do!"

When Paula followed Mrs. Turner into the kitchen, the older woman closed the door to the dining room. She plucked at the cardboard box that held sets of kitchen ware. "I wanted to get you off alone, where Adele couldn't hear us."

What now, Paula thought with misgiving. "What is it?"

"I hate to ask you," Mrs. Turner minced.

"It's all right," Paula assured her.

"I'm afraid Adele's going to be lonely off in Dallas, and get homesick," the mother said.

Paula nodded in sympathy. "I know."

"I just wondered if you'd let me buy your button box painting for her," Mrs. Turner blurted out.

Paula frowned and stared at her, obviously surprised at the thought of selling her winning painting. It had been in her possession for nearly two years and she intended to keep it.

"It would mean so much to her, Paula. Something dear to her heart from home and especially, from you, her best friend."

Paula's gaze shifted.

"How about one hundred dollars? Would that be enough?"

"One hundred dollars! I hadn't thought of selling. It's one of my favorites."

Mrs. Turner stood mute, her brown eyes turned soft and pleading.

"I guess I could sell it."

"I want to give it to Adele as a surprise after we've moved. It'll mean so much to her. She's always loved your work and her button box, especially."

Paula nodded and gave Mrs. Turner a sweet smile. "It's a lovely thing to do. All right. I'll sell it. It will be my very first sale and I'd rather sell to you for Adele than to anyone else I know."

"Oh thank you, Paula!" Mrs. Turner pulled out two fifty dollar bills from her apron pocket. "Here you are! I'll come after it this evening on some pretext to get away. You'll be home?"

"Yes," Paula said, accepting the money. "I'll have it wrapped for you. And thanks very much. I hadn't expected anything like this."

Later, after the Turners had moved, Paula missed "The Button Box" painting. A part of her was gone. It was almost like losing her own child. The one hundred dollars was some consolation, a good fee. The painting had gone for a good cause, for poor Adele had no consolation in the loss of her baby and her husband. When people asked about Adele, Paula merely said that she was staying with her parents because Fred had been transferred. It was generally assumed that he was slated for overseas duty.

Paula, keenly aware of the heartbreaking divorce proceedings, never mentioned the tragic trespass of events that had ruined her friend's life. There were more than enough divorces and rumors of divorce without her adding to the scandalous and the unthinkable. Young people, snatching at life in wartime, married in haste and then too often wound up broken, disillusioned, divorced. Paula was determined that she would never become such a victim.

Adele was gone.

Paula grieved for her sake and over her own loss of her bosom friend to a city far away.

Chapter Seven

During the next few evenings, Paula concentrated on serving at the USO to bring as much cheer as possible to the boys away from home. The USO was within walking distance of her apartment, one block off Chadbourne, the main street, on East Beauregard. It was a separate, one-story structure that had been converted from an office building by the women of San Angelo and the American Legion.

As one entered, homey smells of coffee, hamburgers, and hot cinnamon rolls pleased the senses. Scattered card tables and chairs invited servicemen to sit down and eat or play cards, or to just bull. A couple of davenports and a studio piano completed the atmosphere of a large living room, while to the left, a high counter separated it from the kitchen.

All of the furnishings had been donated by the townsfolk, including the taupe carpet, the refrigerator, and the gas range. It was typical of USOs across the country, its initials standing for United Service Organizations. Folklore had it that the idea began in Chicago, but that was in the Midwest. Out on the West Coast, they touted the first USO ever as having originated in Hollywood. That didn't make any difference. Wherever servicemen were stationed, they were bound to find a friendly USO nearby and they took advantage of it, at times going so far as to ask a motherly matron to help write letters to their sweethearts back home.

Paula often took Mary with her to the USO. She needed encouragement and Paula needed companionship. Mary Nesbit, the

Baptist minister's only daughter, had dishwater blonde hair, was peculiarly sway backed and had buck teeth so that she was nearly always pressing her lips together or hiding her smile behind a hand. Paula reassured her. She was a nice girl, after all, and smart. She told Mary that some cadet, a Bombardier or Navigator, was bound to take a liking to her, if she'd just make herself more available.

One evening the girls had been behind the counter frying hamburgers for two hours, their faces flushed from the heat, when Mary, grinning so wide she displayed her protruding teeth, gave Paula a nudge with her elbow.

"Look! Over there! He's the one I want."

Paula looked, then quickly turned her head. In that instant, she had seen how elegant Cadet Garner Cameron was compared to the other young men. His serious demeanor, his erect, muscular body, greater in height and dignity, gave him a nonchalant air of nobility. Some men were simply born that way, she mused, like Sam Houston and other founding fathers of the Republic of Texas.

Mary nudged her again. "He's coming this way. He's looking at *you*." She gripped Paula's arm and looked her in the eye. "You'd better grab him if you can. Don't be so high and mighty or you'll wind up losing out, period." Heart pounding, Paula shot a glance at Mary, then bravely faced Garner, answering his greeting with a smile.

"Hello! What'll you have?"

Smiling in return, his gaze sparked a light of amusement. "I think it's you I'm after. It's about closing time, isn't it? I'd like to walk you home, if I may."

"I'm Paula's roommate," Mary spoke up. "I'm so glad you asked, because Joe and I are going to close up here and then..." She broke off, nodding over at a young man seated at a card table. She shrugged, her eyes holding a plea.

Garner grinned. "That settles it, then. I'm glad I came by."

Later, while Paula and Garner strolled away from the business district under the streetlamps, Mary's warning reverberated in her mind. But it was so hard to know what to do. No one knew how it would all wind up. The United States had to keep the mad Japs and Germans from taking over the whole wide world and Air Corps pilots were on the most dangerous course of all. Besides, she didn't know anything, really, about Garner Cameron, who he was or his ancestors. And Arkansas was foreign to her. Servicemen sometimes painted a bright picture to get a girl and then took off like a rabbit, leaving her stranded, broken hearted. It was too frightening.

Cadet Cameron was quiet beside her.

She did not notice his silence until they came to an intersection, where he took her elbow and guided her across the street. Then the thought intruded, *He's just the right height for me. My head fits into his broad shoulder.*

She sighed.

Garner looked down at her. "Glad to get a breath of fresh air?"

"Oh yes. It feels good." *And especially with you beside me.*

"The men really appreciate your dedication, your work."

"We're glad to do it," she replied. "We all have to work hard to win this tremendous war, women included."

"Yes, the womenfolk will have to do double duty on the home front. It won't hurt to tell you that you're important and the men trust you. You're the reason we're fighting. And we won't let you down, either." Impressed, Paula looked up at him, so stalwart in his cap and uniform. She had never heard anyone else volunteer such a sentiment.

She slowed her pace as they came near a small, white cottage, half hidden in the shadows. A tall pecan tree stood beside the house and Paula explained that she lived in the garage apartment. They turned into the driveway with its dual tracks of cement pavement, and stopped in front of the white, clapboard garage. A regular house door was set off to one side. Paula rummaged in her purse for the key.

"Here. Let me help you." Garner took the key and unlocked the door, opening it for her. "Must see the young lady safely home."

Her reserve vanished and before she knew it, she was inviting him in. She flipped the switch and the light bulb, hanging from the ceiling on a green cord in the middle of the room, came to life. Its glare revealed a double bed, a chest, and a small, green table and two chairs near a sink and four-burner gas range. The ceiling of exposed clapboard slanted down toward the chest and a make-believe closet that hid clothing behind a flowered curtain.

"Some garage!" Garner exclaimed. "Where's the bathroom, outdoors?"

Paula laughed. "We're lucky to have it. No, there's a bathroom complete with baby elephant tub right here under this alcove." She indicated a closed inside door only four feet high, opposite the kitchen area. "Originally, this was a chicken coop." She hoped he didn't notice the cloying chicken odor that seeped through the smell of fresh paint.

Garner hooted. "Couldn't keep away from the chickens, huh?"

Paula's ire rose.

"There are twenty-five thousand people in San Angelo now, counting the men at both air bases and their wives and families. Before the war, we had a population of only ten thousand, so you see, there are fewer chickens."

"And fewer places to live," Garner said, hastening to correct the situation. "How about giving this ol' rooster a cup of coffee?" He took off his cap, tossed it on the bed, and pulled out a chair, seating himself at the table.

Paula regained her good humor. "I'll just heat it up. There's plenty left over from dinner. She served the coffee and joined him. In her best company manners, she asked if his father ran the stone quarry before he died. Alerted, he shot her a sharp glance.

"I never told you my father was gone."

Paula wanted to sink through the floor. Her face grew hot. *He knows I've seen his Confidential record.* She took a gulp of hot coffee, scalding her mouth.

He pretended not to see her discomfiture. "I guess you surmised it from the way I talked," he said.

She met his gaze. "It wasn't what you think. Colonel McIntyre asked me to go over the folders and make corrections."

Garner chuckled low in his throat. "The old fox! To answer your question, my father did run the quarry, but he was a high school teacher. He taught Science, Manual Arts Training, English, History...in fact, he pinch hitted wherever he was needed. He used to read poetry to me when I was a kid. He could quote reams. He also ran the stone quarry. Teachers didn't make enough to support a family."

He continued, freely discussing the family's fortunes and misfortunes. Not long after his father died, the worked out quarry, forty acres of farmland near Dorsett, and the house in town were all that were left from his part of the Cameron fortune. His paternal grandfather was one of three brothers. At one time, they owned much of northern Arkansas, sections of southeast Kansas, farmland, cotton gins and dry goods stores. But one brother had only one son, whereas the other two had ten children each. So that one brother, thinking he was being cheated, asked that he be given his share of the family fortune. They divided everything up three ways, and that was the beginning of the disintegration of all their combined enterprises.

"Now I'm the third generation," Garner concluded, "and they say that prosperity comes to the third generation after the loss of a family fortune." His intense gaze lingered, as if to say he intended to be prosperous one day.

She listened, attentive.

He spoke again.

Like a true Southerner, he was proud of his ancestry. "I'm a descendant of Donald Cameron," he said, "the gentle Lochiel, a Scottish chieftain. I don't know whether he was knighted or not, but I expect so."

Fascinated, she gazed into his eyes. Under the dim light, they were as black as Apache's tears with no distinction between the pupil and iris. How unusual! A shaft of fear struck her. Why so black? What were his other origins? She suddenly felt left out, barred, unable to see within, to fathom him.

As if trying to bridge the gap that had inexplicably risen between them, he said, "I can tell what you are just by looking." He paused and searched her comely face, the pretty mouth and high, smooth forehead marked with a delicate widow's peak. "You're a purebred, Paula. And I like your cute, turned up nose."

She took exception to that. "My nose isn't turned up. It's as straight as yours, only a little shorter. And I'm a thoroughbred, not a purebred."

He grinned at her. "A filly. You said it, I didn't." He rose and picked up his cap. "I'd better go. Some cadets have been invited to Mr. and Mrs. Morrison's home next Saturday night for a get together. There'll be food and dancing, and a good time for all. One of my buddies has a car and asked if I'd like to go. He'll be glad to take us. It would be a welcome change from the USO, don't you think? Could you come?"

"I *could*," she said, accompanying him to the door.

He stopped and faced her.

"Do I detect some frost around the edges?" He paused to assess her reaction. "I must apologize, Paula. A girl like you, there's bound to be someone else." She hesitated long enough to give doubt to her reply.

"Why, no."

"Some rancher, a Texas cowboy?"

Under his scrutiny, she blushed, furious at herself, afraid he would misinterpret her contrary feelings.

"Or he's in love with you, but you're not quite taken, or know for sure if he's the one." He was being helpful and astute at the same time.

"Yes," she admitted. "I grew up with him out on the ranch." Garner seemed relieved at this news.

"Those things seldom work out, Paula," he said. "I had a similar case. Grew up with a pretty girl everybody in town took for granted would some day be my wife. Then she went off to college and found her true love. End of story."

In a swift movement, he swept her in his arms, his cap tumbling to the floor. He found her mouth and she responded to his kiss, aware of his pounding heart. Shaken, his passion imbued her with a rising emotion, imperative. Desire answered desire and Paula yielded in his embrace. He gently released her.

Tenderly, he kissed the tip of her nose and retrieved his cap. "I'll pick you up Saturday evening at eight."

Chapter Eight

Paula had the blues.

The miasma was one that could not be thrown off in two or three days. The comfortable frame of her life had collapsed. Adele, her bosom friend since the first grade, had been yanked away in a pitiful stroke worse than death, never to return. And she must wait one whole week to see Garner again. But she should not think of him, and if she would be true to herself, she dare not think of Burl, either.

She dangled in agony.

These were feverish days before Garner would leave for Advanced Pilot Training. Soon he would be gone forever. Forever gone! Thoughts of Garner and his passionate kiss formed the insistent drumbeat of her yearnings and she hated herself for this weakness. In silent weeping, keeping the damage to herself, she bore the misalignment within the ventricles of her heart, careful to utter no word of her misery nor show sadness on her countenance.

In anguish, Paula wrote long letters to Adele, always when Mary was not about, even in her absence using control to keep the tears from falling. At length, she bought a new record of Glenn Miller's marvelous swing music and every day after work, she put it on her portable record player, dancing and singing "Little Brown Jug" over and over again, making up the words as she went along. Mary was vaguely aware of her deep seated sense of loss and made no comment. Her place was to remain cheerful and keep things steady.

Then one afternoon at Goodfellow, when Paula was returning to the office from the cafeteria, she saw Garner coming toward her.

Her heart bounded at the sight of him. She was startled at the sheer symmetry of his face and figure. He stopped and briefly told her he had corrected his record by attaining an *A* in Math, which his instructor had substituted for the onerous *B*. Then he casually said, "See you Saturday night at eight!" and trotted off, while her congratulations faded on her lips.

Paula had been flattered by Garner's maneuver to meet her and was well impressed that he had followed through to make good on his special dispensation. But this chance meeting only served to emphasize the bleak outlook where he was concerned. She regretted the date for the party. The only thing that seemed to matter to Cadet Cameron was his record with the U.S. Air Corps. She had been taken in, after all. She would go to the party and have a good time and that was that. No more fooling around with that egotistical cadet.

Nevertheless, when Saturday arrived, Paula found herself shimmering in her veins, her nerves atingle, aglow with the anticipation of being with Garner again. This time her dancing was for joy, an exultation, and Mary was happy for her, but said she'd miss her at the USO. Paula didn't tell her that this would be her last date with Cadet Cameron, only that they were going to a party at the Morrison's. It was a preamble to the Christmas season's rounds of open houses and dances. Paula assured herself that after tonight, if she wished, she could prance around with Burl. She intended to shake the blues and her natural exuberance caused her to float free.

For tonight, she shampooed her raven, silky hair and set it on large rollers. Then she sat down at the open door of the lighted gas oven, head bent, neck craning this way and that to dry her hair evenly. It seemed an interminable process, since her hair was quite thick, but she read a book for awhile, then tired of the awkwardness, and thought her time could be better served by manicuring her nails, since the heat would dry the lacquer, making it an easy job.

She stood up and pulled out the top drawer of the chest, where in the left-hand corner she kept costume jewelry and other small personal items accumulated through the years. For her eighteenth birthday when she was a senior in high school, her Aunt Carol of Atlanta, had sent her a box of five bottles of glamorous nail polish that took her breath away. They were in opaque colors, like paint, and she cherished each one, the Rich-Yellow, True-Blue, Grass-Green, Pure-White, and Wicked-Black. All were more startling than any red or pink. She hoarded them, adding acetone to keep them like new, and not wearing any of these special colors except on sophisticated occasions. She picked up each bottle, noticing that the blue and green were nearly empty. The black would match her hair and her spike heeled pumps. Runny nylons! But the dress could be any color. With a muffled chuckle, she chose the Wicked Black.

She painted her oval nails with the daring black lacquer, thinking of Garner's black eyes. Would he notice? Would he think her a hussy or that she was the most bewitching of all the girls? And the most desirable? Would he be startled out of his usual serious composure and laugh at her guffled genie? She giggled to herself, going so far as to paint her toenails the shiny black as well. Garish against her white skin!

During warm and hot weather, Paula dried her hair outside in the sunshine, playful as she toweled and basked in its warmth, but it took hours over the oven door. Accordingly, she hadn't planned to eat dinner at home. Mary left for the USO at five, so there was no need. Finally, two hours later, her hair was dry. She ducked into the tiny bathroom and gently unrolled her hair before the mirror above the lavatory.

Paula had occasionally gone to a hairdresser in Austin, but the habit of frugality was ingrained and she was accustomed to trimming her own hair and taking care of it herself. She had observed the work of the professionals and adopted their technique to achieve a beautiful coiffure. Now she combed out her curls with such vigor that a friend, watching, might think she was trying to pull it all out. Satisfied with this, she picked up her Fuller brush and brushed her locks, smoothing, curling under, smiling all the while. Ah! Perfect! Her hair, thick and glossy, fell into a halo about her lovely face. Everything would be perfect when Garner arrived tonight.

There would be no cooking odors, and she would be beautiful.

Excitement rose in her breast as she put on her makeup. She chose a princess style afternoon dress of magenta velveteen, mid-calf length with a square neckline and slightly puffed long sleeves. As she put it on, she recalled the fun she and Adele had had at the Sigma Chi Christmas tea dance. Then her nostalgia yearned back to the student dances on Friday and Saturday nights, where they double dated and made nearly every one. Her black velveteen floor length dinner gown with the gold buttons was too formal for tonight, but this dress was just right. The skirt flared out when she jig-jagged and spun in the jitterbug. How she loved to dance!

Paula was ready when Garner arrived. His eyes sparkled at the vision she presented, far surpassing his fondest dreams. He had a strong urge to claim her for his own, but managed to control himself. He leaned against the door for support. She was alluring from her tiny waist to the round forehead and its delicate mark of good breeding. She scintillated under his entranced gaze, enormous blue eyes liquid with the *joie de vivre* of her bright spirit. He worshipped the smooth column of her ivory throat and the shapely, slender hands as white as snow against the startling black enameled nails. She was a work of art. Beautiful in rich velveteen!

"You're ravishing," he breathed. He made to grab her, but she veered with a mischievous smile. He grinned. "Better not spoil your makeup. Here, let me help you." He eased her into her black, woolen coat.

Paula snuggled into the grey wolf collar and thanked him. Once again, she had pleased her escort. She was a carefree young miss back in college, oblivious of the Great Depression, luxuriating in the lively warmth of the fur, which in San Angelo she seldom had occasion to wear. The only thing lacking was a corsage for her shoulder. But Garner's company more than made up for that. Suffused with an elevated sense of well being, she treasured as a rare pearl the iridescence, the quiet excitement that made her pulse race in his nearness.

In the ambience of mutual pride, they greeted Dick and Nancy Harrow and climbed into the rear seat of a 1938 Ford sedan. Dick switched on the ceiling light and turned around to introduce his wife. Nancy was tiny, reminding Paula of a cherubim with her smiling dark eyes and her fluffy bangs and curly brown hair around a piquant face. Her voice was a soft soprano as she greeted them in her Southern accent. Paula liked her instantly, and Dick, too, who was of sturdy English blood, well proportioned but not tall like

Garner. He was good-looking with a nose that bespoke of long thoughts and clear blue eyes beaming intelligence.

Paula was pleased to be double dating. She felt safer this way, and in spite of the uniforms, she could forget the war tonight.

"This is Mr. Morrison's second car," Dick explained. "He's letting us use it while we're here, even furnishing the gas. He knew my father back in Louisiana and calls me his second son."

They drove west past the City Park and a mile beyond, till they came to a neighborhood of nice homes and the Morrison house, a two-story frame home lighted up inside and out on the wide veranda. Other cars were already parked in front. A wreath of holly with red berries hung on the front door, standing out against the impeccable white paint.

Mr. Morrison, who had been watching for Dick and Nancy's arrival, came forward with hand outstretched and broke into a delighted smile the minute they stepped inside. In his sixties, he was trim, bearing an attractive silver-grey mane molded to his head in close fitting waves. Dapper, Paula said to herself as she smiled during the introductions. Mrs. Morrison complemented her husband. She was a vivacious, bleached blonde, exuding hospitality in a pink chfffon hostess gown of rippling-ruffles. Her husband sparkled at her, suave in his charcoal suit, a pink carnation in his buttonhole. They were quite an admirable pair.

The entrance hall, from which rose a curved staircase of polished wood, was larger than a gentleman's den. Paula glanced to her left and saw a spacious living room, then accepted her hostess' gracious invitation to the dining area on the right. The room hummed with the laughter and murmuration of male voices interspersed by the occasional counterpoint of young ladies' responses. The young people were gathered around a lavish spread of holiday dishes on the buffet and colorful hors d'oeuvres and punch bowl on the table, shining in white damask.

The eggnog, giving off the mixed aroma of cream, bourbon and nutmeg, was tempting, so rich, but dangerous. Paula was wondering if she should drink it on an empty stomach, when before she could demur, Mrs. Morrison offered her a cup from the cutglass punch bowl and set it on her ovoid party tray. She helped herself to the dainty hors d'ocuvrcs, stuffed dates, and colorful cookies of all kinds, from German balls, flaky and covered with powdered sugar, to dark chocolate brownies, to bits stuffed with mincemeat, Paula's favorite. And the fruitcake! She tried to control herself over the dark cake of applesauce base, filled with red maraschino cherries, black raisins, candied yellow lemon peel and green citron, all moist and munchy-good with pecan meats. Too delicious for words.

Garner was amused at her elation over the festive food and drink, After a time, he suggested she try the generous buffet for some real food, ham and turkey, to give her more staying power. He was keenly aware of the surreptitious glances from other cadets and servicemen as they flickered at Paula and then cast glances at himself, which said, You lucky devil! Lucky indeed! And he intended to keep it that way. But as time passed, he became more and more uneasy. He was taking a risk with this gorgeous creature. Unknown to her, he couldn't dance, and he didn't know how he was going to break it to her. It would be a bit awkward, but it was a minor thing, because she couldn't help but have a good time.

He was distracted by a member of his group who wanted some advice and when he turned back to rejoin Paula, she was engaged in conversation by a big clunk of an officer, Bull of the Woods, whom he knew only upon sight. At first, he was disturbed, then he calmed down and headed toward the other end of the buffet to talk with Dick and Nancy. Now was the time to enlist Dick's help, a perfect opportunity. He approached his best friend with urgency and a worried gleam in his eye.

"There's something I haven't told you," he said.

"What's that?" Dick asked, slightly alarmed.

"I can't dance."

"You're kidding! You haven't learned yet?"

Garner met his disbelief. Shaking his head, he assured his friend, "No. I can't dance."

"You can't dance! Why, you're crazy!" Dick responded. "You brought Paula knowing that? Trying to lose her, huh?"

Garner's jaw tightened.

"Of all the stupid things! I suppose you've told her."

Wordless, Garner shook his head.

"You must have lost your mind."

"I was hoping you'd ask Paula for the first dance. I think enough of the other fellows will cut in to keep her happy."

Dick grimaced with disapproval. "You can bet on that."

"I'm not afraid of the others," Garner put in with some asperity. "I wanted to show her a good time. You see, I don't have much time left to let her know all about me."

"Serious, huh? Okay. I'll ask her for the first dance," Dick agreed, with a questioning look at Nancy.

She smiled at him. "I won't mind, honey. I'll be glad to sit it out with Garner."

"This may mean curtains for you, buddy," Dick warned him.

"Yeah, I know, but thanks," Garner returned. He was on shaky ground and at this crucial moment, couldn't understand why he'd taken such an unnecessary risk. His attention was drawn across the room to Paula. She was animatedly chatting with the monumental instructor. "How about letting me have the keys to the car?"

Dick grinned at him. "I see you have other designs." With a glimmer, he pulled out the keys from his pants pocket and placed them in Garner's open palm. "Old habits are hard to break! Just you be sure to run the engine for the radio and the heater."

Garner grinned back. "Who needs a heater?" He tossed the keys and gave a quick snatch, a flippancy meant to bolster.

"Yeah!" Dick laughed and turned to his wife. "Looks like it's time to put our little scheme into action. I think I hear ol' Tommy Dorsey's record in the ballroom across the way." He stepped aside and let Garner take her arm, while he eagerly sought Paula. When they reached her, she was wearing a mask of nonchalance but at the sight of Garner, they noticed the light of relief behind the intended camouflage.

"Please excuse me," Dick said to the ersatz swain. "I hate to interrupt, but I came to let you know, Paula, that Garner has given me permission to have the first dance with you." He gave her a charming, triumphant smile, and no young lady could have resisted his pleased astonishment.

She darted a glance at Garner. A lady always reserved the first dance for her escort. But when she saw his encouraging smile, she exclaimed, "How nice!"

Dick crooked his arm for her and they paced as one through the entrance hall into the living room. The carpet had been rolled back and the hardwood floor gleamed with an inviting polish. Dick led her to a clear space and they began dancing on the beat. He proved to be a light dancer, quick on his feet with an instinct to follow the mood of the music. Paula forgot Garner as she swung and jitterbugged to the fast rhythm.

Dick, however, had more on his mind than the dance. When he swung Paula to him, he said, "You know, Garner doesn't dance." She was whirling around on the rebound when she realized what he had just said. *Doesn't dance!*

Mentally, she knew there were some people who didn't dance, yet in her heart she could not believe it. All people were meant to dance and sing. One evening when she was a little girl helping her mother in the kitchen at their chicken ranch, her parents had spontaneously broken into an Irish jig. She was so enamored that she begged them to teach it to her, but they merely shook their heads. That was how she knew that God had made everyone to dance for joy. It was only natural and even the aborigines did it. What was wrong with Garner? Her heart sank at the terrible thought of living with a man who didn't dance. She faltered and missed a beat. Dick caught her and skipped a step to match her rhythm. Dancing smoothly again, Paula skimmed as though on ice, her mind rigid in resolution. Everything was botched up. An appropriate ending. This was her last date with Garner.

Dick, noticing her serious mien, spoke again as she whirled and he pulled her to him. "Garner wants you to have a good time. He thinks you've been working too hard and not having much fun."

"Oh, he does, does he?"

She jittered away with new energy and he took his turn at a whirl. When she returned once again, he added, "He told me plenty of cadets will cut in and you can dance all night. That means I'll get to dance with you again. You're a good dancer, Paula."

She ignored his compliment, as sterile as the cold ground. Her eyes darted this way and that, as if to escape. The number ended and they parted, clapped in appreciation, then took their place again when the second number began. There were three numbers to a set and Dick hoped he could change Paula's attitude during the gentle

"Missouri Waltz." He held her close, dancing cheek to cheek, giving her a sense of security as he suddenly went into a spin. She bubbled with exhilaration, carefree as a child. He dipped her with a graceful flourish, making her once more a coed on the floor. The spin was surely the most thrilling of dance steps and any dance partner who gave this special pleasure became a hero to Paula.

Dick was enjoying himself. He brought her down into a flowing, smooth glide, holding her away, but still guiding with command. "I've known Garner a long time," he said. He had her interest now. "I'm from Bastrop, Louisiana, a small town. One time when Garner was about fourteen, his family visited some kinfolks in Wilmot, about three miles north of the Louisiana state line. Bastrop's fourteen or fifteen miles south of the border and both towns are just off the Bartholomew Bayou. A mighty fine place to hunt ducks."

"Is that what you did when you were kids?"

"Yeah. That and snakes. Lots of snakes in that bayou country. We're a lot like the country boys of Texas."

"How come you dance then but Garner doesn't?"

"In high school, I'd run into Monroe and dance there and then when I went to college, I just kept it up. Garner'n I sort of kept in touch through the years. When the war broke out, we both decided to try for pilot training."

"Why aren't you an officer?"

"I just had a couple of years of college and didn't go in for ROTC. Nancy and I wanted to get married, so I took a job. She's been with me through all my training."

Paula's heart warmed to him. He was obviously so cheered to have his wife by his side.

"But I'll tell you one thing," he continued. "Garner's the finest marksman ever, probably in the whole South, and that's saying somethin'!" He tipped his head, as proud of his friend's accomplishment as though it were his own. "But, you know, he never learned to dance because where he came from, they mostly played country music, and Garner didn't go for that."

"Oh yes, the whiny stuff," Paula sympathized. "I don't, either. Does he ride?"

"I don't think he ever owned a bike." He crinkled at her and she laughed. "Oh, you mean a horse! All country boys can ride a horse, but not like cowboys. Garner has a cousin who trained his horse to do tricks. It can do fancy steps and dance, count to ten, take a bow, and roll over just like a dog."

"And it must sing."

A slow smile crept over Dick's face. "Yes, of course it sings. It's the greatest thing to hear it in the spring when the pussy willows come out. It prances around for joy, singing in high wavering voice like an opera star. I've seen it rub up against the pussies, then dash away and burst into song. They're so soft, you know. Made for love, not whipping."

He had captured her. "Yes," she murmured. "I love them, too. "

"And Garner can do other things. For one, he's a fine taxidermist."

Paula was surprised.

"He's a naturalist, really," Dick explained. "But he's always been set on finishing the work of his father...."

The officer called Bull of the Woods cut in. Dick relinquished her and Paula wished she could have stayed with him. What was it that Garner's father had wanted to do? She knew he hunted for recreation and taught and worked the stone quarry to make a living. Garner had never mentioned anything special. Perhaps it was to lecture or go into politics. But she couldn't spend her time wondering about Garner's ambitions. Better enjoy herself with this attractive hunk. But there she met with disappointment. He wasn't a good dancer like Dick and the floor was becoming too crowded.

Two more servicemen cut in and Paula found herself bored, looking for Garner as she tried to pay attention to her partner's lead. She should forget Garner. If she let her eyes find him and feast upon him, her heart would be lost. Unable to desist, she discovered him near the grand piano talking to Mrs. Morrison, and that lady was supremely happy with the young man's devoted attention. With a pang, Paula tore her gaze away. He was her date, after all, and it would be only *noblesse oblige* to spend the rest of the evening with him.

The music for that set ended and the instructor returned her to Garner.

"Having fun?" he asked, a caring in his question.

"Oh, yes!" she responded cheerily. "But right now I'm too hot and the floor is jammed. It's so hard to dance."

"Better cool off for awhile. Others are bound to quit and then you can try again."

Mr. Morrison joined them and told entertaining stories of New Orleans, where he and Dick's father cavorted as young blades.

Contrary to their expectations, more and more servicemen arrived and the place became packed with the mass of young men, high toned thoroughbreds from both Air Corps fields. Paula and Garner were overwhelmed by the fill of swaying bodies and the stomping noise, which nearly drowned out the music.

"Please excuse us," Garner said to his hostess. "I think Paula needs some of your delicious punch."

Mrs. Morrison graciously nodded, pleased at the compliment.

Garner took Paula's elbow. They squeezed and pushed their way back to the dining room. The punch was a welcome thirst quencher but the revelers were nearly as thick as in the ballroom. While Paula was sipping her drink, Garner excused himself again. After a little while, he reappeared with their coats over his arm, prepared to leave.

As she set down her empty cup, he bent over and murmured in her ear, "Let's disappear like they do in the movies." She saw his mischievous glint. "We can sit in the car and listen to the radio and talk," he added. She was relieved at the prospect. It would be much better than feeling like a jilted girl at the prom while her date refused to dance with her. She smiled and let him hold her coat for her. He shook himself into his greatcoat and they skittered away through the entrance hall and out the front door. Once they were down on the sidewalk with the faint sound of the merrymakers behind them, Paula became aware of the sudden quiet. She stopped. Free! They were alone together in the depth of the cold, crisp night.

She breathed in the fresh air and gazed up at the stars, enlivened till she stood on tiptoe in awe. Oh! The mysterious glory of God! She dreamed that each of the billions of stars was one of God's brilliant thoughts and in this manner, she herself had burst upon the universe. A heavenly spark! At the speed of light, she had sped from a vast distance down to earth, born again, to stay a minute in the time of eternity. At the appointed moment, she would leave this place and spin away to her heavenly sphere to shine again, to sparkle for the Lone Star State, her Texas! Her people would be reassured at her steadfast gleam and know that God was watching over them. And she would be a true part of Him and the other billions of companions, forever fulfilled.

Garner followed her gaze and pressed her arm close to his side. "Glorious, aren't they? There's the Big Dipper in Ursa Major. I feel as if I could reach up and touch it, or bring..." He paused. "No, I wouldn't want to bring it down."

"I know," she murmured. "You feel like you're part of it. And you want to keep the stars for yourself, to be one, to shine as brightly as they do."

Amazed at her comprehension, he put his arm around her. They stood, enchanted by the magnificence of the heavens.

Then Paula looked at Garner. "I'm in the cup, pouring out plenty upon all who will worship. How about you? Where are you?"

"I'm connected to you," he answered, his bass voice hushed. "Thrilled to be part of the handle, the important sensor to guide the largesse you would provide." He looked down at her and seeing the sparkle in her eyes, was stilled, his heart nearly bursting.

She perceived his worship and smiled upon him with an intense fervor. "It's a wonderful night!"

Skimming along in a rarefied atmosphere, they progressed to the car and settled in the front seat. Garner started the engine and turned on the heater. Paula switched on the radio and they felt secluded in their own private world with the green light from the radio adding an approving, helpful presence. As Paula tuned in, she caught KGKL and was rewarded with the strains of Glenn Miller's "In The Mood."

How appropriate, Garner mused, *I'm certainly in the mood. But I've got a tricky hurdle first.* He had not only flaunted his own shortcoming in the lack of a social grace necessary to court the most desirable girl in all of West Texas, or in the whole world, but in doing so, he had committed an unforgivable faux pas. *Work up to it. Easy does it.*

"I expect Dick told you I can't dance," he said, sounding cool-headed although he felt a tightening in his gut. "I'm sorry it happened that way. I was going to let you know on the drive to the

Morrison's, but I didn't want to interrupt the conversation. I was just thinking that you should have a good time and it didn't really matter, since I knew there'd be plenty of men who'd jump at a chance to dance with you."

"You should have told me in the first place, when you invited me."

His smile was ingratiating. "I know, but I was afraid you'd turn me down."

She gave a low laugh. "I probably would have. But I'm glad I came. You can learn to dance any time you want to."

He shook his head. "I don't have the talent. And I never seem to have the time, either. Maybe you could teach me."

She considered that for a moment. "It's unlikely. If we weren't at war, it would be different. By the way, do Dick and Nancy have a baby?"

"No. Nancy says she won't have any children till after the war. She's following Dick until he goes overseas. I think they're both happy with that decision."

"We all want children, but I'm like Nancy. I've decided not to have any until after the war. That's why I'm not going to get married until then, either."

He gave her a surprised look. "That doesn't follow."

"Pretty much!" she disagreed.

He changed the subject and they talked and listened to the music, growing warmer and warmer till Garner said he was too warm. He took off his coat, then helped her pull out of hers. He spread them full length on the rear seat.

"That's better." He reached over and put his arm around her saying, "If you get chilly, I'll keep you warm." She snuggled up to him. "There's one thing I wonder about you," he said in a puzzled tone, piquing her curiosity. "How come you don't have much of a Texas accent?"

"You don't have much of a Southern accent, either," she countered. "Or an Arkansas accent."

"That's probably true," he admitted. "My father was a stickler for correct pronunciation and he deplored careless speech. Besides, my mother's people are English and they keep to their pride in the English language. What's your excuse?"

"Similar to yours," she replied. "My folks are from Virginia and so far as I can tell, they don't have any accent. They just talk plain American, and I do, too."

"Say that again. I like the way you said it."

"What?"

"Virginia."

She turned toward him with a faint smile and said, "Virginia."

He kissed her at the precise moment the shape of her mouth was most tempting, her lips soft and receptive. Overcome, she responded from the depths of her soul, pliant in his embrace, her strength melted away in rapture. He turned her around so that she faced him as he cuddled her in his left arm and as natural as a waterfall tumbling to the rocks below, she put one arm around his waist, marveling that it was not much larger than her own, then curved her other arm around his neck, drawing him to her.

For a time and time again, they kissed, mingling with the stars of heaven. *I love you* burst in Paula's mind, and with abandon, she released her passion, holding nothing back in her desire.

"I love you, Darling," Garner murmured. "I want you for my wife."

The words, I love you, were singing in her heart, but she dare not utter them. She dammed up her confession, unspeakably miserable, trying to recover her equanimity. If she acknowledged her love for him, then she would grant his every wish because that was what love brought, a selfless devotion. This was a woman's position in life, but more than that, she could never deny Garner anything and in today's dangerous statocracy of militarism, she had no choice but to assiduously avoid the final step. The bond of marriage could be fatal. She took a deep breath, consoled that she had already told him she would not marry until after the war. It was a sensible decision and she had to stand by it. This would be her last date with Garner Cameron.

He was waiting.

Her smile chided him. "You've only known me for about two weeks."

"I knew you were the girl for me when I first saw you. And I've known couples who got married one week after they met and they get along just fine."

"Some, maybe. But don't forget, you're a pilot soon to fly off to war."

"I know. If you won't marry me before I go, we should become engaged and marry when I return."

This was something she had stored in the back of her mind, but she still didn't know enough about him to take the risk of tying herself up in such a hurry. It was the dangers that were hidden, such as unwanted genes, that were the worst of all. She shivered with remembered horror. And what would an engagement bring? Only nerves without consummation of their love. But marriage was an eternal bond no matter what happened. In agony, she perceived the promise of paradise slipping away.

Absorbed in his yearning ardor, she gazed into his face, so appealing with the cleft in his strong chin, and she softened. She would have one more date with him and...no! Too risky. *I love him too much already.*

He smiled into her eyes. "There's a good movie on at Goodfellow next Wednesday night. How about dinner and the movie?"

"I can't," she fibbed. "I already have an engagement."

Panic seized him. They had so little time left to be together. He would soon be transferred to Kelly Field and he may never see her again. Fool! Fool! She's getting back at me for the stupid hick that I am. I should never have let her see me at a disadvantage or treated her the way I did tonight.

Oh God! Oh God! What can I do? She's more than my life to me! Help me work out a new strategy! I cannot let her go! I've got to nail her down before I fly overseas!

"Our love is something that cannot be denied, Paula," he said in a tight voice. "I wish you weren't so afraid."

They heard a tapping on the window and at the sight of Dick's knowing grin peering through the glass, they quickly disengaged and drew apart.

Chapter Nine

Paula was relieved to see the Harrows.

Their company on the drive home offered an opportunity to stiffen her resolve not to date Garner again. Mental discipline was the only answer. Self preservation was an imperative, since come hell or high water or war, there would be a future. No mistake about that.

When they reached her apartment, Paula bade Dick and Nancy good-night and Garner accompanied her to the door. He murmured her name and bent down to kiss her, but she bristled and turned away to unlock the door. He opened it for her and when she had stepped inside, she said, "Thanks for a lovely evening."

"I'll give you a call," he responded.

Paula closed the door. Safe! She stood in the dark, throat contracted, eyes moist with unshed tears, a numbness taking over. She had just thrown away her love, her life, her *raison d'etre!*

Slowly, she came out of her trance, aware of Mary's muffled breathing and the ticking of the clock. She realized she had been holding her own breath and deliberately expanded her diaphragm to inhale. She could not escape life that easily. She must carry on in all her ways as if Garner had never appeared, as if he didn't exist, because for her, he couldn't. She would date others and Burl. He was steady and dependable, not elegant and not the Southern gentleman that Garner was, and surely not the lover, but he was crazy about her and they were good friends. Life with him would be better than remaining a secretary all her life and better than a life of anxiety or sorrow or emptiness, all of which could be true if she gave in to her impossible desire for Garner.

❧ ✳ ☙

Two feet of snow had fallen on New York City and the storm was moving on up toward Maine, hindering transportation and causing seven deaths. Another system of blizzards came down from Canada into the Midwest, all the way to St. Louis. But San Angelo's skies remained clear and cold. 'No weather' was daily reported from Meterology at Goodfellow and the training planes continued to fly in favorable winds.

Paula flew her soul's course in the same medium, flashing under the sun, mindful but trying not to be overcome by the turbulence of war. Seated at her desk in the office, she was thankful for her job, a steadying force, and she liked working with her particular officers. It was three o'clock in the afternoon, break time, and Colonel McIntyre and two of his buddies stood nearby. She overheard them discussing Ernie Pyle, best loved of American war correspondents.

"Too bad his column doesn't run in the San Angelo paper," the colonel said, "but I have his latest book, 'Here Is Your War,' and it's a humdinger." He picked it up from his desk and held it out to the other men but they both said they'd read it. Then Colonel McIntyre noticed Paula listening with interest. "Here," he suggested, "I think you'll like it."

She accepted the book with a smile and he generously added a copy of Yank magazine.

These special morale builders will expand my horizons, Paula mused. Garner's words, "I wish you weren't so afraid," were hard to set aside. Maybe I should learn more about the war. But a brief perusal was all she needed of the battlefront reports.

Colonel McIntyre was the daddy of them all and he took a certain paternal interest in Paula, too. Before he and the other officers left for flight time, he opened the book to a page near the middle and said, "Here's a good insight for you. I'll be back by four-fifteen."

Caught up with her work, she began to read where he had indicated. What she read was more reassuring than she had expected. It was clear that now, over in Europe, Pyle expected the Allies to win. Turning the page, she read:

> Our men can't change from normal civilians into warriors and remain the same people.

He further explained that the time gone, the maturing that took place during that absence, would bring change.

> Add to that the abnormal world they had been plunged into, the new philosophies they had to assume or perish inwardly, the horrors and delights and strange wonderful things they'd have experienced, and they are bound to be different people from those you sent away.

She felt he was talking to her. Fascinated, she read on:

> They are rougher than when you knew them. Killing is a rough business. Their basic language has changed from mere profanity to obscenity.... Our men have less regard for property.... They are fundamentally generous, with strangers and with each other. They give or throw away their own money and it is natural that they are even less thoughtful of bulk property than of their own hard-earned possessions. It is often necessary to abandon equipment they can't take with them. One of the most striking things to me about war is the appalling waste that is necessary....

She closed the book. *There is reason to be afraid.* Garner returned would be a different person, changed. He would not be the Garner I know now, even if he miraculously escaped injury or loss of limb or sight or hearing. The outlook is even more dire than I had let myself believe.

The aftermath of the war was something everyone skimmed over, blinded for self protection from the dregs of war, the horrors to be found in the bottom of the intoxicating elixir of miracles performed and bravery displayed in the all out effort to save the world.

And especially to keep America the beautiful free. To keep her from the ravages of war. Blind sacrifice was the order of the day.

Garner was expendable. All the fly boys were expendable. And not only fly boys, but all of the Army, Navy and Marines, the nation's finest youth, and the Seabees, too.

Sobered, Paula picked up the copy of *Yank*, the weekly magazine written by and for enlisted men of the Army. She read letters from G.I.s and the funny cartoon, "Sad Sack," laughing at his Catechism:

> If it moves, salute it.
> If it doesn't move, pick it up.
> If you can't pick it up, paint it.

She'd go for that last one.

It was just as the Old Man always said, "You can't beat the G.I.!" The G.I.'s sense of humor and inventiveness were unmatched anywhere in the world. On this more positive note she returned the book and magazine to Colonel McIntyre's desk, repeating to herself: *The difficult we do immediately. The impossible takes a little longer.*

With Pyle's insight into the effects of war on fighting men, Paula's patriotism was stimulated. America's women were not expendable. Their part and her part, along with them, was to make the boys happy while they were still here on their home soil. And to give them something to come home to. That was what they were fighting for, their women and their homes. If Garner called, she could accept a date when convenient and simply let him know that she was dating other men, too. It was the customary thing for a girl to do and it would give them both a better perspective.

꽁 ✻ ફ

Chadbourne, the broadest street of the town, was festive with Christmas decorations in the store windows. Large, fivepointed, silver stars stood atop each lamp post in remembrance of the bright Star of Bethlehem. These were lighted by night, each united to its mate across the street with furry strands of synthetic greens so that either by day or night, the people's spirits were elevated to a sense of dignified procession as they passed below, their thoughts turning to the divine birth of Christ, their saviour.

Paula noticed and yet scarcely saw the embellishments. Her mind was not on the Christmas season, something that happened every year, nor did she look upon her family's traditions with anticipation. She was waiting to hear from Garner. Suffering the passing days when he did not call, a low fever possessed her. She looked for him at Goodfellow. She hesitated at the corner where she turned to walk to the cafeteria and again, she slowed her pace at the end of the Headquarters Building, looking toward the observation tower, where she hoped to get a glimpse of him. It was all in vain. She felt foolish but assuring herself that he couldn't do without some sort of relaxation, she went to the recreation hall one day, ostensibly to deliver a War Department memo to the Officer of the Day. No Garner and no Dick, either.

Had she hurt Garner's feelings? Better forget him.

When Burl called on Thursday and insisted that she could give up the USO this one Saturday night, she was relieved to be asked for a date and accepted with enthusiasm.

※ ※ ※

The Corral, out four miles west of town, was the only roadhouse in the vicinity. Paula had never gone there because she didn't drink beer and didn't run with the beer drinking crowd. But she would be safe with Burl. And it would be a new experience, she told herself. To go all out, she dressed in her cowgirl outfit of full beige skirt, leather vest with its fringe and tooled designs of a cowgirl lassoing a scampering dogie, and hand tooled, oxford brown cowboy boots. Burl would be pleased, since he always wore cowboy boots with his ranch togs.

The Corral was a low, single story frame building, its windows painted black like a real dive, its name above the front door in bright pink and blue neon. It was surrounded by a gravel parking lot, which was level and large enough to accommodate a good sized crowd. There were only two other cars when they pulled up near the front door at about nine o'clock.

When they entered, the sickening, sweet smell of beer, mixed with the odor of cigarette smoke, accosted Paula's nostrils. The place was dim with only occasional lighted sconces along the plastered walls. Folding chairs were lined up along the front of the hall and at the end to the right, a middle aged man was in charge of the counter, where he sold snacks, beer and cigarettes. Several soft drink machines and a fancy beetle organ stood nearby with their bright white, red and blue lights offering an irresistible invitation.

The white wall along the back, above a row of cozy booths, gave meaning to the place with a mural of cattle that lowered and bellowed, tearing away from determined cowboys in a Texas corral. Paula half expected the floor to be covered with sawdust, but when Burl guided her toward the booths across the way, she was pleased to find it smooth and not too slick under foot. She glided in rhythm, as though already dancing, and Burl, laughing, took her in his arms and waltzed her to a booth in dark mahogany leather, where laughing, they fell in a heap opposite one another.

As though inspired by their antics, from the next booth there rose a thin, weathered grandfather cowboy, his bones showing through his blue cowboy shirt and worn bluejeans. His wide black leather belt down around low slung hips, hung on through tenacious grit alone. Shod in boots, he went over to the beetle organ, put in a quarter, and nodding with satisfaction, returned with a grin on his lined face, while the easy strains of "Red River Valley" filled the hall.

"Dance?" Burl asked Paula.

She shook her head. "That's for listening, not dancing."

"Want something to eat?"

"Not really. A coke will do."

"I'll get you one and a beer for me."

He returned with the drinks and lighted up a Camel. He was thoughtful enough not to blow the smoke in her face and Paula was glad she had come. Burl was tanned and fit, his blond curly hair close against his well formed head, his lopsided smile just different enough to be interesting.

"Cool, Clear Water," by the Sons of the Pioneers came over the record player next and they realized that there would be three more songs that were more for listening than dancing. Burl leaned forward.

"Paula, I think I've made some progress," he said.

"What do you mean? Something I don't know about?"

"I visited the Draft Board again this week." He stubbed out his cigarette and continued, his gaze intense. "And there's one man who's sympathetic."

"Well, I'm not!" Paula was alarmed. "Don't you know you're more valuable at home than you would be out there getting killed or worse?"

Burl jerked his head away, chin lifted to take the assault. "You don't know what it's like having to sit it out while all your friends and cousins have gone into the service. My dad can run the ranch."

"You know he's not well. He's getting old, Burl, and the ranch is more than he can handle alone." She was silent for awhile, then spoke in a small voice. "We need you here. Not just to raise the cattle."

He gave her a long, discerning look and asked, "You need me?" His bass voice had turned soft.

"Why yes, I need you. We all need you." She hadn't realized till now just how much she depended upon Burl. "There are so few men left," she added. "Young men, anyway." Then she laughed. "And think of the advantage you have here at home with all the young fillies waiting for your whistle, you ol' fossicker!"

Burl blinked. "Shucks, ma'am, ah don't even know what a fossicker is, but it sounds turrible individual."

"I guess! It's some gold digger...I mean gold miner...who digs around, you know, in the rubble of an old mine for leavings."

"Leavings! Hey! Is that what you think of me? I'll have only the best plump nuggets at my table. And you're the shiniest one I've ever seen."

Paula grinned at him. "Thanks for the compliment. You say the Draft Board turned you down again?"

"Yeah. "

"I'm glad. I don't want you to go, Burl."

His glance took on a new sparkle. "That calls for another beer!" He heaved himself out of the bench. "Want something? Some pretzels?"

"Okay!"

Paula watched him at the counter and saw him put a quarter in the beetle organ, then heard the melody of "Old San Anton'." She tapped her foot to the lively beat, glad that Burl wanted to dance. He cut an impressive figure among the few local and Air Corps men on the dance floor, being taller and more broad of shoulder, carrying himself in an easy saunter. In this dim light she couldn't see the white skin of his forehead where his Stetson shaded from the sun, but could see the strong jowl. For some reason, it was the thing about him that attracted her most. His jowl wasn't heavy like a Neanderthal man, but just right with muscular strength. A real man's jaw. And his lopsided smile or grin gave just the whimsical touch that made Burl approachable in spite of his superior size and build.

He grinned at her after he arrived at the table, set down the package of pretzels and can of beer, then arms akimbo, gave a rousing, "AAANNH HAANH! OLD SAN ANTON!"

Laughing, Paula rose at this blatant invitation to dance, and held up her arms, which he speedily filled, grasping her around the waist and swinging her nearly off her feet. They clomped around the dance floor with exaggerated high stepping at a fast pace like a couple of kids proud of themselves and the fun they were having. On a fast turn, Paula bounced face to face with Dick Harrow, the slender, graceful dancer, Garner's friend. She backed off, causing Burl to stumble.

"Oh!" she cried. "We nearly ran into someone!"

Dick had recognized her and embarrassed, she had smiled an "Oops!" at him.

Burl caught her up again and they were off at a safer tangent. Paula glanced about, but she did not see Garner. Of course. He didn't dance. He had a specialty of another kind. She wished she hadn't been reminded of it. In remembrance, she shuddered at the thought of Burl's calloused hands and wondered if she could bear his caresses.

☙ ✳ ❧

Burl was polite and handsome enough in a down-to-earth way, but the evening had lost its charm for Paula after her encounter with

Dick. She remained pleasant and smiling for the duration and in spite of Burl's smelly breath of beer and cigarette fumes, she let him kiss her good-night. She made it brief, but was satisfied that her patriotic effort had given him much pleasure. He deserved it and more for sticking it out on the ranch and raising beef for the sustenance of the country's brave fighting men, Garner included.

One whole week had passed and he hadn't called as he said he would. No doubt he was just another fly boy on the fly. She shouldn't have taken him so seriously. Fellows developed all kinds of lines to keep the girls in their clutches. She knew that. It was a good thing she had decided to let him go.

On Sunday, Paula resumed her place in the kitchen of the USO, where she worked hand in hand with Mary until late afternoon. They had just stepped into the apartment, when the telephone rang. Paula threw her purse on the bed to answer and heard Garner's melodious "Hello." Her nerves vibrated.

"Paula! I'm glad I caught you. I need to see you. Do you realize that next Tuesday will be our three weeks anniversary? That calls for a celebration. Let's take in the movie out here at the field. I also need your advice for my sister, Diane. She's depending upon me."

"All right," Paula replied, trying to steady her voice. "If I can help, I'll be glad to."

"Would it be convenient for you to eat at the cafeteria first? The show starts at seven-thirty."

"No. I'd better come home after work, then take a bus out later."

"I'll meet you at the theater around seven-fifteen, then."

"Fine!"

They hung up and Paula tried to calm down. He had called! He had remembered the day they first met. And he needed her advice. Garner was a very thoughtful young man, the kind women yearned for. She should forget all about that,though. Here she was, all atwitter over the prospect of seeing Cadet Garner Cameron for only the fourth time, not an impressive record. He was probably dating someone else.

◈ ❋ ◈

The motion picture theater was a barracks building adapted to accomodate a projection room, auditorium and silver screen. It had a satisfactory business but nothing overwhelming, unless an unusual film came along, such as one featuring the Marx Brothers or Dottie Lamour or Betty Grable. Most pictures were propaganda films about the war and servicemen tended to avoid them. Paula made it a point never to see one. She lived the war every day and that was more than enough.

Garner was there when she arrived and he hadn't changed. Somehow the change in herself had made her think he would be different, not the wonderful young man she dreamed of, especially since she hadn't seen him in ages. Ten days was more than a lifetime.

He had already purchased the tickets and they went inside.

Paula chose seats in the center of an empty row toward the rear. Once settled, Garner took her hand, sending a thrill through her. He gave her an intimate smile in the gloaming light from the Fox News screen and gently squeezed her hand. She smiled and squeezed back in return. Then she realized what she was doing. She withdrew her hand and pretended to adjust her coat. She must remain aloof for the rest of the evening and not encourage him.

The motion picture was a war story of the Navy at sea. Paula sat oblivious to it, putting herself in overglide far above the surface of reality. Once, calling herself back to Garner when he shifted in his seat, she gazed down at his hand on the armrest. It was such a strong, thick hand, capable, with long square fingers. She was startled. Being an artist, she made it a habit to observe the peculiarities of form in the constitutions of individuals she knew or came in contact with. She had never seen square fingers before.

Negroes had slender hands with long, tapered fingers, quite beautiful. At this comparison, she reminded herself that Garner still had the blackest eyes she had ever seen. This made her wonder how Adele was getting along.

Garner's peace was disturbed in an inner alarm. Paula could so easily slip away. There was something, something beyond the war she could not divulge, something that held her in its thrall. If he could only break through, he could win this ephemeral battle. Every time he thought he had her, she would veer away to a never-never land he could not enter. And yet, he knew their love was mutual and it was real. Was there some inherited disease or insanity in the family? He was determined to find out, to overcome this shadowy avenger. They could face it together, whatever it was. He would have to convince her of that. And fast.

After the show, they moved along companionably with the other movie goers and a portion of the crowd streamed toward the cafeteria for refreshments. They entered with the others and Garner said, "This is where we first lunched together three weeks ago. Remember?" Her heart melted at the lovelight in his eyes.

"Yes, I remember."

"You said you were a poet and I said I'm an artist."

He nodded, his gaze more intense. "That must be what brought us together. We're soul mates."

She tore away from his gaze. That first meeting of the minds would be a highlight in her memory forever, more precious than anything else in her life except for his continued presence. But she had no right to encourage him.

They ordered chocolate nut sundaes and began to make small talk while they spooned the delicious ice cream fruit mix of pineapple, maraschino cherry and chocolate dip covered with pecan nutmeats. Then Garner paused.

"Paula, Diane is thinking of joining the WAVES."

"The Navy for women?"

"Yes. It bothers me. She's only twenty and I don't want anything to happen to her."

"You're probably worrying for nothing. No doubt she'd stay stateside and have some clerical job. What does she do now?"

"She's in a munitions factory up at Fort Smith."

Paula's eyes widened. "That seems more dangerous to me than the WAVES."

"Could be, but that's not all." He pulled an envelope from his breast pocket. "I've had a letter from my mother. She sends her love and some news I think you'll find interesting." He handed it to her. Reluctant, yet curious, she accepted it and read:

Dear Son:

I'm so happy that you have found the girl of your dreams. Do give her my love and a kiss from me. I also have good news. I'm sure you'll be tickled that I've been accepted into the Women's Army Air Corps in the Medical Division. I'll be stationed at Pueblo, Colorado for Basic Training. I'll report for duty on the third. I have rented the house and I'm sure everything will be taken care of here at home.

Your sister—

In consternation, Paula let the letter fall on the table. "Your mother a WAAC!" she exclaimed. "Whoever heard of such a thing! How old is she, anyway?" Garner gave her a faint smile.

"She's only forty-two and nurses' aids are needed. I know she's in seventh heaven. She felt so useless at home all alone and with no real job, just a bit of practical nursing."

Paula became thoughtful. "I wouldn't want to be in the WAACs."

"Or in the WAVES? But why should you? You're already doing your part right here at Goodfellow Field and at the USO. I've told you that before. I'm just not certain about Diane."

"I wouldn't worry about her, if I were you. I'd be more concerned for your mother." Sympathy rose in her heart for this young man whose family was being threatened, for the trepidation he felt at the possibility of losing his womenfolk to the war. How many other families were going through the same thing?

"If that's the way you feel," Garner said, surprising her, "I'll tell Diane to join the service. It would be an adventure for her and she'd have a much better job. Also, I wanted to give you Mother's love." Paula smiled her thanks, mentally wincing, wondering how she was going to end this evening without becoming more involved.

She changed the subject and when they were once more out in the cold night air walking to the bus stop, Garner invited her out to Goodfellow for their special Christmas Day dinner on Saturday.

"I'm sorry, Garner. This year it's my family's turn to have Christmas Dinner with the Steins. It's a custom that began years ago when they were our closest neighbors out on the ranch. We alternate every other year."

"But this will be my only Christmas in San Angelo! Couldn't you make an exception just this once?"

"My folks and everyone will be expecting me. And I haven't seen my own folks for some time."

The small city bus, its interior lights showing empty seats, rattled its way toward them.

"I'll miss you," Garner said. Paula did not reply.

The bus drew up to the curb and he courteously handed her into it. She needn't have worried, she thought, when she said good-night. There had been no trouble in remaining aloof.

No trouble at all.

❧ ✻ ☙

Christmas Day came on a Saturday this year, quite propitious, since it meant that not one extra day would be lost in the war effort due to the holiday.

Mary was spending the weekend with her widowed father, leaving Paula free, except the irony was that she was never free of thoughts of Garner. He was real, not a figment of her dreams. She was filled with deep emotion and desire. This love was too powerful, overwhelming all else. It frightened her. She had had no idea that love could be so all encompassing, an ever present entity, demanding, tenacious, self-righteous, burning like an inextinguishable flame, warming and coloring all else to a near oblivion. Nothing else mattered.

And yet it did. Ralph, Bonnie's husband, was far away, fighting the Japs in the Pacific. Bonnie and her little Douglas would not be with the family gathering this year, because they were to spend the day with his folks.

As planned, Paula accompanied her parents to the Lazy S ranch for Christmas dinner with the Steins. Sorry that Garner could not be with them, she made an effort to forget him. This caused her to miss her sister all the more and she sensed that this could be the last one of these gatherings. She made an effort to be charming and tried to bask in Burl's attentions, but it was too much for her and she subsided into a dull conversation with her folks, greatly relieved when she could get away and return home.

The next morning, already dressed for church, Paula was having a leisurely breakfast over the Sunday paper when the phone rang.

"Hello, Paula!" She was surprised to hear Garner's warm voice. "I must apologize for this belated Merry Christmas. I tried to get you late yesterday afternoon, but you weren't home. I was so bushed from hitting the books, I went to bed early. I've got a pass for the day. How about dinner at Ma's Cafeteria?" He paused. "Before you say a word, let me remind you that the twelve days of Christmas have just begun. I have a Christmas present for you."

Never too late, he was saying. Paula thought it had been too late for them before this romance had ever begun. She dangled the telephone cord, then twisted it around her hand. "Bonnie and I are going to spend the day with our folks, Garner. I'm sorry."

"Couldn't you make it this evening?"

"I could make it by six o'clock, if that's all right." She wondered what the gift could be, instantly thinking of the photographs most cadets were ordering. Surely he would not be so bold as to give her his portrait. If it were some kind of ring, she would of course, refuse it. But it if were his photograph, she'd be in a quandary. A photograph was the next thing to an engagement ring, like being pinned by a fraternity man in college. Or just about. She hadn't thought of buying anything for him.

"I'll come by for you at six, then."

"That won't be necessary," Paula quickly responded. "I'll already be in town, so I can meet you at Ma's."

"In the foyer at Ma's, then, at six," Garner agreed. "Have a good time with your folks."

Paula winced. She hung up thinking, Why didn't I just invite him to come along to my folks? I couldn't, yet it seems inhospitable to leave a stranger out, alone at Christmas time, and a fine cadet serving his country, even more so. I didn't really mean it like that. It isn't my fault he told his mother about me. The least I can do is to be friendly, like a true Texan. Friendly, but not sentimental. Garner will soon be gone and then, as the officers at Goodfellow would say, everything would be back to situation normal.

She heaved a deep sigh and poured herself a cup of coffee.

※

Paula, dressed in her dark blue suit and rose blouse, walked at a fast clip up East Beauregard Street toward town. Her heart was pounding with the excitement of seeing Garner soon, her nerves tense. She breathed in the bracing air and concentrated on her surroundings. Soon she would arrive at the town's business hub, where Beauregard and Chadbourne Streets intersected. She loved the broad streets and recalled riding her Palomino horse in the Old Settlers celebration, the High School Band playing, the Texas Rangers and city officials all prancing in ranch and official uniform regalia. Cowboys and rodeo performers brought up the rear, sometimes driving their Brahma bulls and Longhorns before them.

The buildings on the high plateau of San Angelo did not have wooden overhangs to shade the streets like the stores in southern Arkansas or in some East Texas towns. Out here, where the wind blew continuously, delighted to stir up the dust, the people were eager for the sun. Most of the settlers had come from the midwest or the east to regain their health from such respiratory illnesses as tuberculosis, asthma, emphysema, and hay fever. Floyd Roncourt had brought his family here because of his asthma. It seemed strange that asthma sufferers found relief in the perpetual dusty atmosphere, but it was pure dust, pure air bathed in sunshine the year round. And it was uncontaminated with fungus and pollen, since there were few plants and scarcely any moisture. The warm sunshine was worshipped and sweat from the summer heat was whisked away in the breeze along with the people's ailments.

The annual parade streamed down broad Chadbourne Street headed south past the San Angelo Drug Store, which stood on the northwest corner at Beauregard Street, and on past the hardware store and Ma's Cafeteria.

Life was nearly eternal in San Angelo. Around the corner from the drug store, a block away on Beauregard, stood a dark brown hut that had been there from time out of mind. It was the home of a centenarian couple, man and wife, who no longer participated in the town's celebration.

The hut stood on the edge of a parking lot across from the St. Angeles Hotel, near the finest jewelry store. Every day precisely at noon, the ancient couple came forth from their dark haven into the glaring sunshine. No more than five feet tall, they were tiny figures, their skin permanently tanned like parchment. Their movements were protracted, their step a mere shuffle, small feet clad in handmade, leather moccasins. Dressed in black, homespun clothing of several thicknesses, the woman's full skirt nearly swept the ground. On her white hair rested a battered light straw hat whose fancy, embroidered flowers on the brim and blue ribbon around the crown were faded. The man's shirt and pants were of the same homespun material. He usually wore a dilapidated cowboy hat that, although black in its earlier days, was now the dull hue of graywacke.

Citizens on the street took time out to watch this ritual, loving smiles on their faces, smiles mixed with deep respect and wonder. Everyone stood aside, exchanging bright glances, careful to let them pass. With tender attention, the ancient gentleman held his wife's arm to support her, matching his step to hers. Once out on the parking lot, the couple nodded to those nearby and in return, received courteous smiles and nods. No word was spoken. A rare felicity filled the air, the scent of devotion and eternal life a heavenly sensation.

Paula recalled these remarkable occasions, wondering about the couple's lives in their elementary hut. They reminded her of the wooden couples that came out from German clocks at appointed times. These old settlers never varied their routine and every day at noon, activity in their corner of the town was arrested in their honor. They must be in bed now, for it was nearly six o'clock and dark.

While she crossed the broad street of Chadbourne, walking toward the drug store, she surmised that the pioneers probably ate at Ma's Cafeteria every day. She kept her mind off Garner and absorbed herself in her surroundings. The drug store was attractive with its buff brick facade and Christmas decorations in the window. Paula passed it and continued with heightened interest toward the hardware store next door. It was closed but lights blazed in its interior and in its large plateglass windows. The store was a marvel, bearing the latest of modern conveniences and the tools and supplies necessary for cattle and sheep ranchers. The one story building, painted an immaculate white, invited the passer-by to stop, look at its wares, and come in. Paula slowed her pace to take it all in. The window on the right contained tempting household equipment, among the items, irons, toasters, colorful rag rugs, quilts, bridge tables and chairs, telephones and sets of china. The window on the left held fascinating generators, windmill parts, ranch tools, barbed wire, buckets and shiny harnesses and spurs. She was crazy about the hardware store. She wanted to go in and stroll down every aisle, looking at each item and then, finally, to examine the bins of screws, nuts and bolts, nails, paint brushes and rolls of linoleum.

But the store was closed. A great calm came over her and she observed the cafeteria as though seeing it for the first time.

Ma's Cafeteria was quite different from any of the other places. You'd never suspect it was some sort of restaurant. It was inconspicuous, a one-story frame building twice the width of the hardware store. It grew from the dun colored sandy soil in a shade darker and it had only a plain wooden sign above the door with the legend, MA'S CAFETERIA, painted in black. The one small window to the right of the front door held a Christmas wreath and red candle, the only acknowledgment of the season. If there hadn't been a street lamp nearby to shed light on the low building, one could go by without ever noticing that it was there.

Ma was another town fixture, a middle-aged character too generous to become well-to-do. She liked to cook. After her husband died, her affections turned toward the townsfolk. She took great pleasure in cooking and feeding them well at modest rates. This was her aim in life and it was for this reason that she had a steady business with no need for a garish neon sign or any advertising to proclaim her location and superior services, nor any gourmet culinary splashes. She served dependable, hearty Texas food. And no down-and-outer ever left her place hungry.

In a way, Paula knew that she was to meet Garner here, yet she was separated from that self. Not wishing to intrude or give encouragement where none was due, she had exchanged herself for another person. In this altered state of unutterable calm, she pushed open the door and entered the foyer of the cafeteria.

At first, she could scarcely see anything in the contrasting dark, illuminated only by one spotlight in the ceiling. Then she heard the murmur of people lined up and made out men in olive drab ODs, some accompanied by young women, and a few local couples. She sensed Garner's presence before he spoke to her and looked up into his charming face. It was lime green. She thought it strange but accepted the anomaly. *"C'est la guerre,"* she mumbled to herself, at the same time noticing the flat Christmas package he was holding at his side.

It did not concern her.

With pleasure, she wafted in the aroma of roast beef mixed with the smells of onions, brown gravy, pinto beans and hot breads. Sliding her tray along with Garner close behind, Paula had a sensation of *deja vu.* She glanced about the place with a slight grimace. There had been no attempt to make it attractive. It was dark with a few candles on the square tables set with red or blue checkered tablecloths. The ugly, untreated struts and beams were in clear view overhead, unrelieved by paint or decoration. There were no windows to give light or give a glimpse of a garden or some other outdoor scene. It was no wonder she seldom came to Ma's.

Moving away from the food line, Paula found a table for two against the wall, which afforded some privacy. Garner seated her, then set their dishes on the table and returned the trays to the stack nearby.

"Ma Goodwin must have her own cattle ranch," he remarked, as he sat down. "I hear she always has plenty of beef for her customers."

"That's the rumor," Paula said in a normal tone. "I don't know how she does it, but rationing doesn't seem to bother her any." She looked at him and he was still lime green. She turned her attention to her dinner.

Garner, in his customary sober mien, was more loquacious than usual. "When I was a boy, we used to have game for Christmas dinner. My father taught me to hunt. I became a pretty good shot for small game, squirrels and rabbits, and for ducks, too. But I never wanted to kill a deer. And bears were getting scarce by the time I came along."

Separated from herself and him in some strange way, Paula watched herself eat slowly while she listened to his hunting adventures. She glanced at the family dining at the table off to the right and saw that their faces were the same shade of green as Garner's.

She didn't know what was wrong, and detached, as if some other person had taken her place, she perceived that nothing could be done about it. It became obvious, or not so obvious, that the young lady was listening and not listening, interested in the young man and yet estranged.

Garner paused, aware that Paula had not said a word. She was far away where he could not follow. Her face was immobile, like an owl gazing at him from some knowing dimension. Her eyes were dilated, great round velvet-black drops with only narrow bands of blue showing around the edges. His heart raced. *What's wrong? What's happening? Nothing's wrong! Hasn't this happened before? She's waiting for her Christmas gift. I'd almost forgotten. It's bound to bring her around.*

He reached down for the package leaning against a table leg and brought it up, attractive in dark green Christmas wrapping paper and tied with a wide red ribbon and bow. "This is for you, Paula. I hope you like it." He handed it to her, his gaze full of affection. "Merry Christmas!"

Paula was grave. She knew what it was. She took it in her slender, white hands. Desperate to have it, she thought it could not, should not be hers. Better refuse it right now, but how could she when every atom in her deepest desire cried out for it? With trembling fingers, she untied the red satin ribbon and carefully opened the package. She drew out an eight by ten inch photograph and lifted the flap to reveal the portrait.

The veil in her temple rent.

Paula felt the inner adjustment, a settling like that which occurs after a devastating temblor.

There was Garner in exquisite hand painted color, large, deep set eyes shining with intelligence in his sober face. He was wearing his fleece-lined, dark brown leather aviator's cap, flaps down, and the jacket to match, a white silk scarf at the throat. Paula's eyes moistened, her heart bounding in response to the young man's pure beauty. This is what she would have to remember him by, to keep in her heart and in her most secret hiding place for the rest of her life. Yes, yes, she must have it.

"It's gorgeousl" she breathed.

Garner was relieved to see her so touched. He chuckled. "The artist made me a glamour boy, real handsome with those rosy cheeks."

Paula looked up and smiled at him, startled that his face was no longer green. She gazed into his eyes, lingering in a reverie, deep thoughts of the future wrapped in warm sympathy.

"Darling," Garner said, turning serious. "The time has come. I have only ten days before Advanced Pilot Training. I'll soon be gone and I haven't met your parents yet." He took her hand in his warm, strong clasp, sending a thrill through her veins. She tried to quell her emotions by giving her attention to the photograph again. In a smooth motion, she slipped her hand out from under his and put the photograph back in its wrapping.

"I'd like to meet them, Paula," Garner said calmly, watching her. "I've done my best to introduce you to my family."

She deftly put the ribbon back on, as if the gift had never been opened. She was torn. He needed a surrogate father, someone like her parents, someone back home he could write to, someone who would be in the same place through the months away from home. *Be kind to the orphans and widows.* But such a meeting as he suggested was fraught with danger. She hesitated, holding the photograph in both hands, knowing she should return it, understanding she should not accept this marvelous gift, yet unable to refuse it.

Garner sat unmoving, as still as a 'possum hanging on a limb, fearful for its life, his senses alive to the nuance of her slightest action. The seconds expanded into eons.

Then in a swift, decisive movement, Paula put the package on her lap. "I'm sure they'd like to meet you, too," she said with a certain formality. "How about next Sunday, New Year's Day? Why not meet me at the USO after church, then I'll take you to see them."

Garner beamed at her. His scheme was working. "Great! I'll meet you there. And don't think you're getting rid of me just because I'll be leaving San Angelo so soon. I'll still have six weeks in San Antonio."

Paula hadn't thought of that.

Chapter Ten

At 1020 hours Tuesday morning, Paula, seated at her desk, answered the telephone. The C.O., officer's cap in hand, was just leaving through the door.

"Colonel McIntyre," she called on a rising inflection, "it's for you! Major Reams from the War Department in Washington."

The C.O. hastily returned to his desk and picked up the phone.

Alerted, Paula and Captains Tidwell and Kaminsky stopped work and listened to the one-sided conversation. It was most unusual for anyone, even the C.O., to receive a personal call from Washington. Fear of something gone wrong suffused the atmosphere. Questioning glances were exchanged as they tried to think what grievous error had been committed, or what important regulation had been overlooked.

"Yes, this is Colonel McIntyre."

The C.O. was silent as he listened, his expression intense, growing more and more concerned. He paled and sank down into his executive chair. "When, did you say?" There came a long pause. "I see. I see." He choked on his words. "Good of you to call. Thank you very much." He replaced the receiver in its cradle, hand clinging to it, and sat slumped, stricken, staring into space.

Everyone remained still. Then Capt. Alan Tidwell, Administrative Assistant, rose and spoke his name. "Colonel McIntyre?"

He looked up. "I've just received word that my brother, Gerry, has been killed somewhere near Tarawa...exact location not given. Over the South Pacific." He paused. Then, eyes glazed in shock, he muttered, "Gone! Gerry went down...in his Navy plane...never found...I'll never see him again."

Gloom filled the office.

It was so sudden. This death touched home. The sensitive wings of these Goodfellow pilots felt a sharp wind-shear. Gerry, the C.O.'s brother, a Navy pilot in battle on the other side of the world! Swallowed by the ocean! For a time, everyone was silent, immobilized. At length, the colonel looked up again, stunned disbelief in his gaze.

Paula and the officers took over, rallying to their Old Man's support. Within the hour, she had made arrangements for his flight to New York, leaving by 1600 hours, and filled out the papers for his bereavement leave of one week.

What a sad way to spend the holidays! Paula was profoundly affected. Garner would leave for Kelly Field on Wednesday, one week from tomorrow. So little time! She tried to put that thought out of her mind, the loss of her love and his own vulnerability as just now illustrated. So little time!

This is Tuesday, our four weeks anniversary. It was meant to be our good luck day. Under normal times, we'd be celebrating.

While she worked at her desk, half of her attention was given to the hall door. Unreasoning desire caused her to expect Garner any moment. He'd emerge and invite her to lunch at the cafeteria. She reminded herself that he was in constant danger, even here at Goodfellow. He was probably flying right now. Or he was studying. Oh, she'd forgotten! He'd said that he had to work harder than usual. Instructors were more demanding, not only in the air, but also in the classroom. They were trying to wash out any weak links at the last minute before Advanced Training. And Garner's standards were so high, he couldn't abide anything less than near perfection. He would not take any chances now. Once a cadet entered Advanced Training, his commission was virtually assured.

Better resign herself. Garner would soon be gone to San Antonio and there was nothing she could do about it. Nor what might happen to him after he went overseas. But there was one thing she could do for him before he left. She must keep her promise to introduce him to her parents. If he wanted it, that would give him a personal connection back home, a stability he might need.

Garner did not appear nor call all day.

Colonel McIntyre took off safely for New York in an Air Corps plane. Disconsolate, Paula and his immediate staff closed the office early and headed for home.

While she sat on the hard, green simulated leather seat of the small bus, jiggling her way to town, Paula worried about how she could approach her mother. She would call right away, but what could she say? This young man was just a friend? When she and Bonnie were in high school, her mother had warned them not to marry too hastily or worse. They were not to bring a baby home for her to take care of. She had let them understand that this was simply not to be done. She didn't want her mother to worry that she'd marry some stranger. Garner'd be leaving in a week. That should calm her mother down.

When Paula got home, she put her black purse on the table and hung up her coat. As she did so, she caught a glimpse of Garner's portrait standing on the chest of drawers. She picked it up and gazed deeply into his dark, intelligent eyes, pouring out her love for him. Tears welled up and she wiped them away before one could fall on the beautiful photograph. She set it up on the refrigerator, where she could see it from the cooking and dining areas.

Fortunately, her mother was home when she called.

"Hi, Mom! I'm just calling to see if you and Dad will be home Sunday afternoon."

"Nothing planned so far," her mother replied.

Paula licked her lips. "I've got a friend...he's a cadet out at the field...and he'd like to meet you and Dad. If it's all right with you, I'd like to bring him by after church."

"That's fine. I'm sure it'll be all right with Dad."

Paula gained more confidence. "He's going to be leaving for Advanced Training on the fifth. You see, his father died when he was just a boy and now his mother's in the WAACs and his sister's in the WAVES, so he's pretty much alone."

"What a patriotic family!"

"Yes, you could say that."

"Has he asked you to marry him, Paula? Is he in love with you?"

Sometimes her mother could be too discerning and at other times quite cynical. "Well, yes. He's given me his photograph. But I've told him I'm not going to get married till after the war.... whenever that is. I feel sorry for him, Mom. He's going off to Kelly Field and won't be in the States much longer."

"You sound downhearted."

"I am. Colonel McIntyre's brother, a Navy pilot, was killed over the Pacific. He just got word today. We're sad over that and the grim statistics on our men. Did you know that half of our pilots are killed in action? And there are many casualties besides, not to mention those taken prisoner."

"I'm sorry, Paula." Mrs. Roncourt's voice was muted. "Are you in love with this young man?"

Sorrow engulfed Paula, rising from the well of her deepest feelings. Gulping, she swallowed her tears and brushed the hair away from her face. She didn't know what to say. Why had her mother been so direct? She searched for an appropriate reply, but her mother would know if she lied to her. At length, scarcely audible, she murmured, "Yes, I am." Then she drew in her breath and bravely faced the admission. "But that doesn't matter, Mother. I'm still not going to marry until everything's back to normal. I'll never see Garner again. It's best to break off before he leaves. I don't want to write to him. The odds are against our ever getting together again."

Esther Roncourt became firm. "Dad and I will be happy to meet your young man, honey. I'm afraid you can be too headstrong at times. You've had a shock, but it's best not to try to foresee every little event in your future. We often figure out exactly how our life will be according to our own desires and plans. I wouldn't be too hasty about giving him up if you truly care for him."

Paula was silent.

"Remember, many pilots will return unharmed. I'd write to him if I were you."

"I'll think about it," Paula responded. "Anyway, we'll come by around one o'clock next Sunday afternoon."

"Fine! We'll be looking for you."

Although Paula liked Mary and felt close to her as a roommate, she was grateful that her conversation with her mother was concluded before Mary came home from work. At times, a garage apartment was simply too leaky to hold water. And this place wasn't much larger than a rowboat, she thought wryly. If there was anything she detested, it was to have her private affairs known and bandied about as some people liked to do in matters of the heart.

The first thing Mary did was to comment on Garner's elevated status with his photograph up on the refrigerator. She picked it up and facing it at close range, she made outrageous love to his image, googly eyed, cooing, "Oooooh! Garner, Heart of my Heart, I adore you!" Then in a show of helpless passion, she made to kiss the mouth, and overcome, she was fainting dead away, when Paula, jealous at her wicked teasing, called a halt.

"Stop it! I was feeling bad. Colonel McIntyre's brother was killed in action and Garner'll soon be off to San Antonio. So I put him up there till he leaves. Do you mind?"

"Oh, I'm so sorry!" For a moment, Mary seemed truly contrite, then a devil danced in her eye. "I was just trying to hold him for you till you came to your senses."

I'll bet! Paula thought, suddenly imagining pretty girls falling all over Garner wherever he went. It was a good thing she was sensible and would soon be free of him. "Whatever that means," she said.

Mary replaced the photograph, but still relentless, she posed like a vamp with her right hand on her hip while she fluffed her blonde hair. "It means," she said from a corner of her eye, "leading Burl on while you're in love with that noble cadet!"

Paula was aghast. "It's a free country, isn't it? I'm just dating Burl and Garner, too, until he leaves Goodfellow."

No more was said, although Paula wondered if she should tell Mary that she was going to introduce Garner to her parents. She'd probably take it wrong. No need for further disagreement.

❦ ✻ ❧

At 0800 hours the next morning, Paula was at her desk again. The atmosphere in the office was subdued and quiet, spirits at half-mast. Now and again someone would come in and request that she convey their condolences to Colonel McIntyre when he returned. She wrote their names down on a list for that purpose and assured them she would. Otherwise, there was little to do.

When the phone rang and she heard Burl's hearty gust, it was like a fresh wind in her face off the wide open spaces of the Lazy S.

"Paula! Can you talk?"

"Yes, Burl. It's all right."

"I've just come from a meeting of the Cattlemen's Association here in the St. Angeles. We're putting on our annual New Year's Eve dinner and dance at the hotel for the men and their wives, and I'd like to take you." The implication she gathered from his statement caused her to recall Mary's rebuke, but she dismissed it.

"I'd love that. Shall I wear my cowboy boots?"

Burl chuckled. "I will. Wear whatever you please, But the women'll be all gussied up in formals and their high heeled slippers, I expect. It's the posh affair of the year,"

"A good way to usher in the New Year."

"The dinner's at eight. I'll pick you up around seven-thirty."

The invitation cheered Paula. It was good to have Burl to depend upon. Furthermore, the old platitude that trouble comes in threes had been disproved. Gerry McIntyre's death and Garner's imminent departure were enough. The powers that be sought to bring some alleviation to her dejected mood. She would forget everything except the fun she'd have at the New Year's Eve bash. For the remainder of the day and all day Thursday at work, everything went along smoothly. Paula looked forward to Friday night's social gathering.

The next day after work, Mary was sorting the mail at the kitchen table when Paula entered with a bag of groceries. She set the bag down on the counter by the tiny range.

"Here's a letter for you from Adele," Mary said, handing it to her.

Adele! How was she getting along? The sound of her name unsettled Paula, bringing memories of Fred's betrayal, her own part in the cover-up of the shocking birth of Adele's baby girl, and her grief and divorce. Paula took the letter, covering her feelings with a slight smile. No breath of Adele's underlying horror would ever come from her. She hung up her coat, then sat on the bed and tore open the envelope.

Dec. 28, 1943

Dear Paula,

How I wanted to be with you back in San Angelo for Christmas! I nearly died all alone here. I hate my job at Dad's insurance office, filling out forms, taking statistics, and keeping records. So boring and I never see anyone interesting.

Everything is so empty. No men left. They're all gone. And Fred's gone, too. Forever gone. No Fred...no ba...(There was a big splotch and heavy pencilling obliterated the rest of the sentence.)

I keep dreaming of him, Paula. I miss him so terribly! How can I ever get over him? It gets worse as time goes by. What am I to do? I feel like committing suicide. But that would bring disgrace to my folks. I can't live any longer without Fred. He's all that matters. No one can make me eat.

I'm sorry to carry on this way. I do hope you and Garner are happy. Why don't you come up to see me? You would cheer me up, I'm sure. Please come, and soon!

I'll try to stay alive till you come.

As always,
Adele

This was an SOS. Adele desperate, suicidal. Paula dropped the letter and bit on her thumb, trying to stifle the sobs shaking her body. Tears streamed down her face. She had saved Adele from being ostracized by society, only to have her bereaved, lonely and wishing to die.

Alarmed, Mary cried, "What's wrong?"

Paula wiped the tears off and jumped up. "Adele wants to commit suicide! I've got to get to her right away."

Mary picked up the letter and put it on the table, an habitual housekeeping gesture performed while her frowning gaze centered on Paula. "Suicide!"

"That's what I said." Paula drew up to Mary, their faces only six inches apart. She grabbed her arm. "Mary, you've got to help me. I have to get to Dallas as quickly as possible. You didn't know it, but I have a date with Garner to visit my folks on Sunday. I'll stay with Adele as long as I can. I hope I can save her. I'll have to come back to work on Monday. Call Garner out at the field. The Officer of the Day can get a message to him. Tell him what's happened. Call my folks, too."

"Just a minute!" Mary backed up and retrieved a small notebook and pen from her handbag. "I'll write it all down. Just a minute!" She scribbled, murmuring, "Call the field for Garner. Call the Roncourts. What about the office? Colonel McIntyre isn't here."

"No, but the second-in-command is taking care of things while he's gone. You can call the Air Inspector or just call my office and tell whoever answers that I've gone on sick leave for a day."

"Sick leave! You've never been sick a day of your life. They know you never take sick leave."

"Okay. How about saying there's been a death in the family and I had to go to Dallas. I'll return on Monday."

Mary's pen wavered as she considered this prevarication. "I suppose that'll have to do. It's not exactly personal business and not any of their business, either, but there was a death." She wrote in her notebook again. In her anxiety, Paula was becoming impatient.

"I'll miss the New Year's Eve ball. Will you please call Burl for me and tell him how sorry I am? I was really looking forward to it."

"Sure!" Mary glanced up, pen poised in mid-air, and Paula was struck with a bright idea.

"Why don't you tell Burl I said you could go in my place? You'd like that, wouldn't you? What the heck! It'd be a change from the USO bit and you'd have a good time."

A joyous light filled Mary's face only to be quelled by apprehension. "But Burl wouldn't want *me!* He might prefer to go alone or stay home."

"I doubt that. Tell him I suggested it. And have a good time, Mary."

Flushing, Mary wrote in her notebook again. Paula pulled an overnight bag out from under the bed, flung it up onto the bedspread and opened it. In a frenzy, she packed enough changes for a few days, plus her cosmetics.

"I'll call a taxi." Mary said. "Are those all the calls I'll need to make?"

"You can handle the USO," Paula replied, beginning to calm down. "Just don't let them take away your New Year's Eve celebration at the St. Angeles."

Mary grinned at her. "Okay." Then she made the call for a Yellow Cab.

Paula was all packed and ready to go when the taxi arrived, her coat pocket bulging with a Jonathan apple that Mary had pressed into it at the last moment.

By fifteen minutes past six o'clock, Paula was settled in a front seat of a Trailways bus rolling northeast toward Dallas. Oh! She snapped her fingers, causing neighbor passengers to smile. She hadn't called the Turners to let them know she was coming. Too late now! She had their address and could take a taxi. It was awful having to appear on their doorstep after midnight, but it couldn't be helped. Adele had turned to her. They were as close as sisters. They had always shared their most private secrets. As children, they had often played in the forbidden shelled corn bin when Adele visited at the chicken ranch. And one time, with bated breath, they had watched the slow process of an egg being laid by a white-Leghorn hen, keeping the secret from their folks. She dreaded seeing Adele so low again. She didn't know exactly what she'd do or how she could cope. She was no psychiatrist. It would probably be best to play it by ear.

The gods have not relented after all. I hope they stop at three troubles. I don't think I could stand any more. I've been taken away from the two men I love, my friend and my true love. What does this portend? Maybe it was meant to be this way. Five more days and my life will be changed. Garner'll be gone. I'll become a hollow shell living a faceless anominity in a maze of rigid hours, monotonous duties, a shell for appearances only.

Paula asked herself if she were being perverse in anger at her disappointments and frustration. Was she trying to destroy her own hopes first, denying Garner before he was injured or killed? Yet marrying and establishing a Christian family was paramount to society and the nation. And to herself. It was only prudent to be careful in such a crucial matter. There was risk even in peace time.

She sighed. It seemed impossible to avoid risk of some nature. The gamble was that no other man could ever satisfy her after having known Garner Cameron. A state of remaining single, an old maid, haunted her.

No! That won't be my life!I have my talents to be developed and expressed. Never forget that! Maybe I won't be a state senator like my Uncle Paul, but I can be a neauvelle artiste. And nothing says I can't be both at the same time.

Look at Mary Cassatt, our American woman painter who worked in Paris. She was a close friend of Degas and joined the Impressionists. Maybe I emulate Cassatt's work because in her "Women Admiring a Child" and other paintings, a woman who resembles Mother often appears. But not really. Her work in pastels is excellent and she made a lasting contribution to art, and in politics of a sort, she made Impressionism popular in the States.

Sadly, though, she had no real political clout. Paderewski is the artist-patriot to be admired in that respect. He was a wonderful composer-musician. And he became prime minister of Poland! Eventually, he was a hero of two countries, Poland and the United States. But he was a man. I don't know of a woman in the world, artist or musician, who has ever achieved as much.

In our country glory belongs to men. Men like Garner.

An inner voice cried, *Don't give up, Paula! Never give up your vision.*

With renewed energy, she told herself, *I'll have a family and I'll have my art and then later, I can enter politics to make a change for women. My art is important. Time dissolves when I stand before my canvas absorbed in creating a scene or an abstract. This is my intrinsic self in action, my fulfillment. This is my flight to the stars, to becoming a star in the heavens. Like Garner! He must follow his dream, too. If we only could have been together, we could have become binary stars in the blue beyond of the universe. Pilot-Poet and Artist-Politician!*

Garner's face appeared before her, his eyes full of love, and she wept silently in secret.

After a time, she quieted and recalled dancing with Dick at the Morrison open house, how he had said Garner had a dream, his biggest ambition to finish his father's work. Someone had tagged just then and she never had a chance to ask him what it was. Now she would never know. If she ever did see Garner again, she must remain aloof. He was no doubt mad at her for standing him up. She was sorry that they were forced to act under the war's proscription, under the limitations of contrary circumstances. Pitiful little was left for maneuvering. The Depression was better than this. At least, one could starve to death in peace. This terrible war threatened their lives, their country, their freedom.

Nothing was worth anything without freedom. And love.

Paula didn't want to become like her friend, bereft, suicidal. Adele's case was unusual, but nevertheless, there were bound to be more divorces, and divorce was worse than death.

She relaxed against the headrest, closed her eyes, and tried to put herself in neutral. Perhaps the suggestion that Mary attend the New Year's Eve dinner-dance with Burl had been a mistake. Mary greatly admired Burl.

Chapter Eleven

Saturday, the New Year's holiday, was a long day for Garner.

He could hardly wait to see Paula again and had to resist the urge to call her. His plan was working. The next step was sure to further his courtship for her hand in marriage, but he must remember to play it cool.

That night, he found himself restless. He took a hike under the stars from one end of Goodfellow Field to the other. There was no rush, he kept telling himself. He had all the time in the world. This was his way of handling emergencies or obstructive turn of events. Give it time and things would work out. Yet it was hard to fool himself. Time was of the essence. A man had to jump quick sometimes, even if he did have eternity, and especially if the girl, like Paula, was the most gorgeous, tantalizing female on earth. The appointment with her parents must certainly let her know how much she meant to him. He'd made good progress with the photograph. Once he got into the good graces of her parents and family, he would have smooth sailing. He mustn't let her see how her reticence disturbed him. Instead, he should continue to let her know his love was true.

He'd be smooth, really smooth, like those lovers in fiction. She'd come around. She wouldn't be able to resist him. After their visit with her folks, he could make a formal proposal with an engagement ring, everything proper. But only afterwards, when he felt assured of her parents' approval.

He turned into the barracks to retire, absorbed in how he would propose, holding her in his arms, kissing her, telling her how much he adored her, how he couldn't live without her, how she meant more to him than all else in the world and he wanted her for the mother of his children. Calm, enjoying the scene, he was unaware of undressing and getting into his cot. He stretched out, turned on his right side, and imagined himself nuzzling into her fragrant hair and kissing her in the hollow of her throat.

He fell asleep only to awaken hours before dawn, nerves on edge. So much depended upon how the Roncourts received him. Paula was the kind of young woman who would take her parents' attitude to heart. Sleep didn't come so easily again.

He was too excited. This was the most important day of his life. Everything hung on the outcome of this most important visit. He must give the impression of great potential, for what else did he have to offer? He must be self-assured, but not overbearing. He must be friendly and courteous, that was the thing, and show that he truly loved their daughter and would take good care of her. Oh, how he loved her!

Garner thought the sun would never come up.

He forced himself to stay in bed until six o'clock. Then he rose, dressed in his fatigues and went outside, where he huffed and puffed through a set of calisthenics and trotted ten laps around the P.E. field, the cold wind in his face. He showered and gave himself a close shave with a safety razor. His beard was heavy and black and today he must look as clean as possible. He slapped on Mennen's After Shave Lotion screwing up at its sting, then applied shaving powder. He carefully wiped it off with the towel so it wouldn't show. He didn't want to appear unmanly. He dressed in clean olive drab undershirt and boxer shorts, laundered shirt and his cadet uniform.

Garner didn't go into mess for breakfast. It would be better to go into San Angelo a little early and have a late breakfast at the USO. That way, he'd be certain to meet Paula on time. He read the Sunday paper for awhile, then caught the ten o'clock bus to town.

When he swung the door open at the USO, he was engulfed with the wonderful aroma of hot cinnamon rolls, coffee, bacon, and sausage, all blended in a heavenly smell. He was hungry. How could he be hungry at a time like this, he wondered, but on second thought, the food would calm him down.

Garner was tickled to see Mary when she came forward to take his order at the counter. She greeted him with a special welcome in her pale blue eyes, her lips closed in a charming smile. He pulled out a couple of bills and some change and ordered orange juice, scrambled eggs, a sweet roll, link sausages and coffee. The works, he told himself. He recalled the scant breakfasts he and his mother and sister had shared in the Depression after his father died. He was only eleven, but the years of digging in the vegetable garden and raising chickens and milking a cow they owned with his Uncle Ned, had formed a permanent crease down his middle. He gave full attention to his food, a habit he had formed in the cadets, and was nearly halfway through eating when Mary appeared with a pot of coffee.

"Want a warm-up?" she asked. Then she added with sympathy. "I expect you're feeling lonely without Paula." He nodded with an oblique glance, watching the dark stream fill his mug.

"Thanks," he said.

"Did you get the message about Paula?"

Garner looked up. "No. What message?"

"She had to make a quick trip to Dallas. She left hastily yesterday, around seven o'clock in the evening."

Garner straightened up and gave her the eye. "We were supposed to meet here by one o'clock today."

"Oh I'm sure she's sorry!" Mary was eager and half apologetic. "She asked me to tell you she'll be back in time for work tomorrow. It was an emergency. She had to see a friend in Dallas."

"Back tomorrow!" Garner scowled, lips pressed in a straight line, eyes flashing with anger and disappointment. "Why'd she have to make such a trip, anyway?" He'd been stood up. He saw the light.

So that's it! That explains the mystery. She's not telling me or anyone else about her man in Dallas. It's not the rancher at all but some smooth city slicker about to get away from her.

"I don't exactly know what it's all about," Mary lied, suddenly discomfitted and confused at his reaction. "But I do know Paula's the loyal kind, so she must have had a good reason. She said it was an emergency."

Some emergency, Garner thought, noticing how flustered Mary was. Irate, his face flushed, he spurted, "We were supposed to call on her parents this afternoon." *Off in the wild blue again,* he steamed. Then he took himself in hand. *Calm down*! He gave a whimsical smile to Mary. "I'd hate to disappoint them. Paula didn't give me an address. Do you happen to know where the Roncourts live?"

Relieved that he was not to be put off, she grinned like a jack o'lantern. "You're practically there! I'm sure they'd love to see you. And they'll be home from church about now. When you leave here, turn right, go three blocks, and it's the last white house on the same side of the street." She flounced as though she'd made the arrangements herself. Garner thanked her and finished his brunch.

Once outside in the fresh air, he felt better, glad to be taking some action. He formulated his story, rehearsing what he would say. If he could, he'd find out just what kind of man this was that Paula was so attached to. The Roncourts could surely give him an indication as to whether or not he'd have a chance with her in the long run. After the war? He laughed bitterly at himself. Just who did he think he was? It was no good leaving anything to chance where Paula Roncourt was concerned. He'd have to nail her down before he went overseas. Or else. Or else live without her for the rest of his born days, a misery he didn't like to contemplate.

When he came to the white clapboard cottage, he was glad to see a black 1938 Chevy sedan at the curb. He knocked on the front door and an average sized gentleman in his late forties opened it. Smiling, he spoke a friendly hello, while Garner briefly took him in, a pleasant fellow with a round, tanned face and bald head, hazel eyes and a short, straight nose like Paula's.

"I'm Garner Cameron, Sir. Is this the Roncourt house?"

"That's right. I'm Mr. Roncourt." His voice was mellow toned. He opened the door wider. "Come in! Come in!"

"Paula got called away, Sir, but since you were expecting us, I decided to come on alone."

"Glad you did!" Mr. Roncourt declared with enthusiasm. "Glad to see you!"

Garner doffed his cap as he stepped into the modest living room. "I can only stay a few minutes."

The atmosphere was homey with the delicious smell of onions and roast beef permeating the air from the kitchen. The comfortable furnishings in ivory and pale blue bespoke a pervading calm. Garner noticed with pleasure the finish of a Queen Anne mahogany dining table and long buffet at the end of the room. It was much finer than the furniture he had made in Fort Smith. Must be from South Carolina. A studio piano matched the polished furniture and lent a quiet contrast to the pale hues of the walls and draperies. A large painting of extraordinary beauty, golds and blues in abstract, hung above the buffet, adding a touch of enchanting oppulence.

"Mother, this is Cadet Cameron," Floyd Roncourt said.

She was sitting on the divan at the front window and remained seated while she gave him a cordial, How do you do?

With a lurch of his heart, Garner responded with a smile. This striking woman was so like Paula, though the daughter was more beautiful. The mother's face was long and more narrow than the contour of Paula's lovely oval face. But they had the same arresting coloring, the white skin, blue eyes, black hair and the same delicate widow's peak.

"Won't you have a seat?" Esther Roncourt invited. She indicated an overstuffed armchair opposite her husband, who was taking a chair next to the Atwater-Kent radio console. Garner accepted the courtesy, striving to regain his aplomb.

"I'm sorry Paula couldn't come," he said. "She left early yesterday for Dallas, to see a good friend. An emergency, her roommate said." He looked from one to the other and husband and wife exchanged glances.

"Yes, Mary told us," Mrs. Roncourt remarked.

Garner did not answer and an awkward silence filled the room.

At length, Esther Roncourt addressed her husband in a deliberate manner. "Something must be wrong with Adele. Did Mary say Adele was ill or had an accident...in the hospital?" There was some anxiety in her expression. Garner assured her that Mary had made no mention of anything specific.

"Well, then!" Mr. Roncourt smiled broadly. He settled back deeper into his chair. "You know how Adele is, Mom."

Mrs. Roncourt nodded. "Adele has had a great tragedy," she told Garner. "Her baby was stillborn and just at that time, her husband was transferred and the next thing we all knew, they were divorced. The Turner family moved to Dallas. Very sad." She shook her head at the memory of these grievous events.

"When was that?" Garner asked.

"Just about a month ago."

Garner felt deflated, his food a heavy burden in his stomach. This had happened around the time he and Paula had first met, yet she'd never mentioned anything about her best friend's troubles. She'd treated him like a stranger. But maybe somehow this could account for her fear of getting married now. He wished he'd known about this sooner. He'd have to convince her he'd never divorce her, no matter what happened. But for right now, he'd better use military tactics, be bold, make a surprise attack.

He leaned forward and in a confiding way, said to Mr. Roncourt, "Paula and I are in love. I've come to ask for her hand in marriage."

Floyd Roncourt blinked, taken aback. Then he glanced over at his wife. Garner followed his gaze. Esther Roncourt's brows lifted for a moment and she smiled at her husband with an I told you so!

"I know this is sudden," Garner said, "but we don't have much time. I'm leaving for Advanced Training this Wednesday at Kelly Field. I assure you I come from a good Christian family. We're Methodist and Democrats."

Mr. Roncourt nodded, breaking out in a large grin. "Well, then! It looks like we're all on the same beam!" He gave his wife a questioning look and she smiled her approval. "If Paula loves you and says yes, that's good enough for us. She usually knows her own mind."

That's for sure, Garner thought, grinning in return. He glanced up at the oil painting. "Even in the abstract?"

"Yes, that's hers," Floyd Roncourt said with pride.

"It has a remarkable beauty," Garner commented, his gaze softening with appreciation. "I knew she was an artist, but this is the first of her work I've seen. It sets off the room just right."

He got to his feet and the Roncourts followed suit.

"Sir," Garner earnestly addressed his elder, "before I go, I'd like you and Mrs. Roncourt to know that Paula means everything to me. I promise to take good care of her if she'll have me."

"Don't rush off!" Mrs. Roncourt implored. "Won't you stay for dinner? It's in the oven ready to be served."

"Thank you, ma'am, but I've just eaten at the USO."

Mr. Roncourt hastened to add to his wife's invitation. "I understand Paula will be back tomorrow. Bring her around to see us before you leave."

Garner turned his cap in his hands. "I'm not sure I'll have time, but I'll try."

Floyd took out a small notebook and pen from his pocket. "In case you can't make it, here's our address and telephone number." He jotted them down and tore out the leaf, handing it to Garner. "How long will you be at Kelly?"

"I should graduate after six weeks and get my pilot's wings then."

Floyd's face expanded, all smiles. "If you ever want to come back for a weekend, you're welcome to stay here with us."

"Yes," Esther Roncourt said, "we'd love to have you!"

Touched, Garner responded with a courteous thank you and shook hands with his prospective father-in-law. "I might just do that!"

He departed, head high, his step a vigorous beat in a lively cadence. But his thoughts belied his demeanor. Could he have been wrong about another man? Her parents didn't seem to know of anyone else, but they were often the last to know. He still had an awful feeling there was a man somewhere in the equation. Perhaps Paula was at the apex of a triangle, hung up on guilt and remorse.

Nevertheless, he was glad he'd trusted his instinct to call on her parents. They were nice folks and he'd made a good impression on them. He had done all he could. Only God could work out things between himself and his dearest love. And God might have a hard time of it.

Chapter Twelve

The woman taxicab driver carried Paula's bag for her to the front porch of the two-story red brick house. Paula paid the fare and a generous tip, thinking she wouldn't like a job like that. In contemporary style, the home attempted grandeur with pseudo ionic white columns, heavy white front door with a cunning brass knocker in the shape of an oil derrick, and upper dormer windows trimmed in white. The bedrooms would be upstairs.

It was nearly 1:00 a.m., the witching hour. Paula hesitated, then pounded the door with the knocker. She hoped to rouse someone without alarming them or awakening Adele. Silence. She knocked again and called, "Mrs. Turner! It's Paula! I've come to see Adele!" She knocked harder. No sound came from the house. She stepped down from the porch and was considering throwing a rock at a bedroom window, when she saw a light come on.

"It's Paula!" she called again. A dark, bulky silhouette appeared in the window and Mr. Turner raised it and leaned out.

"I'll be right down." In a few moments, he admitted her into the entry hall.

Paula saw that he was the same man she had always known, a tall, heavy man with large features and black, bushy brows and curly hair, now graying. Mrs. Turner, hastily putting on a luxurious blue satin negligee, rushed forward.

"Oh, Paula! I'm so glad to see you!" Memories of their earlier hospital experience sparked between them.

"I'm so sorry to arrive at such an ungodly hour," Paula apologized, "but I had an SOS from Adele."

Mr. Turner grunted, "I'm goin' back to bed." He abruptly took his leave.

A small voice cried out from above. "Mother! Mother!"

Without a word, Paula picked up her bag and Mrs. Turner led the way upstairs to Adele's room, the second door down the hall. She opened it and quickly turned on the lamp resting on a student desk. "Adele, Paula's here," she said softly.

Adele, golden brown hair touseled, turned toward her and squinted at her, not understanding, still shadowed by sleep.

Paula glanced about and murmured, "What a beautiful room! It's twice as large as my whole apartment."

She glanced around, her artistic sense warmed at the sight of the drawn draperies and bedspread of a graceful fern design, silvery fronds against a verdant tint. She felt the thick carpet of a darker hue underfoot and noticed the triple-mirrored vanity against the inside wall, a cedar chest beside it. The built-in wardrobe and shoe closet of fruitwood, handmade, must have been the work of the same artisan who had fashioned the desk. She set her overnight bag down, looking at the slight figure in the bed, seeking recognition. Adele blinked.

With a poignant cry, Paula rushed to her. "Adele!" Her heart turned over when she saw how wan her friend looked, how thin her precious face.

At first, there was no response. Then Adele gazed into Paula's eyes and she asked faintly, "Is it really you?"

Paula nodded to reassure her. "I'm here! I came as quickly as I could after I read your letter." She took Adele's hand and enclosed it in her own two hands. This touch and warmth of human love enlivened the young, bereaved woman.

"How long can you stay?"

"Three whole days," Paul replied. "Tomorrow's New Year's Eve already. We'll bring in the New Year together."

"The New Year," Adele gasped. "I don't want to see another day or another year." She closed her eyes and withdrew her hand.

Paula gulped to ward off the tears, determined to hide her consternation. "Someone's gonna have to light a fire or you're gonna have to let me in bed with you," she claimed. "I'm so cold right now that I don't think I'll ever see another day or another year."

Adele's eyes flew open.

"Well, don't just lie there! May I come in or not?"

Mrs. Turner moved to the foot of the bed. "Paula, have you had dinner?"

"I'm just cold," she answered, shaking her head.

"Get in bed, then," Adele said.

Within a few minutes, Paula was in bed, hugging Adele around the waist. They settled in spoon fashion, warming themselves like little foxes in their den. Mrs. Turner adjusted the covers, snapped out the light, and left.

They soon fell asleep.

Later in the morning, Paula had begun to stir awake when Mrs. Turner, her dark eyes showing pleasure, came into the bedroom carrying a breakfast tray of hot, homemade cinnamon rolls, orange juice and fragrant, steaming coffee. Paula jumped out of bed and shook Adele's shoulder.

"Wake up! Sit up! It's breakfast in bed for your royal highness." Adele opened her eyes and yawned, preparing to turn over, when Paula jerked her pillow out from under her head, plumped it at her back, and pulled her up. "There! Now I can get back in bed and join you. I've never had it so good! This is the way to start the trail for a scrumptious New Year. An omen for the whole year, I hope."

Mrs. Turner set the tray down between the girls and said, "Now, if there's anything else you want, just let me know. There's plenty more in the kitchen." She drew the fernrest draperies aside, letting the cheery sunlight stream into the room.

"I'm sure this is enough. Thank you, Mrs. Turner," Paula said. Seeing that her daughter was perking up, Mrs. Turner left, leaving the door open behind her.

Paula buttered a roll for Adele and offered it to her, ignoring the pallor on her face made more apparent by daylight. Then she ate hungrily. "I haven't had such marvelous cinnamon rolls in ages." Her enthusiasm was catching. Adele drank her orange juice, then ate one whole roll with hot coffee.

When they had finished, Paula set the tray on an end table and stepped over to the clothes closet. She tugged the Jonathan apple from her coat pocket and with a mischievous grin, held it out to Adele on the palm of her hand. "I've brought you something."

Adele laughed and plunged for it. It was their private joke. When they were in the fourth grade, on the day before a test, they would take an apple for their teacher, Miss Comstock. They had never been sure, but hoped this practice was an influence for good grades. Paula called it "politicking." Adele played the game with her because she noticed that Paula seemed to get along well with everyone. And it was fun.

They dressed and spent the rest of the morning visiting with Mrs. Turner. Mr. Turner had gone to his office, but he had given Adele a two-day holiday to spend with Paula.

Paula was expansive. The women were free to talk as they wished without any consideration of a male presence, but more than that, Paula was delighted with the large, comfortable, living and dining rooms, which were decorated in one continuous mode. The colors of beige and royal blue, with touches of magenta in the flowered pattern of the carpets, appealed to her. Overstuffed chairs in brown, gold and blue harmonized with the gold draperies. And the dining room, furnished in rich, black walnut, was a special delight, for it had a window seat that overlooked the lawn and garden of border flowers. Once, she had peeked out and was faced with the velvet eyes of innocent pansies in bright yellow, magenta and deep purple, giving her pause. Such beauty! Truth in a simple yard. Then a gray and white mocking bird suddenly appeared, its tail seeming about to drop off as it flitted from branch to branch in the bare limbed sycamore tree. It's song was loud and clear, varied into many songs with accurate notes of other birds. What a treat! San Angelo's doves and ducks were its only birds of any account.

Lunch was a tasty shrimp salad. Paula told Adele she need not eat all of it if she would eat her apple. This bargaining appealed to Adele and she ate down to the quick of the core. After lunch, Mrs. Turner repaired to the kitchen and the young ladies sat in the window seat in quiet intimacy.

Adele was eager to divulge her feelings never mentioned in her letters. "Paula, I get so discouraged. You don't know how people treat me."

"What do you mean?"

"The people in the office know I'm a divorcee and there's one man who's an important salesman. He's been after me, making innuendos about being lonely in bed, trying to get me cornered in the supply closet. Because of his position with the company, he expects me to submit to him with special favors. It's awful! I don't dare tell Dad. He thinks the world of Howard. And Paula, he's old enough to be my father. He's at least forty-four."

"The old creep!"

"I just don't know what to do."

"We women have to handle things ourselves," Paula said firmly. "There's no other way. I just give a bright, sometimes nasty smile, and stay out of reach. Don't let him ever get the idea you're afraid of him. He has to be careful because of your father. It's a matter of attitude. Be like a porcupine who's gonna throw its quills any minute. He'll get the message,"

"I don't know...." Adele fingered her silver belt buckle. "It's so tiresome!" She heaved a deep sigh.

Paula's sympathy was stirred. She gazed at this troubled young woman, seeing her anew. "I know one thing you could do. Get yourself a sophisticated coiffure. You know, those fluffy bangs make you look years younger than you actually are." She reached out and swept Adele's bangs away to reveal a smooth, high forehead, pleased with the result. "You should see yourself! You look much older and not so vulnerable with your hair up. See? Like this. It makes you appear taller, too."

Adele pulled away, shaking her head. "I've always worn my hair this way. My forehead's not pretty like yours. It's much too high. It's ugly."

"Where'd you ever get that idea? It is not."

They smirked at one another, holding at a stand-off like two wary children. At length, Paula shrugged and said, "I was just trying to help." Maybe Mrs. Turner could be enlisted to bring Adele around to a new look. "A new coiffure can do wonders. I think it would give you more self-confidence."

"I do feel self-conscious all the time," Adele admitted. "Like everyone's looking at me, feeling sorry for me."

Paula nodded with a knowing look. "Yes, and that's probably what that creep Howard thinks in the back of his cotton pickin' mind. Did you know that some men think you're actually dying for their attentions?"

Adele's eyes widened. "What makes them think that?"

"I don't know! They floor me!"

At that, they burst out laughing.

Mrs. Turner came into the dining room, smiling at the happy sound. "What are you girls laughing at?" They looked at one another and laughed again.

Then Paula spoke up. "We were laughing at Adele's reediculous bangs. I think they make her look childish. She needs a new hairdo."

"I like my bangs," Adele said. "I just need a shampoo."

"Look at your mother, how smart she is with her hair sleeked back, showing her high forehead. You could be much smoother, more sophisticated, like her."

Mrs. Turner sat down on a dining chair, facing them. "Thank you, Paula. Such a nice compliment!" She gave a pert smile. "A high forehead indicates great intelligence."

"Yes," Paula said with a gamin grin, "and it's well known that men avoid intelligent women."

Mrs. Turner darted a look at her daughter. "So that's it! You don't want to seem like a helpless divorcee, do you?"

"Of course not, Mother! I want to look like the gay divorcee that I am!" This sarcastic remark opened her eyes.

Later, Paula accompanied Adele to a beauty parlor not far away and upon their return, Mrs. Turner greeted them in her dark green dress protected by a full length apron.

"Adele, you look wonderful!" She gazed lovingly at her daughter, seeking a changed recognition. Adele's countenance had become an elegant poem in statement declared by the high forehead, the adequate English nose, and balanced with a beautiful smile. Her golden brown curls had been coaxed into flattering waves off the forehead, the smooth locks falling gently around her face. "Would you girls like a piece of hot apricot pie?"

"Yes, ma'am," they declared, following Mrs. Turner into the dining room. They soon sat at the table covered with peach linen, already set with shining silver, handpainted china and crystal goblets.

Mrs. Turner served the coffee and beamed at Adele. "Your new coiffure is so becoming!"

"Thank you," Adele replied. What was it about a coiffure, she wondered. It could make a woman regal or dowdy or, yes, flirty. But it could change appearances only. Did appearances affect the person? Would she become a new person now? She thought not.

Without warning, Adele burst into uncontrollable sobs. Alarmed, her mother remonstrated, "Don't cry!"

Paula rose and hugged Adele against her breast. "No," she said gently, "let her cry. That's what she needs. 'Weep with those who weep.'" She caught her breath in spasmodic snuffling. Then, gaining control of herself, she said, "Come on, Adele, Let's go up to your room."

She put her arm around her and led her away, murmuring, "It's all right. Cry all you want." Adele, submerged in her grief, sobbed in broken hearted gusts as they climbed the stairs. Paula took her to the bed and helped her lie down. Picking up a pink and white afghan from the cedar chest, she covered Adele with it, then took her hand and sat on the bed beside her.

Adele hid under the afghan from the bright light of day. Paula rose and quietly drew the silvery green draperies; then she resumed her former position. Adele's weeping gradually subsided. She talked about Fred, of their love, their plans for a large family, and their grand hopes, now vanquished.

Paula listened.

After a time, Adele, emotionally spent and fully exhausted, drifted off to sleep. Paula eased away and pulled up a chair beside the bed to watch over her. She remained there till late afternoon, when Adele awakened and gave her a sweet smile.

"Do you feel like going down for dinner?"

Adele nodded.

Paula perceived that Adele realized for the first time that her husband was truly gone and she would never see him again. She was subdued at the dinner table but she ate a bit of everything that was served. Her folks were aware of the subtle change that had come over her. It was like a break in a life threatening fever. The crisis had passed and there was new hope for recovery.

On New Year's Eve, they retired early before midnight, which brought a sense of well being the next morning with cheerful cries of HAPPY NEW YEAR! ringing through the house. After breakfast, the girls chatted with Mrs. Turner in the kitchen while they cooked candied yams, made Waldorf salad, and helped make Parker House rolls for New Year's Dinner. Paula took on the added job of punching whole cloves into the face of the Virginia ham to be baked.

"Umnn! Everything smells so good. Spices and apples and brown sugar and yeasty bread. I could feast on this aroma alone," she declared.

Adele stirred the red-gold glaze on the yams, making sure the butter-syrup did not stick. "Once it's on the table, you'll want to taste everything like the rest of us," she commented.

"After dinner, I'll expect some music from you," Paula rejoined. "I haven't heard you play for a long time. I miss it. Where's your piano?"

"In the parlor," Adele answered.

"The parlor's on the other side of the stairway," Mrs. Turner explained, "opposite the living room."

"Guess I missed it," Paula said. "Well then, I'll be company this afternoon and expect to be entertained."

Adele laughed. "If you insist."

After the sumptuous dinner, the family repaired to the parlor and hushed, listened to the charming rushes and melodies of Debussy and Brahms as interpreted by Adele's sensitive touch. At first, Paula marveled at her masterful technique and overwhelming expression, till overcome, she lost herself in the glorious music.

Adele finished on a treble, tinkling run, sat motionless, then turned around and dipped her head at her audience.

There was a long minute of silence.

She lifted her head and smiled and they broke out into applause.

"Oh, I love your 'Clair de Lune,' her mother exclaimed.

"I swoon over the Brahms," Paula said in a low, full voice. "Pure music! How I wish I could play like that."

"It's a gift," Mr. Turner said, shaking his head with pride. "But you don't need to play an instrument, Paula, you have your art. "

"That's true. But you know, Adele can sing, too. And I'm not very talented that way, either."

"Adele hasn't been playing much lately, or singing, either," her mother said.

Paula rose. "That's understandable. There're times when I don't draw or paint, either. Thanks for playing for me, Adele. Let's go up to your room so we can talk. Will you excuse us, please?"

"Surely!" Mr. Turner boomed. "It was good to hear you play again, Adele."

Adele's face flushed with pleasure. "Thanks! I didn't know whether I could or not."

"Now we know," Paula remarked on their way out. They disappeared up the staircase.

"I'm surprised you're not singing in the choir," Paula said, when they entered the bedroom. Still playing the part of a guest, she seated herself facing out from the desk, while Adele flopped on the bed. "It'd give you something to do besides work, and it's uplifting."

"I'm a stranger here. I hadn't thought of it."

A light came into Paula's wide blue eyes. "You know, that's a good thing. You're lucky! No one knows you've ever been married or divorced and no one need ever be told."

Adele sat up, alert.

"Don't you see? You're Miss Adele Turner. You work for your father, Mr. Turner. It's a natural protection. And it's more professional in the office. You're surely not Mrs. Thomas in the office."

"Why, no! Everyone calls me Adele."

"I'm called Miss Roncourt. That's as it should be."

"But I can't ask my father to call me Miss Turner."

"Maybe not. But you can answer the phone that way."

"I wouldn't want to. Mrs. Thomas sounds much more mature and professional, I think."

Paula shook her head. "No. Back east, even when the women are married, they use a *Miss Something*. It doesn't have to be their own name, just so it's *Miss*."

"How do you know?"

"My folks are from Virginia, remember? And remember, too, the men wouldn't take you for an easy mark. You could get acquainted with some girl and by next summer get your own apartment together. Share expenses."

"My folks wouldn't like that."

"Oh no. They'll be glad to see you return to your independent, outgoing self. Anyway, it's something to look forward to. Eventually. And a better job."

Adele was shocked.

"Life goes on! It just doesn't stand still no matter how much we'd like for it to at times."

"But how could I get a better job? I can't even take shorthand!"

"Well, then, go to school and learn. You're already learning the insurance business and with good Gregg you'd soon be an executive secretary."

Adele seemed to retreat into herself.

Paula became dismayed, remorseful. "You see, Adele," she said softly, "yesterday at the beauty parlor I sort of received a shock when I saw your check printed with *Mrs. Fred Thomas* on it instead of *Miss Adele Turner,* or *Adele B. Turner,* as I had expected. You have an excellent chance to make a new start here, that's all." She was quiet for a space, but Adele made no answer. Then Paula jumped up and said, "We need to get out. Why don't we go by the USO for a little while?"

Adele frowned, her mouth turned down. Paula realized it was the thought of servicemen, a reminder of Fred, that had triggered her stricken look. "I'm sorry!" she exclaimed. "I work at our USO every week. Guess it's just a habit."

Adele relented. "We could drive by," she offered. "It's only a few blocks."

"Why don't we walk, then? A good, brisk walk would do us good. We won't go inside. I just want to see it."

The walk took them six blocks away toward the Trinity River, where the three-story building stood across the street from the riverside drive. It was an attractive site and quite convenient for Adele, Paula thought. Maybe she should try to get her inside before she left. They turned around and walked back the way they had come and when they entered the house again, Mrs. Turner greeted them.

"Isn't it wonderful what fresh air can do? You both look invigorated and the color has returned to your cheeks, Adele."

"Yes, Mother. I feel much better. I wish Paula could stay longer."

The thought of leaving her the next day made Paula resolve to try again tomorrow.

᠅ ✻ ᠅

The following morning at church, Adele was perked up, greatly cheered by the message of the New Year's sermon: All things are possible through God who strengthens us. At the dinner table, Paula remarked that she'd like to go to the USO for a little while to see how this one in Dallas was run. Maybe she could learn something to take back to San Angelo. Besides, she missed it. Adele, forgetting herself and noticing Paula's sincerity, said, "That's a good idea. I'll go with you."

Paula, exulting within, dampered her enthusiasm and merely nodded. "Good!"

"You girls go on," Mrs. Turner said in a generous gesture. "I'll clean up and do the dishes."

"We can at least clear the table," Paula said, rising and stacking plates to take into the kitchen. "We won't be long. Going to the USO is sort of like going to church. You could say it's a cross between church and home." She avoided Adele's gaze but sensed that her remark had struck the right chord.

The Trinity USO took up half of the space on the second floor of the red brick building, the forefront overlooking the river. Similar to the San Angelo establishment, on the left it had a Pullman kitchen along the inside wall, and was furnished with comfy davenports and overstuffed chairs, a piano, and tables and chairs for cards in the recreation room. As Paula and Adele entered, they were pleased with this familiar atmosphere, but surprised to hear the recorded swing music of Benny Goodman's band and the shuffle of energetic feet dancing in an adjoining hall on the right. They peered through the doorway and saw servicemen and girls dancing the swing and jitterbug with smiles on their carefree faces, bouncing to the snappy rhythm.

"I wish we had a dance hall." Paula exclaimed.

"But dancing on Sunday?"

"Why not? It's just like a dinner dance on campus."

"But the San Angelo USO is next to the church."

"We could dance after church! Fun in the afternoon!" Paula said. "Let's go get a coke."

At the long counter they were greeted by a tall, spare matron who served them bottle cokes and glasses half filled with chipped ice. The woman's thick lenses made her brown eyes oversized in her thin face. She wore a startled expression, much to the young ladies' amusement, till her gaze came to rest on them.

"Are you girls new?" she asked, her voice sliding up in abundant enthusiasm.

Adele looked down at the foam in her glass.

Paula smiled and said, "Yes and no. I'm from San Angelo visiting my friend. She's new to Dallas. I often work in the USO at home and wanted to see what you have here. This is really nice with an impressive view over the river. Our place is quite small compared to this. Of course, we have all the services, except we don't have a dance floor."

"We encourage the young people to dance. It makes them feel more at ease. Our servicemen are mostly a long way from home and they feel lonely, you know."

"Yes," Paula answered. "That's why my roommate and I work at the USO."

"We need more young ladies like you," the woman said, wiping the beads of water off the counter. Her great eyes settled on Adele. "Would you like to help sometimes?" Adele looked at her, surprised.

"Why, I don't know. I've never been here before and I wouldn't know what to do."

"That's no problem. When we need a fourth at bridge, you could fill in. Or dance if you feel like it. And there're shifts for working here at the counter. Mainly, just come in and fill in wherever you see a need. Unless you're signed on for a specific time in the kitchen."

Paula chuckled. "Yeah, home on the range. That's where Mary and I shine."

Adele glanced at her but remained quiet.

A couple of Air Corps men approached the counter and the woman left to take their orders, saying over her shoulder, "I'm Mrs. North. Think about it and if you want to help, just give me a call."

Paula and Adele took their drinks to a table near the doorway to the dance floor and listened to the clarion music of Harry James, Artie Shaw, and Goodman, and mellower renditions of Glenn Miller.

A couple of G.I.s in O.D. uniforms, one with the stripes of a staff sergeant, came over and asked if they'd like to dance. Adele flickered at them. Paula smiled and said, "We're taking time out." When they had left, she told Adele, "That would have been fun, but I don't think you're ready for it. And I didn't want to leave you alone."

"I'll be all alone the rest of my life," Adele said bitterly. "No one has ever gone through what happened to me. I don't know what's happening to my baby and I won't ever see my husband again." She was on the verge of tears.

"I know, Adele," Paula said sympathetically, "but you won't get any better feeling sorry for yourself. Beware of self-pity. Other people are going through things just as bad or worse... maimed, deaf or blind. You just don't know."

Adele flashed back at her. "Are you going to marry Garner?"

Paula sobered, lips compressed. "No. I'm not going to get married till after the war. I want children, and children need a father."

Adele flushed with an effort to hold back the tears. She sniffled and swiped at her eyes. "I hope it's not because of me."

"No, no, no! I made that decision the night I fell in love with Garner. A clean break is best for now. Or any time." She swirled her straw in the rattly ice. "The thing you can be thankful for is that your baby has a devoted grandmother and Fred loves her and will take good care of her."

Adele thought that over, then hooked Paula with a forceful eye contact. "I think you're afraid to marry Garner because of what happened to me."

Paula's chin lifted. "Not really! It's the war. I've only seen him five times within four weeks. I'd be a fool to marry a virtual stranger. Besides, when he flies overseas, he'll have the most dangerous job in the whole wide world, just asking to be killed. The Air Corps has good reason to stand against hasty marriages. They make their men, cadets included, go through a set of hoops before they'll grant permission. You know that!"

Adele's eyes changed. "I'd forgotten. Fred and I dated for six months."

Paula sighed. "We'll both just have to give ourselves time. I'm working in pastels, trying to improve my technique and maybe I'll attempt an impressionistic style, like Cassatt. I need a challenge."

Adele responded with a faint smile. "You're right about self-pity. It's just so hard...!"

"They say the best thing is to do something for someone else," Paula said. Then she changed the subject and discussed her father's real estate business, how it was practically nil. Cattle and sheep ranches were like mints, nearly as lucrative as oil wells, so nobody wanted to sell. No houses under construction and no listings to be had. Everyone was hanging on to what they possessed. And her folks, too. "But by golly," she ended on a positive note, "we're here in Texas, the greatest state in America, and no one has bombed the United States yet."

Mrs. North hurried over and presented a small piece of paper to Adele. "I forgot to give you my telephone number. If you have any spare time, give me a call. I think it's a shame when the boys have to scrounge in the kitchen for themselves. There should be some place where they can just relax and let others do the work for a change."

Paula smiled and suggested, "You're probably shorthanded because of the holiday."

"That's so. But I can vouch to you at times it gets as busy as grandma with a hoe and two snakes!" She rolled her eyes, head swiveling in comic dismay.

"Thank you," Adele said, picking up the note and putting it in her purse. "The music is great." She rose. "It's time we got on home."

"Come again!" Mrs. North urged. "I'm sure you'd enjoy mixing with the young people."

The phrase, 'mixing with the young people,' echoed in Paula's mind during their walk down the stairs and on out to the sidewalk. That's what they both should do, forget everything except having a good time. She hoped Adele would take Mrs. North's invitation to heart now that she had accepted the fact that her divorce was final, a *fait accompli*. And she hoped it wouldn't take her too long to put her grief aside to make forays into servicemen's company. Paula devoutly wished she could be on hand to accompany her, but Adele must surely know some girls at church who could go with her.

Quietly, they walked along the Trinity, savoring the fresh, woodsy scent and nature's peaceful balm, occasionally hearing the cry of a kildeer. Once, the sudden whir of a quail's wings startled them as it rose from the grass near their feet. The silvery river wound away to some mysterious destination where they could not follow. They regretfully stayed on their straight, narrow course among middle class houses for another three blocks, then arrived home in time for dinner.

Paula was happy to see Adele eat with a good appetite, taking helpings of everything. They had had a good holiday together.

Everything was working out perfectly. She had not been obliged to introduce Garner to her parents after all. Perhaps this was meant to be. Yet, even as she ate and talked, a twinge of deep regret gripped her heart at the thought of Garner's leave-taking on Wednesday.

After dinner, the young women repaired to Adele's room, where Paula finished packing for her departure at seven-thirty. She put her cosmetics in the bag, saying, "I'll write, Adele, and you keep on writing to me. When you have your vacation, come and spend it with me. We can stay at Mom and Dad's house." She came across Adele's SOS letter and held it up. "See this? I'm throwing it away right now." She tore it in half. "And I don't want to ever hear you talk like this again."

Adele grew somber for a moment. Then she turned, grabbed her purse, and pulled out her checkbook. She yanked the checks out of their cover and threw them into the wastebasket.

"Aha!" Paula exclaimed. "I see you've made a new start! Good for you, Miss Turner!"

Adele grinned. "Paula, you've saved my life!"

Paula looked intently into her friend's eyes and said, "And you've saved mine."

Chapter Thirteen

Spanish moss dripped in her soul, exotic scenes of small, swarthy, black headed humans peopling the narrow warm streets with its placid canal, winding, circling the city to reflect the steeples of Catholic aspirations in its blue water. Foreign utterances sounded from those dark throats, incomprehensible. Equally incomprehensible were their wending ways in the hot humid atmosphere so alienated from the self-directed energy flowing from the tall, sturdy folk of Germanic and Scotch-Irish blood hard at work in the high dry playful wind of her native town. This was indeed a foreign country, an exotic city, San Antonio, down two hundred and fifty miles southeast of San Angelo, down on the edge of the low country unaware of the Edwards Plateau to the northwest.

Paula had never seen it. She sat recalling impressions of shapes and colors from the pictures and descriptions in a geography book, ochre adobe buildings unlike the wooden structures of home. Everything was different. When Garner left for that strange land, he would be in a land of Mexico or Spain, not in the familiar surroundings of the United States. He would disappear, be gone forever, swallowed up in a foreign country. Her heart bowed, trailing in tune to the Spanish moss.

Two more days. He would be gone. Two more days.

※

Paula absentmindedly colored in the triangles on her chart, her mind engrossed with her beloved. It was nearly 1100 hours Monday morning. She was at her desk alone in the office. Colonel McIntyre was back and his staff had taken him out for a warm homecoming at the Officers Club.

She seemed to hear Garner's melodious bass calling, saying her name. How she loved his voice! She'd never forget it. It came again with more urgency and she looked askance. A glimpse, a vision of his shining presence stood before her. The sunshine fell upon his tall, erect figure, a brightness upon the black brows and smooth face, illuminating his smile to reveal gleaming white teeth. Brass buttons shimmered at her. The sunshine glowed in fiery enthusiasm, yet was outdone by the bursting light from Garner's brilliant eyes. Pure joy poured forth from the vision toward Paula, suffusing her with an unspeakable happiness. She gazed fully, her eyes flowering.

Garner's heart leaped, the blood rushing hot at her beauty. "Paula!"

Her startled comprehension at their sudden reunion gave rise to an awareness between them.

At length, Garner spoke again. "I'm glad you're home. Your father asked me to bring you over to see them."

Stunned at the news, Paula sat as one entranced. *He went to see my folks. And now he's more optimistic than ever.*

"But I'd rather take you out to dinner this evening, if I may. I'll be tied up tomorrow getting ready to leave early the next morning. Final tests and all." He stood still, waiting for her answer.

"This evening." She put her pencil down.

"I'd like to celebrate. Is there anywhere we can go better than Ma's Cafeteria?" Garner, tense, tried to relax.

"The St. Angeles," she replied, barely moving her lips.

"The St. Angeles then. I can come by for you in a taxi at six o'clock. Is that all right with you?"

Paula was fully alert now. "No need for a taxi. We can walk. "

"Okay. I'll see you later." He smiled a farewell and left before she could change her mind.

Exultant anguish invaded Paula. Would that this cup could be taken from me. But I must see Garner again, one last time to tell him good-bye. Strange the way things have worked out. I will be dining at the St. Angeles after all. Mary had a good time with Burl at the Ranchers Club Dinner Dance. Now it's my turn to make a tangential evening in the same place. It's strangely appropriate, since Garner doesn't dance.

⋅ ✻ ⋅

The St. Angeles Hotel possessed the atmosphere of an old distinguished establishment redolent of pungent leather in rich, dark furnishings. Time nearly stood still in the large lobby, where every afternoon during the winter months, tall, wealthy ranchers gathered, sinking into the deep leather chairs, long legs stretched before them while they joshed one another. During these pleasurable hours, their wide brimmed Stetsons remained on their heads, the same as always. The desk to the right glowed in dark green and black marble, the colors carried throughout, which sustained an intimacy appreciated in such a large room. To the left, a staircase led up to the mezzanine, where the Mutual Broadcasting System housed its local radio station, KGKL. The St. Angeles was the glamorous watering hole of its dusty surroundings.

As Paula made her toilet and prepared herself for the swank evening, she thought it best to be silent about *fait accompli de mal,* accomplished deeds of evil for which there was no remedy. Gerry McIntyre was gone and many others like him. She need not mention this to Garner, who would soon take up the battle, placing himself under fire for his country. She brushed her midnight tresses to a scintillating sheen, put on fresh makeup and dressed in her royal blue suit highlighted by a white blouse with a frilly jabot. Tonight she would be practical and not hide behind a foreign language. She would only speak English to herself. She must remain in control of her feelings. But she would enjoy herself, for how could it be otherwise in Garner's company?

Nascent problems were whisked away in the brisk air of their companionable ten-minute walk to the hotel. They entered the subdued elegance of the dining room and were seated at a table for two, brightened by candlelight. A dinner of choice T-bone steaks sizzling on piping hot plates was quickly served. They both chose pecan pie and coffee for dessert to come later.

Garner cut open his baked potato, releasing its aromatic steam, and placed a thick pat of yellow butter in the flaky midst, working it with his fork. Paula followed suit, remarking that she liked the skin.

"I just got to your folks by my skin," Garner returned. "I like them very much, Paula. I knew they'd be disappointed if I didn't show up."

"But I had asked Mary to call them."

"I know, but parents always want to see their children, don't you agree?"

Her eyes changed at the inference. "Or their children's friends," she amended.

"Yes." He cut a bite of steak. "You never have said what was wrong with your friend in Dallas."

A shadow fell across Paula's face. "It was too tragic to discuss. She was on the verge of suicide. I received a letter from her begging me to come. I had to go. If I didn't go and then something horrible happened, I'd never forgive myself."

Garner nodded in agreement. "However, it's unlikely she would have attempted suicide, but you did the right thing, darling."

Her heart skipped a beat at the endearment, but she chose to ignore it. "Anyway, everything turned out all right."

Garner grinned. "It surely did! While I was visiting your folks, I asked for your hand in marriage."

Stars were supposed to fall over her head like they did in the comics, but Paula felt nothing. She simply looked at him, then took a bite of green beans.

Undeterred, Garner elaborated. "They invited me to come spend a weekend with them while I'm down at Kelly Field."

Paula smiled. Just what she'd hoped, yet she felt like a hypocrite. "That's nice! Sort of like a home away from home."

"Don't you want to know what your folks said?"

Paula faced him with a bland expression.

"I told them my family are Methodists and Democrats and that was nearly enough for your dad. But they said it was up to you, that you had a mind of your own."

Paula lowered her gaze and Garner perceived that she was pleased, nearly smiling. He attacked his steak again. Why did he feel so helpless when the tide was in his favor? This was neither the time nor the place for his proposal.

"I saw your beautiful abstract, Paula," he said softly.

She looked up, her eyes wide, attentive.

"You're a very fine artist. Maybe sometime in the dim future, you'll do a painting for me. Abstract or landscape or anything. I'm sure I'd like it."

"Thank you," she murmured. Thoughts of making a small drawing to give him before he left flitted through her mind. *Careful! He nearly hooked you that time!*

She related her experiences in Dallas, describing the Trinity USO and how Adele seemed at last to accept the fact of her divorce and that she would never see Fred again. Over dessert they discussed the possibility of the First Methodist Church allowing the USO in San Angelo to use their Fellowship Hall for dancing. Garner was of the opinion that they would never allow it. Paula said it would be worth a try.

All the while, she wanted to let Garner know that she had come on this final date because she wanted to tell him good-bye. Yet she could not broach the subject, nor could she disturb their intimate tete-a-tete. It would have to wait. Better to savor this moment without anticipating the inevitable.

She showed her delight in his company by praising the excellent dinner.

On the way back to her apartment, they walked arm in arm in communicating silence, aware of the precious nearness of one another, tasting these fleeting moments. Still, Paula did not speak. Before she could retrieve the door key, Garner took her in his arms, finding her eager, pliant and soft in his embrace. Flushed in the warmth of hot blood, she surrendered to his demanding, yet tender depth, lost in their long, fervent kiss. He held her tight. He would never let her go. She gave herself, transported in passion.

At length, he released her, murmuring, "I love you, darling. I love you more than life itself."

I love you. I love you! sang in her heart.

"Garner!" she moaned, unable to declare her love, restrained by the decision engraved in the forefront of her mind. She must not mislead him.

"Marry me, Paula!" He drew out a small square box and pressed open the rounded lid. In the dim streetlight, she saw a tiny sparkle and knew it was a diamond ring.

She gazed up at him mute, somber, full of misery.

"Well then, let's get engaged."

"I can't!" she exclaimed, choking in anguish.

"Of course you can. We mean too much to each other to let anything come between us. There is nothing that can ever separate us anyway, not the war or anything else!"

"You remember," she blurted out, "that night under the stars? How I said I wasn't going to get married until after the war?"

"Yes, but you can change your mind. You mustn't let what happened to Adele affect you. I would never divorce you, Paula, no matter what happened. Come hell or high water, I'll be true to you forever. And I'd expect the same of you."

Her heart was rending, yet she stood adamant. "We don't know what's going to happen to you, Garner. But you're bound to be changed when you get back from the war."

"We're not talking about the war and its hazards. We're talking about our love, the only thing that counts. Our love eternal!"

She had never declared her love. She'd been honest with him. "I came tonight because I wanted to see you one last time to tell you good-bye," she said.

His gaze bored into her with a force that was nearly physical. "You won't consider an engagement?"

"There's no point. We have no idea when we could ever get married."

Snapping the ring box shut, he put it in his pocket and stalked away, speaking to the wind. *"I picked a lemon in the garden of love."*

Stricken, Paula stood gazing into the black, empty night, where Garner's tall figure had vanished never to appear again, his bitter words echoing in her mind, *"I picked a lemon in the garden of love."*

Chapter Fourteen

Bull of the Woods would soon be shipped out. Virtually everyone at Goodfellow had heard. In San Angelo, over and above the gusty winds below, only the great lst Lt. William Hodges of Montana could cause storms of fresh movement in concepts inimical to the directives of the War Department. His flights often took new cadets ahead of themselves, scared. His stomp on the stairs punctuated three at a time, his large presence obvious before he appeared in the doorway, his ranging voice and influence, marked him as stalwart as the Rocky Mountains themselves. He stood a pinnacle to contend with.

Although more sensitive men winced at Bull of the Woods' earthy proclamations, and they often felt a certain relief at his departure, he was nevertheless well loved. He was the moose, the monarch of the mountains and forests, and admired as such.

The women on staff had little to do with the moose. He was a man's man who in a past generation could have filled the role of young gold prospector or better yet, lone fur trapper. He was made of the pioneer stuff of America. No civilized woman could tread where he dared to go nor venture to lay her head next to his. But today, on January 4, a few young women were especially invited to attend a surprise birthday gathering in Lieutenant Hodges' honor. It was to be held in the glass enclosed observation deck beneath the control booth of the forbidden Control Tower. Colonel McIntyre, the Old Man himself, was the one who issued the invitations. He explained this unusual procedure by saying that Bill Hodges liked girls.

That had occurred to Paula. He was always more than courteous toward her when he came to see the C.O. and he certainly made himself felt that night at the Morrison's, tagging in when she would have preferred to dance with Dick. He was interested in girls, all right, but to her, he was simply a male animal of another species. And the day was Tuesday, the five weeks anniversary of the day Garner had walked into her life. But now at her own stipulation, he had walked out never to return, leaving her desolate.

In her chaotic state, Paula welcomed the distraction of the party. She wondered who would be coming. Joyce, the lovely blonde secretary to the Air Inspector, and probably Emily, staff assistant to the Technical Sergeant, and who else? Only three or four, the colonel had said. Paula felt honored to be included, although she knew it was because of her position and the fact that Lieutenant Hodges was partial to her. Admitting this, she was satisfied to be wearing her soft, thick woolen skirt suit in mauve-blue and a violet blouse that enhanced her eyes. Bull of the Woods deserved a lovely final sight of feminine pulchritude and she was only sorry that her legs were encased in cotton lisle hose instead of nylons. At least, that was better than thick, glaring rayons, which slid down her calves to wrinkle at the ankle. And her skirt was short, just below the knee, a definite plus.

The few chosen were to leave their desks an hour and a half before quitting time and go to the Control Tower situated on the edge of the field near the airstrip. They would climb the stairs to their rendezvous. This was a momentous occasion. Nothing like it had ever happened before and since there was only one Bull of the Woods, a moose who looked upon regulations as so many twigs to be trampled on, such a violation of certain rules would probably never occur again.

While Paula worked at the typewriter, she noticed an air of expectancy. A sudden twinge of sorrow assailed her at the thought of losing 1st Lt. Hodges. He would leave another blank space, a hole in the portrait mural on the Goodfellow wall, a larger place than those left by lesser pilots. Smiles were exchanged and light made of any glitches during the day's business, making the hours pass quickly. At the three o'clock coffee break, Paula felt a rising excitement. She went to the restroom, smoothed down her hair and applied lipstick, then tucked in her blouse. No need for coffee this close to the party.

Paula was aware that the Control Tower was a dangerous place. That was the major reason only authorized personnel were allowed to climb the tower stairway. The other reason was that those in control must not be disturbed, diverted from their job. They must be alert at all times. Stories were told, and they were true stories, of how some crazy cadets would buzz the Control Tower, counting it coup to fly low with its apex between their trainer's wheels. They were grounded for that. Shipped out, transferred to another division of the service. Yes, the Control Tower was always in jeopardy. Young, reckless would-be pilots continued to come as the older, tutored and wiser cadets left.

Then too, an accident of another sort could occur. It was possible for a plane to hit the Control Tower through poor flying or mechanical failure. Anything was possible. A gust of cross-wind or even air sickness could be the cause of such an accident. But Goodfellow had a good reputation for safety, better than most pilot training bases. The weather was mild and not too windy. Tornadoes were unheard of. And so far as the Control Tower was concerned, Goodfellow had a perfect record of no hits.

Paula kept herself well informed and she felt safe enough in accepting Colonel McIntyre's invitation. 1st Lt. Hodges was a fine instructor and he deserved their spontaneous recognition. It would be exciting to socialize with him and the top echelon of the base. It would be exciting to enter the Control Tower, the parapet of Goodfellow Castle from which civilization's newest gladiators could be observed in their jousting. This afternoon they would jockey for perfect landings. Solo! They would ride against the wind, against the sun, against their nerves and certainly, against gravity. And she would observe their landings or skewed mishaps—a crash?--from on high.

All this would be hers without danger or concern for her own safety, while she and her friends fawned over Bull of the Woods.

Paula wondered if the other girls in her office were invited, but she never mentioned the party to anyone else and no one except the

C.O. mentioned it to her. After all, it was a surprise party. She left the office alone and walked across the field toward Building 2, the Air Inspector's domain and location of the Control Tower.

When she rounded the corner of the building to reach the stairway facing the apron, she saw Cadet Garner Cameron in his full regalia of matching brown leather, sheep-lined cap and jacket. He was headed for the hangar. She caught her breath, trying to still her heart, and quickened her step to escape his notice. He did not glance her way and she quickly scaled the stairs and entered the spacious reception room. *Garner will be flying! I'm sure he flies all the time and that's no concern of mine. I'm sure to have a good time and forget everything else. I see my friendly Kansas office mate, Captain Tidwell, and he's smiling at me.*

Paula was heartily greeted by the neat Midwesterner of fair complexion and well assembled features. He was not handsome, but he was well proportioned in every way, including his philosophy and amiable attention to duty. He was safely married and that made her feel comfortable in his company.

"I've never been up here before," she remarked to the captain. She looked around at the spare furnishings, a couple of end tables and a few straight chairs, plus a sofa against the solid wall. The floor was of pine plankboard painted beige, as was the trim around the huge plates of glass that ran from floor to ceiling on all three sides. Someone from Mess had brought up a coffee urn, cups and saucers, and cream and sugar. Bottles of Coca Cola were immersed in a tub of ice nearby.

"Where's the birthday cake?" she asked.

Captain Tidwell chuckled. "I'm not sure! There was some debate about that and I think beer may have won out."

"More Bull's style, huh?" She grinned. "I hope they've got some pretzels. I like them with coffee."

Her gaze roved again. She spotted Colonel McIntyre, a civilian airplane mechanic, a couple of other familiar faces, and a small young woman who was a stranger. She was sleek with close-cut black hair.

"I don't see Bull of the Woods anywhere," she said.

"It's his day off. I understand one of his best students is up for solo landings with another instructor."

"Oh?" She tried to sound nonchalant.

"Perhaps you know who I mean," Captain Tidwell elaborated with a wide smile.

"Not really," she replied. She moved toward the window on the right and Captain Tidwell followed her. "I think we can see from here," she commented. They looked down at the hangar and over the airstrip but all was deserted except for one trainer off to one side between the hangar and Building 2. Paula congratulated herself on walking up to the bugaboo she feared. There was no need to fear her emotions after all, no need at all. She could remain quite calm about Cadet Cameron.

The view was that of severe emptiness, the airstrip stretching off into the distance, growing smaller and smaller until it disappeared into the level horizon. The sky, still blue in the afternoon sun, dominated the scene. They could see for miles and miles. No aircraft could be pinpointed. All was emptiness, till gazing down to the far left, Paula saw the crash truck standing by. She was startled, then reassured herself that it was simply for preparedness and it was always stationed there.

"How about a cup of coffee?" Captain Tidwell asked. "Lieutenant Hodges is bound to appear pretty soon. He has to consult with the controller about his personal flight pattern today. He thinks he's taking off for some flight time of his own."

"Thanks. I'd like a cup," she responded. He courteously served the coffee for her, then poured for himself, and they joined the small group by the sofa. Paula met the petite brunette girl, Donna, and learned that she was the wife of the civil service man, a tall, lean Texan.

"Listen!" Donna said, pressing a forefinger to her lips. They all hushed. Then they heard the familiar clomp-clomp of a heavy tread on the stairs. "Bull's coming!"

They remained still and silent as he topped the stairway, then continued on the inside front stairs to the control booth, never glancing their way. With mischievous grins, the party makers silently congratulated themselves at this strategic success. Then the Old Man did a strange thing. That easy going C.O. assumed command in dignity and stance. He raised an orange-red bullhorn to his lips and blared out:

"COME ON DOWN HERE, BULL OF THE WOODS! YOU HAVE INSULTED YOUR COMMANDING OFFICER BY PASSING HIM UP WITHOUT A PROPER SALUTE."

Silence.

"WHAT THE HELL! SIR!" came a lofty bellow. Bull tromped down the wooden stairs in double-quick flight. Once down, he stopped, his long face turning, his long nose sniffing until he spied his tormentor. His deep-set, grey eyes widened, alert, and fastened on Colonel McIntyre. He braced, stood as thick and straight as a Ponderosa pine, and gave a stiff salute. "SIR!"

"HAPPY BIRTHDAY, LIEUTENANT HODGES!" the colonel replied.

A foolish look of disbelief covered Bull's face, mashed into a great grin. He lunged forward. "You son of a gun! Always keeping track of your crew!"

"The bullhorn's all yours," Colonel McIntyre announced. "See that you use it well. You can bring down the whole Luftwaffe with this."

"You're damn right!" Bull grabbed the horn. He danced around, broadcasting his message. "YOU HEAR ME, KRAUTS? I'LL BORE KNOTHOLES IN YOUR MESSERSCHMITTS TILL THEY LOOK LIKE SLABS OF CHEESE! BULL'S EYE!"

Satisfied with his proclamation, Lieutenant Hodges took his place as the center of attraction. He looked straight at Paula and launched into his hunting stories.

"I've got a license to hunt," he confided.

Confused, she shot a glance at Captain Tidwell.

"Quail?" the civilian asked with a wicked grin.

"No," the captain flashed back. "He's a big dame hunter!"

Everybody laughed.

"But you gotta be careful!" Bull said, wagging his head. "One time, I went hunting for deer—not the slippered kind—and this buddy of mine was drinking too much. I shot a deer and he got mad, jealous because he was always missing. Suddenly, he pointed his gun right at my heart." He stabbed himself in the chest.

Alarm was visible on the faces surrounding him.

"What happened? Did he shoot?" someone asked.

"He couldn't!" Bull declared. "I had my finger over the hole."

Laughter again. Paula was relaxed and laughed with them.

Colonel McIntyre spoke in a solemn manner. "One of my neighbors shot himself twice, cleaning his gun."

"Heavens! Was it serious?" Donna asked.

"Well, the first wound proved to be fatal, but the second wasn't so bad."

Yeah, everyone laughed.

Then someone asked Bull if he had any luck hunting bear in Montana.

"Yep!" They leaned forward to hear this one. "I didn't meet one!" he quipped. Then he said, "I could have shot a bear one time when we were hunting."

"Why didn't you?" Paula asked.

"I didn't like the look on his face. He wouldn't have made a good rug."

"That's what we all need," Donna's husband said. "A good furry rug and a long legged, sweet little a...."

"Our bombers are the best," Captain Tidwell cut in. "Nothing can beat the U.S. flying carpet for fun and games!"

Lt. Col. James Ecklund, the Air Inspector, offered Bull his advice. "Just fly 'er right and watch out for the Brits. Remember, they're high on rank. Don't go shooting at them. You'll have to salute them instead."

"Naw," Bull said, "I'll just honk my horn!"

Paula thought she heard a plane in the distance. She turned away, drawn to the window. She noticed that Joyce and Emily were talking together to one side, while the men continued their bantering. But Donna, the married girl, was off to herself, looking lonely, shunted aside.

Paula went over to her. "Let's see if any of the planes are coming in," she suggested. "I think I hear one and it'll be fun to watch it land." Donna appeared grateful for this considerate overture and the two of them sauntered back to the spacious window on the hangar side.

They watched a lone plane coming in, gradually losing altitude, and making a perfect three-point landing. The pilot was not Cadet Cameron.

"Ed is divorcing me," Donna said.

Paula simply looked at her with no show of alarm.

"I'm too small for him."

Paula remained quiet. Donna seemed quite resigned and accepting of the situation. Paula was sorry but thought it was too bad they hadn't thought of that before their marriage. It was an obvious thing just to look at them.

"What will you do?" she asked.

"I'll keep on working here."

"We can have lunch together," Paula said. "I'm not married, myself, and I'm going to wait till after the war."

The roar of more planes revving up caught their attention. Three planes were taxiing out, lining up for takeoff. From the height of the Control Tower, Paula could not see well enough into the cockpits to recognize the fliers and she had missed seeing any student pilot climb up into his airplane. She wondered if Garner were one of them. Then she chided herself. *What do I care?*

"Come and watch the show!" she called to Joyce and Emily. The two young women joined them and for a few moments they exchanged details of their personal histories.

The men remained in a huddle, only two drinking beer while they exchanged slightly off-color jokes and stories of their flight experiences.

The planes took off in good form, one after the other, leaving the runway to two more that rolled out from the hangar. Keeping her eyes glued to the open side of the hangar, Paula thought she saw Garner talking with one of the mechanics. It was Garner! He was preparing to take his plane up for a solo flight and practice landing.

Garner retreated into the hangar and she lost sight of him.

Just then, Colonel McIntyre approached her. "Miss Roncourt, could you tell Captain Kaminsky about that last CFTC memo? You know, the one about the latest rules concerning cadets' excuse from flight training in case of illness."

"Yes, Sir," she answered. "I remember."

Captain Kaminsky was the Medical Administration officer and he had interpreted the memo in a way that was opposite to the intent for washing out a cadet in case of several bouts of illness. After some discussion with him, Paula promised to send him another copy of the memo, along with Colonel McIntyre's interpretation.

The memo was quite clear, Paula thought, but perhaps Captain Kaminsky took exception to it. At length, she was thanked for her assistance. Sorry she had missed seeing Garner take off, she told herself she would watch him land. But which plane was his? She returned to her observation post and greeted her new friends with a roll of the eyes. They snickered in sympathy and the foursome turned their backs against the male heads. "Thank goodness he's not my boss!" Paula said.

The men took their lead from Lieutenant Hodges, who was interested in watching the student pilots come in for their solo landings. They sauntered over to the window and gathered together, Bull settling beside Paula.

"I was going to get in some flying time for myself today," he told her in a voice that was surprisingly gentle. "I completely forgot that it's my twenty-third birthday."

"I'll soon be twenty-three, myself," she responded. "That'll make us twins!"

He laughed, showing his large, perfect teeth. "I hope not! I'd like to think your beautiful self will be here while I'm up there bombing the Germans. Will you be waiting for me to come back home?" She heard a wistful note in his low voice and gave him a warm look of understanding, enveloping as a comfy blanket.

"Yes, I'll be here. And I'll be praying for you, waiting for you to come home. We all will." He thanked her with his eyes, lowered his head for a moment, then straightened up.

"This is one birthday I'll never forget!" he declared, resuming his bigger than life persona. I'll never forget it, either, Paula told herself, thinking of how Bull of the Woods had volunteered for overseas duty. He was eager to serve his country. It was what he truly wanted, but it would take all he had to give. It would take guts, stamina, leadership in battle, and dedication. She prayed, *Bring him back safely to us, God!*

During this fervent exchange both of them had forgotten the 'air show.' From their deep awareness, they were startled by a shout.

Look! Three coming in for a landing!
Three?
That can't be!

From the public address system, they heard the controller directing in urgent commands. They saw one plane circling overhead and two others coming close together, one above the other in the same circling approach pattern, decelerating, losing altitude. Coming too fast! Joining its fellows, the third plane quickly headed downstream behind them, losing altitude at a rapid rate. The buzz increased to a roar.

"Oh my God!" It was Lieutenant Hodges, horror spread across his face, long fingers gripping the bullhorn. The two planes were locked in, one above the other, neither able to see the other, the student pilots unaware that they were headed on a certain collision course.

Paula froze.

Which plane was Garner in? Something crazy had come over the student pilots. Each acted like no one else was up there in the air except himself. Paula strained with all her mental power. *Pull up! Pull up! Let the lower plane land first!*

Suddenly, the third plane veered up and curved away. He had seen! Was that Garner? Her cup clattered in its saucer and for a dizzy moment, Paula watched her trembling hand, a thing apart. Then comprehending, she steadied it with her left hand and looked out again.

The two planes were dipping, dipping down, the upper plane slightly above the other in precise formation to land on top of the lower plane in a deadly crash. With a blood chilling wail, the ambulance sped away toward the planes, accompanied by the fire truck sounding its siren. Then the roar of jeeps followed, bearing mechanics and other rescue personnel.

Paula could no longer stand still. She slipped away to the serving table and set her cup and saucer down, then she dashed down the stairs to run out front. In the excitement, no one paid any attention to her. She ran, not caring why she ran, only following an instinct to relieve anxiety, to help if possible, scarcely aware she was running, not knowing what she would find or what she could do. It was enough that she was running toward the oncoming crash.

She heard the breaking, rending crash on impact. In a flash, her vermillion imagination pictured the collision. The dead bodies! Horrified, she stopped alongside the ambulance and watched the planes crash, converging. The lower cockpit and its pilot were crushed. The wings broke into pieces. Tangled. The fuselages swerved, grinding toward her on the tarmac, ready to bellow flames at any moment, a cruel mangled monster.

Garner! Garner!

Terrified, she was speechless. Devoid of will, she stood unable to move, the crash coming at her.

A mechanic sprinted out from the hangar, olive drab coveralls flapping around his legs. Alarmed at the sight of Paula transfixed, waiting to be killed, he rushed forward and grabbed her arm.

"Here! Get back! Get back!" he yelled. She offered no resistance. He steered her back between the hangar and Building 2. Safely out of the path of the disaster, he held her arm fast while they mutely watched the planes burst into flames.

The tip of a wing penetrated the fuselage of the lower plane. Sirens wailed above the frantic voice from the Control Tower. The wreck, crackling and burning, twisted, and then finally ground to a halt.

Two medicos jumped out of the crash truck and ran to the rescue. Two other servicemen rushed from the fire truck and poured water in great arching spouts onto the flames.

Paula was dazed. She glanced at her protector, eyes glassy with horror. She jerked her arm free and he quickly pulled her back.

"Stay here!" he commanded. "There's nothing you can do."

Her face was white, great eyes pleading, but he shook his head in sad recognition of the tragedy.

"They're both dead. There's no way either of them could get out of this alive. It's just an exercise....just an exercise. Too bad!"

Garner gone in an exercise!

She wished she'd stayed upstairs, inside. She didn't want to see. She didn't want this smell of death! The fuel and smoke! The hiss of steam! The heat of Hell! She whispered in a trembling voice, "Do you know who the cadets are?"

"No, but they're off base now."

Off base. Yes, off base. Off base forever.

They saw a couple of medicos carry a stretcher bearing a body covered with a white sheet and watched them lift it into the ambulance. Then they helplessly stood about, waiting for the fire to be brought under control. Other men climbed up into the cockpit of the upper plane, a difficult job, since it rested at an awkward angle, sticking up with one wing down.

Miraculously, the student was alive. The medicos, one on each side, carried him down between them, till they slithered down to the tarmac along one wing. The pilot, bent over double, stumbled forward out of the debris helped by his rescuers. He was alive!

Was it Garner?

Paula strained to see, bobbing her head this way and that, till finally, she got a glimpse of him. No! He wasn't tall enough! All of a sudden she felt ill, weak. *Who was that on the stretcher?* She began to faint.

"Here!" The mechanic put his arm around her shoulders and led her toward the hangar. "That wasn't a pleasant thing to see. But you weren't supposed to be out here, you know. Just rest a few minutes, Miss. It's all over now."

Yes, all over. All over for me. I don't belong here. He's right. What am I doing here?

"I don't know what came over me," she said.

"We all get uptight," her protector said, "but from now on, you'd better stay away. Against regulations, you see."

"I thought it was a cadet I know. I'm still not sure..."

"You could go to the hospital. They'll know."

She nodded, not sure she wanted to find out who was killed. She thanked him and he resumed his business with another worker, while she slowly moved to return to the party.

Paula had not gone far when she heard a familiar deep voice calling her name. She spun around and saw Garner coming toward her. "What the devil are you doing out here?" he demanded. "You were in danger!"

"Garner! I thought you were killed!"

She ran to him and leaped into his arms, pressing her cheek hard against his face. "I love you! I love you!"

Chapter Fifteen

Garner crushed her to him.

Alive!

They clung to one another united, safe, a single being—one blood, one mind, one spirit. Fears dissolved, they kissed in a passion kindled by anxiety, their desires turned into triumph.

After a time, Garner pulled away and held Paula at arms' length. "It's me you love, isn't it?"

He was a god standing in supernal joy before her. An exultant shining filled his face, lighting his eyes and covering his shapely head. Awed, grave, humbled, she cast aside.

"I thought you'd been killed."

He took her chin and tilted her face to meet his gaze.

"It's me, dead or alive, isn't it?"

At the word *dead* she slowly looked about, overwhelmed by the black smoke, the charred odor of the shattered-scattered airplanes, the smell of oil fumes, the stench of horror and death they had so narrowly escaped. The huge explosion on the tarmac had left a dark blot on the souls of those involved in the tragedy on this innocent, sunny afternoon.

Garner's attention stayed riveted on her face, never wavering from those staring, deep blue eyes. His own expression hinted a smile of victory. She loved him for himself—his serious intent, his earnest loyalty.

He watched her inner light flow into mystical initiation, turning, wandering, adjusting to the realization that through death or life, true love was a new, permanent order, a heaven brought down to earth in a magnificent revelation. She would love him no matter what, because he was who he was and the way he was.

"You will be Mrs. Cameron, won't you? You will be my wife before I go overseas."

His urgency recalled her, doubling her own infinite longing. "Yes, oh yes, Garner! We won't wait until after the war! We'll get married before you go overseas!"

He kissed her again, tenderly, holding her gently, his beloved, sealing the promise of their lives to be lived together in love and respect, and in trust, no matter how far away from one another in distance or in air miles, no matter how long the separation—no matter the weeks and months—until they could be together in their own home forever.

"Sorry I gave you such a scare," he said. "I was scheduled to fly, but my plane had engine trouble. I was in the hangar kibutzing with the mechanic when the crash occurred."

"I saw you go in, but later, I didn't know where you'd gone." She shook her head. "I'm a nervous wreck."

"I know. It sure gave me a scare when I saw you out here on the airstrip. That was a dumb fool thing to do!" He took her arm and led her away. "I don't know which cadet got killed. My flight was cancelled. Now all flights'll be cancelled. Let's go over to the cafeteria for dinner."

Under bluish fluorescent lamps, they were soon settled at their favorite table for two against the wall.

"I thought I'd never see you again," Garner said. He covered her hand with his warm, thick palm. "I'm glad you came looking for me." Her regard wavered. "I'm not ever going to crash, Paula." He held her gaze with an inimitable confidence. No training exercise, no enemy, no nothing could intercept or modify his steel intent. The rod of his will would carry him through many battles and on through the war. She glimpsed the courage it must take, the indestructible control a pilot must maintain during those awful bombings.

Should she tell him she was at a party for Bull of the Woods? Why diminish his dominance in any way? Instead, she brightened and accused him. "You peeled me down to a pulp!"

He grinned at her. "Look who sliced me up first!"

That silenced her and she began to eat. Garner followed suit.

After a small interval, Paula smiled with a mischievous glint. "You forgot something!"

"What's that?"

"It's Tuesday!"

"Our day!" He laughed. "I had forgotten! Tuesday will always be our day. And this is our Fifth Week Anniversary, the preamble for many to come."

Delighted he'd remembered, Paula sobered. "But you're leaving tomorrow morning. Or are you?"

He nodded. "This won't make any difference. Another crew for the new class will come right in behind us."

Paula wondered if he still had her engagement ring. "We'll get married when you get your wings," she said with a spurt of enthusiasm.

"Oho! You don't feel like marrying some nobody, huh?" Garner polished his brass buttons with his knuckles. "I don't blame you. But I'll warn you. I'll have my wings and my commission in six more weeks."

"Six weeks!"

"You know the Advanced Training course is six weeks long."

The final day of parting that had been looming somewhere out of sight now threatened Paula. Soon gone. Just when they were married. She couldn't bear it. She put down her fork and addressed the problem.

"But the Air Force chaplain at Kelly Field will have to officiate, won't he?"

"It'll be close," Garner said. "We'll see if we can work it in before I fly off into the wild blue yonder."

Her face fell in dismay.

"Don't look at me! I'm only going along with you. That's what you said, when I get my wings. Then there'll be little time indeed before I shove off."

"Couldn't we get married sooner, so we'll have some time together before you go?" she pleaded. If only she could postpone that terrible day, rub it out into nonexistence!

He smiled at her.

"I'd like nothing better. I can arrange that. And I think you'd rather be married here in San Angelo in your own church, wouldn't you?"

"Yes. That's what we'll do."

They congratulated themselves, clinking their water glasses. "Here's to our church wedding in San Angelo!"

Paula promised Garner she'd visit him in San Antonio within two or three weeks, whenever he could get a weekend pass and a couple of hotel reservations.

The next day in a cool, brisk wind out at Goodfellow, on Wednesday, January 5, 1944, she kissed him good-bye, whispering their private code, "See you Tuesday!"

Chapter Sixteen

The fence must be down at Amarillo. That had happened a year ago when the temperature dropped to five below zero, catching townspeople and ranchers unprepared. Pipes had burst. Young animals on the range had frozen. Burl Stein consulted the thermometer and then the barometer hanging on the north side of the big red barn. The barometer was falling. No doubt about it. A Norther was coming all the way down the Great Plains from Canada, whistling through North and South Dakota, along the steep Slopes of the Rocky Mountains of Colorado and curling its way in a big swirl on Amarillo. But there was nothing to stop it. San Angeloans could tell when the fence was down in Amarillo.

It would be cold tonight, this most important night of his life. His heart was icy hot while he reveled in the cold wind stinging his face and watched the white clouds of his breath flow in and out on the air. This was nature's way of bracing him for the big event tonight. The sparkling, perfect blue diamond as large as a pea was snuggled in its midnight blue velvet box among his bolo ties in the upper drawer of his chiffonier, just waiting to be placed on the finger of the most beautiful young lady in the world.

Burl called his dog, Shep. He'd have to round up the herd of one hundred Herefords and bring it into the corral, the little dogies into the barn. He'd never lost a steer in the cold yet. And he wasn't about to now. Everything depended upon this herd he'd bought for the spring market. He was pushing it to bring this herd onto his land, but it was for a short time and he figured he had enough money to buy the fodder needed to avoid overgrazing. He was taking a gamble, but it was worth it. When he netted a ten thousand dollar profit in the spring, he would indeed be a hard down suitor worthy to be Paula Roncourt's husband.

He mounted his horse and Shep barked for joy, jumping alongside until they fell into a long gallop, coursing in a companionable rhythm together. Heading north, their dark shadows moved along with them, casting shade and light in lively forms among the sage and yellow rocks, which were fast growing dim as the sunlight waned in the closing of the day.

The sun's lowering but it's rising in my heart.

Burl lifted his voice in song. "Oh, give me a home, where the buffalo roam.... and the skies are not cloudy all day...." The black and white dog keeping pace at his side, glanced up in appreciation. Then he again faced the business at hand. Shep liked nothing better than to work at his master's side or to be trusted to work on his own, loping off to distances far away from the main herd to bring in the wandering cattle too dumb to know better. He was a five year old shepherd dog, experienced and avid in handling the bovine beasts and he took pride in his work.

An unfamiliar odor assailed Burl's nostrils. A storm was coming! Black clouds in long swaths darkened the sky and he felt a freshening, cold blast on his face. Damn! Could it be a blizzard? He'd never heard of snow in this country and knew his grandparents had never seen snow. Just the same, he'd better hurry and get the cattle in. Those clouds were traveling awfully fast. Now they were over him, slate-black, shutting out the sun, making the evening as dark as night. A needle-point of ice, then another and another, came right at him, horizontal, speeding to intercept his passage. They were cold, piercing, threatening.

He spurred his horse to a fast gallop in urgent need to outrace the storm and was relieved when he spied the herd not far off. "There they are!" he shouted. "Come on, Shep, let's hurry!"

Shep needed no urging. He was already out far to the left running close to the ground, ears back, tail down, going around behind the herd to bring them forward. Burl swung off to the right, whirling his lasso overhead, whooping in counteracting control. The cattle responded with a slow, ponderous trot. Then they broke into a heavy gallop, their hooves making loud thuds against the earth, causing it to shake.

The icy particles were turning into thick, white flakes. Snow! Damnation! I won't get to see Paula tonight! Dad and I'll be up all night keeping the water melted, pitching hay for the cattle. It's a blizzard, all right. Too cold to take any chances with the herd. They sure take a lot of looking after.

Burl knew if a man wanted butter, he'd have to be willing to churn. It might take a little more time, but he was a-churnin'!

៛ ✻ ៩

Paula hung up the phone, relieved.

She and Mary had been home from work only half an hour when Burl called to cancel their date to go out to the Barbecue Restaurant and then to the monthly meeting of the Democratic Party. Snow was falling and it wasn't letting up. He had sounded harrassed and disappointed. After the brief business session, the Democrats were going to listen to the re-broadcast of President Roosevelt's annual message to Congress. "It's his Economic Bill of Rights. Very important," Burl had said, then in a lower tone, "But not as important as seeing you."

She had been given a reprieve, but it wasn't final. How she wished she would not have to disillusion him! They had been so close for so many years, it would break her heart to break his. Yet she would have to tell him about Garner and it was a good thing they couldn't appear in public together tonight. But she would miss him.

She had given a hint, telling him she'd like to see him before a little trip to San Antonio.

"What's going on down there? I haven't heard of anything," Burl had replied.

"No. Well, it's personal. I'd like to tell you about it."

"Sure, honey! I hope it's not bad news."

"No, nothing like that."

"If you need any help, you just say the word."

She'd been all primed and now, although she was relieved, she regretted she'd have to bolster herself up again.

Mary glanced at her sober face. "Burl can't come in."

Paula shook her head. "No." Then she gazed with disbelief into Mary's pale blue eyes. "It's still snowing!"

Mary laughed. "Terrific! We won't have to go to work tomorrow."

"Oh, the snow'll melt. Whoever heard of snow in San Angelo?"

Mary rushed to open the door. "Look!"

Thick and white in the yellow streaming light, the feathery flakes were falling, falling as if they would never stop.

"It's already two inches deep!" Mary exclaimed.

"Shut the door. It's colder than I thought. We should keep the oven on all night to keep us warm. We can stay in and listen to Roosevelt's speech."

"It'll be nice and cosy like one of his fireside chats," Mary agreed.

They hurried through a light supper and settled down to listen, Paula at the table and Mary on the bed.

Mary had become more interested in politics through her association with Paula. She was pleased to show off before her roommate. "The newspaper said that he is adding economic security as a political right to Jefferson's ideals of liberty, equality, and self- government."

"Maybe women will be included to get their fair share," Paula remarked. "Wouldn't that be something?"

"Yeah. You'd better get your notebook. This will be one to remember."

"Even if it isn't," Paula said, laughing, "I'll enjoy hearing Roosevelt's mellow voice in his aristocratic Eastern accent." She grabbed a stenographic notebook from the top drawer of the chest. "It won't hurt to take down the salient points, as my Political Science professor used to say."

"Quiet!"

The President was introduced and he launched into his address:

..... IN THIS WAR, WE HAVE BEEN C0MPELLED TO LEARN HOW INTERDEPENDENT UPON EACH OTHER ARE ALL GROUPS AND SECTIONS OF THE POPULATION OF AMERICA. AND I HOPE YOU WILL

REMEMBER THAT ALL OF US IN THIS GOVERNMENT REPRESENT THE FIXED-INCOME GROUP JUST AS MUCH AS WE REPRESENT BUSINESS OWNERS, WORKERS, AND TEACHERS, CLERGY, POLICEMEN, FIREMEN, WIDOWS, AND MINORS ON FIXED INCOMES, AND OLD-AGE PENSIONERS. THEY AND THEIR FAMILIES ADD UP TO ONE-QUARTER OF OUR ONE HUNDRED THIRTY MILLION PEOPLE.

IF EVER THERE WAS A TIME TO SUBORDINATE INDIVIDUAL OR GROUP SELFISHNESS TO THE NATIONAL GOOD, THAT TIME IS NOW.

He cited actions taken in 1918 as lessons to be followed.
"Good history lesson," Paula commented. She put down her pen and listened.

THIS REPUBLIC HAD ITS BEGINNING, AND GREW TO ITS PRESENT STRENGTH, UNDER THE PROTECTION OF CERTAIN INALIENABLE POLITICAL RIGHTS.... AMONG THEM THE RIGHT OF FREE SPEECH, FREE PRESS, FREE WORSHIP, TRIAL BY JURY, FREEDOM FROM UNREASONABLE SEARCHES AND SEIZURES. THEY WERE OUR RIGHTS TO LIFE AND LIBERTY. AS OUR NATION HAS GROWN IN SIZE AND STATURE, HOWEVER.... AS OUR INDUSTRIAL ECONOMY EXPANDED....

Paula picked up her pen again, and concentrating, she took down his words in shorthand.

....THESE POLITICAL RIGHTS PROVED INADEQUATE TO ASSURE US EQUALITY IN THE PURSUIT OF HAPPINESS. WE HAVE COME TO THE CLEAR REALIZATION OF THE FACT THAT TRUE INDIVIDUAL FREEDOM CANNOT EXIST WITHOUT ECONOMIC SECURITY AND INDEPENDENCE. 'NECESSITOUS MEN ARE NOT FREEMEN.'

Paula flashed an exultant glance at Mary, her pen moving with speed in heightened patriotism and love for her President.

....REGARDLESS OF STATION, RACE, OR CREED. AMONG THESE ARE:

THE RIGHT TO A USEFUL AND REMUNERATIVE JOB IN THE INDUSTRIES OR SHOPS OR FARMS OR MINES OF THE NATION. THE RIGHT TO EARN ENOUGH TO PROVIDE ADEQUATE FOOD AND CLOTHING AND RECREATION. (Imagine! Recreation!)

THE RIGHT OF EVERY FARMER TO RAISE AND SELL HIS PRODUCTS AT A RETURN WHICH WILL GIVE HIM AND HIS FAMILY A DECENT LIVING.

THE RIGHT OF EVERY BUSINESSMAN, LARGE AND SMALL, TO TRADE IN AN ATMOSPHERE OF FREEDOM FROM UNFAIR COMPETITION BY MONOPOLIES AT HOME OR ABROAD.

To these the President added the rights to adequate medical care and the opportunity to achieve and enjoy good health, the right to adequate protection from the economic fears of old age, sickness, accident and unemployment and the right to a good education. Then he spoke with a renewed emphasis:

ALL OF THESE RIGHTS SPELL SECURITY. AFTER THIS WAR, WE MUST BE PREPARED TO MOVE FORWARD IN THE IMPLEMENTATION OF THESE RIGHTS.

AMERICA'S OWN RIGHTFUL PLACE IN THE WORLD DEPENDS IN LARGE PART UPON HOW FULLY THESE AND SIMILAR RIGHTS HAVE BEEN CARRIED INTO PRACTICE FOR OUR CITIZENS. *FOR*

UNLESS THERE IS SECURITY HERE AT HOME, THERE CANNOT BE LASTING PEACE IN THE WORLD.

Paula and Mary gazed at one another scarcely breathing at the scope of Roosevelt's statesmanship, the depth of his compassion, and his fine intentions for the people. Paula feverishly flipped a page to keep up.

OUR FIGHTING MEN ABROAD....AND THEIR FAMILIES AT HOME....EXPECT SUCH A PROGRAM AND HAVE THE RIGHT TO INSIST UPON IT. IT IS TO THEIR DEMANDS THAT THIS GOVERNMENT SHOULD PAY HEED RATHER THAN TO THE WHINING DEMANDS OF SELFISH PRESSURE GROUPS WHO SEEK TO FEATHER THEIR OWN NESTS WHILE YOUNG AMERICANS ARE DYING....

EACH AND EVERY ONE OF US HAS A SOLEMN OBLIGATION UNDER GOD TO SERVE THIS NATION IN ITS MOST CRITICAL HOUR.... TO KEEP THIS NATION GREAT....TO MAKE THIS NATION GREATER IN A BETTER WORLD.

The announcer came on and Paula turned off the radio. Her President had called for greatness in peace after the war. She closed her notebook and deep in thought, sat down again.

She turned to her roommate. "Ours will be greatness, Mary. A glory after the war. You and I will play a large part in it, just as we are working in the home force today. The men have their glory in war, but we women will have our glory in peace."

Mary shook her head at the optimistic prophecy, but Paula believed Garner would share her expectations and be as eager as she to take part in the grand effort to come, the struggle to bring the nation up from the Great Depression and the war into a marvelous new prosperity.

※

God had passed a miracle.

Moisture, that most precious of His gifts on earth and so rare on the semi-arid plateau, had come in a marvelous form to cheer and comfort the hearts of the people of San Angelo.

The next morning when Paula and Mary peered out the window, they were amazed and filled with wonder. The snow was a foot deep. The world stood still, hushed in pristine white, snow piled up on the black, bare limbs of trees and bushes, covering the rooftops, the yards and streets, making the mundane beautiful. No one was astir. No bird nor human being in sight. The clouds had disappeared, leaving the sky a bright, cerulean blue and the air crisp. The Texas sun shone with laughter at the scene, causing sparkles in the snow dazzling to the eye.

"It's heavenly!" Paula exulted. "Let's put our boots on and go out and play. You were right, Mary. No work today."

She snatched up the broom and with much effort, swept the fluffy stuff away from the door. They played like children, making snowballs and throwing at one another—dodging, falling and laughing all the while—and managed to keep score till they were tied and both flat on their backs making their angel wing impressions on the universe. They wound up rolling a snowman so proud of his carrot nose, prune eyes and red radish mouth. His round head was too big for a hat and they happily left him bald. Paula inscribed, BRAIN, on his round forehead. He was their ideal snowman.

The sun shone from above and as the day waned, it grew warmer, back to normal. The snow gently melted, enough for the Goodfellow bus to run its rounds the next day.

❧ ✳ ☙

Paula was nervous, expecting Burl to take her out to dinner at the new Barbecue Restaurant. She dreaded the ordeal of telling him about her forthcoming engagement to another man. She must be delicate, use a *frottage* of tact. A tracing is never as harsh as the bold original.

She had made no effort to be glamorous tonight. She hadn't changed from the tan gabardine suit she had worn at work and had not put on fresh makeup. It would be wrong for her to give a come-on signal, but lounging around, waiting with nothing to do, made her all the more nervous.

Mary was sympathetic. "It's not your fault, Paula," she said. "Remember, Burl has known all along that you weren't in love with him."

"I know, but I have a strange feeling. Like something's going to happen tonight."

"It is! Believe me! Don't you chicken out and not give Burl the real skivvy. He's an okay guy, but you and I know he can't hold a candle to Garner. Burl's more my type, while Garner's...." She shifted her eyes back and forth, trying to think of the right words to say. "You know what I mean. He's superior in every way. I'd never make it with a man like that. But he's perfect for you."

"Maybe you and Burl should get together," Paula said with new interest.

Mary laughed, embarrassed.

"Why not?" Paula urged.

"You have a great deal in common. And Burl's really a fine person. You know that."

In her attempt to cover her feelings for Burl, Mary was vociferous. "How in the world could Burl want me, when he's been crazy about gorgeous you all these years?"

Paula considered, then she replied, "People do change, Mary. And adapt."

"I don't want some man adapting to me!"

"What I mean is that when circumstances change, people usually change with them."

They heard a loud knock at the door and Paula rose to answer it.

"Hi, Paula," Burl greeted her. "Better wear your coat."

She thought Burl looked snappy himself, in his fine black Western outfit with silver bolo tie, his black Stetson and fancy black boots. He was a bona fide cattle rancher and cowboy, a young man who was successful in his calling. But she mustn't weaken and let him influence her.

Burl helped her into her rose woolen coat, a mohair mix that made it somewhat shaggy, much to Paula's secret delight. She related to animals of all kinds and tonight the shaggy coat made her think of buffalo out on the range. She was going to be a buffalo, stand her ground, and not be driven off the cliff.

The new restaurant was roomy with exposed beams, a few tables near the counter and booths along the windows. Spicy aromas from the kitchen tantalized and Paula found herself hungry. She chose a booth away from the front door with its drafts of frigid air.

As Burl hung up her coat on a tree rack, he also took off his hat. He remarked with a grin, "A cowboy never takes off his hat except at funerals and maybe a wedding. But this is a special occasion." He seated himself opposite Paula and gave her a meaningful look, his sky-blue eyes bright and spirited under straight brows.

Burl sometimes appeared or could look mean with those straight brows of his, having an aspect of a bald eagle, but tonight his cheery, lopsided smile alleviated this stern look. Paula was uneasy about his reference to the special occasion. That probably accounted for her strange feeling earlier.

The waitress came and Burl ordered draft beer, asking Paula if she'd like a glass. He should know she couldn't stand the smell of beer and had never tasted the rotten stuff in her life, and furthermore, was never going to taste it. But not showing her disgust, she courteously declined. How could she have forgotten that Burl drank beer and smoked, and he liked sauerkraut and weiners, all of which were anathema to her? She was glad he'd ordered the beer. It reminded her that the Stein in him did not match the Reid or Roncourt in her.

She asked for coffee and thought of Garner, realizing that he never smoked and he didn't drink beer. He drank coffee, or milk, like her. And he ate the same things she did. Almost invariably when they dined out, they chose exactly the same entres and vegetables. Even the desserts. At this wonderful discovery, she smiled.

Burl was encouraged to see her so pleased. He'd made good points with her by taking Mary out on New Year's Eve. He was sure she'd come around to having a glass of beer with him yet.

Soon spicy racks of barbecued beef ribs, pinto beans seasoned with chili, and cole slaw were placed before them on thick platters, accompanied by hot sourdough bread and butter.

"Looks good enough to eat, doesn't it?" Burl asked.

"Yes, it does. And the prices are reasonable, too."

"They'll do well. I wonder if this meat came from one of my steers."

Paula laughed. "Could be!" She took a bite of the meat. "Delicious!"

Burl joined in and as they ate, each was absorbed in personal concerns. Paula hoped Burl would give her a lead so she could broach the subject of her trip to San Antonio, while he was trying to figure out how he could propose and present the engagement ring.

"Honey," he said between bites, "everything's jake out at the ranch. This cold snap sure kept us humping for awhile, but Dad and I kept the cattle watered and fed, and not a one lost."

"I'm so glad."

"You know, I bought a hundred head of Herefords. I was thinking of you when I bought them. I'll sell the herd in March and figure it'll net me ten thousand dollars." He lifted his brows at this thought.

She remained quiet and took a bite of beans.

"That's a good chunk of money and you can spend it any way you please."

She looked up in surprise.

He reached into his vest pocket and brought out a dark blue ring box decorated in gold and held it out to her.

"Honey, I found this big diamond, which I hope is beautiful enough for you. I'm proposing now because at last, I have plenty to give you. Everything I have will be yours and our marriage will be perfect. You'll never want for anything, Paula."

An inner softening shone from his gaze, but Paula sat mute, not moving. At first, he didn't notice. Then he snapped the box open and presented it again with an urgency she could not ignore.

Her face was taut, pale in sentient dismay. "It's a beautiful diamond, Burl. I'm so sorry, but I can't accept it."

"What do you mean, you can't accept it?" He was turning angry, his look forbidding. "Here! Take it! It's yours!"

"I can't! Don't you see? I cannot accept an engagement ring from you. I like you, Burl, you know that. And I love you as a friend."

"More than a friend. We've always been closer than that. I insist! This is your ring!"

"No, Burl. It isn't. That's what I wanted to talk to you about. The reason for my trip to San Antonio. I know this is sudden and I'm so sorry."

"But we've always had everything in common."

"I know. But you see, I'd met someone else. A cadet. And I broke off with him just two days after New Year's. Then an unusual thing happened. You remember the day that cadet was killed at Goodfellow?"

Burl looked stunned, frowning in disbelief at this preposterous refusal.

"I was there at a birthday farewell party for one of our instructors," Paula continued. "And when the planes came in and I was afraid they were going to crash, I ran down to the tarmac, because I'd seen Cadet Cameron out there and I was afraid he was one of the students coming in for a solo landing."

Burl kept holding the ring box out to Paula, determination growing as his frown deepened.

"I didn't know who was killed," Paula said. "Then I saw Garner coming toward me, and all of a sudden...." Her voice broke. "It was something I couldn't control. I ran to him and right then I knew I was in love with him."

"And I love you."

She stopped speaking, relieved that it was said at last.

"That was just a reaction," Burl said. "You're infatuated, that's all. A fly boy and all. This is your ring. I bought it for you. Don't you want to try it on?"

"No." Paula dipped her head.

"Let's see if it fits." Burl took the ring out of the box and started to take her hand.

Paula looked him in the eye and drew back. There was a humming in her ears and under the table, she ran her forefinger around her thumbnail, holding on. She called up her vision of a bison standing against a blizzard, head down, patient, withstanding the storm. She would not be moved.

Burl jerked the ring up under her nose and involuntarily she glanced at the glorious diamond. It was gorgeous. She swallowed, then became intensely interested in her plate.

"I'm sorry, Burl," she mumbled. "I just cannot accept it."

"It's yours, anyway," he said hoarsely. He dropped it in front of her plate. "I'm sure I don't want it."

She looked up and calmly said, "You could save it. You'll find another girl you'll want to marry. Or if you'd rather, you could return it to the jeweler and get your money back."

"Never!" He gave her a long, searching look, then quietly asked, "That's it, then? You're sure you don't want to marry me?"

She nodded, miserable, tears starting to glisten.

Helpless, he heaved a great sigh. "I'll keep it, honey. In case you change your mind. I want you to know I'm waiting for you and this ring is definitely yours. And don't forget. I'd be a good husband to you."

"I know, Burl," she said with compassion. Then after a pause, "I'll be going to San Antonio in a few days to visit Cadet Cameron. He's in Advanced at Kelly Field now. I'll let you know how it comes out."

"I'll be waiting for your call." He closed the box and put it back in his pocket.

Paula was relieved. It hadn't been so bad after all. And she had been spared an attempt at a beery kiss. She started a discussion of President Roosevelt's new Economic Bill of Rights. That was something they could completely agree upon. That, and the sweet, nutty pecan pie for dessert.

Chapter Seventeen

Paula swung through the main door of the San Antonio Hotel and heard the murmur of men's low voices replete with the tinkle of young women's laughter. Cadets from Randolph and Kelly Fields and their wives and girl friends swarmed about the lobby in good spirits, hugging and kissing in their happy reunions.

The lobby was spacious, elegant with furnishings of heavy, dark wood carved in Spanish style, quite different from the severe, leather ranch style interiors of the hotels in San Angelo. The warm air was soothing and soft, also quite different from the dry, crisp atmosphere she had just left.

Adobe clay walls, subtly worked in artistic swirls, formed a gracious enclosure of rosy pink, echoing the curved alcoves, which contained graceful statuary. The alabaster figure of a young girl in gently draped clothing adorned the center of the area, a pleasant plash of the water fountain spilling out from her oblong jar. Paula had entered a foreign world, a reflection of Spain itself. She was amused at the thought that the choice of her pink woolen dress had been perfect for blending in with this exotic scene.

She glanced at her watch. It was five-thirty. Garner should be here. She stopped beside an empty easy chair, set her tan overnight bag down and glanced about, searching for him.

Where was Garner?

After a few anxious moments, she saw him entering through the doorway to her left from another street. He strode with dignity, carrying his cap and a small duffle bag, his figure as straight and erect as his principles. Paula swelled with pride at the sight of him, this man soon to be her husband. Only four more precious weeks and he would be gone.

He caught sight of her and their eyes met.

Quickening his pace, his smile sent shafts of delighted welcome as he honed in on her. She wanted to rush to him, but made herself stand still and wait like a lady.

He greeted her with a kiss and took her bag, then escorted her to the desk to confirm their reservations. It had taken him nearly two weeks to get their rooms, hers a small single on the third floor, his a larger, double room on the fifth floor. They would have the night and all day Sunday together. They signed the register and Garner took the keys with a private remark to Paula that it was a good thing their rooms were on different floors. When they arrived at her door, he handed her the key and said, "Lead me not into temptation."

She made enormous eyes at him and said, "I didn't invite you in."

"For just a little while," he pleaded.

In a swift movement, he took her in his arms and kissed her a lover's kiss, which caused her to lose herself and all sense of time.

Then he placed his cheek next to hers and said in her ear, "I promise to be good."

She moved to face him and with a forefinger smoothed his wide, black brow. "It's not you I'm concerned about," she murmured.

He grinned down at her. "That's good enough for me. I'll come to take you down to dinner at seven. All right?"

They dined in the hotel restaurant so engrossed in one another and their wedding plans that they scarcely noticed their lovely surroundings of crystal chandeliers and ivory damask draperies and fine china. Garner explained that it was tougher to get permission to marry shortly before he was to be shipped out for overseas duty, but he thought he could get permission from his C.O., because he was a friendly Texan. And he would manage to get time off in another couple of weeks to return to San Angelo for the ceremony. He hoped his mother could come down from Pueblo, too, but Diane couldn't come from California. They set the time and date for the wedding at four o'clock in the afternoon of Saturday, February 5.

Confident and happy, after dinner they ventured out into the night. No sooner had they left the hotel, than they were arrested, their souls filled with awe, illuminated by the silent and mysterious rising of the large orange cycloid of the moon, visible behind the edge of the earth, dominating the sky and the city. Hushed at the night dawn, they watched the bright, golden full moon slowly rise, fascinated as it cast its ethereal light, beautifying, changing the dark mundane to an ineffable glory.

Paula glanced up at Garner and he gazed down at her sweet, oval face, dreamlike, bathed in fairy light, partaking of a rosy hue from the moon and her pink dress. This heavenly moment a visible disclosure of the ecstasy they found in one another! He worshipped her.

"You're beautiful!" he whispered.

He took her arm and helped her down a few steps to a cabana, where he hired an oarsman and his boat for a leisurely cruise along the winding San Antonio River. They stepped into the boat and sat down in the stern, while their guide untied the rope and seated himself at the other end, facing outward. He began to paddle in shallow drafts, which moved the boat along in a slow, smooth glide. In intimate privacy, Garner put his arm around Paula and she snuggled up to him. Enchanted, overcome at Garner's alluring countenance in the moonlight, she gave him an ardent kiss, her full lips soft, quivering with passion.

"I adore you, darling," Garner murmured. "You're my inspiration. You've already said you'd marry me, so now, we should become engaged." He brought forth the jewel box he had offered before, opened it, and presented the diamond ring again, shining in yellow gold, nestled in velvet. "Hold out your left hand."

She did as he bade and he slipped the ring on her third finger. "We are now properly engaged to be married," she said, holding out her hand in admiration. The small diamond, less than half the size of the one Burl had wanted to give her, gleamed faintly, but to Paula it was far more desirable and far more precious. "I love you!" she exclaimed, and kissed him again.

They glided along with the soft, swishing sound of the water, embraced in their own paradise between heaven and earth, exulting in the brilliant eye of the full moon above, travelling with them to light their way.

❧ ✻ ☙

The next morning after breakfast, Paula and Garner bought a Sunday newspaper and repaired to her room. It was small, but warm and sunny and they felt like children playing house. Pretty in a shirtwaist yellow dress, Paula spread the full skirt around her as she settled on the bed with the funnies. Garner sat down in the chair beside the table with several sections of the paper. To him, this was like home away from the military base. He turned on the radio and the tension of the outside world invaded their peace.

The news concerned speculation as to the decisions to be made during the Casablanca Conference now underway, two months after the successful Allied landings in North Africa. The Big Three Allies, headed by Roosevelt, Churchill and Stalin, were to meet together to plan their future war strategy, but Stalin had sent word that he found it necessary to remain at home to direct the Russian campaign.

Paula and Garner let the newspaper fall from their hands and they gave full attention to the newscast. Decisions made at the Casablanca Conference would directly affect them.

Paula looked at Garner in consternation. He met her gaze, then he bowed his head, ear tuned to the news.

The announcer continued:

> THE MAJOR ISSUES OF THE CONFERENCE ARE SUBMARINE WARFARE AND THE NEXT ALLIED THRUST AFTER VICTORY IN AFRICA. IT IS KNOWN THAT EVEN BEFORE THE AFRICAN CAMPAIGN, OUR MILITARY LEADERS WANTED TO PREPARE FOR A LANDING IN FRANCE. BUT IT HAS BEEN RUMORED THAT CHURCHILL WISHES TO ATTACK SICILY AND THEN INVADE ITALY. HE HAS CALLED IT 'THE SOFT UNDERBELLY' OF EUROPE.

WE CAN ONLY SPECULATE AS TO THE ALLIED FORCES' NEXT MOVE AND AS TO WHERE THEY WILL STRIKE. THESE DECISIONS WILL NOT BE MADE KNOWN UNTIL PRESIDENT ROOSEVELT CALLS A PRESS CONFERENCE, AND THEN ONLY IN THE BAREST OUTLINE, BUT WE MAY BE CERTAIN OF ONE THING: IT WILL BE BAD NEWS FOR THE GERMANS AND ITALIANS....AND THE JAPANESE.

Garner turned off the radio and Paula spoke up.

"We don't know where you'll be sent," she said, "but I'll bet Roosevelt will prevail and France will be our next target. It makes the most sense. France is next to Germany and certainly more important than Italy."

Garner disagreed. "I think Churchill wants to get rid of Mussolini, Hitler's pal," he said. "And you know as well as I do that the British have a way of getting their political will. Besides, it's really Churchill's war. We're just along for the ride."

"Don't say that!" Paula flared. "Your ride is not going to be anything easy!"

"Never mind, darling. I'm studying those enemy aircraft till I can identify them coming and going. And I'm also studying the railways, highways, rivers and hills and the cities of both France and Germany."

"And Italy?"

"Yes, the whole schmear. I'm familiar with the B-17, too."

Paula sighed. "At least, we know you're not going to fly over China." Garner was silent at that. He had an uneasy feeling that he could not know what his future held. Paula, sensing his unspoken qualms, hastened to add a word of encouragement quietly, in a low voice. "I know you'll be the best pilot in the whole U.S. Air Corps."

He gave her a quick smile, dismissing the subject, and they returned to the paper, then made plans for the rest of the day. Paula suggested lunch outside the hotel and then a visit to the historic Alamo, where in 1836 a small group of determined fighters for Texas Independence from Mexico fought against Santa Anna and his army and took a heavy loss. Paula knew the Alamo was the turning point, for it broke Santa Anna's power and the Texans eventually won. She was all too familiar with the cry, "Remember the Alamo!" She hoped there would be no similar cry for the American forces in Europe. "Remember Pearl Harbor!" was surely more than enough.

Garner left to freshen up in his room, leaving Paula to prepare for their outing. She changed into her dark blue soft woolen suit and blue blouse and put on a pair of old Girl Scout oxfords she had worn as a girl. Her mother had recently found them in a box in her bedroom closet at the Roncourt home. She'd forgotten all about those dark brown, all leather shoes and was tickled with the find. Though they were scuffed and disreputable looking, they still fit and were ideal for walking.

When Garner saw her touring outfit, he looked down at her feet and for a moment she had a turn, a misgiving as to what he must think of her tacky old shoes unfit to accompany his own highly polished shoes. But the sight of her oxfords brought back memories of the many hours he'd spent as a boy tramping through the forests of the Ozarks, hunting for squirrels and quail, his rifle ready for a quick shot.

"Say! Those shoes are just the thing! You're as good as a hillbilly!" he exclaimed with a grin.

She could not share his enthusiasm. "A hillbilly! I'll have you know these are Girl Scout shoes."

He kissed her widow's peak. "I'm glad you're a Girl Scout, then." He gazed deeply into her wide, blue eyes. "To me, you'll always be a good scout and a dependable one."

This was more than she had hoped for so early in their sworn fidelity to one another. More than anything in the world, she wanted to be a good wife and the mother of his children. She would be fiercely supportive of her husband come what may, and his companion and partner in their endeavors to establish a fine, Christian family. She smiled and said, "I'm ready!"

The Alamo Museum brought back to mind the trials of the early American settlers and sacrifices made to form the nation. Paula and Garner were receptive to the images of bravery and courage impressed upon their minds and they were glad they had come. They returned to the hotel by mid-afternoon and Paula glanced at her watch.

"It's only three-thirty," she said. "I brought my sketch pad and pastels, Garner. We have time to go on our own little exploration in the park across the river. I'd like to sketch our hotel, the river and park and a few city scenes as a remembrance of our engagement interlude."

Filled with chagrin, he said, "I should have thought of that." They took the elevator up to her third floor, talking as they went. "You take your time and don't mind me," Garner continued. "I'll strike out alone while you sketch....say about forty-five minutes, if that's enough. That is, on one condition."

"What's that?"

"I want one sketch for myself to stash in my cap." They had arrived at her door and he unlocked it for her. "I'll keep it there no matter what. I'll know it's there and you with me. Whenever I get lonely or flak crazy, I can look at it and think of you and our moonlight engagement."

She was intrigued with the idea. "You'll keep it secret, won't you? Don't let anyone else see it." She glowed at the thought. "What scene wouLd you like?"

He became thoughtful. "I don't know yet. Why don't you do whatever appeals to you and I'll look them over."

The scenes Paula sketched with her pastels were clear of line and composition. The first was the Catholic cathedral near the hotel, which rose in a steeple with a cross on top, the colors in gold and magenta. Then she sketched the winding river running along the park like a canal, with the low, city buildings in shades of ochre, the Trailways Bus Station off to the right, with figures of servicemen and young women at its entrance. Another was of the park itself, showing trees, benches, and grass, and children at play, a water fountain in the background. She worked rapidly in sure strokes, inspired by the purpose of her pursuit.

Before she had time to start another scene, Garner sat down on the bench beside her. Rather proud of her creative interpretations, her use of color and line, and the variety of the scenes, she showed the sketches to him.

"How do you like them? Do you see the one you want?" she asked eagerly. He considered, but was slow to answer, and a black doubt entered her heart, making her anxious.

At length, he replied. "I like all of these. They're good. But you forgot. These are too large. I need a small one. It must be only about six inches by five, or smaller. And now I realize I had my heart set on a picture of the moonrise over the San Antonio River. But I'm sure that'd be too hard to catch. No one could paint the marvelous experience we had last night."

"Consider it done! If I waited long enough, I could have the moon for a model, but I'm afraid it'd be too dark."

"You remember, don't you?" he asked in an intimate way that thrilled her.

"Yes, I remember very well," she murmured. "But please don't watch me. I'd be too nervous and I want to surprise you."

He left again and Paula smiled, watching him saunter over to a group of boys and begin to play catch with them. Her art must be fine this time. Small, precise strokes, the moon bright, the earth not too bright, but somehow reflecting the red-gold of the rising moon. With the background to her satisfaction, she brought the winding river forward. She put a streak of gold in the stream as it reflected the moonlight. Then she added a few black strokes indicating a rowboat, a man and woman in the stern and a boatman paddling up the stream. It was a lovely vignette, complete.

When she had finished, elated, she hurried to gather up her artist's kit and went to find Garner. He saw her halfway to the water fountain and smiled at her lithe walk, the beauty of her slender figure coming ever closer, enhanced by her long, black pageboy swinging in excitement.

They met and he took her hand, their pulses in accord while in silent speech, their eyes spoke of love, exulting in one another. They stood thus for a moment.

Then Garner expressed their feelings. "You've got it!"

Paula nodded. Without further speech, they went to a bench near a curved walk and sat down. Paula brought the kit up to her lap and opened it, then drew out the small work of art, careful not to smear it. "Don't touch it," she warned. "It doesn't have the fixative on it yet." She held it flat on the palms of her hands for him to see and watched for his reaction.

Garner took in every detail, amazed pleasure suffusing his gaze. "How did you do it? You've caught the mysterious beauty of the moonrise, its mystic light fading away into infinity." His deep voice was hushed. Then he looked at her in wonder. "This is truly a work of art, worth more than any amount of gold. I'll treasure it always, darling. And you, the gifted artist, even more."

"Do you see us?" she asked, her enormous eyes fringed in black curled lashes, so appealing to Garner.

He nodded. "Yes."

Satisfied, she returned the small piece to the kit and placed tissue paper over it. "I'll spray it to make it permanent for your cap, a fitting cover for your poetic, intelligent mind."

He sobered. "I've written some poems in my passion and angst, but I tore them up.Some day I'll write more worthy poetry for you."

The sun was lowering, the brilliance of the sunlight fading in late afternoon, and a waft of cool air brought the scents of pinks, bluebonnets and green grass to their attention.

Paula rose. "I'll look forward to it," she said with a smile. "I see it's time for us to go eat before you catch your bus out to Kelly Field."

"Yes, back to our worldly life and its troubles," Garner said, "but this has been perfect, a time to cherish forever."

Since time was short, they dined in the coffee shop of the hotel. The conversation turned to Garner's duties and his overseas assignment.

"General Jimmy Doolittle will be a strategic commander in the European Theater, I'm sure," Garner commented. "I want to serve under him."

Paula saw his enthusiasm, the male scenting of the battle to come and its trials fraught with adventure in the presence of danger. "Yes," she said quietly, "if I were in your place, I'd want the same thing."

He noticed the shadow over her spirit, gave her a smile, and changed the subject to plans for their wedding, a more pleasant prospect.

Chapter Eighteen

After her return to San Angelo, Paula lost no time in telling Burl about her engagement. She invited him to the wedding, repeating the time, date and place in her eagerness. He took it with good grace and wished her all the happiness she deserved.

During these hectic war days, elaborate weddings were out of style. Life was stringent with little extravagance, indeed. Most weddings were quite simple with a few members of the family gathered together in a church, if the bride were married in her home town. Otherwise, and this was often the case, vows were exchanged before a Justice of the Peace or before a military chaplain wherever the groom was stationed.

In keeping with the custom of the times, Paula wanted her own wedding to be informal. She thought that too much folderoy would take away from the deep meaning of the ceremony. For her, the important thing was to be married in the church. Marriage was not only the most serious step in a person's life, but it was a solemn sacrament to be blessed by God. Paula earnestly prayed for God's approval of her union with Garner and also for His continued support of their marriage in the future. Their lives would begin as a unit before the church altar. In their hearts they would seek their heavenly father's blessing, as well as give their vows of fidelity to one another.

Paula and her mother were soon busy with preparations for the wedding. Esther Roncourt sent a special invitation to Private Alma Cameron in Pueblo, Colorado and another to Garner's sister, Diane, who was still stationed in San Diego. Diane sent her regrets, but Mrs. Cameron accepted the invitation with great delight. Arrangements were made for her to stay with the Roncourts and Paula was looking forward to meeting her. She was eager to become acquainted with Garner's mother who had borne and reared such a fine young man. She would love Garner's mother as her own.

Paula was grateful to her mother for offering to make the wedding dress. She chose a princess style pattern in a lovely, white taffeta moire fabric, which would emphasize her small waist and at the same time afford a full skirt with a feminine swishing whenever she moved.

On a Sunday afternoon in the brittle January sunshine, Paula walked to her mother's house for a fitting. She was soon standing in the middle of her former bedroom, trying to hold still while her mother made an adjustment in the front panel seam. Esther took in a half inch and Paula approved, saying that felt better.

"Now you've got to decide on the length," her mother said. She sat down in a nearby chair and looked at her daughter.

Paula's expression showed conflict, her lips moving as if to speak, then compressing in indecision. Tradition dictated that the wedding gown be floor length in front, bearing a long train in back. She knew her mother would like to see her in such a gown.

"Mother," she said in a conciliatory manner, "don't you think it would be nice to make it informal? Say below the knee, not mid-calf, but a little longer than usual, like a tea gown. Then I could wear it later on Sunday afternoons and for other social occasions."

Esther Roncourt's glance showed her disappointment. "But I think you should have a real wedding gown. There's enough material here. You'll be a beautiful bride, Paula, and this is the one time in your life when you should make the most of your beauty."

Paula tried not to show surprise at her mother's unusual praise. This from a woman who always said, "Beauty is as beauty does."

"But I won't be having a veil, Mother. I'll just wear a corsage at the shoulder. It will be simple and elegant, don't you see?"

"Bonnie didn't have a real wedding, either," her mother responded. She sucked in her lower lip, then added, "I was hoping that you would get to have one."

"I know, Mother. But I'll tell you what we can do. Why not use the extra material for a half slip? That'll give a luxurious rustle as I walk down the aisle."

"Oh Paula!" Mrs. Roncourt shook her head at such a deplorable scene. Where was the stately dignity her noble daughter deserved? Then in resignation, she said, "All right. Whatever you say."

"Speaking of Bonnie," Paula said, as her mother measured the hemline with a yardstick, "is she coming over?"

"Yes, after little Doug's nap." Her mother took another straight pin out of a small cushion strapped to her left wrist and inserted it near the edge of the turned up fabric.

She had nearly finished the pinning when they heard the chatter of a one-year-old baby. Bonnie appeared in the doorway, holding her son in her arms.

"Hi, Paula! Already a bride, huh?" she teased.

Bonnie, with her round face, nearly always exuded a sense of cheer and now her face shone with happiness for her older sister. Her figure was round like her face, not heavy but more substantial than Paula's slender form. Bonnie was fair with blonde hair and sky blue eyes. She resembled her father and unless they knew otherwise, strangers took the two sisters to be unrelated, mere friends.

Paula was glad to see her. Preening with pride, she asked, "You like it?"

"Gorgeous! But look what's in it!"

"All right," Esther said, satisfied. "Let's take it off and go into the kitchen. I want to go over the guest list with you, Paula, while we have a cup of coffee."

Floyd stuck his head in the door and gave his approval, then offered to take the baby while the women attended to their important business.

The guest list for the wedding and reception to follow was kept to a minimum. Paula wanted to invite Adele and a few of her friends from church and Goodfellow, but she didn't have room for Adele to stay with her. Bonnie said she would love to have her and that was settled. Then Esther said she thought they should invite the Stein family, since they had been neighbors for so many years.

"I've already invited Burl," Paula said. "But I'm not sure he'll come."

"Why not?" Esther asked.

Unsmiling, Paula and Bonnie exchanged glances.

Esther cast Paula a knowing look. "Did he take it that hard?" Paula flushed with embarrassment.

"Yes, why not?" Bonnie asked in her outgoing manner. "He Just might take a liking to Adele for a change."

"Yes, wouldn't that be nice?" Esther joined in. "Don't you think it would be a nice thing for both of them, Paula?"

Paula was uncomfortable at the way they played with her private intentions, her sometimes jealous leanings. She tossed her head. "I don't think so, Mother. You know that Adele and Burl have very little in common. He's a rancher and she's a city girl."

"Well, who knows ...?" Esther said, shrugging her shoulders.

"Yes, who knows?" Bonnie echoed. "But I know you, Paula. You're something else. You're too stingy and too generous all at the same time."

"Of course we should invite the Steins, " Paula said. "Burl can come or not, just as he chooses. I really don't care.

"That's right," Esther said, dismissing the fribble. "The Naomi Circle will put on the reception and Dad and I will put on the dinner at the St. Angeles for family members only. I'll mail the wedding invitations tomorrow."

"And I'll lend you the something old," Bonnie told Paula, her eyes bright.

"What is it?"

"My one and only pair of nylons," Bonnie said triumphantly.

"Oh no! I couldn't! You've been saving those for a long time for Ralph's homecoming. Thanks anyway, Bonnie."

"Your wedding's just as important. Well, almost. I know how careful you are, Paula. You won't get a run and I insist. You can't walk down the aisle in those awful cotton things."

"Are you sure?" Paula asked, capitulating with wide eyed pleasure. "They would look nice with my dress and my pumps." She gave Bonnie a loving smile. "I never dreamed I'd wear nylons for my wedding."

※

The days passed swiftly and soon Saturday, February 5, dawned clear and cold, a perfect wedding day.

Garner arrived from San Antonio and checked into the Concho Hotel. Then he called the Roncourts. A few minutes before noon they came for him and the three of them met Pvt. Alma Cameron at the bus station. Floyd drove them home in his old Chevy and the family had a convivial lunch of fried chicken, Southern style, lightly turned in flour, salted and peppered, and fried in margarine, crisp on the outside, moist inside, the delicious aroma floating up in steamy goodness with each bite. The candied yams, garden peas and tossed green salad were equally delectable and not too heavy for a satisfactory lunch.

Paula did not join them, since according to tradition, she was not supposed to see Garner before the wedding. Mary, in eager attendance to her friend, did the cooking and kitchen work in order to give Paula time to do her hair, pack her bag, and put on the final touches of her toilet. She had finished manicuring her nails and was painting her toenails with bright red lacquer when the phone rang.

Mary answered and said it was Adele.

Paula replaced the nail polish brush, screwed it in, and picked up the receiver. "Hello, Adele! Where are you?"

"I'm here in Dallas," came Adele's muted voice. "I'm so sorry! I wouldn't miss your wedding for anything, but I promised to work at the USO and can't get out of it."

Paula instantly thought of Lt. Fred Thomas and was glad that Adele had taken her advice. "That's all right, honey," she said. "We wouldn't have any time together anyway, and I'm glad you're helping at the USO. You have fun and I'll write later and tell you all about it."

Adele wished Paula all the happiness in the world, said she would call Bonnie to let her know, and they hung up.

Mary, all aflutter, was getting nervous. "Did you put your marriage manual in the bag?" she asked.

"No, I didn't," Paula answered. "I have it all in my head."

Mary gave her a wise look. "I'm not sure that's where you'll need it."

"Don't worry, Mary." She chuckled and Mary laughed with her, relieving her tension. "We'll get along all right. And I trust Garner. We're not going to have any children until after the war."

"That's what they all say."

Paula ignored her. "I'm ready. I think the walk to the church will do us good."

"Let me carry your wedding dress. I'll be real careful with it. I like the long, slender sleeves."

"Okay. I'll carry the bag. It's good of you to do this for me." Paula gave her roommate a warm smile.

"Bonnie may be your Matron of Honor but I'm your Personal Maid, a privileged character," Mary said, with a pert twist of her shoulders. Paula understood that she was putting on to hide her true feelings of devotion. She was grateful to have such a congenial roommate.

When they arrived at the church, Paula was surprised to find her mother and Mrs. Cameron waiting for her in the Bride's Room, ready to assist her with her wedding dress. She introduced Mary to Garner's mother, then said, "I'm Paula. I'm so glad you could come."

Private Cameron smiled at her, showing her dimples. "I would have known you anywhere," she said.

Paula noticed how different she was from her own mother. This lady was tall and slender, attractive in her khaki U.S. Army uniform. Unlike Esther and Garner, she had blonde, wavy hair and a turned up nose. Her large, blue eyes shone with intelligence and a sincere welcome to Paula as a daughter-in-law. There was an instant rapport between the two, for they loved the same man with all their hearts.

Paula hearkened back to her dreadful doubts as to Garner's lineage and was amazed at herself. This woman was so different from what she had imagined. With a sense of one freed from all fears and with confidence in her future, she basked in the attention lavished upon her.

Amid much gaiety and laughing chatter, the women dressed Paula for her wedding, pinning on the corsage of pink carnations as the finishing touch. Animated, she stood before a full length mirror and gazed at herself, thrilled with her new image. Then she saw the reflection of her mother approaching from behind with a dainty tiara and white veil in her hands.

Esther lifted the tiara and said, "Turn around, please."

Paula whirled about and faced her mother, waiting.

Esther placed the tiara on her head, making her the princess she truly was. She fluffed the veil back over her daughter's head, which covered her raven hair, the veil falling down to her waist. The tiara was cunningly made to fit her head, the frame adorned with two rows of sweetheart roses made of the white moire' taffeta, seven mounds rising from them, forming a peak in the center, these also made of the same fabric white as snow.

Paula gasped. "Mother!"

Her mother gently took her by the shoulders and turned her around to look in the mirror again. Paula saw not herself but an enchanted princess ready to be swept away by her prince, a U.S. Army pilot, her fly boy poet in disguise. Enthralled, the princess' gleaming eyes held a mysterious light, candles of love dancing to the pulse in her throat, red mouth curved in dreamy visions of love-making, the black hair framing her sweet face in beauty, contrasting with the white purity of her adornment. She was crowned with the promise of fulfilling love and devotion.

The women stood by, a look of wonder on their faces at the transformation. Paula the Bride, the Princess Bride!

Then she spoke to her mother in the mirror with a hushed tone. "You made this for me?"

"It's my wedding gift for you, Paula." Esther's voice was soft, as were her eyes, full of mother-love.

"It's beautiful! And it just fits. You're so artistic."

"You're the artist!"

Paula swirled around and gave her mother a fervent hug, clinging to her for a long moment. "I'll walk down the aisle on air," she whispered.

There came a tap-tap-tap at the door.

"It's time, Paula," her father called.

In grand tones, the organ began Lohengrin's "Wedding March" and in stately pace, Floyd Roncourt proudly escorted his beautiful daughter down the center aisle to the altar. He then seated himself on the front row, where Esther joined him. Garner, in his cadet uniform, was sponsored by Colonel McIntyre, who marched beside him and left him at Paula's side. He then seated himself across the aisle from the parents.

Bonnie, lovely in rose chiffon, took her place beside the organ, facing the congregation. She looked and sang like an angel, her sister's favorite love song, "Because God Made Thee Mine, I'll Cherish Thee."

Garner smiled down at Paula, pledging with his eyes, and she returned the promise, thrilled to the depths of her being.

When Bonnie finished singing, the silver haired minister came forward in his black robe and opened the Holy Bible in his hands. Solemnly, the young couple exchanged vows to cherish one another, forsaking all others, to have and to hold from this day forward, for better or worse, for richer or poorer, in sickness and in health, until death did them part.

Garner placed a slender, gold wedding band on Paula's engagement finger, saying, "With this ring, I thee wed. "

"You may kiss the bride," the minister said in blessing.

Garner embraced his new wife and kissed her tenderly, yet with an exuberance he could not hide.

The organ ripped off in stirring consumation to which the bride and groom floated back up the aisle, Paula clinging to Garner's strong arm. Their smiles were reflected back to them by their friends and family whom they could now see and acknowledge. Paula glimpsed the Steins, Burl's head and shoulders above those around him. She smiled at him as she passed by, but later, she noticed that he wasn't present at the reception.

In a hum of congratulations and best wishes for happiness, the wedded couple stood in the receiving line, then Paula cut the towering wedding cake decorated in white rosebuds and miniature vines embellishing the upper edge of each layer. The cake was topped with a replica of the young couple in white wedding gown and military uniform. Wedding gifts in ornate wrappings were arranged on a long table in the corner of the hall.

Floyd Roncourt, beaming at his daughter, said he and her mother would take the gifts home with them, and they could open them there, since she didn't have enough room in her apartment.

Paula finished serving the cake and was soon surrounded by former classmates and church friends, while Garner was off in a different group, a few cadets from Goodfellow Field. Standing near his father-in-law, Garner caught Paula's eye and winked at her. A sensation of wickedness came over her. She gave him a wanton glance in return. They were married!

After everyone finished their refreshments, the new bride and groom bade their guests good-bye, then Paula retired to the Bridal Room to change into her going away clothes. Garner waited for her, his attention centered on the closed door.

Paula finally emerged and appeared in a long sleeved, powder blue dress of fine wool crepe fashioned with a flattering peplum around the hips. Like jewels, black velvet buttons set in silver, edged the round neckline and trimmed the self-fabric belt. Garner caught his breath, stunned at the elegance of line and color, the beauty of her transparent skin, her eyes fringed with black lashes, and ebony hair.

"From bride to model!" he exclaimed in admiration. "I didn't know I'd married a fashion plate."

"Not a plate," she returned, arching her neck, haughtily looking askance. "A dish!"

"Definitely, a dish! I could eat you up any time of day or night!"

"You'll have to wait awhile, Cadet Cameron," she answered tartly. "First, the gifts, and then the dinner. By that time you'll have lost your appetite, I'm afraid."

"Not on your life!" He started for her but she parried his advance.

"Ah, ah, ah!" she warned. "Let's be on our way."

Mary was included in the family group subsequently gathered in the Roncourt living room. She kept tabs on the gifts and their donors as they were unwrapped. Very little was expected, since Paula had told her friends not to give anything because she wouldn't have any place to put it and wouldn't need it, anyway, with Garner going off to war. She blinked away tears moistening her eyes as the packages were opened. They included a sandwich toaster, sheets and pillow cases, a towel set, a linen tablecloth and six napkins, a blue woolen blanket and lovely etched, crystal candlestick holders and oblong candy tray to match. Small kitchen utensils and a set of carving knives brought smiles to her face. She loved to cook.

When all the presents and wrappings were placed on the buffet, there came a momentary hush. Paula looked around at everyone, then at Garner, and said in solemn recognition of their new position in society, "Now we're set up for housekeeping. We'll take good care of these things and have them for the rest of our lives."

He nodded with a smile. He knew how much these articles of affection and usefulness meant to her. "Amazing the variety," he said. "And just what we needed."

"Yes," Esther said. "And isn't this woolen blanket the Steins gave, a wonderful gift?" Paula smiled as her mother ran her hand over its softness. "We'll keep it here for you Paula, and the other gifts except for some of the kitchenware you may want now."

"Mother," Floyd said, glancing at his watch, "it's time we went to dinner. Do you have what's left of the wedding cake?"

"Yes, we mustn't forget that," Bonnie said, "especially if we want our wishes to come true."

"That's for the bride," Mary said. "You'll have to put a piece under your pillow and sleep on it, Paula."

"I've already taken the cake," she replied with a meaningful glance at Garner. "You can have my piece." Everyone laughed in good humor.

They all piled into the Chevy, four in front and four in back, Paula ensconsed on Garner's lap, for the short drive to the St. Angeles. There they were soon seated about a round table in a private dining room, with little Douglas in a high chair placed next to his mother.

The young waiter poured light amber, bubbling champagne for everyone except the baby. Floyd rose and lifted his glass.

"A toast to the bride and groom!" he announced. All conversation ceased and everyone except Paula and Garner raised their glasses.

"May you live a long, happy life together filled with as much happiness as on your Wedding Day. May you have as many children as your hearts desire. And may you never move far away from Esther and me, but come visit us quite often."

"Hear, hear! To the Bride and Groom!"

Glasses clinked around and across the table in effusive enthusiasm.

Amused, Paula addressed her mother-in-law. "A sneaky toast, don't you think? Our lives planned complete."

Alma Cameron pursed her pretty mouth. "Just a mite," she said. "But these are sneaky times, times to defend ourselves. Even if a bit selfish, I'm sure your father was sincere."

"Thanks!" Floyd joined in. "I'm sure you're sincere, too, Mrs .... I mean, Private Cameron. Sincere in your boot camp training."

"You have no idea how sincere," she replied with an exaggerated smirk.

"Tell us about it. We admire you greatly for what you're doing."

"I'm in the Medical Division of the Air Corps, as you know. But at the end of a day's workout, I often feel like I'm the one who needs medical attention. At first, it was simply awful." Alma bugged her eyes in remembrance. Then she continued.

"I came in dead one day, absolutely ready to quit. The sergeant was there for inspection and I didn't think I could stand up, much less stand at attention. But I managed, and passed muster. Then one of the girls told me of the standard joke going around: A private asked, How do I know I'm not dead? And the sergeant answered, Two ways: If you are hungry, then you know you're not in heaven. And if your feet are cold, you know you're not in the other place. My bunk mate said to me, 'Ask yourself if you're hungry and see if your feet are cold.' I told her, 'Are you crazy? I already know I'm in the other place!'"

Everyone laughed heartily in sympathy. Baby Douglas crowed, gazing from face to face, and clapped his chubby hands.

Servings of roast rib of beef, whipped potatoes and gravy, green beans and fresh ground cranberries seasoned with raw orange rind, were served, followed by salads of winter asparagus on lettuce leaf, garnished with strips of pimiento, red against the white vegetable tinged with green. The baby clapped again, when he was served in his warming dish.

"What a happy child!" Alma exclaimed.

"He keeps me busy and happy," Bonnie said.

Mary passed the rolls to Garner with the comment, "You and Paula should follow Bonnie's example."

Garner turned to Paula and she said, "We're not going to have any children until after the war."

Bonnie braved her own opinion. "But just think, Paula, if anything happened to Garner, you'd be left all alone, with no part of him."

Paula blanched, her eyes flickering to Garner then back to Bonnie as she secerned this hypothetical tragedy. "But that wouldn't be fair to the child. Every child needs a father. I think yours is a shortsighted view of the whole thing."

Bonnie's eyes flashed but she held her tongue, hiding her feelings as she gave Douglas a spoonful of potatoes. An uneasy silence fell around the table.

In his deep bass voice, Garner broke the impasse. "Nobody has asked what *I* think about this," he said. "I want to be present when my baby is born. And I want to be his or her father from the start, too. So I agree with Paula. We've discussed it and have decided to wait and have our family after my return. The way I see it, we're both young and have all the time in the world." He smiled a slow, loving smile at his bride and Paula glowed. She could have kissed him for standing up for her.

"Everyone has his own viewpoint," Esther said, ending the discussion, "and there is no right or wrong in the matter." She was nevertheless secretly pleased at Garner's caring attitude and she admired him for supporting Paula.

Floyd engaged Garner in conversation about the war and America's future.

"We'll have a revolution in the United States with as far reaching change for the world as our Revolution of 1776," Garner said, his eyes sparkling. "America will lead the way for the world. The war is bringing forth amazing new technology. It's going to be a place we'll hardly recognize. A better place. A wonderful place, where we'll be proud to rear our children."

"You two will get along fine," Floyd said. His round face expanded in a genial smile at the young couple and then around at the others. The family responded in kind with encouraging murmurs of affirmation.

In this gentle euphoria, the party broke up. Paula hugged and thanked her mother and father for the finest wedding a girl could ever have, even better than her dearest dreams.

֍ ✳ ֍

Garner had obtained a modest room in the Concho Hotel, which was unpretentious with only a small entry at the desk. They entered the elevator and went up to the fourth floor. When they reached Room 415, Garner unlocked the door, slipped the key in his pocket, and turned the knob. Then he picked up his bride, while she put her arms around his neck, smothering him with kisses till he couldn't see where he was going. He carried her across the threshold, shoving the door open with his elbow, and once inside, pushed it closed with a foot. But he didn't let her go. He took advantage of the ritual, kissed her soundly, then set her down.

"Welcome home, darling!"

He helped her out of her coat and hung it up in the alcove closet, then seemingly from nowhere, he produced a wedding gift and presented it to her. What a gracious surprise! She read the dainty card: For my beloved wife on our Wedding Day. Love eternal, Garner.

The medium flat box was wrapped in glossy paper decorated with silver wedding bells and angels and tied in a blue satin ribbon. Paula opened the package and spread the white tissue paper apart to reveal a pastel blue scarf. She picked it up and shook it out, delighted with its sheen in light weight rayon. "It's lovely! Just what I've always wanted. How did you know?"

She was truly surprised at the gift and Garner was pleased he had guessed right. She put it across her shoulders and swung around, showing it off. "It just matches my dress. I've got to see."

She flew into the bathroom, and standing before the mirror, covered her head with it, tying it on one side under her right ear in a fetching manner. She returned, head tilting this way and that, modeling her new style.

"I didn't know about the dress," Garner said, "but it goes with your beautiful eyes."

"Garner!" Paula was pleased, but suddenly disappointed in herself. "The moonlight sketch was my engagement gift for you, but I didn't get you anything for a wedding gift."

"You didn't need to. I didn't expect anything," he assured her. Then with a devlish grin, he said, "Don't worry. I'm going to collect what I want."

He grabbed for her and she twirled away in skittish alarm, allowing him to catch her before she reached the bed. He picked her up and sat down in the easy chair, holding her on his lap. She took his face in her hands and began nibbling his brows, his nose, his cheek, his chin, all the time, moving toward his mouth.

"Here! Not so fast!" he protested. "At least, let me take off your scarf first."

She bubbled with laughter and held still like an obedient child, while he unknotted the scarf and carefully, so as not to muss her hair, took it off. He folded it and laid it on the table.

She nuzzled him and he found her mouth, his ardor rising in a long, deep kiss. She came up for air and he nibbled on her ear.

"How long can we hold out?" she murmured.

"I don't know about you. But I'll bet I can hold out as long as you can. After all, we have all night."

She straightened up and put her forehead against his and looked him in the eye. They rubbed noses Eskimo style, grinning playfully.

"My what big eyes you have!" she exclaimed.

"The better to see you with, my dear!"

"My, what big teeth you have!"

"The better to eat you with, my dear!"

Garner began to gobble-gobble gobble her and eat her up and before she knew it, she was nearly gone. The moment their nude bodies met in loving, embrace, she sighed in ineffable ecstasy. He tenderly, ever so gently, with care and longing, made her his, their bodies and souls becoming one.

Chapter Nineteen

During the Casablanca Conference, Churchill's long cherished plan to attack Sicily and then invade Italy won out, as Garner had predicted. At this news, Paula was disappointed, thinking that this tactic meant a delaying maneuver for getting at the Germans, the weightier enemy. This would probably make Garner's assignment all the harder and longer.

Yet the build-up in England continued. Planning for the major invasion of Europe proceeded while the Italian campaign relieved some of the military and political pressure on the Allied Command. It was reported that Gen. Dwight Eisenhower, supreme Allied Commander of the invasion forces, had set a tentative date for May. The great invasion was near.

Paula tried to dismiss her underlying concern and all thought of the days and nights to come when Garner would be gone overseas. He miraculously secured a room for her near the hotel where they had stayed before, and she asked for two weeks off from work for a honeymoon in San Antonio.

The small city swarmed with servicemen coming in from Kelly, Lackland, Brooks and Randolph Air Corps Base, the latter located nineteen miles northeast of town. More were added to these numbers by the personnel at Ft. Sam Houston, a military hospital inside the city. San Antonio was a popular place overwhelmed by these installations of young men and their courageous womenfolk who spawned upstream for each precious hour stolen from Uncle Sam.

Paula was intrigued by the remarkable mixture of Spanish-Indian Mexicans and the servicemen and their families of various nationalities from across the country. She often overheard these strangers comment on the native automobile drivers and how they caused a fearful risk in crossing the street on foot. She counted this a visitor's exotic experience while skipping through the crowds and close traffic on the curved streets.

The continuous honking was a constant irritant. Each driver seemed to think he was the only one with the right of way. Aside from this cacophony and danger to the other pedestrians and herself, Paula once again enjoyed the beauty and peace of the winding river and its park, so calm and quiet in contrast.

The two weeks flew by, yet seemed like a thousand days, each moment etched to an intaglio of scene and event enlivened by her heightened emotion. There were exciting moments when Garner came in to spend the night with her. Then there were challenging times when he could not come in and she was left alone. At such times, she ate in the coffee shop and attended the movies or dallied along the streets window shopping and sauntering through the department stores, each activity deemed a precious part of her honeymoon and impressed upon her mind as with an indelible pen. But the times she enjoyed the most when alone were spent with her pastels. She made new sketches for her scrapbook to be perused in the future and to share with her children some day. A real legacy.

Paula would return to San Angelo after Garner received his commission on Tuesday, the twenty-second, their Tuesday. They had decided there would be no point in her following him for his brief training and final assignments of his plane, his crew, and their secret destination.

That Monday night, their last night together, they clung to one another in vows of eternal love. As they lay in bed with Paula's head on his shoulder, Garner murmured, "I won't be so far away, darling. Barksdale, Oklahoma isn't far and I'll write every day. But even after I'm gone overseas, I'll still be with you all the time. You're always in my thoughts. You're the fuel my engine runs on. I'll live till the day we can be together again."

They made love, slept, awakened and made love again, and at length, fell asleep an hour before reveille. But Garner didn't rise at the big boom that day. He was not required to check in at Kelly Field until 1000 hours, or ten o'clock civilian time.

At eight o'clock they rose and Paula dressed, paying meticulous attention to her appearance. She must be beautiful for her husband. The way she looked would be his last impression of her before their lengthy separation.

She chose a form fitted mauve dress with a jewel neckline and sheer, full length sleeves. The snug bodice showed her youthful curves and high bustline. It ended mid-hip length with a binding that held a full, pleated skirt, at once feminine and smartly chic. Her necklace of large beads in a deep shade of violet, enhanced the color of her eyes and made a delightful completion to her costume. She used pink tones of makeup and brushed her hair to a gleaming ebony in a perfect, long pageboy.

"You're gorgeous!" Garner approved with a light in his eye. "Straight from heaven!" He pressed her to him and kissed her on the forehead.

Paula smiled up at him, savoring his pleasure. "And you're my Adonis, the handsomest man on earth."

She picked up her coconut hat, put it on, and then took her art kit and purse. Garner looked disappointed.

"Not yet!" he exclaimed.

"Afraid so!" she said. "Time for breakfast and then the bus to Kelly."

He glanced at his watch and gave a sober nod. "You're right."

At Kelly Field, Garner took Paula to the recreation building and left her on her own, a good-bye before the final farewell, for he was restricted to the field that night. She had left her overnight bag at the hotel already packed, ready to check out by five o'clock. She was glad she'd brought her art materials. Sketching would ease her rising sorrow at the thought of losing Garner for months to come, possibly for the rest of her life.

Paula ate sparingly at lunch time. Later, she found a strategic place among other wives and relatives to observe the military ceremony. She stood in the dappled shade of a tall cottonwood tree at the edge of the parade ground.

Kelly was as green as its name. The Texas sun shone brightly, warm and proud of her finest sons in their hour of successful training and recognition. These were the USAAC pilots who would be out front, over and above, giving and taking hellfire on the wing, protecting their own, destroying their enemies. These were the men who held in their hands and minds the leadership for the destruction of enemy planes, bridges, roads, and armament factories, and for softening the enemy's will so that the U.S. Army and Marines could go in and mop up.

At two o'clock, on the expansive greensward, the platoon of prepared cadets and their officers marched to their designated place in front of the audience. Paula spied Garner among them, fifth from the left in the front row, standing at attention.

One by one the cadets stepped forward to receive congratulations from their Commanding Officer, while he pinned on the silver Air Corps wings. With happy smiles, family and friends applauded each recipient.

Paula quickly sketched the memorable moment Cadet Garner Cameron stepped forward to receive his wings and his commission as Second Lieutenant.

When the last cadet was served, the Commanding Officer saluted and called, "Dismissed!" The men, now officers of the largest military Air Corps in the world, rushed to their loved ones.

Exuberant, Garner approached Paula in swift stride.

She greeted him with a slight tip of her head in swank formality, her face half hidden under her coconut straw hat. "Congratulations, Lieutenant Cameron," she said. "I'm proud of you."

He stopped before her and looked at her with a quizzical grin. Then he grabbed her by the shoulders. "You can't get away with that. For all the trouble I've been through, I deserve a kiss to kill."

Paula chuckled, then dissembled and offered herself in a lengthy, passionate kiss. It would be their last embrace for an aching eternity.

PART TWO

BROKEN WINGS

Chapter Twenty

Garner's life changed abruptly.

All at once, he had to adjust to more responsibility as an officer, to real practice missions in the B-17 Flying Fortress, and at a time when he had to leave Paula's warm embraces and forego her encouragement. What a brief honeymoon! He sorely missed her.

In spite of their separation, Garner carried Paula in his blood stream, in his pulse. She was his raison d'etre, a fundamental force in his thoughts, even when his mind was occupied with immediate concerns. She was always with him and he intended to return to her whole in mind and body, ready to take up their lives together after the war. It was strange about war, he mused. Men were animals, yes, but self-deceiving animals unlike nature's beasts. With a wry admission to himself, he vowed to keep Paula for himself, his own private war.

He couldn't bear the thought of her becoming wife to another man, of being replaced in her passion and affections. Before parting, he had not told her she should marry again if he were killed. He'd see to it that he didn't get killed. It was a matter of determination. And faith. No, he didn't mention death, and neither did she. Instead, he vowed to keep alert, to keep God on his side, for 'If God be for me, who can be against me?' He would be counted among that fifty percent of the pilots who survived. And he would survive in good shape. With God on his side, whatever he decided would be done. This was no self-deception. This was his creed.

Yet, springing forth from this drumming decision, at times, he was overcome by his body and soul's yearning for his love. Again and again during loneliness of night, he envisioned the contours of her lovely face, the high cheekbones, the large blue eyes, muril, like the clear, innocent gaze of a doe, or loving, intimate, alluring, filled with desire. Then he would nuzzle into her soft, white throat, absorbing her warmth, the scent of her hair, the round pillows of her breasts and limbs, and at last her soulful kiss, culminating in ecstatic ejaculation, silent, secret. Something of the purity of lovemaking in absentia brought comfort for a time and its peace remained with him.

Garner was ready for war. His overt, conscious effort was focused on his new responsibilities at Barksdale, Oklahoma, where he was assigned his flight crew. Barely twenty-two, he was put in command of a new B-17 Flying Fortress outfitted with .50 caliber guns. Their destination was kept secret, but he hoped they would be assigned a base in England to bomb installations of France and Germany. 2nd Lt. Max Gibbons, his co-pilot, was with him there. Garner liked Max, a steady, level-headed fellow from Carthage, Missouri. With his muscular wrestler's physique to back up his demands for honesty and justice, an aura of no-nonsense surrounded him. They had been in class together and they would work well with the crew.

The afternoon they were assigned, instead of meeting in the crowded mess hall, Garner gathered Max and the seven other men around him in the enlisted men's recreation hall. The place reminded him of Goodfellow with the desk for the C.O. Of-The-Day, a pool table, where men were playing, causing smacks of the hard balls to sound, along with the male kibitzing, and two or three tables and chairs near a tall coke machine against one wall. He bought cokes for everyone and they crowded around a plain oak table.

Barksdale is just another bleak place compared to Arkansas, Garner thought fleetingly, but this is where we'll complete three weeks of our practice missions before shoving off to war. It's the men who count. My crew, my men.

He was satisfied with each one, all young like himself, all American from different backgrounds. He glanced at Navigator

Staff Sgt. Edwin Eiler of Milwaukee, an efficient cuss typical of his German blood. He'd make their raids worthwhile, with Bombardier Jack Cross to follow up.

Next to him was Flight Engineer George Stefaniski, top gunner in a vulnerable spot. He was the quiet one. Too serious? Would he crack? There was something perhaps too sensitive about him.

Garner thought of how he could boost the morale of these men. There were bound to be rough moments. His gaze shifted to the five other gunners. Tail Gunner Charlie Scanlon, a small, wiry Slovak from New Jersey who was sometimes hard to take. He cussed over nothing, a constant bitcher. But Right Waist Gunner Martin McAuliff from Ohio, a good looking, slender fellow who was self-assured, cooperative, and perhaps the smartest of them all, made up for Charlie. And he liked Belly Gunner Pete West, the bug eyed, long faced joker from El Paso. His wit was welcome.

"Men," Garner said, "we've all met and know we can depend upon each other. I assure you I'll be thinking of your safety and mine all the time. But the mission comes first." They looked at one another, giving a subtle salute to their commander. "Now before we go on our first practice mission, let's seal a pact among ourselves as to who we want to take charge of our belongings, our mail, and someone to write to the relatives of any who might be killed in combat."

Pete West said, "Yeah. We've already discussed pact and impact. Charlie and I have teamed up."

"Good," Garner approved. "Max and I will team up. Ed, how about you and George?" They nodded in agreement. "And since we're uneven in number," Garner added, addressing Nose Gunner Doyle Ingres, "how about you joining them?" Then he concluded, "That leaves you waist gunners as a pair."

This was fine with everyone.

Garner took charge again. "Let it be understood that if your partner gets killed, you have the right to any of his clothes and the wearing of them will be an honor in memory of your buddy. But you will also be responsible to handle his mail and to write the wife and the mother and father. And if you can, visit them when we get back home." He turned to his co-pilot, a question in his gaze.

"Yes, I agree to all this," Max responded. In return, the men nodded in solemn acceptance. Then he surprised them. "But before we do anything else, we've got to give our fortress a name." His tone was insistent and the suggestion lifted the spirits of the crew.

They bounced several ideas around the table, *Special Delivery* and *Bearcat* among them.

"She's a bearcat of a plane, all right," Garner said. "I swear right now to get my thirty missions and take out twice as many of the Luftwaffe!"

"Aw, we don't want any tiger-bear!" Ed declared. "It's gotta be a gal's name like the rest of 'em. I'm with Lieutenant Cameron. Let's call her *Greedy Gertie!*" His bright blue eyes shone as if he imagined his bomb-sight aimed straight at a munitions target, his wide grin asserting a healthy appetite.

"Sounds good to me." Garner approved.

"*Greedy Gertie* it is!" Max agreed with enthusiasm.

Later that day, Flight Engineer Stefaniski, the quiet one, used nearly a gallon of orange paint for the huge rounded letters curved just so on the grayish, olive-drab nose of their great four-engined, armor-plated airplane. Under the curved name, he painted smacking lips in brilliant red. *Greedy Gertie* was thus baptized in good faith. Thirty missions to go. But practice first. They were primed to get started.

On their first practice time out, a submarine search mission over the Gulf of Mexico, they glimpsed something—the gray shape of a whale or a submarine—and the crew revved up with excitement. Garner circled, nose down, losing altitude, while all eyes watched, fascinated. He descended to the minimum 3,000 ft. altitude and there she was! A German U-Boat, all right! They could see it on top of the ocean, its hatch and shape distinguishing it as German. No doubt about it! Garner's scalp tingled as the killer instinct took over.

"Glad you wheedled those two depth-charges out of the boys at Barksdale," Max told him.

As his words faded, Garner made his run over the target. "They see us," he announced into the intercom.

The German U-Boat began to submerge, disappearing. Just then, Sergeant Eiler did a sweet job of laying those ashcans right alongside. Garner ascended and circled back. They made a pass over the spot where the sub had been and saw a big oil slick in its place.

"Got him!" Garner called. Elated, the crew congratulated Ed.

Max finished the job by calling in the Coast Guard to send out a patrol boat, and in high spirits, Garner said, "Let's hit home base!"

Yessir! They had learned how to do prectsion bombing in a rare chance on their first practice mission. Back at Barksdale, they received a deserved citation for their exploit. 2nd Lt. Garner Cameron's fort had earned its new name. The men had faith in *Greedy Gertie*. Although no targets appeared during subsequent practice missions, this peerless beginning became a portent for their future combat missions.

The men were continually seeking good portents in the rumors that circulated at the base. One piece of good news was that forty-eight year old Lt. Gen. Jimmy Doolittle had been assigned to the Eighth Air Force Command. Garner and Max were having lunch in the Officers' Mess Hall, seated at a round table near President Roosevelt's portrait, when another pilot brought the news. The other officers at the table quickly finished their meal and drifted off in the quest of more poop, leaving Lieutenants Cameron and Gibson, who were engaged in conversation.

Garner's eyes gleamed at the mention of Jimmy Doolittle. He leaned closer to Max and said, "I hope we'll be assigned to the Eighth. We'd see plenty of action under General Doolittle."

Max chewed on a bite of bread, his square jaw working with his small mouth closed. He swallowed and said, "You bet! He's the one who commanded the raid on Tokyo from the Hornet two years ago. That sure boosted our morale."

Garner leaned back, thoughtful as he took a drink of milk. "I first knew of him as a kid," he said, thinking it was a long time ago. "He surely inspired my father. That was back in 1932. Doolittle was a racer, you know. He set the world aircraft speed record. That was when my father, who was older than Jimmy, built his own airplane. A monoplane."

"A monoplane?" Max set his fork down, his food forgotten.

"Yes. His was a new design, you see, since bi-planes were all they had in those days."

"How'd it pan out?"

Garner lifted his gaze, pride and anger glinting from his dark brown eyes. "It was in the middle of the Depression and Dad didn't have enough money to buy the engine for it, so he went to the bank for a loan. They knew him, and his father had been a wealthy man. But those creeps thought my father was crazy and they wouldn't lend any money at all." His gaze dropped down to his plate.

"Didn't he ever get to fly it?"

"No," Garner said, shaking his head. Then he looked up again. "It was a good design, though. It would have flown. But my father was killed in an accident shortly after that."

"Too bad!" Max frowned. "How old were you?"

"I was only eleven,"

"No wonder you wanted to be a pilot."

Garner smiled at Max. "How about you?"

"My father was a druggist. I just wanted to get into the best military service, a cut above the army or navy. I worked in the drug store before the war." He took a bite of steak. "What did you do?"

"I had a business course that did no good and went to work in a furniture factory in Fort Smith. It was sort of like home in a way, joining and gluing pieces of wood together. He turned his milk glass back and forth. "Sometimes I imagined I was building an airplane."

"Maybe you will some day," Max said. "Ol' Doolittle has come a long way. He's been in the thick of things for a long time. I hear he flew twenty-five missions from Africa, including the first raid on Rome."

Garner perked up again. "Yeah, and he made his first Eighth Air Force Command sorties in January against Kiel and Elberfeld in Germany and then to Tours and Bordeaux on the same mission. He's a living legend!"

This heart to heart talk sealed the friendship between the two men. After that, they stuck together and exchanged bits of information about the action in Europe.

Things were moving fast, and military personnel with them. General Spaatz was given command of U.S. Strategic Air Forces in Europe, with headquarters in the United Kingdom. He now had overall operational command of both the 8th and 15th Air Force Commands.

Rumor had it that there was a tremendous build-up of bombers, both B-17s and B-24s, at Seething Airfield in North Anglia just southeast of Norwich, and that was to be *Greedy Gertie's* home base. And so it proved to be.

Chapter Twenty-One

In the dawn of March 16, Garner and Max took their crew of seven other neophyte warriors and rose with widespread wings in their Flying Fortress headed east toward the sunrise. A feeling of elation to be at their job at last rode with them. At the same time, they realized this B-17 would be their new home for some time to come. No one knew how long.

Their course was toward Seething, USAAF Station No. 146. From the air it was muddy, flat, strange looking. A thousand feet below them was an aerodrome with empty hard standings, handy turnarounds, and three broad crossing runways. A winding taxi strip circumscribed the open fields around the end of each runway. From the perimeter track, short, paved turnarounds stood out both into the open field and into the surrounding woodland, the trees leafless. In one corner of the field was a bunch of arch-roofed buildings of war-drab color, longer than American Quonset huts. From that area, they could see roads leading to many similar structures in a scattered pattern. They later learned that the first group of Quonset-like structures contained Headquarters and Operations facilities. The other buildings were used for the living quarters of the various squadrons.

Garner pointed to the only building that could be seen on the airfield proper. It was a small square structure of two stories with a walkaround on the upper deck. This was the Control Tower and instantly, Garner remembered that day at Goodfellow when Paula had run down from the Control Tower out on the tarmac, alarmed at the impending crash. He'd been petrified with the fear of losing her, but she had rushed into his arms, clinging to him, and had declared her love. That was the turning point in his life, a turning point for love and laughter, for a happy future. The loss of his father had been more than enough. He was afraid losing Paula would destroy him. The crashes on this airfield would be many times worse than those at Goodfellow, but at least, he knew that Paula was safe.

Greedy Gertie came down in perfect style into the northwest wind and the men were soon assigned their places. At first, only twenty-five missions were required before airmen could return home to the States. Then the number was raised to thirty.

Garner and his crew got in under the deadline before the number of missions was raised to thirty-five in April. This was big news. Now all incoming crews had to fly thirty-five missions. *Combat flying must somehow be getting safer!*

Bad weather kept the airfield muddy all the time. They had had a six-inch snow early in March before *Greedy Gertie's* arrival. Storms accounted for some collisions with friendly or enemy airplanes. Other crews and bombers were still being shot down, lost during a raid, or sudden storms came up over the Channel on their return trip, holding them up, running out of fuel, having to bail out into the unknown. Every mission was filled with danger coming from ME 109s, ground defense fire, and threatening weather. They were surrounded! They had to fly high above the clouds with limited oxygen, keep in formation, hit the target and turn to home base as quickly as possible. Garner was grateful for the U.S. Air Corps P-38 Lightning Fighter escort. Those fighter planes were like mosquitoes. Hard to pinpoint, they were so fast. They made the enemy nervous!

Due to bad weather, two or three times in March the missions were called off, which wise decision saved their lives. But then the rate of sorties picked up and missions became fairly smooth, the fifth much like the first. By April 13, Garner was almost complacent about his sixth mission, another milk run.

Twenty-four aircraft were dispatched to bomb Pforzheim near Ludwigshaven, which was only one hundred kilometers north of Strasbourg, France, on the Rhine. The briefing had been handled at

0400 British Double Summer Time, so it was still dark. At 0909, due to weather, a recall option signal was received, but the squadron commander judged the situation to merit a continuation, and the formation carried on. They were to return across the northern part of France, an easier pass than over Germany.

Immediately after takeoff, Garner discovered that the tail wind was much stronger than forecast. This made the bombers early in spite of their deliberate dog-legging course. Colonel Thompson was determined that the bombing that day should be accurate. Garner followed his lead as he made three passes over the target. Eventually, at 1104, the lead aircraft dropped and all followed except for two that had been shot down on the way.

The target was bombed to hell. Munitions! Ed did a bangup job as always. Garner concentrated on that, ignoring the black bursts of flak from anti-aircraft guns while trying to veer clear of enemy fighters and still stay in formation. They turned west, tightened, the roar of engines and gunfire in their ears, and regained combat wing formation. Then, Garner headed south with the others, and once over France, turned west by northwest. He was soon over the French Coast.

Then out of the sun an ME 109 appeared head-on! Guns flared. Props spun a roar in Garner's ears. He pulled up but flak hit No. 2 Engine with a crash. Garner jumped in nervous reaction. He took a quick look at Max as the ME veered away, *Greedy Gertie's* guns after it.

"I'm okay," Max assured him, his features fear bitten. "No. 2 Engine got smashed is all."

The ME 109 disappeared in a cloud. We're okay, Garner told himself. He ascended to resume his place in the squadron formation. One engine gone. No matter. We're on our way home.

Out of the blue, the Messerschmitt was back, spitting fire. *Greedy Gertie's* cannons and guns boomed and blasted back all around. No. 1 Engine was struck and died.

Garner held onto his nerves, turning aside from the Nazi pilot, sure of the massive strength of his B-17 in spite of flak holes. But another ME, camouflaged to look American, joined the attack on the other side. No. 4 Engine conked out!

Greedy Gertie caught a burst of gunfire in the right cockpit, hot red blood splashing over Garner from his buddy and from his own wounds as the Plexiglas shield was pierced. Shards flew! The smell of cordite and smoke filled the cockpit! Max fell back as Garner slumped over with a loud grunt. He burned inside. His heart raced. Doubled up, he was blinded with blood and anger and pain. He couldn't see! He hung on to the wheel for dear life. Max! Max! He swiped his eyes and saw that Max was mortally wounded. Face turned away, the side of his head was a bloody mess, brain matter exposed.

Garner shuddered.

He felt the cold wind pouring in.

He gulped the fresh air to keep from passing out. The enemy was gone. Only one engine left! Oh God! Oh God! I've got to save my crew! Not down in occupied territory! Help me! Help me! Save us!

Max is dead!

Greedy Gertie was losing altitude!

He brought her up to make a swooping, gentle fall from the sky. The Nazi pilots were satisfied with their kill. They were gone. And now he was out of range of the antiaircraft fire along the coast. Garner gathered his remaining energy.

"Prepare to ditch!" he called in a low voice.

He saw the water and it looked good, a haven. No Messerschmitts, no coastal guns, a clear landing surface!

The crew threw out the .50 caliber guns, unhooked the inflatable rubber dinghies and tossed out everything else that wasn't nailed down.

"Mayday! Mayday!" Garner called. *Only one engine!*

George sent out the message over VHF for ASR, Air Search Rescue, back at Seething.

Garner hung on. Hot blood ran down his chest and back. Warm, so good! He went woozy. Don't pass out! I'm dying....dying....like going to sleep.... He closed his eyes, drifting off....so peaceful....let what will happen, happen.... No! No!

I've vowed to come back to Paula!

His mind and body jerked with a mighty effort, straining, fiery with pain, till superanimate courage overtook him. Save the crew! Stay alert! Stay alive!

I am alive!
It's close now! Come down easy!
"Prepare to ditch!" he screamed.

Wide awake, chilled and burning, he scanned the choppy waves, circled, held on and lowered into the stiff breeze. Too fast! Set her down easy! Easy!

Greedy Gertie responded, her great wings parallel with the horizontal waters.

God, save us!

Down she came, all crewmen ready for action. On impact, the ball turret broke free and water rushed in. The deluge sucked Max's body under.

Garner let go of the controls. He shook at the slam of the cold, stinging saltwater in his wounds as he plunged headfirst into the billowing sea. With a gigantic effort, in frantic strokes, he came back up. *Safe!* Safely away from *Greedy Gertie!* If he could keep his head above water, he'd make it! Gasping for air, swallowing great gulps of saltwater, he bobbed away from the plane.

It was every man for himself. The rich green smells of seawater and of oily fuel spurred their desperation. They scrambled, kicking hard ass, two of them grabbing the dinghies. Now clear of the B-17, they were thankful for their Mae West life jackets. Ed grabbed to help George, who had been shot. Ed managed to haul him into his raft.

Garner, between rafts, bobbed up and down as he looked around to count his men. Max was killed and nowhere in sight. His friend gone! Where was Pete, his funny belly gunner? *He's gone! Killed on impact!*

Stunned, Garner instantly subsided into a weak dog paddle, his impetus for survival forgotten. Only a subconscious will remained.

All of the other men were in the rafts and Martin, right waist gunner, saw a distinct blush of red surfacing behind his commander. In an energetic sturt, he yelled, "Come get into the dinghy, Lieutenant! Gotta get outta that cold water!"

He dived into the sea and swam over to Garner, grabbed him around his collar bone, and pulled him over to the raft. The others helped him get the long-legged pilot into the dinghy.

"What in God's name do you think you were doing?" Martin demanded, irate. "You're bleeding to death!"

Bent in the middle, Garner looked up at him, his eyes clouded, a suffering stubbornness flaring. "I'm all right," he muttered between stiff lips, his face a ghastly blue.

Martin struggled to set him down in the middle of the raft, while Garner hindered by trying to do it himself. Finally, he got him half seated.

"Sit stilll!" Martin ordered. He jerked a tourniquet band out of his medical pack and wrestled Garner's Mae West off of him, then unzipped his jacket. He peeled away his clothing down to the skin. Pale, with a deep frown and lips clamped together, he looked at the bullet wound in Garner's chest. Then he examined his back and saw where it had come out, tearing the flesh, bleeding. "How could you be alive? I can't understand how you could ditch the plane. It's a Goddamned miracle you're still alive!" Working fast, he tugged, binding the tourniquet tight. "Gotta stop this bleeding....can you breathe?"

Garner winced but did not cry out as Martin helped him into his cold, clammy clothing. "Feels better," he mumbled. His breathing was shallow and fast like a dying stag. *Paula! Paula!*

Martin grimaced and hastened to wrap Lieutenant Cameron with the wet silk of a 'chute. "Trying to get us eaten by sharks, huh?"

Garner glittered. "Not a bad idea!"

"We're safe away," Martin told him. "You just rest now."

"Pete?" Garner asked, his gaze dimmed with anguish.

"Yeah. Pete's gone. George.....he's not gonna make it."

They glanced over at Ed, cradling George in his arms. It wasn't like the way they thought it would be, coming in on a wing and a prayer, Garner thought. It was a cold, murderous mish-mash.

Ed bowed his head on George's chest. His shoulders heaved in wrenching sobs. George was dead.

His face ashen, Garner straightened up as best he could, and sat nearly erect in the yellow raft. "Ed, you can let George down overboard for his burial at sea." He paused, panting in shallow breaths. "I'll say a prayer for him. And for Max and Pete."

Ed took the Mae West off George. Then he picked him up and knelt, facing the mother of graves. He rocked his flight mate, swaying with the waves, tears rolling down his face. Then he murmured in George's ear, "Good-bye, Buddy." He lifted the limp body and gently rolled it over into the deep. A splash greeted their ears and George sank down out of sight, leaving a heavy weight behind him.

Sharp pain seized Garner. He shook in a rigor of stabs and grief, the cold, the loss of life, the stupidity of it all.

He swayed, overcome.

Sorrow, stunned awareness, fear, silenced the crew, all eyes upon Lieutenant Cameron. They waited. He gained control of himself and said in a strained voice, "Sergeant McAuliff, bring the other dinghy alongside. We've got to keep together."

The waves from the concussion of their eagle fall had dropped to a more normal surface motion. Martin reached out and Bill Gunn, left waist gunner, grabbed his hand when McAuliff made a close pass. They pulled till the dinghies bounced against each other. Charlie Scanlon, tail gunner, and Nose Gunner Doyle Ingres were the only others in the dinghy with Bill.

Six of us left, Garner thought. A third of us lost, and the Fortress, too. I've got to be calm and steady. Ignoring the deep ache and excruciating pain of his wounds, he lifted his head and said softly, "Let's bow our heads."

It was quiet. The noise of battle had ceased. The early afternoon sun sprinkled dazzling glints of gold upon the waves. He looked at his men and they all bowed their heads.

"Oh, Eternal Father," Garner murmured with enlivened spirit, "God of heaven, creator of earth and sea, we are a long way from home." He paused, panting for breath. "We've lost Max and George and Pete in battle. They won't be going back home now. We ask that you take them home with you. We also pray for their loved ones. Comfort their families and us. And help us to continue with our missions in honor of these brave Americans, our buddies. And give us the victory. In Jesus' name. Amen."

Rocked in the deep.

He gazed up into the sky, overwhelmed with the silence. No gunfire, no cannon, no roar of airplane engines, no voices. No nothing. Only a free quiet, a few cumulous clouds and higher strata swathes above in the northern spring air, a filtered blue in the pale gold sunlight. It was so peaceful! But there remained *Greedy Gertie,* wounded beyond life, beyond repair. Garner felt a surge of sorrow for his men lost and regret over the loss of their Flying Fortress, symbol of a staunch warrior in battle hovering nearby, unable to give up. Her burial was next.

He made no signal, nor said a word. None was needed.

The crew stayed near *Greedy Gertie,* waiting for her burial at sea. Doused, glad to be alive, but cold to the bone, under shock, they sat in their yellow rubber rafts and watched the battered fort, waiting. She hung in there, wings widespread. Gently jouncing, they waited. She didn't want to go down! They shivered, miserable in their wet suits and leather jackets. Silent, they waited.

Then they began to note the time: 1315. They still sat, waiting.

An hour passed.

Then *Greedy Gertie* tipped her nose down.

They saluted with tears in their eyes.

Her tail shot up and *Greedy Gertie* was gone!

The two dinghies stayed together.

Garner told his men they were pretty close to Dunkerque. "That means Ramsgate is forty miles away and another one hundred air miles to Norwich," he said. "We're only about ten miles out from Dunkerque. The logical thing is to go to Dunkerque and give ourselves up." He struggled for breath, then added, "Let's check the rafts."

No provisions. In their emergency medical kit, they found a Mars candy bar, morphine, gauze, salve, bandaids and binding for a tourniquet. Nothing else. But they did have paddles. Garner refused the morphine when Martin offered it.

"Jesus Christ! What'll we do?" Ed swore. His teeth chattered as he hunched over with his arms folded across his chest. "It's cold as hell and getting colder and nothing to eat!"

"We've got paddles," Garner huffed.

"Yeah! But forty miles?" Ed grumbled.

Martin broke in with a wry laugh. "We'd warm up in a jiffy if we paddled all the way to England!" Then he lightened up. "But being a prisoner in occupied France could be even warmer!" He rolled his eyes with an oooh-la-la!

Garner gave him a stern look. He then gazed at each in turn. His mouth was taut as he considered their dilemma. He would hate to surrender. He had multiple wounds. How bad were they? How long could he last? If they tried for England, they might be shot out of the water and end up in the sea like George and Max and Pete.

Doubts raced through his mind, but he said, "Someone will probably pick us up in an hour or two. This is a little unusual, but rather than telling you what we should do, I'd like to put it to a vote."

"Yeah," Bill said. "That's the democratic way."

"A simple majority then," Garner said. "Aye for England. Nay for Dunkerque." Struggling to keep his voice steady, he called off their names. The ayes had it.

"We'll be coming in on a paddle and a prayer!" Garner announced with renewed power in his deep voice. He grinned, proud of his men. "I'm sure we'll make it!"

These words braced them and they paddled with a will, headed west, taking turns on and off. Hypothermia had set in but they never let on and never let up.

They had been elbowing it for a couple of hours, when they espied a fishing vessel. Excited, they paddled toward the boat. They made good headway, but somehow they did not get any closer. The boat was skittish. It moved off to the right, then off to the left, hovering, keeping its distance.

Then it came closer, but it stood a hundred yards off.

Unable to paddle, Garner could only suffer, trying to sit erect to give his men courage. He felt blood vessels breaking inside, the hot blood coursing down through his body.

God, it's hot! Burning inside, cold outside!

He shivered with the freezing wind plastering his wet uniform against his injured torso, his back stinging with pain. Jaw set, he remained inured to the draining, aching assault on his life force.

Members of the crew, their teeth clattering with the cold, began to cuss. Would that damn fishing boat never get here?

"Goddamn those shitty nincompoops!"

"The bastards! They see us all right!"

"You just go to hell!" Charlie hollered. He stood up and shook his fist at them, rocking the dinghy. "We'll get to England before you can cut bait! GOD DAMN YOU!"

Then right before their angry glares, the fishing vessel suddenly turned and sped toward them.

"What the hell!" the men cried in unison. They gaped at one another in disbelief and the paddlers stopped, lifted their paddles into the rafts and rested. The fishing boat drew near. They sat grinning, waiting for it to pull up alongside.

Garner felt faint. It was hard to breathe. He was nearly paralyzed. He moved his arms to hold his bleeding insides, but that hurt too much. He couldn't stop the internal bleeding. He'd hold up, get his men safely to Seething. That was the thing. Then he'd check into a hospital. Mustn't pass out.

A fisherman hailed them. "Ahoy, there!"

"What took you so fucking long?" Charlie responded, still put out.

"Are you Yanks?" came the reply in British accents.

"Hell, no! We're Americans!"

"You're welcome to come aboard," a mate called. "At first, we thought you were Krauts! But we heard you cussing a blue streak and knew you must be Yanks."

"Glad to see you Limeys!" Ed yelled. "We've got a wounded pilot here."

Chapter Twenty-Two

The disinfectant smell of a hospital ward greeted Garner's nostrils when he awakened. He lay flat on his back on white sheets. He missed the roar of airplanes. Oh yes, he remembered. He was in the Norwich Hospital but he never knew how he got there. He must have passed out, then slept after the X-Rays.

Garner turned his head and looked around. Sunbeams were streaming in from high windows above the beds lined up along the walls, an aisle in the middle. There were ten beds in the ward, each one occupied. He didn't like what he saw next to him, an airman with his head, face and arms bandaged, a mummy in white gauze, no doubt a burn victim. He turned his head back again and gladly looked at the ceiling.

His back hurt. He couldn't breathe. He hoped he wasn't paralyzed. Somehow, he felt he couldn't move, yet he had turned his head. *Oh God! I hope I'm not paralyzed!* He'd felt paralyzed in that dinghy. Frozen stiff. Now here he was. He'd have to face whatever the doctor had to tell him. He heard a moan two beds down and felt like moaning, himself, but he kept silent. Take your medicine like a man, he admonished himself. The worst is yet to come.

A nurse in white, starched uniform and cap came by, shook a thermometer, and placed it under his tongue. He hated the thing, wanted to bite it off, but after rolling it around with his tongue, he settled it at an angle. He waited, careful to avoid her eyes. She took it and shook it again, read it, and noted a number on her chart.

Without a word, she hooked the chart back onto the end of the bed and went to the next patient.

She might have told me how I am! What a baby! I know I'm not dying. Just paralyzed.

Time passed.

Garner tried to breathe, but the excruciating pain hindered his diaphragm muscles. Still, he was alive. Just barely. This was agony, waiting for the verdict.

Might as well go to sleep and dream of Paula. Drift off...off into the blue....across the ocean....across the country all the way to Texas.....and my wife....dream of Paula.....

A warm hand pressed his shoulder. He woke up with a deep resentment. Anger flared as he gazed into the gray eyes of a British doctor.

"There you are, young man," the physician said with a friendly smile. "Nothing to get alarmed about." He held a couple of large, black negatives in his hand and at the sight, Garner's chest heaved with a start of fear. "I have something to show you," the doctor said.

Garner wanted to whip the X-Rays to the floor. Destroy them! His right arm involuntarily moved, but he controlled himself. The physician looked at this stalwart serviceman with a sense of wonder in his kind face.

"Son, I've never seen anything like this. It's utterly remarkable. See for yourself." He held up a negative and handed it to Garner, who disbelieving, took it. Nevertheless, he could move his arms and hands. But it was his back, his insides he was worried about.

"Hold it up against the light," the doctor said. "See this path right here?" He pointed to a place in the thorax where a pencil of light lay nearly straight downwards, then disappeared. "You were shot with a bullet that entered here and went through your body, coming out down here." He held up the other negative. "This shows where it came out in your back. Unbelievable! The bullet missed your lungs, your heart, all of your internal organs. After a rest of three or four weeks, you'll be up and about again. Your body will absorb the blood from your internal bleeding and the blood vessels will heal nicely. You'll feel a bit weak, of course, because you've lost quite a bit of blood, but your strength will come back and no harm done."

The doctor was triumphant, as if he had worked the miracle himself.

Garner searched the doctor's face with an earnest intensity.

The older man cocked his head and said, "I don't understand it, either. Your guardian angel must have been looking after you."

"Yeah," Garner responded, "but most likely the Old Man, himself." He became solenm and asked quietly. "You sure a nerve wasn't hit or something around my spinal column? I won't be paralyzed?"

Again, the physician showed the negatives to Garner and pointed out each detail, showing where the spinal column, lungs, heart, liver and other organs were and exactly how the bullet had passed through at such an angle as to miss them all. He had only to rest and let himself heal.

Garner heaved a sigh of relief and made a gutteral sound at the pain before he could stop himself.

"We've bound your chest to help stop the bleeding," the doctor said. "You stay quiet, take shallow breaths for a day or two. We've used iodine disinfectant and I'll check your wounds tomorrow. We don't want any infection."

"No," Garner murmured. "Doctor, do you know how the rest of my crew are?"

"They're fine. Were checked over and released at Seething Airfield. A few days' rest and they'll all be flying again. They can visit you three days from now. You must have complete rest for awhile."

"Thank you, doctor." Garner's gaze signalled his gratitude and relief at the good news the doctor had bestowed upon him. The physician's glance, in return, evinced a feeling of appreciation for being in the presence of a remarkable young man. His battle wounds could scarcely be expected as one in a million cases, an anomaly in medicine.

Garner caught this thought in the doctor's puzzled expression and gave him a penetrating smile. He drawled with a dry wit, "I may have a hole through my middle, but I'm not just a whistlin' Dixie. I keep the Master Pilot on my side."

The doctor smiled with an understanding nod and left to continue his rounds.

Garner went back to sleep. His resentment flared when the nurse came again and stuck the thermometer under his tongue, rudely awakening him. But he was grateful to have the bedpan, painful as it was. He tried to keep his irritation down, especially when he heard the yowls and moans of the other patients. On the second day, "the mummy" was taken out on a stretcher. He didn't make it. Then more than ever, he was determined to control himself, to ignore the sounds of the nurses' urgent footsteps, the quiet commiseration of the doctors, the swish of changing sheets, the bringing in of trays of food, and the expletives of those servicemen who were well and clamoring for release.

Garner put his mind in neutral and closed off his ears for sleep, healing sleep. On the third day, he was allowed visitors for half an hour.

Ed and Martin came by. They took chairs on the same side of the bed and kept their voices modulated, both showing concern at the sight of the lieutenant's pale face.

"How you feeling, Garner?" Ed asked.

"For some reason, I'm kinda puny." Garner gave a faint smile. "I'll be here awhile. Got a hole in my middle, but the bullet missed everything. All I'll get out of this is the Purple Heart and loss of time after those Germans."

"You deserve a medal for ditching so well and wounded at that," Martin said.

"Don't make me laugh," Garner rejoined. "I'll be laid up for more than a month and lose my chance for a promotion. And hardly started on my thirty missions at that."

"Yeah, but the main thing is that you're alive," Ed said. "It's a good thing the bullet didn't hit your heart."

"I'm lucky, all right! Maybe I need a blood transfusion, but I think a transfusion from Paula would do me more good."

"Have you heard from her?" Martin asked. Garner jerked his head and faced him.

"No. I haven't. And I can't write to her or Max's folks."

"Have the Chaplain write for you."

"The Chaplain's been busy," Garner said with a meaningful look, and the men glanced down with solemn nods.

"We'll be glad to write letters for you," Ed said.

"Thanks for the offer, but I'm sure the chaplain will do it. Are you okay and back on your runs?"

"Sure!" Martin answered. "But we miss you, Lieutenant."

A nurse entered the ward and warned visitors that it was time to leave.

Ed and Martin rose and Garner thanked them for coming. "I'll remember you on my future missions," he told them. "Hang tough no matter what and I'll do the same. We'll grind those Germans in the dust!"

He watched them leave and was glad they were still alive. His thoughts turned to his good men, Max and George and Pete, who had been shot down. *I pledge you, I pledge myself to avenge your deaths with twice as many Germans!* With this vow, he made haste to heal as quickly as possible, eager to get back into action. But he did not forget Paula and his promise to Max. He asked the Chaplain to write for him.

As he lay in bed recuperating, other airmen came and went, bringing him the latest poop. Late April brought good news. The effectiveness of the Air Sea Rescue Service was improved to the point where the chances of being rescued from the sea were now considerably greater than when he had ditched *Greedy Gertie.* The Eighth now had its own ASR on Boxted Airfield with a PBY Catalina and other amphibian aircraft as a supplement to the much augmented British ASR services. Two full-time specialist ASR officers were appointed at Seething, which illustrated priority now being given to Air Sea Rescue.

This was heartening news that made Garner have more faith in the earlier rumors, when there had been great excitement over a travel restriction clamp-down and practice defense alerts. The airmen thought this must be the first signs of invasion preparations. Bad weather prohibited missions and Garner figured he wasn't missing much.

He finally received a batch of letters from Paula and learned that his letters had been unnecessarily censored, but at least she knew he was in the hospital. His mother was serving in a Medical Unit of the WAACs in Boulder and doing well.

One afternoon, Ed came by to give him more news. Sitting up in bed, Garner asked where he got his expert knowledge.

"Didn't I tell you?" Ed asked. "Navigators are training to be reliable record-keepers and Bill Vermont is almost compulsive about it. I see his diary nearly every day."

Garner was sorry he missed the first raid on Berlin on the 29th. But maybe it was just as well. Ed told him that it was a brutal day. Of the twenty-seven aircraft that made it to Berlin, six were lost. The formation was unmercifully attacked by fighters on the leg home. 2nd Lt. William Ponge went down forty miles east of Dummer Lake. Three of the gunners were killed but the other crew members survived. Five miles farther east, 2nd Lt. William Rogers' aircraft disappeared in the poor visibility and crashed.

The litany was too long and Garner said he'd had enough. He was saving his for D-Day. His wounds were healing and he was growing stronger eating whole meals and gaining weight. He felt a strange sensation, an itching inside. Maybe this was because he was itching to get back to bombing missions again. He had not known that the healing process caused a real physical itching as the blood vessels mended.

On May 23, four weeks and one day after his sixth mission, 2nd Lt. Garner Cameron was released from the Norwich Hospital. He wrote to Paula that it was a Tuesday, their day. He was assigned a new crew, including a navigator, and this time, a B-17 Flying Fortress. Like him, his new men were survivors of other combat missions. He got along well with them all, but his co-pilot was the nervous type. Gunshy? He would need watching.

Everybody knew the big invasion was imminent. Airmen who had the good fortune to get to London were peppered with questions on their return to base. Is the place empty? Are there many paratroopers in London? The returning men told stories of the British countryside roads jammed with trucks, half-tracks and tanks, all moving south, and of passenger trains withdrawn from regular runs to speed up the movement of troops. England was packed with troops.

From June 2 to June 5, the bombers hit the French Coast. It was a good sign that the important day wasn't far off. On June 3, the weather was tricky, and Garner was in one of the two squadrons of the 448th's that managed to do any bombing on coastal batteries.

The next day, the radio news was good. Rome was captured by the Allies. Hooray!

On June 5, General Hodges came to inspect the 20th Combat Wing HQ. The unit was thoroughly ready for his visit. The Commanding General had come for a last-minute check-up. Big things were in the air.

And then it came! The long desired day of invasion!

Late that same Monday afternoon, Colonel Mason returned to Seething Airfield from a meeting at Ketteringham Hall, the 2nd Division HQ. Immediately, orders of restriction were passed to all units and the crews were encouraged to retire early to rest in their quarters.

At dusk the air above began to tremble with the sound of hundreds of in-line engines. The RAF bombers! Lancs and Halifaxes! *This was surely it!*

Then the Field Order came in. Shortly afterwards, the Tannoy blared: "Lead crews, pilots, bombardiers and navigators report to S-2 immediately!"

This was for special briefings.

Garner listened to the briefing with his mind envisioning each bit of information as he committed it to memory.

Colonel Mason and the Air Executive, Lt. Col. Hubert S. Judy, stood on the stage. They called for quiet. Then the C.O. spoke, reeling off the statistics.

Four million men. 5,000 troop carriers. Six battleships. 30 cruisers. And within the next hour, 1,100 Royal Air Force bombers would drop 6,000 tons of bombs on the beach defenses. Then at first-light, the Eighth would go in with 1,300 bombers and 7,000 tons of bombs.

"After the heavies are finished," he said, "the B-26s and B-25s will take over. Then when they have done, the fighters will go in under tactical cover and attack anything that is left."

Zero hour was 0630.

"Landing craft and troops will be 400 yards to 1-mile offshore as we attack," Colonel Judy explained. "You are to strike the beach defenses at Cerisy, dropping your bombs not later than two minutes before zero hour. If there are any aborts, you are to leave the formation before crossing the English coast and fly back below 14,000 feet. The sea traffic to the invasion coast is one way. If you ditch then, only ships returning to England from the beach-head will pick you up."

Aircraft aborting must make the decision before departing the coast. All aircraft returning over the Channel through lst, 2nd or 3rd B corridors would be fired on, regardless. Garner was assigned to the Ist B corridor.

"It will be congested in the air and with large masses of surface vessels, which will appear on your....the Allies star....will be displayed on the largest horizontal surface available on all friendly ships participating in D-Day."

There followed details of the color codes, radio call-signs, and all the paraphernalia of the massive plan.

At the end of the powerful briefing, Colonel Mason took the center of the stage. He smiled broadly, and with his easy charm said, "Do me a good job today, boys. It's my birthday."

Garner had been present at a few of Colonel Mason's 'birthdays.' He and the others knew what was required of them.

The initial briefing was over.

More briefings followed, four in all.

After the final briefing in the early morning of June 6, trucks waited in a long-line outside the briefing rooms to carry the crews to their planes. Garner climbed up into his plane, alert as an owl, seeing everything in the dark, blood throbbing in his veins, feeling himself flying already.

He and the 1,299 other bomber pilots ran up their engines, breaking the stillness of the countryside with a roaring crescendo. At 0140 in Norwich, the roar of the Liberators' Twin Wasp engines could be heard coming from all directions. The tremendous roar ranged across the whole of East Anglia!

Lieutenant Cameron was an American eagle, expectant, avid to cripple the enemy, kill if necessary, decimate the German war machine. Honor that sang in the blood was more precious than life itself. Freedom, liberty, democracy all depended upon how well he and the massive Allied assemblage handled themselves and their weapons.

Sitting high above the ground in the cockpit of his B-17 Fortress with his instrument panel before him, Garner felt exalted. We're all heroes, he thought. He recalled a poem from an old English playwright that his father used to quote:

> Ruby wine is drunk by knaves.
> Sugar spends to fatten slaves.
> Rose and vine-leaf deck buffoons;
> Thunderclouds oft in wreaths of dread
> Lightning knotted round his head;
> The hero is not fed on sweets.
> Daily his own heart he eats;
> Chambers of the great are jails.
> And head-winds right for royal sails.

Let the head-winds be royal! I aim to stay alive!

Paula, I'll come back to you. But first, I'll bomb. I'll destroy. I'll annihilate the enemy and his maniacs. Those preposterous egos!

Easy! Easy does it!

By just after 0200, the planes formed in two lines, converging at the head of the runway. Each had its navigation lights on. Up in the tower, Captain Beaumont in charge of Flying Control, kept tabs on the time.

Garner noticed his co-pilot, Leo Scarelli, breathing hard, eyes bulging, hands fiddling with the controls.

Garner spoke softly. "Just be patient. Take it from a Southerner, and just relax. The time will pass quicker that way." He hoped to God this Brooklynite could hold up in the battle to come. But Leo responded with a sneer as if to say, What do you, a slow country boy, an Arky from the hills, know?

A chill passed through Garner, bringing new determination. No doubt, no emergency, no virile animosity, no fear was going to veer his royal Fortress wings from the cause in this telling thrust for victory.

He turned away from Leo, his jaw set. He scarcely noticed a thick, black undercast rolling in from the distance behind the Control Tower.

Then he and his crew heard the news over their radio that the lead 446th Group got away exactly on time at 0200.

The waiting became interminable. Eager, alert, Garner's thoughts flew to the change coming as a result of this monstrous effort to invade France and Germany. It all depends upon us. If we can pull this off, quicken Germany's demise, then Japan will soon follow with all our efforts switched to that theater. His blood thrummed with ecstasy, the thrill of battle unpredictable, the knowing that the future of the world lay in his hands and heart and those with him. He knew he was committed to follow in his forefathers' vision for liberty and justice and in his own father's vision for flight, flight taking man to new heights, this time by jet planes and rockets into outer space. Humanity could not be limited to this small earth, bound like a worm in its soil while its soul squirmed under a rock.

No! I'll fly with divine power to kill before being killed, to pulverize the enemy's war machine, to rescue those two-legged ants below from their own mad militant tunnels.

Then, just before 0600, when the second mission of twenty-four aircraft in Garner's twin squadron were to take off, broiling dark clouds moved in, carried by a cold, insistent wind. They billowed overhead, a solid cover. The moon was gone and there would be no dawning, no light from heaven.

This meant radar bombing!

Garner glanced at Leo and saw anger mixed with raw fear and animosity. Their eyes locked. Garner shot a dagger through Leo's soul intended to cut away any mistaken notion of his own place in the cockpit, to cut with a clean slash. The Brooklyn Italian retaliated with a stubborn block and Garner knew he'd have to watch this guy. Handicapped by the weather, he'd have to fly right in his checkerboard formation and keep his eye on the co-pilot.

One crazy move on Leo's part could bring them down.

Chapter Twenty-Three

At first, after their parting at Kelly Field, when Garner was sent to Barksdale, Paula called him every Sunday afternoon those four precious Sundays, and this, added to their letters, sustained her until he was sent overseas. Then she imagined him on his bombing raids and as she did so, her spirit took flight in prayer for his safety.

In her heart and mind Paula followed Garner wherever he could be—flying, eating, writing letters, sleeping. She wrote to him every day, typing on the sheer, pale blue V-Mail letter-envelopes, telling him of her activities, always cheerful, with touches of news events at Goodfellow. When she began to receive his V-Mail letters, she kept them in the upper bureau drawer and often pulled them out to read again.

Then she received four letters at once. They had too many rectangular holes. It was ridiculous to think Garner would give away any secrets. It finally occurred to her that he may have used an acronym, GATW, in referring to their heady dreams of glory after the war and the censors had assumed it was a reference to some classified information.

One evening at dinner during their honeymoon, she had confided her dearest dreams to him. She told him of her deep concern that men continued to cause havoc with wars and she figured they loved war because of the glory they attained through the exercise of unspeakable courage in battle, and their leaders through imposing their will on others to show their power. But she had faith that after this global conflict the glory would pass to the women.

Garner lifted his brows at this new idea and his interest spurred her on.

"Women are making this war possible here at home by working as Rosy the Riveter at Boeing, turning out hundreds of planes per month, and in amunition plants, factories and offices," she said, and Garner nodded, encouraging her to continue. "Of course, I mean we're making it possible for victory. We don't want to make war possible. Wars have always ruined women and families and now civilians are bombed, as well as munitions, ships and cities' factories. Anyone can be killed, not just the soldiers."

Garner agreed with her. He shared her vision of a changed world following this senseless slaughter. "Can't you include me in your revolution?" he asked softly. "Can't women and men work side by side? Can't we share this glory after the war?"

Paula was taken aback. It wasn't in the cards. Nothing in history showed a male propensity to accept woman as partner, woman as important as the man. Only Christian men were sometimes amenable. With doubt, she searched Garner's intent.

"I could accept you," she said, "but I think men in general will not want to go along with us. Women will have a long struggle to bring that about." She paused, lips pursed, then added, "But it is essential. And women will rise up. We've had enough. We'll accept the challenge and eventually bring about great changes in society. You see, war must be outlawed! Men don't understand this necessity. They don't yet comprehend God's plan and how important it is to follow His lead, to work together according to His grand plan."

Other holes in the letters were probably where he had carelessly mentioned time or date. She warned him of these oversights and he stopped giving any further speculation, mostly writing that he was fine and he sent his love. He did mention *Greedy Gertie* and clearly explained why his crew had given their Flying Fortress that name.

One night Paula became restless in bed and unable to sleep, although Mary was quiet and sound asleep beside her. Paula chided herself. She turned over on her left side and comforted herself with the goosedown pillow. But no sooner had she settled once more than a terrible chill engulfed her. Garner! Garner was struck! Injured! He was in pain! He seemed to be rocking back and forth. Cold, cold! She shivered but tried to send a message of love and warmth, holding him close, close. He came to rest, holding a brace, still cold. She repeated over and over again, You're safe! You're safe! Everything's going to be all right!

Then he was gone.

The trouble must be over. Or had he died?

Tense, Paula went into a rigor, shaking the bed. But she must not disturb Mary. She curled up into a ball, trying to hold still. She stopped shaking and merely shivered inside. Garner's chill had entered her own body. Gripped in fear, she became rigid and remained sleepless the rest of the night.

After that horrifying experience, Paula received three more letters from Garner. Then they stopped. Her anxiety rose. She did not wish to mention her dreadful psychic apprehension of her husband's condition to Mary or anyone else, nor to show any sign of trepidation, so she joined Mary in longer hours at the USO. She not only served behind the counter, but often played cards with the cadets.

If Garner had been killed, wouldn't she know it? This question continuously tormented. The days and nights dragged on, till nearly a month of silence passed. Nor did she receive a notice from the War Department. She must hold on! Keep up a semblance of the normal self and never let on that she was crumbling inside. She kept her outer shell animated. Another blow and she would shatter.

Mary noticed her white face, her energetic activity and perpetual smile with laughter at the slightest provocation. One evening at their kitchen table, when they were having a dessert of jello fruit salad, she looked at Paula and held her gaze.

"What's wrong, honey?" she asked softly. "I know you haven't heard from Garner for some time. Don't take it so hard. You know that's par for the course. The mail often gets delayed. This is war. It's to be expected."

Paula's face became a mask. She played with the jiggly, red dessert. "I know that!" she said crossly. "I'm all right." She put a spoonful of jello in her mouth.

Mary touched her shoulder in sympathy. "Well then, calm down. You're too hyper and going too hard and fast. All your worrying won't help a bit. You'll just get run down."

For a second, Paula wanted to tell Mary everything, then she shriveled into herself. People would laugh at her if she told of her psychic experience and Mary would no doubt think she was over-dramatic, looking for sympathy. She couldn't possibly tell her what had happened, that she knew Garner was.....lost....killed....? No, this was her burden and it was not her place to bother anyone else with it. People didn't talk about such things. She straightened up, gave Mary a sweet smile and said, "I know it. I'm sure I'll hear from him any day now."

Mary was satisfied and glad she had spoken. "You're just different from most people, more sensitive," she said. "You can paint beautifully, but I think you also suffer more than others, Paula. I'm thankful I'm just a plain, ordinary person."

They finished their dinner with no more conversation. Three days later, Paula received a V-Mail letter from England. Mary had not yet come home from work and Paula, alone, opened the envelope with trembling fingers. It was from Norwich! She was afraid to read it, but took the plunge.

> Norwich Hospital
> April 25, 1944
>
> Dear Mrs. Cameron:
>
> I hasten to write to let you know that your husband, Lieutenant Cameron, is safe and doing well in hospital. Garner will write to you soon. He sends his love and devotion.
>
> Yours truly,
> Chaplain Harris Olmsby

There were no holes in the letter and relieved, Paula suddenly felt there were no holes in her, either, no riddling of doubts. Overwhelmed, she held the letter pressed against her heart and plunked down onto the edge of the bed facing the table. She sobbed and sobbed scalding tears, unaware that Mary had entered the tiny apartment, carrying her handbag and an armful of groceries. When she saw Paula in such agony, she stopped, woe sketched across her face.

"Paula!" She dumped everything on the bed behind her roommate and rushed to take her into her arms. "I'm so sorry for what I said last night!"

Paula pulled away, feeling guilty, and wiped away her tears. Then she laughed, careful to muffle any hysterics. "I'm okay, Mary." She handed the letter to her. "Garner's in the hospital for awhile. But he'll be all right."

"Oh!" Mary gulped, her eyes bulging. "I thought he'd been shot down! I thought it was a notice from the War Department." She quickly read the letter. "What were you crying about? He's alive! And okay! I'd be tickled to death."

Paula looked at her in disbelief.

Then she laughed outright. "I guess it was all those tears I'd been holding back!"

Chapter Twenty-Four

Paula's life became one long stretch of saintliness; yearning to God in her entreaties; writing cheer to Garner; staying kind to Mary in their garage apartment; and as usual, being considerate to Colonel McIntyre and his staff. She was so sweet and earnest that Garner was sure to get well and remain safe.

One by one, the days of May slipped by until one important day she received a letter from Garner in which he wrote that he was being released from the hospital and would soon be back in action.

Paula listened to the radio every evening. As she had predicted, delays in the Italian campaign held up the relay of landing craft to Britain, necessitating the postponement of the concerted attack on France until early June. Americans everywhere, on the farms and ranches, in offices, in munitions and aircraft factories, in shipyards and in schools and homes, were awaiting the big day, the day of the invasion.

It was understood that the proper combination of tide, weather, and moonlight would determine the hour and date. Yet this was a well guarded secret. And where would they strike? No one knew. Secrecy was of utmost importance for the Allies to catch the Germans off-guard. Paula was only aware that Garner would be among those giving support for the Allied forces.

Then it came! The news was broadcast out of Washington, D.C., on June 7. D-Day! This was what they had all been working toward!

Colonel McIntyre brought his portable radio out to the office and Paula joined the others gathered around to listen, each one personally involved, each one eager to hear how the invasion was going. Would it be a surprise and successful, or would the Germans pull another technical miracle to once again clobber the Allies with a massive slaughter? The Allies met stubborn resistance in a few sectors, but the landing forces speedily secured a strong beachhead and the news reporter told of supplies and equipment being rapidly moved in behind the advance wave.

Later announcements assured the American people that the German comnand had expected the major Allied effort farther north in the Boulogne-Calais area. They regarded the Normandy invasion as a diversionary tactic. Paula was elated at this news. This major miscalculation by the German general staff, combined with the brilliant planning of the Allied command, threw the Germans into confusion and disorganized retreat. At this news, much whooping and pounding filled the office. But Paula could only hope that Garner had come out unscathed.

Then another announcement shook her equilibrium. With limited success, the Allies had been trying to knock out the base in the Baltic where the Nazis were testing the V-1, called the Vengeance Rocket. On June 12, Adolph Hitler's top secret V-1 rockets landed and exploded in London. Garner was doubly vulnerable! The V-1 rockets would surely be aimed at Seething Airfield. He was now in peril more than ever on land and in the air.

The V-1 was described as a flying bomb with wings jet propelled, and pilotless. It was said to carry a ton of explosives at a speed of up to 370 miles per hour.

"Now the British will have to destroy them in the air," the newscaster said. But how, Paula wondered, by fighters and bombers? Land antiaircraft would not be effective. She was excruciated. What bad luck that the Allies had not been able to knock out the base where the new rocket was tested!

Paula gained a new insight into one of Garner's earlier letters when he had mentioned something about jet propulsion.She had put it down as some of his engineering dreaming but now realized he was trying to tell her something, trying to prepare her for this new development. Once again there were no letters from Garner. This time, Paula became numb. Like a dumb animal, she waited for some touch or word. Then, at last, several letters were delivered at once. Garner was alive and well. His missions were checking off on schedule.

In one letter he wrote:

> I found out what was wrong with my Co-Pilot, Scarelli. Just before D-Day, he received a Dear John letter and it tore him up. I've managed to cool him down and we're a pretty good team now. I told him that his girl friend's loss is really his gain. Who'd want a two-timing wench like that?

This time, she danced for joy.

Torrid summer arrived with news reports coming at a furious rate. In France and internally, the Nazis were weakening. On July 20, it was revealed that a bombing attack on Hitler had failed.

Paula and Mary were home that Thursday evening, seated at the small table with the door open to get a breath of fresh air. The dishes had been done and they were listening to the popular H.V. Kaltenborn.

> THERE'S GOOD NEWS TONIGHT!
> ADOLPH HITLER WAS BURNED AND BRUISED YESTERDAY AT HIS SECRET HEADQUARTERS WHEN A BOMB EXPLODED, KILLING ONE AND INJURING TWELVE OF HIS MILITARY STAFF. WHILE HE WASN'T KILLED, THIS IS REAL EVIDENCE THAT THERE IS A SERIOUS RIFT BETWEEN HITLER'S HIGH COMMAND AND THE GERMAN ARMY. HIS FALL IS SURE TO COME! AND SOON!

The telephone rang and excited, Paula answered, recognizing her mother's voice.

"Mom! Did you hear the news? Did you hear Kaltenborn? Germany's beginning to crack! Oh how I wish Hitler'd been killed!"

"Yes, Yes! This is good news," Esther responded. "Dad and I were just listening. But things aren't so good for the Steins."

"The Steins? You mean Burl?"

"Burl and his father. I thought you should know."

"What happened?"

"Dad received a call at the office today. Burl says he'll have to sell his ranch and he asked if Dad would take the listing."

Paula was stunned. "Sell the Lazy S?" As a child and through the Depression, she had always been able to depend upon the Lazy S, the one place that would remain the same forever.

"Things are bad at the ranch." Esther's voice was grave. "His well has gone dry. He tried to witch-stick for water, but no luck."

At this news, Paula lost her voice.

"And his father is in the hospital with kidney stones, which have caused infection in both kidneys."

Paula knew what that meant. He was dying. Poor Burl! To be struck down like that! His father dying and no water for himself or his cattle. "How awful!"

"Yes," her mother responded. "Dad asked if old Mr. Miller would let him have water from his ranch. But Burl has already asked for his help and he's hauling water every day with only two more weeks to go. Mr. Miller's afraid his own well will give out."

"I can see that. Only two more weeks! I've got to do something."

"You can't do anything, Paula. Burl's herd won't be ready for market until October. If he sells now, he'll lose money. There's nothing you or anyone else can do. I'm afraid he's in for it,"

"But he just can't sell. We've got to do something. Could he drill for water away from the house? Maybe that's the thing!" Paula paused, then asked soberly, "But could he find water and drill and have it all done within two weeks?"

"That's a risky and expensive business," Esther said. "You know as well as I do that the last moisture we had in these parts was last January...a rarity at that. How could there be water anywhere else on his land?"

"I don't know," Paula replied. "But the Lazy S covers at least a section, six hundred and forty acres. You'd think there'd be water somewhere else on it."

"If there were, I dare say it would be too far away to be of any use, considering that the Miller and Stein ranch houses are pretty close together."

"Is that what Dad said?"

"Yes. That's his considered opinion."

Paula sighed. If Mr. Stein died and the ranch failed, what would become of Burl? He'd be all alone. Two years ago his mother had been struck down by heart failure and with his only brother deceased at the age of six, his closest relatives were two cousins who were both in service in the Pacific. These thoughts ran swiftly through her mind as she tried to assess the crisis.

"Mom," she said softly, "you remember how Burl saved our whole brood of baby chicks that time? How about Pop Fogel? He's still San Angelo's water witcher, isn't he?"

"Yes, I remember. But honey, old Mr. Fogel died three years ago."

"Oh!" Paula was silent for a moment. "But didn't he have a son, Robert, Pop Two? I think he used to go around with his father. Is he our dowser now?"

"I think so, but he's at least fifty-five, and this is all too problematical."

"I don't care!" Paula said, exploding. "I've got to do something!"

In spite of her mother's warning, the next day after work, Paula called Robert Fogel and told him of Burl's awful dilemma. She asked how much he would charge to look for water on the Lazy S. He said in this hot weather, he'd want twenty dollars a day. She figured the most time they had was five days, so it couldn't amount to more than one hundred dollars. She could afford that. She suggested they start where Mr. Fogel thought there would be water and do it that way instead of making a grid across the land. Mr. Fogel agreed and added that the twenty dollars would be for a whole day or any part of a day, just so he got his twenty. Paula grimaced, but asked him to begin the next morning, a Saturday. Burl would surely give his approval when she told him of her appointment with Pop Two.

That night, Paula gave up the USO. She stayed by the wall telephone in her folk's kitchen, calling the Lazy S every fifteen minutes.

To keep her company, Esther sat at the kitchen table with a glass of iced coke.

Burl was not at the ranch.

At length, at eight-thirty o'clock, Paula called the hospital and learned that Burl had left an hour earlier. Where was he? She became more and more anxious, doubting her wisdom in trying to find water to save Burl and his ranch. Esther remained quiet, neither encouraging nor discouraging, as though she assumed her daughter would not give up until all avenues of action had been exhausted.

Paula rose from her chair. "I'll call the Millers. Why didn't I do that before?"

But Burl was not there, nor had he been there all day. The Millers didn't know where he was. At this, Paula became worried about him. Had he gone off the deep end? A beer bust? No, that's ridiculous! He's been at the hospital. He might have a new girl friend. That's something to consider. After all, I'm married now. She couldn't blame him if he decided to forget her and look elsewhere. She tried to squelch qualms about her true motive. It was nice to have a dependable man like Burl Stein in love with you, but it was up to a Texan to be a good neighbor, wasn't it? That was all she was trying to do. Maybe she should give up.

"Mother, if I don't get Burl by midnight, could I spend the night here?"

"Of course! But I think Burl will be home long before that, if he hasn't gone off to Big Spring."

Paula gave her mother an alert look. "A girl friend?"

"Oh no! A man who could be interested in buying his herd." Esther flashed a look of discernment as Paula turned away, covering her embarrassment by saying she would try again.

It was fifteen past ten when Burl answered.

Paula was so startled, she didn't know what to say. Then she found her common sense and asked how his father was.

"He's in godawful pain," Burl said, anguish in his voice. "It's terrible! And the doctors cain't do anything except give him some pain pills, and that don't do much good. He cain't last long. I just hope it gets over quick!"

"I'm so sorry, Burl! Is there anything I can do?"

"No, nothing. But thanks for calling." He was about to hang up. She hastened to catch him.

"I'm coming out tomorrow morning at seven o'clock, Burl."

"What for? You cain't haul water!"

"I've hired Robert Fogel to water-witch some likely places on your ranch."

"I've already tried that near the house. Any farther is too much of a long shot and a waste of time and money, the latter of which I'll have very little, I might add." Paula heard the desperation in his voice.

"Don't worry about that. I'm paying Pop Two. If we find water, you'll be able to pay for the drilling. We just can't lose the Lazy S!"

Burl groaned from the depths of his soul.

"I want to help, Burl," Paula said. "Just hold on, you hear? We're going to lick this, You attend to your father and the ranch and I'll find the water. There's bound to be water somewhere, and I'll bet, not too far off, I'll find it!"

"There you go, optimistic to the point of perdition!" Burl exclaimed, attempting some humor. "Let me remind you, it costs thousands of dollars to drill a hundred feet or more. And then the laying of pipe..."

"I know. But let's take one step at a time."

Paula heard Burl release an explosive sigh. "Thanks, honey. I really appreciate it. I'll see you in the mornin' then."

Chapter Twenty-Five

Early the next morning, with birds still twittering at the dawning, Paula dressed in a light blue cotton shirt, bluejeans, oxford tan boots and cowboy hat to match, and set out walking to town to meet Robert Fogel at the Concho Restaurant. Unaware of the delightful picture her slender figure made with hat cocked at a pert angle as she swung along, she contemplated the dusty day ahead in the sweltering July heat. Doubts of finding underground water on the Lazy S clouded her outlook. But none of these misgivings was evident in her lively step, for in spite of the risk she had invited, she was determined to engage full energy to a satisfactory conclusion.

She entered the cafe and saw Pop Two standing near the door. She was struck with how much he resembled his father. He was a small, cheery man with fine pink skin and bright blue eyes peering out from under a huge, sweat-stained tan Stetson. He had an air of mischief, seeming to have some sort of prank he was about to pull. Here was the new generation Pop who loved everyone and children most of all. He'd been a Boy Scout leader for many years. His greeting was high pitched and raspy, as though he needed a drink of water, Paula thought. This was incongruous. He was good at his job and she would get her money's worth.

He glanced at his wristwatch. "Six-thirty. You're right on time." He grinned, squinching up.

"We don't have any time to waste," Paula replied. "We have to cover as much ground today as possible."

"Don't worry. We'll get right at it." He held the door for her and they went out to his red Ford pickup.

As Paula climbed up into the cab, she glanced at the box and noticed several coils of rope, a spade, a pick ax, and a strange looking forked stick in the shape of an elongated *Y*. It was gnarled, yet held its utilitarian form. That must be the water-witcher's wand. She wondered about the intuition of this Merry little man who didn't seem serious enough for the weighty task of finding the elixir of life for his fellow Texans. His was a crucial job and one that must take a lot of nerve.

Once Mr. Fogel saw Paula seated in her place, he slammed the door shut, walked around to his side, hopped in and soon had the truck in gear. Paula glanced at him, askance. He didn't seem nervous at all. This critical event, the outcome of which could save or mean the ruin of a family's history of generations in the ranching business and Burl Stein's livelihood, all he had ever known, was brushed off by Pop Two as another routine job, or a game in the mystifying plot of nature. She wished she could take it as calmly as he, but her nerves tingled, her inner electrical impulses flying faster than the pistons in the vehicle's engine. She should calm down. She must simply let Pop Two pop to. He'd do his job and hers was to stand by for moral support.

They were out on the highway now, the mesquite plains rolling by. Paula emitted a long sigh and deliberately gazed at her companion, truly puzzled.

"I see you're not worried about finding water for the Steins," she said. Mr. Fogel took his eyes off the road and cast a quick look at her.

"No," he shook his head. "I learned a long time ago from my father that it never does any good to try to outguess the lay of the land's interior. There're veins of various minerals and water that we'll never know about. There might be a big underground river under the Lazy S. I hope so. I hope we can tap into the main stream or a good branch of it. I want to save that ranch as much as you do."

With that, he gave his sole attention to the highway, and reassured, Paula relaxed and leaned back against the worn upholstery. She made no further comment and asked no questions. Pop Two remained silent and she suspected he was concentrating on the work to be done.

The Lazy S was twenty miles southwest of the city limits and by the time they reached the neighboring Miller ranch, Paula thought the temperature must be around eighty-five degrees already. The day would be a scorcher, at least one hundred and five, maybe even one hundred and ten. She was beginning to wish she'd worn a straw hat instead of the heavy felt. But the wind would blow the straw hat away and the felt would keep her brain from frying. She reminded herself that the experienced dowser was wearing his old Stetson. Her instinct must have been right.

Paula loved being out in the open. She was transported back to her childhood by the limitless grandeur of earth and sky, the heavens golden in morning sun dominating the horizontal stretches. The flat, yellow expanses, windswept, lay barren except for the random sage interspersed with prickly pear and a few spiny mesquite shrubs. She inhaled the pungent scent of the plains, the acrid dust mixed with the spicy semi-desert plants. A sturdy, barbed wire fence followed along the roadside, but no sign of life could be detected, no cattle or sheep, only a vast emptiness of wild freedom plotted to satisfy the need in the human soul.

Then she recognized a slight rise off to the right. "This is part of the ranch right here," she announced.

"Might be a good place to start," Mr. Fogel said.

The land curved to a gentle swell of the high plateau and off in the distance to the west, they sighted the round, winged head of the windmill standing as a sentinel guarding the low, white ranch house. Soon the cluster of buildings came into view, the large red barn not far from the rambling house, which faced south in a slight hollow, protected by cedar and tall pecan trees.

They came to the gravelled road wide enough for trucks to pass, leading between fences to the establishment. Pop Two slowed down and turned in, driving under the great arch of wrought iron letters proclaiming: LAZY S RANCH. His window was already down and now Paula rolled hers down. She breathed deeply.

The blended odors of sage, sand, cactus, cattle and horses filled her with the indefinable recognition of home. This ranch must be saved!

The house was a sprawling frame building behind native gray stone pillars and a wide veranda. It rested in the shade of a large pecan tree, an oasis in the once green lawn now turned brown. Watching for Burl, Paula scanned the scene as they slowly drove along. She surveyed the barn lot, taking in the horses and Rhode Island reds, and the corral where the Herefords stood at bales of hay. Some turned their heads at the sound of the truck. But there was no sign of Burl.

Then she saw his tall, manly figure moving out from the shadow of the barn into the sunshine, a black, wide-brimmed hat shading his strong face, sinewy legs taking long strides. His faithful black and white dog, Shep, trotted at his side. Burl looked up and nodded, unsmiling. He gave a low wave.

Mr. Fogel brought the truck to a stop at the wooden barnyard gate and Paula jumped out and ran over to Burl. It was so good to see him. He was holding up, dependable as always. She felt a rush of warm compassion toward him as he came through the gate, stepping around Shep. The dog, in a frenzy as he recognized Paula, leaped and wagged his whole body, turning this way and that.

"Down! Down!" Burl commanded. Then he stood still and waited for Paula. She rushed over to him, grabbed his arm, and looked up into his face. Her eyes gleamed like deep pools under her hat, her gaze searching his face with a true caring.

"Burl!"

Downcast, he responded with a twisted smile of oblique resignation. Then his gaze met hers. His eyes filled with a copious joy and he grasped her hand.

"You're a sight for sore eyes, Paula," he said fervently. She saw traces of his suffering and grief in the deepened frown lines and the set of his mouth.

"It's good to see you, too,"

After a long moment in which he clung to her, she gently withdrew.

Mr. Fogel joined them and Paula stepped back while Burl extended a hand in greeting.

"I wish I could stay," he said, "but I've just had a call from the hospital. Dad is . . ." He choked with emotion, his Adam's apple working. Tears started and he cleared his throat. "He's not expected to live the day."

They were silent for a few moments, while Burl regained his composure. "There's nothing anyone can do," he said, dolefully. "And the doctor won't let anyone but me in to see him."

"I'm sorry about your father," Mr. Fogel said. "You tell him we're gonna search for an underground river and if it's near, we'll find it."

Burl smiled. "I'll tell him. And I wish you good luck."

"I'm going with Pop Two," Paula said. "May I ride Old Red?"

Burl looked startled. He doffed his cowboy hat and wiped the sweat off his forehead, then smoothed his shock of curly blond hair and settled the hat on his head again. Years back, Old Red had been Paula's favorite when in their carefree youth they rode together over the range. He shook his head.

"You'd better not. You shouldn't be out in the hot sun. You can drive the truck and go along with Pop Two as he works his witch-stick." He aimed a pointed look at her. "And be sure you stay in the cab."

Her eyes widened in disappointment, but she acquiesced without a word.

"Don't worry about us," Mr. Fogel said. "I've brought a couple of gallons of water, one for us and one for the jackrabbits and any stray dogie we might run acrost. Got our lunches, too, with a thermos of ice water."

"How about Shep?" Paula asked. "Maybe he has a nose for water."

"He must have," Burl said with a chuckle. "His nose is always wet. I'm sure he'd be tickled to go along. I'll leave the house unlocked in case you want to use the bathroom or the telephone. No telling when I'll get back." He scooped Shep up and set him down in the truck bed, then opened the wide corral gate. He waited till they were safely through, closed the gate, and waved them off.

Mr. Fogel drove along the fence, rattling at a slow rate across the rough ground.

"How far before we stop and look for water?" Paula asked.

"When we've gone five mile, we'll stop. I'll get out and walk four mile at a right angle. I've got a pedometer on my ankle, no trouble. Then I'll turn in and go two mile, turn again for another four, and so on. I'll make a sort of *S* grid." Pop Two flashed a grin at her, as if to say *S* for Stein.

"How long will that take?"

Pop sobered. "We've got to find a big source. I want to start another piece farther away by around two o'clock."

"About six or seven hours," Paula murmured. "We mustn't get too far away."

"That's right," the man agreed in his raspy voice. "It'd be a wrong gamble to search or drill for water more'n ten mile from the barn."

"You mean, more than ten miles and a new ranch house would have to be built?"

"Yep! The closer the water to the barn and house, the better!"

At this, Paula's determined optimism took a plunge. Reality faced her with a bald glare, hard, round within its own truth, displaying no hint of what was behind its smooth surface. She shook her head and forgot the matter. Her attention centered on the discomfort of bouncing on hard springs, innards jouncing up and down. It became necessary to hold buttock and diaphragm muscles taut to keep her insides from splatting around. Something might break! She put her hands against the dashboard and braced herself.

"Hold on!" Mr. Fogel called, giving it the gas. "We'll soon be there and then you can ooch along, driving beside me or sit 'n wait, if you want." He threw her a quick grin.

Her reply was a weak smile.

The truck hit a deep hole and Paula flew up, losing her grip. Her head struck the ceiling with force, crushing her cowboy hat down over her eyes. On the hard landing, her jaw clamped down with the impact and she felt a grinding.

"Take it easy!" she screamed. "I'm about to lose my teeth!" She pushed her hat up and glared at Pop Two.

He laughed with a capricious cackle.

"Just testing! Just testing! Wanted to see if they wuz false!"

Paula was furious. She rolled her tongue around, examining her teeth and wiped off some grit with her thumb. When she looked at him again, his crinkled face was so funny, she had to laugh in spite of herself. "They're not false yet, but you be careful or I'll have to sue you for damages!"

He slowed down.

She thought of Shep and looked out the rear window. He stood in the middle of the box, panting, ears prick, feet wide spread. "Shep!" she called, tapping the window. He looked at her and wagged his plumed tail.

Suddenly, the wicked water-witcher jerked to a stop. Paula braced herself, her hat tumbling forward.

A devlish imp flashed in Pop Two's grin. "You enjoyed that fun ride now, didn't you?"

Paula glared at him. She straightened her hat, then she chuckled. "You're just lucky I didn't break my neck!"

The skinny fifty-five year old was suddenly all business. "You stay here while I get a start," he said. He jumped out and scrambled up to get his witch-stick, while Shep wagged and nosed his hand with enthusiasm. When Mr. Fogel retreated, the agile dog put his front paws down on the fender and he bounded out of the pickup.

They were off!

Paula scooted over to the driver's seat and watched with fascination. Pop Two grasped the handles of the scalene wand and stooping over, held the prong close to the ground, walking in a steady, unhurried pace, concentrating, all else forgotten except his search. It was somewhat like plowing, plowing a mystery, for how could the stick know where water was deep in the earth? And how could it guide the hand that held it? How could the man be certain? Here was man in and of earth trusting in action and reaction, man and tree and earth become one to work a miracle, to discover the most precious element of the universe. Water! He must succeed!

Paula wondered if she should pray. She doubted it could help in this instance, where the spring of life was wherever it was, and that was that. She didn't expect God to make water on the spot and she was no Moses. Watching the dowser's figure grow smaller, she knew it would do no good to pray for a geological miracle. Instead, she should pray for guidance for Pop Two. And guidance for the wand. She turned on the engine and slowly rolled *bump-bump-bump* over the drought-ridden land. She'd ride beside him to let him know she was pulling for him. Shep stayed to his left. Paula's head hurt. She took off her hat and felt the sore spot. The welt wasn't too bad. The hat had saved her.

The intent man and companion dog trudged along, while the truck rolled nearby, stopping intermittently. In this way for four long five-mile stints and half of the fifth, they tediously covered the ground. The sun roiled in fierce, unremitting, fiery heat. At last, they stopped at twenty minutes past two o'clock.

"Time for lunch!" Mr. Fogel called. His blue shirt darkened with sweat, clung to his body, and his face was flushed. He dropped the magic stick on the spot.

The wand had not spoken.

Shep seemed to understand their disappointment.

Mr. Fogel poured out some water into a coffee can for the faithful dog, then joined Paula in the cab. He gave her and himself welcome drinks of ice water from the thermos jug before he opened the lunch box.

They drank and ate in grateful silence.

This is just the beginning, Paula reminded herself. We can do another area before dark. That is, if Pop Two can hold up.

Heat waves danced off the hot rocks and the dry land, bewildering the horizon. A lizard sped across a rock, reached its miniscule shade, and lay panting.

"I don't want you to have a heat stroke," she told Pop.

He laughed at the idea. "I'm good for another go-round," he declared. "If I get to feelin' queasy, I'll yell, 'Water! Water!'"

He poured himself another cup of ice water and slowly trickled the cold water on his gray head, whooping and yelling like a boy. Then he splashed the water on his chest, for a good soaking.

Paula jumped out of the cab and poured the ice cold water on her black crowned head, then down between her breasts in happy frolic, gasping and laughing at the shock. She took an ice cube and put it down her front, jiggling in torturous ecstasy. And mindful of Shep, she poured the remaining water over his head.

"I'm sizzling!" she exclaimed. Mr. Fogel jerked his head and took a sharp look at her.

"Did you put water in the radiator?" Paula's joy turned into dismay. "I meant to tell you to watch the radiator," he rasped. "We don't want it to boil over."

He got out and Paula hastened to release the catch for the hood. He lifted it up and a thin wisp of white steam rose before him. He gingerly touched the radiator cap. His thumb and fingers burned in quick stabs from the hot metal till he finally got it off and a hissing jet streamed forth.

"Caught just in time!" he yelled. The steam fizzled out and Mr. Fogel returned to Paula and asked for the gallon of warm tap water.

"So that's why you brought this," she said. "Unless it was for a lost steer."

"Or a couple of stranded Texans," he rejoined with a sly grin. He filled the radiator and returned a half gallon to her, then called out, "Shep! Come on! It's time to go!"

Shep leaped into his arms to be lifted up into the pickup again. Mr. Fogel took his place behind the wheel and glanced at his watch. "Twenty-five till three. We'll do another patch."

He drove five miles and braked to a stop.

"I'll stay here while you and Shep look," Paula told him. "I'll move every half hour to catch up with you. That'll save the radiator." Mr. Fogel agreed and she watched man and dog hike off to resume their exhausting search.

Paula prayed under her breath, "Oh God, be with Burl and his father and please guide Pop Two and Shep to water. Let them find it today not too far from the house. In Jesus' name. I thank you."

No answer came but she trusted that God had listened to her entreaty. There was no need to repeat herself. Whatever He decided would be done, but she should have faith that He would answer her prayer. And for her part, she must concentrate on Pop Two in his search. It was for this reason that she had not brought along a sketch pad or a book, but now she wished she had one or the other. In this terrible heat, it was difficult to keep attention riveted on the water-witching. The temperature must be over one hundred degrees. Drowsy, she stifled a yawn. She must keep track of time.

Paula noticed a turkey buzzard circling high in the sky, its wings as still as those of an airplane. It hovered effortlessly, tipping now and then to make graceful, silent returns. It remained high in its surveillance and did not come down near the ground, which was a relief to her. The thought of the ugly bird picking at a dead deer or rabbit filled her with revulsion. It sailed away and she closed her eyes. Relaxed, she drifted off to sleep.

Paula awakened with a crick in her neck. Blinking, she looked at her watch. Three-thirty! She was late! Fear gripped her as she wondered if she could find Pop Two. What if he were far away from the other end of the five miles? She must be certain of the direction. Then she calmed herself. She had been waiting only fifty minutes. At his pace, he'd be about two and one-half miles away.

She started the truck and slowly rolled forward, taking it at ten miles per hour as she ran over the sage brush and dodged prickly pears and rocks. The harsh land was impervious to the vehicle's tread. Within twelve minutes it had traversed two miles. Paula expected to see Pop Two and Shep at any moment.

Neither appeared.

She kept going.

She drove another two miles in the same direction. There was still no one in sight. Then it came to her that Pop-Two had not said whether he was going the four-mile stint or the two-mile sweep. Perhaps he had turned two miles back and was now traipsing off in another direction. She must keep her head. No need to get alarmed. But now she wasn't certain in which direction to go. Probably to the left. Anyway, she couldn't get lost. On the other hand, she must not leave them stranded for long without shelter or water. She wheeled to the left, searching the landscape as she drove.

In her extremity, Paula reverted to a childhood habit and let the pickup have its way as though she were riding her cowpony. Guiding lightly, she earnestly sought her companions.

Still no sign of life! *Where can they be?* Panic rose in her throat. She had lost them!

Paula stopped the truck, turned off the engine, and jumped down from the cab. Looking in every direction, swinging full circle, she called, "Mr. Fogel! Mr. Fogel! Shep! Shep! Where are you?" After each attempt, she waited, listening. There was no answer. Frantic, she climbed up into the box, then on tip-toe, she looked all around, surveying, scanning. No sign of life anywhere! Distressed, overheated, her heart pounding, she jumped up and down again and again, the better to see.

At right angles to the third jump-up, Paula thought she saw a dark lump..... a body..... a mirage......or part of a heat wave? She couldn't tell. Excited, she tried again. Yes! It was something......if only a shadow.....something real. But what?

Hopeful, yet fearful, she clambered down and took the wheel, then angled the pickup off and drove as fast as she could toward the dark spot. As she drew closer, it looked like a mesquite tree and for a moment she tensed, disappointment overtaking her. *Only a mesquite bush!* A large rock lay in her path in front of the bush. She drove around it and continued in her former direction. When she looked again, she was amazed to see the figures of the water-witcher and the shepherd dog a couple of hundred yards away. She rolled toward them, swiping off the perspiration from her face in relief. Soon she could see that Shep was barking furiously. As she drew nearer, she could hear the ruckus made while Pop Two tried to hush him.

She slowed and came to a stop. Mr. Fogel threw up his hands at the sight of her. She rushed over to him. His face was tomato-red. Paula gasped.

"Pop! Pop! Come get into the truck right now! You must get cooled down!"

"Glad you found us!" he shouted. "The goldangest thing has happened!"

"Come on now! You can tell me in the truck. We'd better get Shep in, too. He can lie on my lap." Paula led him away and spoke firmly to Shep so that he followed as commanded.

Once they were all settled, with Mr. Fogel slowly sipping ice water and Paula highly uncomfortable with the hot, heavy dog sprawled across her lap, she said, "Now what in the world were you two doing way off here? You must have run all the way like you were tryin' to get away from me!"

Mr. Fogel huffed for awhile before he answered.

"It was Shep," he said at last. "I was goin' the route and all of a sudden, he saw some vultures off in the distance and took off like lightning! I don't know! Maybe he hates turkey buzzards or thought they were after one of his dogies. But I couldn't let 'im get away, so I ran after 'im. And the vultures were down on the ground right over there." He pointed to a spot not far off, but all Paula could see was the cast-off water-witcher's wand. She could not see any carrion.

"Well sir, when I got there, it was a nest of rattlers right there comin' out from under that rock and the buzzards after 'em! They flew away when Shep went after 'em and the snakes scurried off, but Shep'd been yappin' and diggin' at 'em and I thought he might be after some more of 'em, so I watched till I come to realize it wan't snakes he was after." He gave Paula an owlish look and a cold chill ran down her spine.

Mr. Fogel pointed again. "Look close! What d'you see?"

Paula searched again and gave her attention to a dark spot in the yellow dirt beside the rock. It looked like a stain.

"Water?" she whispered.

Wordless, Mr. Fogel nodded.

"Do you think....?"

"Soon's I catch my breath, I'll find out," Mr. Fogel replied in a wheezy voice. He wiped his forehead with a blue bandanna handkerchief.

Paula took Shep's face in her hands and kissed him, then lay her cheek against his soft, furry ear. "Good dog," she murmured with a loving squeeze. Shep's large, soulful eyes held pure adoration.

Calmed down and somewhat cooled off, they all went over to the snake hole that Shep had enlarged.

Mr. Fogel picked up his wand and held it steady in front of him, weaving it back and forth in a time honored ritual. As he stepped toward the mesquite bush, the prong dipped down, nearly causing him to lose his grip. Then it swung up and shimmied. Mr. Fogel danced in harmonious rhythm with its gyrations, loose and free, letting it have its own way. His face was ecstatic, his smile as a bewitched priest seeing the face of God, transported into a private heaven of his own.

Paula stood enchanted. This was a true dowser, a mystic witch doctor of the earth sent to serve his neighbors and countrymen in need of the living fountain far more precious than gold.

Shimmying, dancing, the wand alive in his hands, Mr. Fogel continued on past the bush until suddenly, the prong pointed straight down and he stopped. No one moved. Not even Shep. Paula held her breath for minutes till she thought she would expire. Then Mr.

Fogel came out of his trance, straightened up, lifted his head and looked around.

"There's no doubt about it," he said, awed. "There's water here a-plenty."

Paula tossed her hat in the air. "Yippeel Yippee!" Then she hugged Pop Two and Shep, who was doing a dance of his own.

They reckoned the place was about seven miles from the windmill, not too far away to be useful to the house, since pipes could be laid at a reasonable expense.

"Can't say how far Burl will have to drill, but I'm sure he won't ever have to drill again," Mr. Fogel exulted, wagging his head. "We've found what we come for. God works in mysterious ways. If it wan't for the snakes and the vultures and that dog, we might never've found it."

"That's right!" Paula exclaimed. "You're a real Indian witch doctor!"

They drove back to the ranch house and Burl met them at the corral gate. When Pop Two had stopped on the driveway, Paula leaped out of the pickup and ran over to him. He was diminished, grief stricken, bowed with sadness.

Paula was brought up short by his mournful expression, sympathy rising in her breast. "How's your father?" she asked softly.

Burl clamped down and merely nodded.

With a troubled gaze, she asked, "Is he....?"

"No. He's still alive. Just barely."

She wanted to take him in her arms to comfort him, but he might misunderstand. Instead, she said with some intensity to get his attention, "Burl, you can give him good news before he passes on. We've found your water. Or rather, Shep did." Overcome with affection and sympathy and a desire to cheer him, she reached up to give him a hug.

In a swift movement, he clutched her with a low moan, bending down to her. She saw a rapt longing in his eyes as he sought her mouth. Flustered, she turned her head in time to avoid the forbidden intimacy. His kiss landed on her cheek and he released her.

She had not meant this to happen. But Paula admitted to herself that she had forgotten how wonderful it was to have a man's arms around her and how appealing this strong man could be. In the future, she would have to be more careful around Burl.

Chapter Twenty-Six

The August heat was suffocating.

When Paula got home from work one afternoon, drained and droopy, she noticed the poinsettia plant at her doorway, its lovely leaves beginning to wilt, and she hastened to water it before slaking her own thirst. The poinsettia was important to her, for its bright red leaves were a talisman for joy at Christmas time and somehow she thought she would expire of too much loneliness if it should die.

That done to her satisfaction, she went inside again and filled a green glass with ice cubes, then held it tipped at an angle, while she slowly poured a bubbly soda into it. She gulped at the dark liquid and spluttered as it fizzed up her nose. She set the glass down on the table, took off her wide, white leather belt, and draped it over the back of a chair. She pulled at her white cotton dress. It stuck to her shoulders, and she tugged till she finally got it over her head and threw it on the bed. Her movements were quicker now as she finished undressing. Relieved to be naked, she took no notice of her slender body, the tiny waist of which she was so proud, or her trim hips and smooth, white legs. She hurried over to the improvised bathroom and stooped to pass through the small opening.

The radically sloped ceiling of narrow, white painted boards allowed her to stand in the spot in front of the lavatory or sit on the toilet, but she had to bend down to get into the old fashioned tub that stood on animal legs with clawed feet. She turned on the water, then tied up her hair with a bright red ribbon, a gaudy contrast to her black hair and her fair skin. With her hair lifted from her neck, she was ready, and once in the tub, she luxuriated in the cool water flowing over her. She leaned back and dipped the blue washcloth in the water, letting it drip over her thighs, then draped it down on her stomach, patting it, feeling the delicious shiver as it clung to her skin, showing a slight depression over her navel.

I'm so flat.

She dipped again, letting the water drip from the cloth, feeling the rivulets trickle down into the crevices between her thighs, transparent globules caught in the curly, black pubic hair. She covered her abdomen again.

Flat. Barren.

She wished that she had let herself get pregnant like Bonnie. She could have managed. Someone would have baby-sat for her while she worked out at the field. Her mother need not have worried so much. She would never take a baby home to her mother. On the other hand, a baby needed its father and Garner was at war, still risking his life going on air raids nearly every day. He was unable to write much to her except that he was fine and he loved her.

As she lay cooling off in the bath, Paula reviewed events that had taken place since D-Day and Garner's part in it. The Germans had been surprised by the Normandy invasion and the newspapers reported that neither the German Air Force nor the U-Boats had been able to interfere. By the evening of D-Day, 156,000 Allies were ashore. The war effort had stepped up to a massive assault on both sides.

What concerned Paula was the letter in which Garner lightly mentioned that he was glad he was too busy to go down to London. The city was under almost continuous fire and Paula knew that Norwich and probably Seething Airfield were also getting their share. Garner was leading a doubly dangerous life. But he never mentioned that. And she never wrote about Burl except that she had attended his father's funeral.

She recalled how she'd been so engrossed with her own problems that she overlooked much of the home front news. Only six weeks ago, as she served hamburgers at the USO, she had overheard some cadets mention the new G.I. Bill of Rights. She prided herself on keeping up on things, and especially anything dealing with politics, so it was with great chagrin that she learned the bill had been passed on June 22 without her even noticing. It was the most far-reaching piece of veteran's legislation in the country's history up to the last third of the twentieth century.

The cadets were excited about it and said that after the war, qualified veterans could receive educational benefits to attend college. They planned to take advantage of it. There were other benefits, too, such as guaranteed insured loans for homes, farms, and businesses. It was a comprehensive plan to help the. G.I.s adjust to civilian life when they returned home.

Paula was glad she had written to Garner about it. He wanted her to look into it further and let him know just what was required for him to qualify for college. He did not have his thirty missions in yet for home leave, but was creeping up into the twenties, he wrote, adding:

> I should be coming home on leave before
> you know it, bright eyes. All is going well
> here. My crew is A No. 1 and we're getting
> the job done.

For Paula, this was the beginning of a period when she was full of confidence Garner would soon be home and their prospects were better than she had dreamed they could be. Garner could go to college. He could take Aeronautical Engineering. They would have a bright future, indeed.

She hummed the melody of the romantic tune, "Poinciana," as she finished bathing and put on a cool, pink negligee.

I don't need to be so concerned about getting pregnant, she told herself. Garner will soon have his thirty missions and come home to stay, if he wants. And our baby will have both parents.

She remained at peace after that, the weeks gliding by unnoticed as she worked at the office days and at the USO nights, doing her patriotic bit. There was some relief from the heat when the days grew shorter and the nights cooler. Life was once more endurable but it was at that time that Garner's letters began to arrive intermittently. Then before long, they stopped coming altogether. Paula assumed the mail was being held up again. By late September, she still had not heard from him.

One afternoon, she hurried home from work eager to get the mail, but she found the mailbox empty. She pushed open the door and kicked off her miserable wooden soled sandals, watching with satisfaction as they rattled on the linoleum and tumbled under the table. That expressed her feelings exactly. Then she noticed Mary sitting cross-legged in the middle of the bed surrounded by the green and white woven bedspread, silently observing her. She sat in the only comfortable place in the room, holding a letter of several pages.

"Hi," Paula said. Then she cast about looking for more mail. "Anything for me?" She placed her purse on the table, then took the batch of mail that Mary handed her. As she riffled through the bills and advertising material, Mary resumed reading her letter.

A yellow envelope dropped to the floor and Paula stooped to pick it up. She instantly saw that it was a telegram—a telegram from the War Department.

Paula stood motionless for a moment, then sank into a chair, her breath coming in shallow puffs. As if struck over the head, she was stunned, given a death blow like that of an unwanted animal. Destroyed! She automatically put the telegram aside on the table, unable to open it. Mary glanced her way and saw the transfixed stare, the face pale, drawn, diminished as in a death throe.

She leaped over to her. "What's wrong, honey?"

Speechless, Paula's wild eyes were full of woe.

Mary saw the telegram. She picked it up and turned it over, examining it. "Look," she said, "there's no black border on it!"

Paula came to herself and mumbled, "No black border?"

Mary shook her head with reassurance. "I'll open it for you. Want me to?" Paula was suddenly angry, the color rushing to her face.

"No! I can do it myself!"

She grabbed the telegram, her hands steady and calm, the hands of a stranger. In one habitual stroke, she ripped the envelope open and pulled out the message. She unfolded it and read aloud:

> WE ARE SORRY TO INFORM YOU THAT YOUR HUSBAND 2ND LT. GARNER DAVIS CAMERON IS MISSING IN ACTION OVER HOLLAND STOP AS SOON AS WE LEARN OF HIS WHEREABOUTS WE WILL GET IN TOUCH WITH YOU STOP
>
> SINCERELY

Her voice broke and she did not see the name of the person who sent it, if one were given. She sucked in her breath and dropped the telegram, shrinking back into herself. *Missing in action! Not dead! Or is he? And I didn't even know!*

Mary sat down facing her and spoke in a gentle, serious tone. "He's probably all right, Paula. You know how well Garner handles himself in any situation. You just keep up your faith. Aunt Ruth said in her letter I should advise you that in order to keep up your faith, you must be patient."

"Patient!"

"Yes, patient. Where is your faith if you cannot hold it and hold on to it?"

The jangling bell of the telephone rang, cutting into their conversation. Mary answered it. "It's Mrs. Quigley." Her gaze was questioning, but Paula nodded and took the receiver.

Mrs. Quigley reminded her that she would be on a holiday over the weekend and she expected Paula to open the USO and be responsible for the food on Saturday and Sunday, and work both days because Gwen Hayes had a cold. Paula already knew she couldn't count on Barbara Diel or Ginny Boston, her other close friends. She hung up with a smirk and a sigh.

"Mary," she said, frowning, "everyone I know is sick or busy. Mrs. Quigley won't be here this weekend so I'll need your help at the USO all day Saturday. And some on Sunday, too."

"All day!" Mary exclaimed, showing her buck teeth in her alarm. "I can't help you at all. To tell you the truth, I have to study my shorthand. You know I'm never going to get up speed if I don't practice," Paula knew that was true, thankful she had taken it in high school.

"All right," she answered. "But we definitely need you tomorrow night for the bridge game at Barbara's."

Mary agreed to sit in to make a foursome the following night and the two young women busied themselves with dinner after Paula had put her telegram away with Garner's letters. They didn't mention him again and both were glad they had the diversion of bridge and extra work, but above her anxiety, Paula was distressed and felt guilty somehow that she had had no inkling of Garner's -- crash? imprisonment? death? How could that be? She kept this secret concern to herself, even when they walked over to Barbara's house the next evening.

Mrs. King, a tall, commanding woman full of railing bones, greeted them at the front door of the large white house. She had dark, almond eyes in a long, horsey face unrelieved by short, brown hair. Mrs. King kept a protective vigilance over her only daughter.

"So glad you could come, too, Mary," she said in her metallic voice. "I have to fill in tonight, myself. We can't let Barbara miss her bridge."

All was pleasant, but Paula thought Mr. King should be there, a part of the picture. As usual, he was probably off with his domino cronies, too selfish to be a real father.

Nearly two years ago, Barbara had received a telegram edged in black that announced with regret the death of her husband, James Keith Diel, over in Italy. Submerged in grief, Barbara had contracted within herself and would not go anywhere nor see anyone except her bosom girl friends. Now Paula found herself in a similar position. What would she do? Perhaps she had done no better for Barbara than her mother. She would not want to shut herself away like Barbara if Garner were never found, or if he were already dead. She wondered if she had been such a good friend to her school chum, after all.

It probably would have been better if I had shunned her, made her find a new life for herself or insisted that she go out, Paula ruminated. If Garner has been killed in action.....I'd suffer like Barbara. I'd need my friends. No, I could never have turned away from her. Just the same, I've got to face the fact that he may be gone. How can one have faith under such circumstances? Is it hot air going up the chimney? I mustn't become like Barbara. Yet, like her, I'd be alone with no child. I would have lost Garner completely except for my memories. If Garner ever.....no, *when* Garner comes home, I'll make sure that I get pregnant right away. That's the only way I can be sure to have a bit of him no matter what happens in the future. Poor Barbara! How in the world can I really help her? Mrs. King is so formidable.

Barbara entered the living room with a dull cadence in her walk and welcome. In a loose fitting, pale pink dress, she had an air of enduring age, a shriveling dryness, which lent a mummified glaze to her sallow skin and lacklustre eyes. She should have been pretty, for her features were fine and her hair, though limp, was a luxuriant golden brown. But her spirit at the age of twenty-two, was as old as the gods. She was painfully thin and Paula noticed that she had not improved, but she seemed glad to see them.

Mrs. King set up the bridge table in the middle of the living room and the girls helped her place the chairs, one off to the side for the rotating Arctic fan, which pleasantly hummed a soft breeze their way now and again, agitating the sheer, white curtains as it swiveled away.

They cut for partners with blue Bicycle cards, Paula and Barbara paired against Mary and Mrs. King. Then Mary took the first deal with a cut of the ten of hearts, not an auspicious beginning for an exciting evening. She was learning the Culbertson method of bidding, so the others did not mind if she talked across the board. Paula had a count of one hundred honors, bid four hearts, and made game, bringing Barbara to life with this good beginning. Amber lights appeared in her hazel eyes as she dealt the second hand with a flourish. Paula's thoughts congealed.

Oh, Barbara! You can't spend the rest of your life dealing cards. Then in a flash, *I could become like Barbara!*

I must stop this.

But in agony, she tried to guess where Garner was right now, icicles pricking her nerves, her mind, making her feel numb. He could be paralyzed, blinded, maimed! Whatever his condition, she told herself fiercely, I will take good care of him for the rest of his life and be true to him even if he is ...

Mrs. King interrupted her train of thought by asking, "What do you hear from Garner?"

Startled, with both hands Paula quickly hugged her cards to her chest. Mary's warning glance to Mrs. King bounced off her nose, not reaching her intellect, since that woman's attention was given to Paula.

Paula kept her poise in play-acting as if on stage. She looked at Mrs. King without flinching. "I haven't been hearing from him lately," she said calmly. "As a matter of fact, yesterday I received a telegram saying he is missing in action over Holland."

With a sharp gasp, Mrs. King's mouth formed a round Oh, her sloe eyes squinched. Barbara shot a look at her friend in livid consternation. Mary consulted her hand, making herself small. They were frozen in silence for a long moment.

Breaking the spell, Barbara murmured, "I'm so sorry."

Paula smiled at her, lowered her fan of cards, and played a three of clubs, second hand low. "Thanks," she replied. "They'll notify me when they find out where he is."

The game was resumed and Paula kept her worries to herself. It's wrong to think bad thoughts. It's seeing Barbara like this that makes me so gloomy, so petrified. I've got other things to think about. Like tomorrow. How could I forget? The USO! And no one to help me.

She regarded Barbara. They were sitting it out while Mrs. King and Mary pondered a one club bid, or was it three no trumps? Paula's gaze became intense and at length, Barbara lifted her eyes in answer.

"Barbara," she said invitingly, "how would you like to help me at the USO tomorrow? Mrs. Quigley is on vacation and there isn't a soul but me to feed those boys."

Barbara shook her head and returned to her cards.

Paula jumped up, jiggling the table, black pageboy swinging as she jerked her head in anger, face flushed. In blazing accusation, she flared at Barbara. "You haven't turned a hand down there! What are you doing lollygagging around here day after day? You might at least think of those lonely guys and try to make it a little easier for them. But no! All you can think of is yourself. Your pitiful self! Well, I don't pity you any more. And you want to know somethin'? No one else does, either!"

She tossed her hand down and the cards flew face-up, scattering across the table, some invading Barbara's lap, others falling onto the floor. Outraged, Mrs. King stood up and faced her, a deep crease between her eyes.

"How dare you! You're always butting into other people's business, Paula. But not here! I won't allow you to talk to my daughter this way. You apologize, and then you may leave." Her eyes narrowed to slits and full of spite, she added, "And you need never come back!" She clamped her mouth down like a zippered pocket.

Paula gave her the scarcest flicker of a glance as she watched Barbara sitting motionless, a stunned look on her face, mouth gaping, eyes staring at her in utter amazement. Her safe shell was cracked. Mary, disturbed, strained at the two, but Paula stood her ground, still accusing. Neither Barbara nor Mary had ever heard such an outburst from her before.

Mrs. King fumed.

No one moved.

Paula ignored Mrs. King. Her intelligent eyes asked Barbara to let the light of self-knowledge in. She must make up her mind.

Slowly, Barbara put her hand down and retrieved the cards from her lap one by one, head bent over the table. She closed her mouth and gazed at the cards a moment, hands stilled, the lank hair veiling her thin face. Then she straightened up and confronted her mother, stretching to a new dignity as she remained seated, a proud lift to her chin.

"Paula's my best friend. And she's right, Mother. I'll help her at the USO. I'd forgotten the Golden Rule." She paused, then spoke with pain in her voice. "I think Jim would want me to help make the boys feel at home."

Paula rejoiced that she had spoken her dead husband's name.

Mrs. King raised her hands to protest, but Barbara pushed away from the table, stood up and faced her.

"Mother, she needs *me* now."

Mrs. King was a loaded howitzer about to explode.

"There's no ready-made rainbow in the sky for any of us," Paula said in a conciliatory tone.

The steel melted and Mrs. King gave Barbara an indulgent smile. "Yes, that's right, honey. That's what friends are for. To help each other." She tipped her head to one side and smiled at Paula. "I'm sorry for bursting out at you that way. I'll be glad to help you, too."

"That's all right, Mrs. King," Paula said with a brief glance her way. "It's forgotten. No, we won't need you. We'll get along just fine, thank you." She was courteous, but firm.

Good for you, Barbara! *Break all the strands right now*, her eyes signaled to her friend.

Mary rose, backed toward the fan a little as she spread her skirt, and said, "I'll be helping during the rush hour around noon. Can't practice shorthand then, anyway, and I sure do like to fry hamburgers."

Paula moved her chair and picked up the cards from the floor, speaking as she did so. "Thanks, Mary. Barbara, you should wear a snood over your long hair and don't bother about leg makeup. You too, Mary. We're not going to a party. It's just like home. Of course, when you're out of the kitchen, you can take off your snoods if you want to." She sat down at the table, gathered up the red deck and started to shuffle.

Barbara sat down and grinned at her. "I'll wear my new white one. It's pretty on me. I should wash my hair tonight."

Paula beamed at her. "We'll leave early, Mary."

The matter was settled and Paula was truly glad when Mrs. King and Mary wound up as winners for the evening. As promised, Barbara helped Paula open the USO at nine o'clock the next morning. They were cheered by the smells of coffee, bacon and buckwheat flapjacks, knowing that this mixture of nurturing odors was dear to the hearts of the servicemen.

The two young women worked in harmony through the breakfast hours from nine-thirty till eleven o'clock. Then Mary joined them in the kitchen at noon and helped through the lunch hour until two. Paula urged Barbara to entertain the servicemen while she remained behind the counter. Rushed, she scarcely noticed that her friend was coming around, shy at first but later finding her niche at a bridge table.

Except for these hectic stints at the USO, the following days and weeks tolled a largo pace for Paula with no further communication from the War Department. Mary and Barbara both advanced in their social lives, making new friends, leaving her to spend the evenings alone.

Paula became jittery. The waiting—waiting-waiting was unbearable! At times, she wanted to scream, to wail and screech until the whole town could hear her. Colonel McIntyre assured her that if Garner were killed in action, the Air Corps would have notified her. She did not trust the Air Corps. She could not believe Colonel McIntyre.

During a bleak night in early November, her nerves became uncontrollable. All the more jittery, her nerves caused her to quiver inside, as though chilled. There was no relief. She told herself that she could not go on this way, not knowing what had happened to her husband. The other girls knew where they stood. They were free to make their own lives. But not her.

Quivering, she lay awake staring at the walls and the ceiling in the moonlight that streamed in through the tiny window at the head of the bed. How faint that light! Faint like her hope. Thin like her patience. And the dreadful shadows at the door. Her faith must be strong enough to cause Garner's materialization, to bring him through that door to her bedside.

Each second was a pillar of anguish leading into uncertainty, sloping off, leaning toward the invisible. Garner could be a prisoner of war somewhere, wasting away...or dead.

Here I am, all alone. If only I had had his baby when we were first married! Now I would have the child, a part of Garner, someone with his brilliant mind, his handsome face. Someone to carry on the family line. To give meaning to my life!

She was rigid, yet trembling inside, scarcely breathing, trying to hold back the emptiness, the tears. She sank into the depths of death as the light of the moon under her woeful eyes ever so slowly moved, faded and disappeared. Darkness! Black darkness! It would be like this to know that Garner was lost forever.

What will I do if Garner has been killed?

Suddenly hot tears flooded her eyes and rolled down the sides of her face. She remained stiff, trying to control herself.

I made a dreadful mistake! If Garner ever does come home, I'll get pregnant the very first thing. I promise myself that. I'll never take a chance again on missing out.

Never, never, never!

Uncontrollably shaking her head, she turned on her side and curled into a defensive ball, wiping away her tears. She quieted herself and felt relieved. I've got to act as though he's coming home. Patience isn't enough. I've got to show my faith. Otherwise, he'll never make it. I won't wait another day. I'll buy a car tomorrow so we'll have it when he comes home. And it would do me good to get out on the ranch and ride the cowpony again. Burl will let me. He'll be glad to see me. But I mustn't go alone. I'll take Barbara with me. Burl and Barbara are a lot alike. Maybe they'll take a liking to each other....

Inaudibly, she heaved a sigh, put her hand under her cheek and forced herself to relax. At length, toward three o'clock, she heard the machinery of the bakery behind the garage apartment and smelled the delicious yeasty bread baking. She sang to herself, "Pat-a-cake, pat-a-cake, baker's man...." and soon fell asleep.

Later that morning, Colonel McIntyre cheerfully granted her the day off. She felt almost light hearted when she drew out twelve hundred dollars from her savings account and deposited eleven hundred in her checking account. It was good to be doing something positive, something to give herself more freedom. Cars were scarce and there were no used car lots in San Angelo. She had saved the one hundred dollars for a trip to Abilene, where she hoped to find something. Colonel McIntyre had advised her to buy a 1941 model because that was the best year before the war and since 1942 automobiles were manufactured only for the military.

This was something of a lark. She boarded the bus for Abilene, excited about the quest all on her own and with the money she had saved from Garner's pay, plus half from her own.

Not knowing that she was due for a pleasant surprise, at the second car lot, Paula was shown a brand new 1942 Willys four-door sedan, a cute little cream colored car with a four cylinder engine that would be most economical to operate. She was immediately enamored of this embodiment of America's experiment with the big-little car. The front seat fitted her, the whole car fitted her, and it suited her needs.

The dealer wanted twelve hundred dollars for the Willys, but when she told him her husband was a pilot missing in action over Holland and she only had eleven hundred, he let her have it for that.

She ground the gears at first try, but soon learned the hang of driving it. It was easy to handle. Elated, she drove back to San Angelo, proud of her new and unique acquisition and the fact that she still had five hundred and fifty dollars in savings, a nice nest egg.

    Mary was not there when she arrived at the apartment. She would have to show her one-and-only Willys in all of Tom Green County to Mary later, but eager to spill her joy, she rushed to the phone to call Burl.

Chapter Twenty-Seven

He answered on the third ring, his familiar voice bringing a warm strength, which caused Paula's enthusiasm to rise.

"Hello, Burl!" she bubbled. "Remember me? I've just bought a marvelous Willys sedan...brand new...a 1942 Model Four-Door Sedan. It's a darling little car, probably the one-and-only Willys sedan in all of Texas. It has only four cylinders and will be easy on the gas. You should see it! It's cream colored with simulated leather upholstery. But it's small. Just fits me! The biggest little car you've ever seen. Really compact!"

"Slow down, Paula." Burl's low drawl came over the wire. He gave an amiable chuckle. "You say you've just bought yourself a little Crosley?"

"Crosley!" Paula spluttered. "I didn't say a midget! I said a Four-Door Sedan, a Willys. You should see it."

"When you comin' out?" He must have read her mind.

"I don't think it's big enough for you," she answered hesitantly. "But the salesman did get in and demonstrate it for me."

"That don't matter," Burl replied in his easy manner. "We could mount our horses and ride where that funny Willys never thought of goin'."

Paula laughed. "That's for sure!" Then she sobered. "Have you heard about Garner?"

"No. What?"

"He's missing in action over Holland."

Burl was silent at the bad news. Then he said, "Oh, I'm so sorry, Paula. But maybe you need to come out all the more. A ride in the fresh air would do you good."

"It'd be good for Barbara to get outdoors, too."

"Bring 'er along," Burl urged. "This lonesome ranch's been ratty for too long. I'll guarantee the horses will welcome you and any of your female friends. You'll be a sight for their sore eyes, and mine, too." His voice held a jest but Paula knew he meant what he said.

She had not seen him since the day of his father's funeral, which now seemed years ago in an innocent age of life. The shattering uncertainty about Garner's condition had warped all sense of time. Yet she was careful to keep her tone light.

"Well, you just tell the rats to move out or the Willys will run 'em down when we arrive Saturday afternoon."

"Say around two?"

"Two it is!"

"I'll serve notice on those long nosed, long tailed varmints right now."

❧ ✻ ☙

The following Saturday afternoon, Paula took her easel and pastel sticks and stashed them in the trunk when she went after Barbara. Filled with anticipation, she was nearly as carefree as a child in her bluejeans, bright orange, longsleeved blouse, cowboy boots and white Stetson. She hoped to have a chance to ride Old Red, wondering if he'd still be glad to see her. It'd been a year and a half since she'd ridden. She hoped Barbara wouldn't be afraid of the horses. They both needed the physical and mental challenge, a welcome relief from nothing but work and worry.

When she arrived at the King home, she entered without knocking and softly called out. Barbara hurried forward dressed in a white blouse, Levis, bobby sox and old oxfords that she had saved from pre-Hitler days.

"You look great!" Paula greeted her. "I like that green scarf in your hair. Makes your eyes sort of green, you know, like they reflected the green grass of the meadow."

Barbara laughed with a snort. "What would you know about a meadow, Paula? You're so romantic. We'll be lucky to see a cactus alive."

"Let's go!" Paula said, laughing at her friend's down-to-earth viewpoint. "I'm the artiste today. An artiste sees only beautiful things, whether they're there or not. In the Old Masters, there's always green grass with lush streams and flowered knolls where nymphs and naked women rolling in folds of fat disport themselves in fanciful frolic."

They reached the car and she opened the door for Barbara with a low bow. "How do you like my new limousine?"

Barbara gave it a rapid onceover, nodded slightly, then got in. Paula closed the door after her, went around to the left side, and settled herself at the wheel. She grinned at her friend in triumph, inserting the key into the ignition switch, and started the engine.

Barbara shook her head and remarked, "You wanna know somethin'? You look just like a West Texan to me." Her glance fluttered over Paula, clearly indicating that she was out of place. Then she gave a faint smile. "I'll have to admit, though, you're a paleface. You *could* be from East Texas."

Paula chuckled and shifted into low gear. To her intense delight, the Willys performed smoothly.

"It doesn't matter what a person looks like," she said, turning the corner and heading out of town. "It's what's inside that counts. I brought my art materials because I'd like to sketch you and Burl on your Palominos, standing 'way out on the land, gazing at the far horizon.....maybe with one of those spectacular rayed sunsets."

"Oh, how corny! They're mystifying in real life, but no one could ever paint one to look like anything. Does Burl know I'm coming?"

"Yes, of course! Actually, I want to ride but if we miss him, I'll do some sketches. We're glad you could come."

Barbara flashed a grin. "I could see you needed a chaperone. His devotion is legendary...or I should say, undiminished...and you've had a long dry spell...nine months, isn't it?"

Paula flushed, the hot blood rising to her cheeks. This was ridiculous. She wished the bit of teasing had not embarrassed her so. She drove on in silence, heading for the highway.

"Don't worry," Barbara snickered, "Burl will be at the gate waiting for you."

"Or you!" Paula came back. "But I'm not trying to he a matchmaker or anything."

"Like butt into my affairs?"

Paula threw her a glance and nodded.

"Mother didn't really mean it, Paula. Like you didn't mean what you said. Furthermore, you might as well know, Bob kissed me last night."

"How was it?" Paula gave Barbara a sidelong look and saw a shyness come over her.

"He was so sweet. I was surprised."

"That's nice. You two get along so well, it's perfectly natural that you'd enjoy necking."

"I was really surprised, Paula. I hadn't expected it!"

"Oh, I see!"

"No, you don't see. He has a girl back home, and besides, he's too young for me and I'm not ready to think of someone else...."

"Never mind, Barbara. No harm done. Just stop dating him and do something else. Practical, I mean. Go into politics, why don't you?"

"Politics! Who me? That's more your kettle of fish."

"When I was a little girl I wanted to be a State Senator like my Uncle Paul, but when I grew up I realized what I wanted most was a family of my own. Nevertheless, you and I could serve on the election board in the coming election."

"That's nothing," Barbara scoffed. "A beginning, you'll say. But you know we can't really do anything worthwhile. At bottom you know that's the way it is."

"Yes, I know that," Paula said, simmering. Then vehemently, "But it isn't really true! It is our duty as citizens to work for good government even if it's only on the precinct level. You could run for Postmistress. You ought to consider that." Then she giggled again. "It could be very interesting knowing what's going on all over town."

"It's all so boring!" Barbara's voice was dry, her mouth turned down.

"It seems just the opposite to me," Paula declared. "Look at the drastic, exciting wars men always manage to bring off. I think things are going to be different after this war. We women have served in the WACS and WAVES, in factories and government offices, given up our men, done whatever the men wanted us to do. For what? Destruction and death! Why let them have all the responsibility for our society? Do you know half the women don't even vote and the other half usually votes the way their husbands do? Women just don't seem to understand how important their votes are!"

Barbara sighed. "No man would ever listen to a woman. I think you might get some place, Paula, with your name and ability. You surely made a good Senior Class president and know how to run things. Why don't *you*...?" She broke off, biting her lip. Then she said softly, "You could do that, maybe, but I hope you'll have the family you want."

Paula turned to her, eyes wistful with a tender longing. "Barbara," she said with a penetrating intensity, "did you know when Jim was killed?"

Barbara's hazel eyes lighted with the new thought of prescience on her part, something she had never aspired to.

Paula went on to explain. "I knew when Garner crashed into the English Channel, was full of pain and cold, oh so cold out in that dinghy bouncing up and down. But now I...I...can't..."

Barbara touched her arm in a comforting gesture. "No," she said quietly, "I never knew when Jim was killed. I didn't feel anything. That's why it was such a shock when I received the notice."

They exchanged heartfelt looks of deep understanding in an empathy to be remembered, a holy communion.

Relieved that maybe she was not so remiss, Paula once again gave her attention to the road. In a small voice, she said, "I didn't feel anything about Garner this time. I thought something was wrong with me or...or maybe he's forgotten me."

"Oh, no, Paula! You mustn't think that. Most people aren't psychic or intuitive like you. There'll be lots of times when you won't know what's going on with Garner. That's only natural. We always want a complete union with our loves and for that wonderful union to be continuous and forever. But that's a dream and sadly, impossible here on earth." She paused, then admitted, "I've had to realize this the hard way."

"Yes, and you've made me realize it, too," Paula replied sympathetically. "I expect it's what's called growing up." Then she mentioned that they would soon be at the Lazy S.

She probed the distances, the sunny grandeur of earth and sky become one, and anticipated the cool wind on her face during her ride on the range.

"I brought a couple of sweaters. They're in the back seat. Take your choice and we'll put them on when we get out of the car."

She saw the new windmill about a mile off in the distance. Burl must have managed to trace the underground stream and bring the windmill in much closer to the house from the spot where Shep had made his discovery.

As she swung into the lane leading to the ranch house, she thought how fortunate she was to have two good, dependable friends like Barbara and Burl. Relaxed and feeling at home, she slowed to a stop at the barnyard gate, where Burl, waiting for them, waved a welcome.

The girls jumped out and put on their cardigans, red for Barbara and blue for Paula. Then Paula rushed over to Burl.

"How do you like my nifty automobile?" she bragged. He tipped his black Stetson and grinned at her.

"It's a nice piece of machinery, but it cain't compare with a real live horse," he told her. Then he glanced at Barbara, who was lagging behind. "Hi, Barbara! Glad to see you all. I've got the horses for you. Ready to ride?" He became suddenly serious and searched Paula's face. She saw concern reflected in his eyes and was afraid she seemed somewhat drawn, somehow older. There were traces of grief in his face from the suffering over his father's death. She was genuinely happy to see him and gave him a reassuring smile.

Then laughing at herself, she cautioned, "I'm not sure I can ride any more, Burl. It's been so long. And I did have my heart set on Old Red. But I know how rambunctious he can get. You can always trust a cow pony to give you a wild ride. Want to look over my Willys?"

"Oh, yeah. Later," he said. "I'll ride along with you. Ol' Red takes his job seriously, sometimes even when he's not on the job. Maybe another horse'd be better, but we wouldn't need to race."

"How about you, Barbara?" Paula asked. "You want to ride?" Barbara seemed so noncommittal that for a moment, Paula almost wished she had not asked her to come.

"A mare will do," Barbara finally responded. "I need something gentle and not too anxious to go, if you know what I mean."

"Right this way," Burl drawled. "It just so happens I've chosen a fine mare for you." He opened the gate and they followed him into the corral. "It's Summer. She likes women because she's a lady, herself."

He brought a four year old Palomino out of the barn and offered the reins to Barbara. She took them and stroked the horse's silky muzzle, looking into her large dark eye. A beauty! Her ivory mane flowing as smooth as taffy, she looked as though she had been recently curried, and the saddle on her back was cinched and ready.

"Oh, she's lovely!" Barbara murmured. "Summer and I'll make a good pair."

Paula smiled at Burl, pleased with her friend's display of pleasure.

Satisfied, Burl retreated into the barn again and returned, leading a golden Palomino proud as a Thoroughbred, with white stockings on all four feet, the creamy tail and mane gallantly flowing, face perfectly blazed, head up, alert, ears prick, intelligent brown eyes regarding Paula. She gasped. This must be Lightning Streak, the Lazy S's prize stock stud!

Burl halted the horse before her and stood, a man as fine and proud as his horse, smiling at her, inviting her pleasure. Caught by surprise, Paula was overwhelmed by his male presence. So attractive! Shy, she turned her head. Burl waited, triumph steaming at a boil, for glory! she perceived him in a new light, as a suitor for the first time. Slowly, she lifted her eyes and gazed into his. He smiled again, proposing, showing white even teeth. Instinctively, she knew a barrier would be breached if she accepted this offering. Yet she was drawn to the handsome pair, the beauty of Lightning Streak and the noble generosity of the man. How could she refuse? She mentally shook herself, trying to back away from the brink.

Barbara mounted Summer with a bit of trouble, and this movement brought Paula back to reality, to safety.

She smiled at Burl and said quietly, "I couldn't. I'm not up to it. Thank you, but I'd rather take my chances on Old Red."

"Whatever you say," he said genially, displaying no disappointment. But Paula saw the secret rejoicing in his blue eyes and knew he was elated to have made an impression on her at long last. He moved to the fence and tied the stallion near her. "I'll get Red for you."

Paula patted Lightning Streak. *It's been nine months since I've seen Garner. How much longer will I have to wait? Indefinitely?*

"I'm goin' on out," Barbara called. "I'm so slow, you and Burl will catch up with me in no time."

"All right!" Paula replied. She watched her command the mare and ride off at a walk across the corral and on out through the open gate to the wide west range. Her mood changed. She talked nonsense to the horse, glad to be here on the ranch once more, but aware that she must be careful around its owner.

Then Burl came leading the big roan and she ran to greet him. He remembered her, whinnying in greeting, nuzzling her, nearly knocking her off her feet with his large head bobbing up and down.

"Hey, take it easy, Red Cowpony!" She threw her arms around his neck and gave him a big hug. "How are you, Old Red?" she murmured in his ear, and he settled down.

Soon they were on the range breezily aware of the horse scent, the warmth and might of their mounts, galloping swift as the wind. Paula, caught up in the exhilaration of it, was free. Free of all cares, doubts, desires, sorrow, loneliness—only aware of the joy in the ride, the rhythm and feel of Old Red under her, running his heart out for her, Burl beside her on Lightning Streak.

A rabbit flashed its white tail up ahead in Red's path. He wheeled. Paula slipped off to one side, dangling, desperately hanging on, the rough sage grabbing at her.

Oh, I see! I'm falling!

Suddenly, in an explosion of energy, she pulled herself upright, and in command, regained her seat in the saddle. Full of self-confidence, she laughed at the look of anxiety on Burl's face as he reined up beside her and grabbed the bridle.

"I'm just fine!" she panted. "Old Red's got all the power and quickness he always had! But I can handle him!"

She was jubilant.

And I can handle myself! I'll take charge of my life as I've done with Old Red. No matter what my mother or anyone else says, as soon as Garner comes home, we'll start our family. I feel it in my bones! He's coming home! He's on his way!

All of her old optimism, her independence, her courage flooded back. Laughing, she struck Old Red on the rump and challenged Burl. "Let's race!"

Chapter Twenty-Eight

Hands folded behind his back, his pale crew cut standing up in alarm, Colonel McIntyre paced up and down in front of Paula's desk, the staccato thumps of his worried steps overriding the roar of trainer planes. This show of nervousness was so unlike the Commanding Officer that it disturbed Paula. When she had come into the office and found him upset, she had quietly taken her place at the typewriter and made herself small, filing and bringing the charts up-to-date.

"This whole base will go to hell if we don't do something quick!" the C.O. declared. Tech. Sergeant Quinn, standing near a filing cabinet with one drawer open, turned and said, "Yes, Sir! What's the trouble?"

"We're losing our good Flight Instructors. Lieutenant Borden's gone and now Lieutenant Morrison's going overseas. Too many pilots killed in action! They're taking our best men and we don't have any career men to fill their slots."

"Yes Sir! We sure do need good instructors," the sergeant commiserated. He put away a file folder, closed the drawer, and gave the C.O. his full attention. "What we should do is get some of our returning pilots to sign up for another tour of duty, Sir." The colonel gave him a piercing look, then crossed over to his desk and sat down.

"You're right, Sergeant! But the pilots experienced in battle want nothing to do with the Air Corps. They're eager to get on with their lives as civilians. And those who want a job aren't qualified, being casualties one way or another. I'm afraid the pickings're nonexistent."

"Just the same, we've got to try."

Colonel McIntyre asked Paula to take a letter. He dictated a request to the Commanding Officer of the Central Flying Training Command for two experienced pilots to be transferred to Goodfellow Field as Flight Instructors. In the second paragraph, he explained his dilemma and the importance of securing these men as soon as possible. Paula had heard rumors that too many pilots were being lost due to inadequate training. She hoped Colonel McIntyre's request would be granted and Goodfellow could maintain its high standards.

Attrition of pilots and their crews had been disastrous these past three years. A full account was not given in news reports, yet the people were aware of what was going on due to their own grievous losses. There was scarcely a street in the country that didn't have a gold star in the window for a son or husband lost in the war, and a good number of those came from the Air Corps contingents.

Paula did not dwell on this, but she avoided looking at the windows of the houses she passed, either while walking or driving down the street. She didn't want a gold star in her window, not that she had a front window in her coop apartment. The day of Colonel McIntyre's letter of request to the CFTC was no different, except that this Wednesday in early December 1944, she wished Garner could have been one of those pilots the C.O. needed. But Garner was a bomber pilot, not an instructor, and he was still missing in action.

With the glimmer of a lost opportunity for her husband's safety, she felt his absence all the more keenly that evening. After dinner, she pulled out the two old shoe boxes she kept under her clothes in the closet opposite the bed. One box contained V-Mail from Garner. The other box held her own letters to him, unmailed for lack of a sending address. She had labeled the latter, Hope Missiles, a humorous epithet for Missives, because she aimed to keep faith that somehow Garner would receive her messages through clairvoyance.

The letters to her husband increased her faith and her secret hopes. They gave her a close connection with him and she planned to give them to him when he returned. She had faith that so long as she continued to write Hope Missiles, Garner was a part of her, aware of her, and he would irresistibly be drawn back home, back to her arms where he belonged.

Besides these earnest aspirations, Paula's letters were an attempt to keep Garner informed about important political events, and this evening, since she was downhearted, she gave only good news. While Mary sat propped up with pillows, reading a Pocketbook novel on the bed, Paula sat at the small kitchen table and wrote her letter:

Dec. 12, 1944

Darling,

Everything is going well here with relief from the summer heat and a tinge of winter in the air. I hope it is not too cold where you are.Please remember to keep dry and warm for me. It's about time you had a Home Leave and I hope you'll be back soon. Then you can bask in our warm Texas sunshine and feel good all over. You must hear the big news.Our hopes have risen to the skies. President Wilson lives again! Last Monday a news report said that forty-four nations have written a draft for the charter of a future United Nations.

We are all hopeful for a better future for the whole world after this war is over. There are also plans for a National Monetary Fund and an International Bank for Reconstruction and Development, so the big-wigs really think the war will soon be over.

Mary and I are still serving at the USO and Barbara is coming out of herself. She's been dating some. In the meantime, when we're home, we listen to Mary's records. This is a great substitute for the war news. I just love Glenn Miller and the Modernaires, especially "Chattanooga Choo-Choo" and his dreamy theme song, "Moonlight Serenade." I couldn't make it without Glenn Miller.

By the way, have I mentioned before that Churchill and Roosevelt have decided to switch their efforts to the Pacific Theater? That proves they think Germany will surrender soon and you'll be coming home to me. I miss you terribly and send all my love and then some.

Your ever loving wife,
Paula

After she signed the letter, she folded it, put it in the Hope Missile box, and read some of Garner's old letters. This practice brought great comfort.

The days passed with the Allies advancing in Germany from the west, while the Russians invaded from the east. Colonel McIntyre had accepted the assignment of one new pilot as Flight Instructor, but he still lacked an adequate staff, which caused Paula to wish all the more for a miracle, a chance for Garner to fill that vacancy.

While at home the following Saturday morning, the phone rang and Mary answered it.

"It's Burl," she said, as she handed the receiver to Paula.

"Hi, honey! Glad I caught you at home!" His intimate voice gave Paula a pleasant sense of his claim upon her. It was reassuring to belong, to have someone who cared, a dependable man like Burl. "Shep and I'd like for you to come out for a T-bone steak dinner and cheer up this lonely old place. Say about two o'clock?"

"I'm sorry, Burl. Barbara has asked me out to lunch. She might be thinking of getting engaged."

"You don't say!" Burl paused at the news. "Maybe you could come afterwards for a ride out on the range."

"No, it'll be too late for that."

"Well, some other time, then. Hope Barbara's not on the rebound. Tell her hello for me."

Paula was glad she had an excuse. In her own loneliness, she might have succumbed to Burl's masculine charm. His attentions were certainly tempting, although no doubt quite innocent, or if not innocent, at least honorable.

Paula still took the bus to work and saved her gas coupons for errands around town. Her gas tank was nearly full when, with Christmas imminent, she decided to call on Bonnie to make plans for the holiday with their folks and to take her shopping. As she drove down the street, she congratulated herself once again on the car's purchase, enjoying the freedom it afforded. A black laborador suddenly ran in front of her and she jammed on the brakes. The dog stopped just short of the front wheel and ran back to where it had come from. Relieved, Paula drove on to Bonnie's house.

When she turned into the driveway, she was surprised to see a truck parked in front of the garage and wondered if Bonnie had bought it. She ran up the front steps and entered the living room without knocking, calling, "Bonnie, are you here?"

Then she saw Bonnie and Burl in animated conversation, little Doug at play on the floor between them. They looked up in surprise.

"Hi, Paula!" Bonnie greeted. Burl rose to offer her a chair.

Paula wavered. A shaft of jealousy assailed her, making her vulnerable.

"My, you're quiet," Bonnie said with a smile. "Come on in."

"I was just surprised to see Burl," Paula said frankly. "I thought maybe you'd bought yourself a truck." That sounded foolish and she covered her embarrassment by accepting the chair.

Burl sat down again. "I was in town for a meeting of our ranchers association at the St. Angeles and dropped by to see if Bonnie needed any help with the house. You know, with Ralph gone, someone needs to look after his little wife." He gave a broad smile, causing Paula to wince inwardly.

"Yes," Bonnie said. "He put in a new light bulb for me back in my sewing room. It was too high for me to reach, even with a chair."

"Just the opposite for me," Paula remarked, "not that I have a sewing room."

After Burl left, Bonnie said in a comforting way, "Burl was just being neighborly, Paula."

"I know that," she answered testily, chagrinned that her possessiveness was so apparent. It had sometimes occurred to her that Burl could of his own volition become interested in another woman. But not Bonnie. And why not? She'd been crazy about him and Ralph might not return from the Pacific. Once again, she was faced with her own dependence upon him for back-up security, necessary because a woman without a man was no woman at all.

※

Christmas Day arrived and Paula still had not heard from the War Department about Garner.

The winter holiday was a clear, bright day at a temperature commonly called suit weather. The poinsettia plant beside Paula's front door was more beautiful than any greenhouse plant, standing two feet tall with bouquets of long red leaves symbolizing the joy of Christmas. Delighted, Paula gave it a drink before she carried gift packages to the Willys and drove off to celebrate with her family. Mary was already over at her father's home.

When Paula entered the Roncourt house, she took a sniff, savoring the aroma of roast turkey, pumpkin pie and Parker House rolls, exclaiming, "Hmmnnn!" Then she noticed the synthetic Christmas tree standing before the front window, brilliant in colorful, twinkling lights and decorated with shiny baubles and icicles.

Bonnie came to help with her packages and to take her coat. When it was revealed that Paula was wearing a bright red dress and Bonnie dressed in green of the same intensity, they laughed at their appropriate Christmas colors.

Smiling cheerfully, Floyd Roncourt started to rise from his easy chair.

"Don't get up!" Paula said. She kissed her father on his bald head and wished him a Merry Christmas. He returned the greeting and told her she was just in time for dinner.

It was so good to be home! Paula relished every bit of the wonderful roast turkey and giblet dressing, candied yams, cranberry sauce, whipped potatoes and gravy, and the dessert of pumpkin pie and ice cream, so different from Depression times.

After dinner, they were gathering around the tree for the exchange of gifts when someone knocked at the front door. Floyd opened it to Burl Stein, alight with Christmas cheer, sharp in black and white cowboy togs.

"Come in! Come in!" Floyd invited, his jovial face showing pleasant surprise.

"I was in town and just wanted to say Merry Christmas!" Burl replied. He advanced in the room and went up to Paula. "I have a little something here for your tree." She smiled in spite of herself, as he tugged at something that seemed caught in his pants pocket. "It's his legs," Burl said.

Then he jerked it loose, pulled it out, and handed it to her. His legs indeed! It was the figure of Old Red, who was a long legged horse, done in roan colored cowhide, smooth muscled, mane and tail in darker strips. Paula set it up on the palm of her hand and held it out for everyone to see.

"Old Red!" she exclaimed. Its features were carved in a remarkable resemblance to her favorite cowpony.

Burl smiled down at her. "He's as much your horse as mine, I reckon."

She glanced up at him with appreciation for this generous thought, meeting his gaze for an instant. "It's a real work of art. Did you make it?"

"One of my Mexican hired hands showed me how," he said.

"It's a fine figurine. Thanks, Burl. It'll make a unique addition to our hand crafted ornaments." *If I won't come to you and Old Red, you'll bring him to me.*

There was an awkward pause between them and Esther Roncourt hastened to cover it. She took the small ornament and hung it on the tree. "You've done a good job on Old Red, now let's see you do justice to some Christmas cheer. Paula, give Burl a cup of eggnog."

Paula served the traditional drink laced with bourbon and offered him a chair beside her father. During his visit, it seemed to her that Burl's presence filled the room. He was large in every way, in his openness as a rancher, in his tawny good health and tall strength as a Texan, and most assuredly in his pure integrity. Burl was steadfast. He'd loved her since he was fifteen. Perhaps she'd always thought of him as that awkward teenager. Now she knew he was a mature man. A strong desire for him to stay surged up in disappointment when he rose to leave. She accompanied him to the door and thanked him again for dropping by and for the replica of Old Red.

"He's waiting for you," Burl prompted. "Give me a ring any time and we'll have ourselves a good ride!"

"Maybe I'll just do that," she responded. Then they said good-bye and she closed the door and sat down on the floor with Bonnie to distribute the presents.

Paula looked at Old Red hanging on the end of a twig nearby and a sadness gripped her, a feeling of lost childhood, a lost happiness, which could never return.

Her father, sensing her mood, turned on the radio for some Christmas carols and handed her a flat package wrapped in shiny, dark blue paper tied with a silver bow. "This is for you from Mom and me," he said with a smile.

"It's special!" she cried. "I just know it. But I hate to unwrap this gorgeous paper!"

"Go ahead," her mother said.

Paula carefully pulled the Scotch tape away and took off the wrapping. When she saw the black leather box and the name, Windsor-Newton, in gold letters, she lifted her gaze to her mother in disbelief, tears starting. She ducked, then looked up again.

"Ten colors!" she exclaimed. "I've always wanted these fine English oils. I couldn't bring myself to paint Garner's portrait with those cheap oils I have. But now I can paint a portrait that will last forever." She held up the box for Bonnie and Douglas to see. "Oh, Mom and Dad, this is the greatest gift I've ever received. My first painting with these oils will be for you."

They smiled at her and at one another in satisfaction.

Bonnie was offering Paula a chocolate, when the music stopped. A baritone voice broke in over the sound of a teletype machine:

LADIES AND GENTLEMEN, WE INTERRUPT THIS PROGRAM. A NEWS BULLETIN HAS JUST COME IN. MAJOR GLENN MILLER, FAMOUS BAND LEADER, IS MISSING OVER THE ENGLISH CHANNEL. THERE IS NO OTHER WORD AT THIS TIME. WE REPEAT, MAJOR GLENN MILLER IS MISSING OVER THE ENGLISH CHANNEL. THIS IS NBC IN NEW YORK. WE NOW RETURN YOU TO YOUR LOCAL STATION.

The family gasped as one.
Floyd shook his head. "Too bad!"
They looked at one another in dismay.

Paula was stunned. Glenn Miller missing! Miller, not even in combat! Garner missing over Holland! Garner, a USAAC pilot in the war! He was missing, shot down, killed, and no one knew where!

Garner, my love, my life! Garner is gone!

She covered her face with her hands and burst into tears.

Chapter Twenty-Nine

The USO was crowded and noisy on New Year's Day, 1945.
Since Mary was visiting friends, Paula took refuge there all day. More and more of the new cadets were fresh out of high school and barely eighteen. To her, they seemed mere children. Perhaps it was because she was growing old beyond her years.

For days a determined search was being made for Glenn Miller. The search extended over a wide swath of miles criss-cross over the Channel. No sign of him or his plane was ever found. He had been on a mission to play for the troops. Empty handed, Americans were all the more grieved, disturbed over his mysterious disappearance and their senseless loss. He was a personal hero to so many, this fine, talented gentleman who devotedly strove to give a new sound, a new music for the enjoyment of his people. A bright star had been extinguished, dimming the hearts of millions of listeners and dancers. There would never be another Glenn Miller.

Paula suffered a dark, subterranean trepidation. Glenn Miller's loss increased her continuous unease about Garner.

It was possible that he was still alive, but she had received no 'message' from him. She had no feeling that he was alive, no knowledge of where he might be. If he were in a prison camp, he could be undergoing brutal treatment, maybe torture, and he would certainly be on short rations, near starvation, near death.

But maybe when he crashed on Dutch soil, he was immediately discovered and shot to death, stripped of his uniform, his boots, and even his dog tags, then his body dumped out of sight in a ditch somewhere or seriously wounded, or he may have been able to crawl to a place undercover in a drain pipe, or in some bushes, and there, unseen, he could have died all alone. His death would have been full of agony and sorrow so far away from home, unable to see his loved ones and tell them good-bye, unable to know whether or not his wife, his mother and sister, both of whom were in the service, were safe and well, unable to protect them any longer, and denied in his inglorious death, a decent burial in his homeland. How bitter! How burdensome his trials, no matter where he was or if he had already died.

Though she knew not the exact toll, his burdens were her burdens. These she must carry in her heart until the mystery of his whereabouts was solved. And if this were never revealed? She put that thought aside and concentrated on pouring a glass of milk for a cadet from Iowa.

※

With the passing of time, Paula's connections with her friends from the University had become more tenuous. She'd lost track of Don O'Grady over a year ago when he was somewhere in the Pacific Theater. And as for her mentor, Prof. Sheldon Brown, he had long since given up placing any of his or her own paintings with dealers or in museums. He had taken on the added responsibilities of assisting in the acquisition of European masterpieces from financially stressed refugees who had escaped from France and Italy with limited funds and a few of their precious art treasures.

American art museums were not buying native art. It was imperative to save what could be gleaned of the European lode. Professor Brown had placed Paula's "The Fairy Dance" with an art dealer in Dallas, but after a year when it did not sell, he withdrew it and brought it home, where he hung it in the Arts and Sciences Library of the University. He had placed a price tag on it of three hundred dollars, but thus far, no buyer had appeared.

He and Paula exchanged Christmas cards and he had been quite sympathetic at the news of Garner's Missing In Action status.

WILD BLUE, First of a series 309

On a Saturday, two weeks after Glenn Miller's disappearance, Paula was home when the mail came. Mary was out. Paula was thrilled to see a letter from the Art Department of the University and she hastened to open it without taking off her coat. She spread out the letter and read:

January 6, 1945

Dear Mrs. Cameron:

It is with deep regret and sorrow that we must inform you of Prof. Sheldon Brown's sudden death. He died of a heart attack a week ago at the early age of forty-five.

Paula sank into the chair at the kitchen table, the letter falling from her hands. She sat shocked, the blood rushing from her face, leaving her pale and distraut. Prof. Brown dead! Her heart palpitated and she panted for breath. Without any warning, a part of her was excised. She couldn't think. The man's light extinguished! He was gone! But this couldn't be! No noise, no fanfare, nothing left of his innate creativity, his knowledge. What a dreadful loss! She picked up the letter again and read through blurred eyesight in blind disbelief:

We have learned that the oil painting,"The Fairy Dance," which has been hanging in the hall of the Arts and Sciences Library for some time, belongs to you. We feel sure Professor Brown would want the painting returned to you. Please be assured that it will be well protected in a wooden crate. The Trailways Bus will transfer it to San Angelo C.O.D. We have given them your name, address and telephone number and they will notify you of its arrival within five days.

Yours truly,
Byron Bergstrom
Byron Bergstrom, Dean

It was all so terribly official. In anguished rage, Paula jerked up, shoving the chair back, and started to tear up the letter. Then she stopped herself. This would not undo the damage. What must Mrs. Brown be going through? She must be under shock.

Forcing herself to calm down, Paula took off her coat and hung it up. Impulsively, she looked up the telephone number of the Brown home and put in a long distance call.

Mrs. Brown answered and Paula gave her heartfelt commiseration, explaining that she'd just learned of Professor Brown's passing.

"It's good of you to call, Paula," Mrs. Brown said. "A couple of days ago I got a letter off to you. Since you haven't received it today, I'm sure you'll get it Monday. Sheldon wrote it to you for a New Year's greeting before he became ill. He included a portion of that lecture you liked so well, 'The Fabric of Human Life.' He said you liked his conclusion."

"Yes, and I appreciate it so much, Mrs. Brown. I'll cherish it always. I'll miss him so much! His art and his teaching will be my inspiration for the rest of my life."

After a few more words, they hung up. Paula ordered a basket of spring flowers to be sent to Mrs. Brown, along with a sympathy card.

Mary was a comfort, helping Paula deal with the shock of her grievous loss. On Monday, she received her mentor's letter and gained consolation from his wisdom and loving-kindness.

Mary sat down across the table from Paula and asked, "Read it out loud for me, will you, please? I'd like to hear it, too."

"All right. I think it's something everyone could learn from," Paula said. Then she read aloud:

The Fabric of Human Life

Art forms the fabric of human life.

An artist's soul is hidden in clouds of color and strata of drifts and lines, angles and swirls, in depth of thought. Thought is transposed to the hand in drafting answer to the spirit's urgings.

How is this spiritual made physical? But if not made physical, how can humanity apprehend the spirit surging within the hidden soul's delight? If it be the artist's hand with brushes of color or the musician's fingers plucking aural tones, or yet the writer's dreams translated into printed words, is it not the spirit made physical? The spirit reaches humanity thus, answering its deepest needs, replenishing its joy, its understanding of life, its direction and purpose. The physical, spirit filled, is honored, raised to a transcendent height.

The transcendent laughter, sorrow, compassion, elation, joy, and sense of completion are emotion-spirit speaking to our peace. The perfect union of the physical and spiritual brings the peace of equilibrium floating free. There is no strain. For humankind there can be no satisfaction without the affirmative spiritual expression in the physical. This is the healing power of the arts. Every individual is an artist. The expression of any personal artform is an unconditional right to the triumphant life that draws upon this wholesome peace.

Art forms the fabric of human life, the artist its interpreter and master. Without art there is no culture, no civilization. The artist is worth more, far more than his or her weight in gold.

The artist is the priceless human gold.

Mary was thoughtful when Paula had finished reading.
Paula asked, "Now you see why I revere him so?"
Mary nodded. "He means the artist is the most valuable person of all."
The phrase ran through Paula's mind. The most valuable of all. *The most valuable—Garner Cameron, Glenn Miller, Sheldon Brown. All lost! Gone! The most valuable of all!*
Suddenly her protective shock cocoon was disrupted, split asunder.

She stared at Mary, unseeing, a wild, other-worldly, eerie light in her eyes. The letter dropped from her hands.

Frightened, Mary drew in her breath. Something had happened...was happening to her roommate.

Paula sat immobile, somewhere off in another world.

"Paula!" Mary cried.

Paula came to herself and gazed at her friend. Then she burst into tears in racking sobs, her body shaking in convulsive waves. Dismayed, Mary got up and led her to the bed.

"Here," she said, "you need some rest. You've been through so much."

Mary had never seen Paula like this before. Attempts at comforting went unnoticed. Inconsolable in her anguish, Paula continued to sob, spinning down, down into a deep depression. More and more frightened, Mary stood by, inert, watching. She knew Paula needed help of a kind she could not give, yet she must do something. Flashes of the hospital crossed her mind but she didn't want that for Paula.

Finally, she went to the telephone and called Bonnie. She answered after the second ring.

"Bonnie! Paula's on the verge of a nervous breakdown! I can't do anything with her!"

"Hold the fort! I'll be right over!"

Nervous, but relieved, Mary told Paula, "Bonnie's coming. I know you'll be glad to see her."

But Paula, out of her senses, didn't hear a word. She contimued sobbing as though without reason, without knowing why, just sobbing, unable to stop.

Bonnie soon came, bringing her little boy, Douglas. When she saw Paula, she swooped her up into her warm bosom, hugging her close, tight, like she'd never let her go. "Let it all out, honey," she crooned. "Cry all you want. You can come home with me and Douglas and stay with us for awhile."

Paula, still torn by wrenching sobs, was like a rag doll. She allowed Bonnie to get her up into a sitting position slumped over and stayed there, limp, while her sister got out her overnight bag. Mary helped her pack a few things and cosmetics for a short visit.

Then Bonnie led Paula out to the truck, with Douglas following, and they drove off to her house.

The baby was a welcome distraction for both of the young women, bringing a welcome breath of innocent life into their midst. Bonnie allowed Paula to sleep late the next morning, while she prepared a light luncheon for her.

Paula picked at her food, but tasted some of the gelatin salad. She was mute, unsmiling, steeped in the realization that her life was over. Her husband gone, her career lost, nothing left but death.

"Paula, Douglas surely likes this cherry pie," Bonnie said.

"Pie, pie!" Douglas cried, waving his spoon about.

"I made it just for you, because it's your favorite."

Paula looked up and saw Bonnie and Douglas for the first time. Douglas spooned a bite and thrust it at her. "Bite!" he exclaimed. "Bite pie! Good pie!"

Paula looked at him and Bonnie was glad he'd caught her attention.

"Aunt Paula doesn't want your piece of pie," she said, "But thank you just the same. Here!" She placed a piece before Paula. "This is for you."

"Thank you," Paula said. It looked tempting but her stomach wasn't normal somehow. Maybe one cherry. She took her fork and put one cherry in her mouth and slowly chewed.

Bonnie was cheered by this overt action, the beginning of a return to normalcy. "You haven't died, honey," she said. "You're just as wonderful an artist as ever. Remember that. You never had to depend upon your professor or anyone else to produce marvelous paintings. Yours is the talent and nobody can ever take it away from you."

Tears began to fall from Paula's eyes again, making Bonnie sorry she'd spoken. She jumped up. "I know what'll do you good!" She crossed to the refrigerator and got out a bottle of Coca Cola and poured it into a glass over ice. "Here! Try this. It'll fizz away those tears!"

Paula chuckled through her tears. "You're so funny, Bonnie!"

Bonnie laughed and Douglas laughed with her. "Funny! Funny!" he cried.

"Yes, we're all funny," Bonnie said, laughing. She sat down again and watched Paula sip the bubbly concoction. Then she said soberly, "I have an important request."

"What is it?"

"I've always hesitated before, but now is a good time, I think. I'd like for you to paint a portrait of Douglas for me. He's two years old, a darling age, and I do so want a portrait of him."

Paula's eyes widened. "I couldn't! He wouldn't hold still long enough for me and besides, I don't know how to do a portrait of a child's baby face."

"I wouldn't care what you do or how you paint it," Bonnie protested. "I just know it would be beautiful and it's something I'd always have, no matter whatever happened to Douglas."

Or Ralph.

Paula's gaze swung from Bonnie to Douglas at this thought, then back to her sister. Bonnie was looking at her, penetrating, piercing her heart. If Garner is truly gone, Paula thought, I'll not even have a picture of our little boy. *What little boy?*

Her great blue eyes, muril, saw Bonnie, her plain common sense, her wisdom, always following her instinct instead of planning every little thing about her life the way she did.

With her gaze fastened on her sister, she said, "You were right, Bonnie. You have Douglas and I have no one. Nothing."

"Oh Paula!"

"No, you're right. I was wrong all along. If Garner ever does come home, I'll let nothing stop me. I'll get pregnant right away. Nothing in life is certain, especially life itself."

They sat silently communing with deep emotion, acknowledging that their husbands were both off at war.

Then Paula spoke again. "All right, I'll try to do Douglas' portrait for you. Bring him over next Saturday afternoon and I'll see what I can do."

They made arrangements for Bonnie to bring Douglas and also his photograph, which Paula could use in a pinch. Working at her palette once again helped her to slowly regain her passion for her art and to restore confidence in her talent.

When Paula was notified of the return of her masterpiece, she was thankful she had the Willys in which to pick it up. Her mother had told her she could put it above the piano or the buffet in the living room at her home, where she would keep it until she had a place for it of her own.

Mrs. Roncourt helped her hang it above the piano and was pleased that the colors harmonized with the blue of her decor.

"Honey," she said, "I think you should keep this painting for yourself. You've sold "The Button Box" and you should have some of your own paintings, especially this one, your masterpiece."

Paula regarded her with a serious look, but remained quiet.

Esther Roncourt surveyed the painting again. In a hushed voice, she said, "I don't know where you got such an idea, but this painting is extraordinarily beautiful. Amazing!"

On impulse, Paula said, "Mom, I'm going to make a copy of Douglas' portrait for you and Dad. And by the way, I'm glad you like my masterpiece."

She smiled to herself.

The fairies of the four year old child she had once been were embodiments of her secret dream, a dream that was real, but hers alone. Everyone needs a private, sublime secret, she mused.

Chapter Thirty

Paula and Mary had stopped playing Glenn Miller records because they were still grieved over his tragic loss. Once in awhile they played a crazy Spike Jones "Tea For Two," but most of their spare time was spent at the USO.

One Saturday afternoon at home alone, Paula worked at her easel, shading in the round chin of her nephew in oils, when a knock came at the door. She opened it to a Western Union delivery boy. "Telegram for Mrs. Cameron," he announced.

Her heart plunged with fear, but she smiled and asked, "Where do I sign?" He handed her the telegram.

"Here, ma'am," The boy held out a blank form on a clipboard and she signed her name in the proper space. He wheeled away on his bicycle and she closed the door. Her nerves tightened and vibrated in a rigor she could not control. She leaned against the door, unable to look at the yellow envelope. Mary isn't here to read it this time. I must open it and read it all by myself.

She took deep inhalations to make her heart stop pounding so hard. Nothing she could do would change the message now. She quickly brought the envelope up and looked at it, marveling that her trembling hand obeyed her will. There was no black border! Who could have sent it? She tore open the envelope and pulled out the telegram.

U.S. WAR DEPARTMENT   18 JAN 1945

WE ARE PLEASED TO INFORM YOU THAT YOUR HUSBAND 2ND LT. GARNER DAVIS CAMERON HAS BEEN FOUND WITH AMERICAN ARMY TROOPS SAFE AND SOUND IN NORTHERN GERMANY STOP TELEGRAM FOLLOWS.

Tears of relief streamed down her face. Then she whooped for joy. *HAPPY NEW YEAR! BETTER LATE THAN NEVER!*
My Hope Missiles have struck home!
Garner is safe and sound!
Paula danced around, waving the telegram, kissing it, and whirling about till she finally settled down. She poured a bubbly soda and held the glass out high above her head. "To Lieutenant Garner Cameron, the greatest pilot in the whole USAAC!" she proclaimed aloud. Then she called her mother and father and Bonnie and gave them the good news.
On Monday, January 20, while at home, Paula received another telegram.

U.S. WAR DEPARTMENT   20 JAN 1945
2ND LT. GARNER DAVIS CAMERON IS GRANTED A SIXTY-DAY HOME LEAVE FROM COMBAT DUTY STOP HE WILL ARRIVE AT GOODFELLOW FIELD ON TUES 21 JAN AT 1400 HOURS

TUESDAY! TUESDAY! OUR GOOD LUCK DAY!
HE'LL BE HOME TWO WHOLE MONTHS!

Sixty days and nights! Paula was in ecstacy, rapt with anticipation. Then she stopped. Where will we stay?
It would be too much trouble to buy furniture and set up housekeeping in an apartment at Goodfellow before they knew Garner's assignment after his Home Leave. They could stay with her folks at first and then Goodfellow later. The C.O. needed Lieutenant Cameron. She needed him. Paula was seized by a palpable euphoria in which she dreamed of connubial bliss. They would be really,

truly married! They would live right here in San Angelo, both working out at the field until the war was over. It would be heaven, baby and all.

Then she caught a glimpse of Garner's portrait standing in its folder on top of the refrigerator. There he was, the handsome, sober young brunette pilot in his fleece lined brown leather cap with flaps down, a white scarf overlapped at the throat of his sheep lined leather jacket. She crossed the room, picked up the photograph, and searched his likeness, looking into those black eyes to see if he was anyone she knew. He had noble features, his mouth carved to perfection, his nose straight, forehead high, denoting intelligence, and a charming cleft in the chin. But did she really know him? She suddenly felt strange.

They had had such a whirlwind romance, a wedding before they could become very well acquainted, where their time was measured in minutes and a few meager weeks, with Garner nearly always out at the base. Their love story was quite different from the normal dating of two or three years followed by an engagement period. Their time together had been brief, passionate, hours spent in making love, while all else was forgotten in the rush of their mating. But now she was faced with reality.

She set the photograph back up in its place, feeling as sober as the young man caught in a serious pose.

I know Burl. I know who and what he is. I know his temper, his likes and dislikes, his good points and his faults. But I know very little about Garner. I must have been infatuated out of my mind.

All at once, this love she had lived for, so yearned for in her loneliness, seemed ephemeral. Could she give herself body and soul to a virtual stranger after a separation of nearly a year? Could they have anything in common? It was up to her to overcome the great gaps caused by the exigencies of war, or to ignore them and pretend they did not exist. She must be resolute. Since they were already married, she would prepare a rendezvous, a private place for their tryst on the afternoon of Garner's arrival. Her own apartment would be best. They could be undisturbed, alone together, yet in familiar surroundings, which would ease any qualms they may experience. Yet she doubted that Garner would have the same feelings as she about their conjugal reunion.

But she must not think of Burl. Then would her devotion to Garner be a mockery. She buried her misgivings by making certain that Mary would stay away from their apartment tomorrow afternoon at least until five o'clock.

The next morning at ten o'clock, the Air Inspector called Paula at her office and reported that Garner's C-47 was expected to arrive at 1410 hours. He invited her to come up to the Control Tower and watch the plane come in. Colonel McIntyre granted her the afternoon off, remarking that she'd be no good on the job, anyway.

Paula had dressed for her husband in her favorite black twill suit, fashionable with its long jacket, the pastel blue blouse with the scalloped collar, and her black and white spectator pumps. Her sexuality was evident in the shiny hair, bright red mouth and nails to match, and an inner excitement that gleamed from her dark blue eyes. The officers near her could not fathom that she had carefully painted her toenails a brilliant red to titillate her lover, yet they would not have been surprised.

She sauntered over to the cafeteria and had lunch with three other secretaries who were envious of her, not only for her good fortune to have a husband, but also for their fabulous, fairytale reunion. With knowing smiles, they wished her good luck when they parted. Paula walked on toward the Control Tower and climbed the stairs to the observation deck. She chatted leisurely with a couple of officers over an ice cold Coca Cola, their strong male presence giving her a certain calm, a reassurance.

During the hour of waiting, her excitement rose in spite of herself. Then she heard the great roaring engines above the controller's voice over the loudspeaker and saw the transport plane swoop down for a landing. Heart beating fast, she ran down the stairs out to the tarmac, forgetting the regulations. Goodfellow had no fence to keep visitors off the landing strip like the ones she'd seen in the movies. Only approved personnel were allowed on the apron, as she so well knew, yet she was there and nobody stopped her.

At a distance of several yards, she watched Garner climb down the steps from the C-47, a tall, spare figure, energetic, a seasoned officer of the USAAC. She took a deep, audible breath in an involuntary "Ohhh...!

He hurried toward her.

"Paula!"

He grabbed her and she clung to him, arms around his neck, aware of his eager embrace. They kissed for a long, fervent moment, then grinned at each other.

"Are you all right?" she murmured. He was so thin!

"Fine as frog's hair. Just hungry for you."

"No broken bones or injuries?" she persisted.

"No. I lucked out when I brought the plane down. A few scratches and bruises, that's all." He gave her a meaningful grin. "I'm all here!" Her face flushed and he drew her close again.

Paula accompanied him during his check-in with the Air inspector, then she drove him to her apartment in her little Willys. Garner was surprised at the small car, but no more surprised than she at his lean frame. As it was, she could scarcely believe that he was here sitting beside her, but he was real and eminently sane, as her mother often described her own relatives, the Crazy Reids. And they were together after nearly a year's long, torturous separation.

The apartment was a small haven, only ten feet wide and twenty feet long, but it seemed large to them, a cheerful love nest with the sunlight streaming in from the south through the narrow, horizontal window above the double bed. Paula lighted the gas oven and left its door open to take the chill off the room, apologizing for the lack of a gas heater.

Garner doffed his officer's cap and moved toward the refrigerator. "I'll put my cap up here for old times' sake," he said. Then he saw his photograph perched there. "What's this! You've relegated me to the cold perimeter of your digs?" Subconsciously wanting to please, Paula's face fell with chagrin.

"Why, no! It's the best place up high, where I can see you when I cook and do the dishes."

Garner picked up the photograph and placed it on the table in the corner beside the refrigerator. He looked at it admiringly and said, "I think I'd rather be right here, where I can talk to you whenever you sit down to eat or write or whatever you do. More on your level."

She was pleased to see that his command had not gone to his head. "Give me your jacket," she said. He obliged and she hung it up beside her own, thinking that that was where it belonged.

When she turned around, he kissed her delicate widow's peak and looked down at her oval face, drinking in the pure, translucent skin, the full red lips, and her dark blue eyes fringed with black curly lashes. She gazed at him with a clear submission, enamored by the love lighting his soul.

He took her hand. "I worship you." His rich, bass voice was melodious to her ear.

Captivated, she responded, "I love you," all misgivings forgotten.

They kissed, pressing close to one another. Soon she was lost in his deep warmth, in the wonder of his caresses, his passion shaping anew their sublime paradise. All strength left her in urgent desire.

"Garner!"

She spoke his name in pleading song and he answered with his soul and body.

※

On their first wedding anniversary, Garner surprised Paula with dinner out and a night in their nuptial room of the Concho Hotel. The furnishings were the same; the double bed, low chest of drawers, overstuffed chair and end table, with its accompanying lamp, and a straight chair, plus adjoining bath.

Garner gave Paula a wooden spoon he had carried with him in Holland and had brought home as a souvenir. She gave him a hand-tooled, leather billfold with a cowboy scene in light tan leather edged in dark brown, West Texas lacing style. He thanked her with a smile that held a trace of suspicion.

"Trying to make a Texan out of me, huh?" he drawled, pulling her down onto his lap. The easy chair squeaked, but neither took notice. She grinned openly at him.

"You could do worse!"

Once again, she'd been impressed with her husband's depth, his vision for the world and his expectations of ushering in the marvelous new epoch to come. She must protect this brilliant young man, and more than that, more than her desire for a child and family of her own, she must see to it that his lineage was not lost. The G.I. Bill had become a compelling force for their future, for it could be the means through which Garner could obtain his Engineering degree. The time was right for her to confide her dearest wish.

"Let's start our family tonight." In the dim light of the lamp, her eyes gleamed with enthusiasm. "Uncle Paul says there's still room at Texas A. & M. or at the University, but maybe all colleges will soon have to close their doors to out-of-state veterans, due to the lack of housing. You can become a Flight Instructor at first and stay right here at Goodfellow until your tour of duty is up and then enter college."

He gently set her down and she seated herself in the occasional chair, the better to gain his serious attention.

Garner rose and looked about, bestirring himself while considering this new proposal. "I see!" he said, pausing before her. "Then I'd be a Texan for double duty and for sure. You're beautiful and I love you." He gave her a tender smile and squeezed her hand. "I'd give anything to be able to stay home with you."

"But you can! Colonel McIntyre is looking for a Flight Instructor right now."

Garner shook his head and released her hand.

"I only have twenty-seven missions, Paula, and fifty are required. It'll soon be up to seventy-five and you see, I don't now have and wouldn't have enough points to get the benefits I'll need for four or five years of college. Besides, I'd have to take Instructor's training and the points would add up too slowly. And there's no cinch about being assigned to Goodfellow."

"It can be worked out," she pleaded.

Garner winced with a quick shake of the head, like a father having to deny his little girl a heartfelt wish. "No. I think I'll take B-29 training and switch to the Pacific. I'd get out of the service quicker and with more points that way."

Panic seized Paula. It traveled from the pit of her stomach to her arms and down to her fingers. "What! You've served your time overseas! I've decided to have a baby!"

"Whatever gave you that idea? We're right in the middle of a mammoth war and you're acting as if nothing's happening."

Paula contained a dam of stubbornness. She didn't want to ever be left alone again without a part of Garner and she had pledged herself to get pregnant the next time he came home.

Garner clammed up and neither spoke of the matter again. But Paula had not given up.

Chapter Thirty-One

Esther and Floyd Roncourt loved Garner as if he were their own son and the reunited couple was happy in Paula's former front bedroom, taking most of their meals with her folks. They had not presumed to bother Garner, fearful of upsetting him with excruciating memories should they ask about his misadventures when he was downed in Holland. That country was in German hands, something they, themselves, did not like to contemplate.

Garner appreciated their thoughtful sympathy, and without their having to question him, one evening at the family dinner table in the warm kitchen, he opened up.

"You may be wondering," he said, "but there's really not much to tell about my being shot down over the Netherlands. You see, we were in on the biggest glider and paratroop operation in the history of warfare. The task of the U.S. and British Airborne Divisions was to take the bridge at Arnhem, the most difficult of three bridges to take and hold, in order to secure a foothold over the Rhine."

"Yes, I remember that push from the newspapers," Floyd said.

Garner turned from him to Paula. "We were sent to make drops of K rations, dynamite, howitzer-ammo, mortars, and infused mortar shells, all wrapped in neat bundles. This didn't count as a bombing mission." His gaze was intense, pointed.

Her eyes widened at this unjust decision upon the part of whichever officers were in command. Satisfied that Paula had understood, Garner continued.

"Our drop zone was in a clearing in a woods close to the town of Garoesbeek, south of Nijmegen. Our B-24 force flew in low at four hundred feet in excellent visibility. As we got deeper into enemy territory and toward the higher ground, we dropped even lower, to one hundred feet. We were so close, we could see the Dutch.... men, women and children...jumping up and down and waving at us. I'll never forget that." He became thoughtful, nodding to himself while he recalled the scene of flat land with its rectangular fields, its orderly homes and barnyards, the people jumping for joy at the sight of Allies come to their rescue. Then his mood changed and he drew his wide black brows together in a deep frown. "Many aircraft were damaged and ours mortally so." He made a wry face. "Or at least, mortally after I crash landed in a wet field you could practically swim in."

"The fields were wet?" Paula asked, surprised.

"Yeah, you could say that. I was dunked again. The Dutch had flooded the fields and we discovered that the water was nearly five feet deep in some places."

"Amazing!" Esther exclaimed.

"That was to deter the Germans. But it deterred us as well. Only three of us got away, the others killed in the crash," Garner continued. "Our Navigator found them and buried them, while we quickly buried all the parachutes and insignia."

"But where did you go?" Floyd asked.

"We hid in some bushes and before nightfall, the underground came and took us in. But we couldn't stay with them for very long," Garner answered, black pupils enlarged, dilated till his eyes shone black in recalling those events. "We had to move about. Scatter. Dodge and hide! We didn't know it at the time, but we'd landed right in the middle of three German Divisions at rest only a short distance away from an entire German army."

His listeners exchanged alarmed looks.

"The Dutch were risking their lives," Paula said, her voice low, hushed.

"Yes. They were magnificent. The Allies all cooperated, civilians and all. Besides them, you know what saved my life?"

"No, what?" Paula asked.

"The French shoes I'd been issued before that assignment. The Air Force found out we were losing too many men because the Germans could identify us by our American boots, so our officers got smart and issued us French shoes to carry along in case we were shot down. This was helpful to the underground, too."

"Many other Americans like you?" Floyd asked.

"Oh, yeah! We kept the Dutch busy, all right. That's why I had to keep on the move," Garner replied, his voice rising at the memory. "One time, I was standing at the edge of the road...been out looking for something to eat in a garden...and a platoon of Germans came by right in front of me. I bowed my head and stood stock still. And they passed on by."

Esther shook her head. "Must have been those shoes."

"Yes," Garner nodded, "and they didn't investigate because of my humble attitude. But I sure sweat that afternoon and all night. I didn't know where to go. I'd be taken in now and then, then go off in another direction, heading south to try to join up with the Americans."

"Starved, I'll bet," Floyd said with feeling.

Garner grinned at him. "You might say that. I surely did drink a lot of water."

"So that's how you got back with the American army," Floyd said. "We're glad you made it, son."

Garner grinned at him. "An Arkansas hill billy knows how to survive off the land, but I'd ha' never made it without the help of those brave Dutchmen." He resumed eating his dinner and said no more.

Paula rose, poured coffee, and served tempting cinnamon slices of hot apple pie, giving her husband a whole quarter. She topped it off with two scoops of vanilla ice cream, remarking, "Now it's time to fatten you up."

Garner gave her a soft, intimate look. "It was all worth it, just to be here with my little wife, at home, and with apple pie a' la mode. My dreams come true."

She kissed him on the top of his head. *And I'm dreaming of a baby boy just like you.*

"Tonight's special," she said, smiling at him. "I have some Hope Missiles to show you." He gave her a quizzical glance and she was satisfied that she'd captured his interest. "I'll let you look at them just as soon as you finish your pie."

She must lose no time. She knew Garner. Once he'd made up his mind to do something, he'd act quickly. She must do everything in her power to tug at his heart and to be practical at the same time. She now had Colonel McIntyre's assurance that he would request 2nd Lt. Cameron to the post of Flight Instructor at Goodfellow, and her love letters would touch him so that he could not refuse.

They repaired to their room and Garner closed the door, then turned on the floor lamp at the overstuffed chair and sat down, comfortable with his belt tight from the generous dinner. Paula stooped down and pulled an old shoe box out from under the bed. She handed it to him.

"What's this?"

She exuded a seductive air of mystery. "Open it!"

"Hope Missiles," he read aloud, then he opened the box to find a stack of letters addressed to himself.

"Those are my prayers and hopes for your safe return. This is the real reason you came back to me."

"Paula!" He reached for her, but she stood aside. "I couldn't write to you, much as I wanted to, you know that. I was in no position and busy every minute trying to stay alive."

"I know," She blinked slowly, the way she did when sympathy overcame her. "And I'm going to make certain you'll never ever be in that position again." They gazed into one another's eyes a long moment.

"You're too serious," he finally said. He set the box down on the floor. "Let's put this stuff away and settle the world's problems in bed." He reached for her again, but she dodged, swerving behind the easy chair, inviting a chase.

With triumph in her laugh, she called, "Colonel McIntyre has promised to request you for Flight Instructor at Goodfellow."

He caught her before she could get around to the vanity, lifted her in his arms, and bore her off to bed. He ravished her mouth in a fiery passion that amazed her, overcame her, making it nearly impossible to pull away to murmur persuasively, "Garner...darling...let's try for a baby. Everything'll work out just fine. You can stay home with me and we can start our family. It's time we had a baby just like everyone else."

He drew away and turned over on his back. "Everyone else is not having babies. Some people just have accidents, that's all."

She absorbed his cold logic, shivering with the chill that coursed through her veins. He said no more and she stiffened, remaining on her side facing him.

At length he said, "We can't. I was going to tell you tonight, but it's hard because it means more sacrifice for you." His bass voice was modulated, solemn with the portent of what he had to say. "I've already signed up for the B-29 Training Course. I'll be leaving Monday, March 12th, for Maxwell Field at Montgomery, Alabama."

Paula, silent, was stunned beyond tears.

"The war is still on. We've got to finish up and I'm an experienced pilot. I'm needed because there've been so many..."

"Killed!" she burst out.

"Yes, we've lost a lot of good men. But Jimmy Doolittle is still in command and I'm on his team. He's still going strong, you must remember, even though he's already led the way from the earliest days after Pearl Harbor, on to Palermo....to Berlin. I expect he'll return to Tokyo. He'll have plenty to do with shellacking the Japanese."

"You don't love me!" Paula flipped over, turning her back on him.

"No, darling, I was just trying to explain that I'll always come through, like General Doolittle. I'll come back to you for sure!"

Paula jumped off the bed raving mad, arms waving, her dark hair swinging with the jerk of her head.

"You Benedict Arnold!" she screamed. "You just had to do it! And you had to tell me when you had me in your fooshywooshy clutches! Now I know how I count with you! You don't love me! You went ahead without consulting me, behind my back! You knew I didn't want you to go to the Pacific. You're not God, you know!" She stopped the harangue and stood jiggling up and down, facing.him. "To hell with you!"

Garner rolled off the bed and rushed to her side, trying to take her into his arms. "Darling! It wasn't like that at all!"

When he tried again, she slipped away from his grasp. His reach was long, but she was quick. She hopped up onto the bed and bounced across to the other side, hatred blazing, face white as alabaster. She would have nothing to do with him.

Garner paused. "Calm down," he said in a gentle, but commanding tone. "The world hasn't come to an end. I told you what I was going to do and why. You knew I didn't have enough points, that I wanted to finish this job. This war isn't over until we whip those heathen barbarian Japs, and you know it. Do you think I want them coming over here? I can't bear to think of what they'd do to you."

"Me! That's just an excuse. No Texan's gonna be hurt by a lousy Jap."

"The war's not over till it's over," he warned her. "General Doolittle needs experienced pilots." He paused and with a changed air added, "Besides, Velocity's out there."

"So you're a hot shot pilot! You've become an ego maniac, that's what. There's plenty of velocity right here at Goodfellow Field."

Garner burst out laughing.

Then he felt bile-green venom streaming from Paula.

He sobered.

"I forgot. We haven't had much of a chance to become very well acquainted, have we?" His manner held contrition mixed with compassion. "He's one of my cousins. The one called Velocity."

Paula stopped bouncing. She folded her arms against her breast and stood suspended in anger. Betrayed! Betrayed by my own husband!

"His name is Charles Bean," Garner continued. "When he was a little boy, he went around with a pea shooter. Then when he got older, he used a sling shot and there was never anyone else like him. He could kill a squirrel just like that with the quick shot of a stone!" He snapped his fingers. "And that's how he got his nickname, Velocity. We call him Vel for short."

"Velocity Bean!" Paula spat out scornfully.

Amusement rumbled in Garner's throat. "You can be thankful he's fighting on our side, a more than accurate fighting Marine." Then, without waiting for another outburst, he began to undress. "I like you better naked," he said softly.

Paula watched while he unbuttoned his shirt, released his pants and laid them across the back of the chair, then untied his shoes and took them off, peeling off his socks and shorts, and finally, his under-shirt, all in the fluid movements of the calm strength she loved so well. Then he stood before her, nude, the beautiful form of perfect man with oval head and face supported by a strong neck from broad shoulders and a deep chest. His legs were equally developed, the body well proportioned with the miracle of a tempting waist nearly as small as her own. She knew full well his soulful, muscular energy now at rest. Immobile, she subconsciously sculpted that perfect figure.

A crack in the drawn curtains let a beam from the streetlight shine on Garner's chest, displaying the mysterious way the straight black hairs formed a star. Paula's aesthetic sense danced at this sign of favor bestowed upon this, her young man. She became aware that she'd hurt his feelings, but he had hurt her worse, hadn't he?

"I can't let him down," Garner said. "I can't let you down. "

"There're plenty of guys being trained right now to take your place. You're just asking to be killed." Her intense gaze pierced him to the bone.

"Paula!" His tone was one of disbelief.

"And what's to become of our glory after the war?"

"But that's why I did it. It's all for you, for our babies, for our family, our future."

"You could still get out of it," she said quietly. But if not, she thought, I could be safe with Burl.

Garner's eyes flashed, his own anger rising. "Don't you think about Burl Stein, Paula! You wouldn't be happy with him. I have every intention of coming back to you. And I do love you with all my heart."

She perceived that he was bigger than life, monumental in principle, independent in action, unconquerable. She shrank before him, a haunting expression on her face, then she jumped down off the bed.

"I'm going to go take a bath."

He longed to embrace her, but her attitude fended him off and she disappeared down the hallway leading to the bathroom, self-pity burgeoning in her breast. Once inside with the door closed, she rallied, mumbling to herself, "It's not over yet, even if my sweet Garner is not quite the man I thought him to be."

She now knew what his strong hands and long fingers with their square, blunt ends meant. They were indicative of his stubborn, bumptious character. There was no twisting him around her little finger! She called it The Enlightenment.

But she had an ace in the hole.

The C.O. could fix the 'enlistment' without much trouble. No problem there. It was changing Garner's mind that must be accomplished. He would listen to her folks. Let him do whatever he's doing now. It'll do him good to be left alone for awhile. Maybe he'll read some of my Hope Missiles, while I talk with my folks.

They'll make him see the light.

Refreshed, calmed down, and fully clothed after her bath, Paula entered the living room.

She heard her parents' voices above the rattle of pans and dishes in the kitchen and followed the sound to her new commitment.

When she passed through the doorway, her mother was hanging up the dish rag and her father was putting away the skillet. "Want some more coffee?" he asked.

"There's plenty left for all of us," Esther said. Floyd sat down at the table, and she poured a cup for him, then another for herself. "Have a seat and join us."

"No thanks." Paula's manner was dour, her voice filled with disappointment. She stood beside the table, unmoving.

"What's wrong?" her father asked. He was more sensitive toward Paula than her sister and the family knew this, assuming it was because Paula reminded him of his wife. They did not consider him partial to her, since impartiality was a strict plank in their parenting agenda. Yet there existed a special rapport between them.

Paula gave him a tight smile, more like a grimace, which was unusual for her. "Garner says he's signed up for B-29 Flight Training and will leave on March 12th for Maxwell Field in Alabama, then go to the Pacific." As if saying the words for the first time made her suddenly aware of the finality of her statement, she drooped, her face full of woe, the tragic look of a woman deserted. She fell into the chair next to him.

Floyd darted a look at Esther, but she remained calm, unruffled.

"What did you say to that?" she asked.

"What could I say? I had it all planned for him to stay here. There's no need for Garner to go back overseas again. Colonel McIntyre told me he could get him transferred to Goodfellow as a Flight Instructor. We could have a baby, and then Garner could attend Texas A. & M. after the war."

"Garner's been gone less than a year, Paula," her father said gently. "He must have a good reason for deciding to continue in combat till this whole thing is over."

A spunky fire had returned to Paula. "He says he's only got twenty-seven missions and already, fifty are needed for an honorable discharge. Then he exaggerated and said it'd soon be up to seventy-five missions."

"He's probably right," Floyd said. In a helpful manner, he asked, "Why don't you ask Colonel McIntyre?"

"There's no time! Garner's all about having enough points to get all the years in college he'll need....four or five...under the G.I. Bill."

"Both reasons well taken," Esther said.

Paula disagreed. "But he can go to Texas A. & M. right here at home and we'll get along fine. I just know it!"

"With a baby?" her mother questioned sharply.

"I expect Garner's thinking of his responsibility for you," Floyd said. "He's in no position to take on a family right now."

"He's already been shot down twice. He won't have a chance over Japan!" Paula exclaimed.

"It's mighty hard to tell a Southerner that," her father declared, wagging his head.

"Yes, Dad's right, honey," her mother said. "Garner isn't just any young man, you know."

"But he'd listen to you," Paula pleaded. "If you asked him to stay and explained it isn't necessary for him to go, I know he'd stay!"

"Paula," her father broke in, leaning forward to reassure her, "the war's going to be over in Germany any day now and Japan will soon follow. Believe me, it won't be long. You're probably worrying over nothing."

Paula was aghast. Her father was siding with Garner.

"Mo-o-ther!" she bleated.

"Now calm down," her mother responded with a maternal love.

Floyd rose and excused himself. "Mom, you try to explain things. This is women's talk. I'm no good at it." He left the kitchen, growling to himself, "Blast this cursed war!"

Esther rose and took a clean cup and saucer from the cabinet, then poured a fresh cup of coffee for her daughter. "Have a cup of coffee," she invited matter of factly, "it'll cheer you up." She sat down again and faced Paula. "Your father is probably right. And I doubt that Dad and I could influence Garner one way or the other. He cannot be outguessed or made out to be a fool. I'm sure that whatever he's decided is the result of a thoughtful conclusion."

"He's full of spit and polish, thinks he's a hot-shot pilot!" Paula sputtered into her coffee.

"He's a Southern gentleman," her mother said quietly.

"Coming from Virginia, you would think that," Paula retorted. Then she paused, her eyelids rapidly fluttering."I'm not like you and Dad. I'm a West Texan!" The fierce sparkle in her eye called up scenes of rough outdoor life, of rustling and herding contrary beasts in harsh weather. "And Garner'd better find that out right now!"

A smile flitted across the window of Esther's mind, but it left a glaring sheet of ice in her pale stare.

"Garner is a blue blood. I hope you realize you're very fortunate to have found him. He is your equal. Burl would be in your power. Maybe that's why you never returned his love. Maybe you're not so West Texan as you like to think. Breeding cannot be bred out in a single or even four generations."

Paula noticed her mother's hand holding her cup, a fine, slender hand. It was shapely and small, yet capable, the smooth nails showing white moons in delicate curves, a patrician's hand. Then she consulted her own hand, so like her mother's.

"And I'll say something else to you," Esther said with a depth of understanding and affection. "Garner is not only a Southern gentleman, but he shows the power of self-assurance. He is always courteous, like most great leaders of men. You must never confuse his courtesy with weakness. To the contrary, it eminently demonstrates his strength of character."

Paula became thoughtful, her large eyes shining with a new appreciation, even as her soul giggled at her mother's use of her favorite word.

In a rare display of giving her own opinion or advice, her mother added, "It isn't easy being the wife of a great man. Garner shows genius. But you have talent in art and another kind of genius. As his wife, you must support him in everything he does. That is your part, your mission in life."

"You mean I don't count? What I want doesn't matter?"

"I didn't say that. He needs your moral support now, especially now when he's caught up in this terrible war. And you should understand that he must remain true to his honor."

Dispirited, Paula hung her head, chin down on her chest. "I can"t go through this all over again! Not knowing whether he's been killed or maimed or what...."

"You can and you must. I have faith in Garner. He'll come back to you. He truly loves you, honey. You must believe in him." Paula was startled. She lifted her head.

"Believe in him! I believe in God!"

"Yes, and so does he. And that is why he is so steady and reveals strength and power. It's both. From God and from who he is."

"I should trust in Garner?"

"Absolutely!"

Paula drew in a deep breath and slowly let it out. "All right, Mother. I'll try."

Esther's gaze held heartfelt sympathy, but she did not reach out to comfort her daughter. She never touched her with a kiss, an embrace, or any sign of physical empathy. It was her husband who occasionally took his daughter's hand or put his arm across her shoulders in fatherly affection and support.

"I know you'll be lonely," Esther said gently, "but remember, Dad and I and Bonnie are here and you can always come home whenever you please. Then too, you have your work and your art. The time will pass more quickly than you think, if you'll let it."

"But Mom! The danger!"

"I know." Esther was solemn, and suddenly Paula wondered if she really did know. Her mother spoke softly again. "Make friends with fear."

Paula was silent, her eyes widening with this unexpected advice. She considered the meaning of this new concept, a strange paradox. Then she spoke quietly, "I don't know how yet, Mother, but I'll try." She appreciated her mother's wisdom and the reassurance of enduring family love.

Paula would fight the Battle of Texas, as the wives and sweethearts of the Air Corps servicemen euphemistically called their struggles, but she thought her mother could never know how much she suffered when Garner was gone. His absence alone, without any fear of cannon or anti-aircraft fire aimed at him, was enough to make her feel bereft. Nevertheless, she resolved to give Garner her approval and moral support. With the grit of a true West Texan, she would believe in him. Hadn't she always believed in him? She idolized him.

She rose from the table and said good-night to her mother, filled with a determination to face the future with more courage, more calm than she had had during these past few months. Eager to return to Garner's warm embrace, she went to the bathroom and slipped out of her pink dress, then stripped down to her white satin slip as a substitute nightgown. Carrying her clothing over an arm with shoes in hand, she entered her bedroom and closed the door.

Seated by the lamp, Garner looked up, eyes flashing an alert.

Why had she not noticed before?

In that moment, his glance showed an illumined knowledge gained through out-of-context experience. The face and eyes revealed what the spirit averred, how it had matured, the aims it possessed, what it planned to do. Here was the antiquity of the soul, for he had given and taken unseemly violence and destruction, much horror and death first-hand.

She perceived this along with the revelation that here was also a free spirit, the spirit of a flyer, a man accustomed to the exalted atmosphere of the heavens, released from the earth beneath, alive in an altered perspective. He had survived through command. A pilot looked out at you as strong as a horse, his eye-beam like the stroke of a quoit. Filled with emotion, the eye obeyed precisely the action of the mind. Her gentle Garner had a strong will. Under dire distress in emergencies, he had made right decisions through the use of wise control. He had commanded his will, the better to command his crew and airplane.

Garner could not now renounce his role in the war against his own precepts, although it grieved him to deny her their shared dreams of a family. Warfare had brought swift changes and an untimely maturing along with unflinching sacrifice. She could not escape into blinded, selfish desires. She was an intrinsic part of her husband and his life's flow. She should not, could not try to bring him down to her small mundane efforts on the Texas home front.

Paula called it *My* Enlightenment.

His rueful expression brought a faint smile to her face. Then she noticed that Garner was in his grey print pajamas with the magenta cording, the pair she liked because it was seamless with no buttons down the front to hurt her. He had one of her Hope Missiles in hand and she gave him a pleased smile.

His gaze fell to the letter and back to her, a subtle pleading intertwined with his comprehension of her glossed over anguish when he was missing in action. Her smile expanded with loving reassurance. He took her in, the spicy, carnation scent of her bath, the beauty of her translucent skin, and her slender form showing full, rounded breasts in an inviting nudity under the smooth, satin slip.

With relief, he returned her smile. He set the letter aside. "Here. I'll take your things." He put the shoes and clothing on the straight chair, then turned to her again.

"Paula!" Her name was a prayerful intonation.

He grasped her shoulders and searched her soul with hopeful questioning. She responded with a sweet, forgiving smile.

"I believe in you," she said with calm conviction.

His eyes changed and he squeezed her so hard, she nearly burst. Then he lifted her in a whirl of joy and carried her back to bed, his passion renewed. Lost in ecstasy, once more they became husband and wife.

At length, Garner withdrew, turned on his back, and pillowed her head an his shoulder. "Comfortable?"

"Umn-hummnn. "

"I love you, darling. I'm glad you understand why I must go. Nothing on earth or in heaven can keep me from returning to you."

※

During the remainder of Garner's Home Leave, Paula maintained her new concept of devotion, eager to please, attentive to his least wish, cherished in his amorous embrace. Time passed nonexistent in their domestic safety and bliss.

As with most expected events, March 12 arrived and they said good-bye again, partially consoled that Garner would be in the States another six weeks for training and not fly overseas until April 23, a Monday. Paula thought it a good omen that it was not a Tuesday, their good luck day, since she couldn't bring herself to believe it was truly good luck for her husband to be going into combat over Japan.

They wrote to each other every day and talked over the phone each Sunday as they had so long ago, the past year's months marked as slow eons. Paula did not go up to Montgomery to visit Garner. She explained that it would be purely unsatisfactory, because they'd become accustomed to living together, and also, it would only mean another soul searing good-bye, which would make her miss him all the more.

The war, the senseless, all consuming war, controlled them both. Paula acknowledged this although at times, she wondered about the male human being's fascination with war and its trappings of uniform, march music and gore. The uncertainty of Garner's return was realistic, a fact of life in spite of his own self-reliance. She missed him terribly once he was gone overseas, yet she was relieved she had not become fragrant, convinced more than ever that a child must have a father. The father was essential to the whole family, not the mother only. Father and mother were one in God's plan. Secretly, she grieved over the loss of her beautiful dream baby, but she hinted of this additional sorrow to no one.

With prayerful resolution, Paula started another Hope Missile box just in case, and braced herself to continue the Battle of Texas, to endure, to make friends with fear.

PART THREE

TASTE OF VICTORY

Chapter Thirty-Two

It was a warm June day and Paula stood in a sliver of shade in front of the window of the flat roofed, cement block Trailways Bus Station. Unaware of her own movements, she swayed with the jazzy rhythm of the San Angelo High School Band music heard from a distance. Trying to be inconspicuous, she was busy watching the scene before her.

Excitement whirled in the elements. Restless as the wind, the townspeople eddied about the small building, some arriving in old cars, others coming by shank's mare. Everyone was smiling or openly grinning. Today the West Texas dust tasted good!

Its acrid odor, mellowed by the fragrance of red and yellow roses, heightened Paula's belief in the reality of this dreamed of moment. Bonnie's sailor husband, Ralph, who had never seen his two year old son, was due any minute. Paula contemplated her sister, surrounded by Ralph's folks and her own parents a short distance from the bus ramp. Bonnie, fair and pretty in her white dress, a must for her "Second Wedding Day," her full face rosy with contained anticipation, would cheer any man's heart. She was all Ralph could desire, but would little Douglas recognize and accept his Daddy? Nevertheless, this was Bonnie's day.

A gust of wind tipped Paula's coconut hat and she held on, watching the yellow dust devils. Spring had come, a different spring, yet the same where the wind, the yellow earth, and the blue-gold sky were concerned. She bent down to control the flared skirt of her blue dress, now suddenly threatening to billow up to her waist in unseemly exposure.

The women, clumped together among the patient men, struggled with their short skirts and straw hats. The lusty wind parted Bonnie's blonde hair, pushing curls into her eyes. She was purposely bare headed. Nothing should interfere when Ralph embraced and kissed her for the first time after three long, empty years.

The blaring band music grew louder. Paula strained to see. Golden fezzes danced in the breeze, then the crowd parted and she saw the brass instruments flashing in the sun and the band strutting in blue uniforms with gold braid, keeping time with the boom-boom of the bass drum as it approached. The sound of horses' hooves clip-clopping behind the band on the pavement of Oak Street cleaved the brassy tune.

Here's Ma Goodwin! Yippee! Look a' there! That banner's big enough for Dallas!

Paula craned her neck, eager to see, yet filled with misgiving. Would Ma Goodwin give her a signal or would she even see her? She couldn't yell out in this crowd, couldn't ask the verdict, and of course, Mary had not ventured to come.

There was Ma Goodwin!

The hefty, gray haired native West Texan with strong features, proudly sat her Palomino in style, decked out in ranch regalia of brown and beige tones, the cream Stetson matching her horse's mane and tail. She looked straight ahead, never glancing toward Paula, proceeding in front of her teammates, a couple of young Air Force sergeants mounted on borrowed Palominos, who held high the huge banner. It bore the legend: WELCOME HOME, BOYS!

Paula stared as they slowly came forward. Was that Sgt. Fuzzy Baldwin? She wasn't sure, but she could see loyalty exuding from their earnest young faces. Those young men knew better than anyone else how Ma Goodwin had helped them and their buddies. She held them together during their hard Bombardier and Navigator training out at the San Angelo Air Corps Base. Pinto beans and sirloin steak were always plentiful at Ma's Cafeteria, even when neophyte 'Bombagators' couldn't pay. Texans take care of their own,

Ma Goodwin always said. There'll be plenty of steak in West Texas, war or no war. And that's the way it was.

Paula wasn't sure she'd know Fuzzy if she saw him. But the banner was fine, not too gaudy. The slender mayor, dressed in a fringed western shirt and dark blue cords, hurried to Ma's side. He helped the stocky woman dismount in a dignified manner and escorted her to the small platform decorated in bunting, where he and other officials would preside. He gave Ma Goodwin the chair next to his, a place of honor.

Paula, her gaze on Ma, took off her hat in a broad sweep. She saw her. Paula nodded sideways at the sergeant in question and Ma acknowledged his identity with an affirming smile.

Trust Ma! She's working on him!

The band and banner-bearing servicemen halted beside the platform. Men of the National Guard carrying the stars and stripes and the lone star flag of Texas, with its white star on a vertical blue background, crossed to the opposite side. The band continued to play, marking time in place.

Paula grinned her approval at Ma Goodwin and put her hat back on. There was no one like Ma. They'd been friends ever since she was a little girl, when the woman, the town grandma, had encouraged her in her art. It was only natural that she go to Ma with her design for the banner and ask for help in making it. Ma had furnished the blue and gold satin and they had stitched the bold letters together, gabbing away, until Paula had brought herself around to telling her about Mary and her broken heart. Now she was glad she'd trusted Ma.

One day, Paula had caught Mary crying, face down on the bed, clutching a pillow, trying to muffle the sounds of her anguish. It was just before dinner, when Paula had arrived home late from work.

"What's wrong?" Paula asked, putting her purse down. She took Mary in her arms and sat on the edge of the bed beside her. "What's happened?"

"Oh, Paula!" Mary sniffled, looking at her, makeup smeared by her tears, a pitiful sight. "I've lost Fuzzy!"

"Fuzzy! Don't tell me.... !"

Mary bent her head, eyes averted.

"What happened? You didn't let him... !"

"Oh no! He wanted to but I wouldn't let him."

"Garner never acted that way with me. You're probably better off without him. A man should realize he not only ruins a girl's reputation that way, but what's worse, he ruins her. I'm glad you didn't give in to him, Mary."

"He told me he loves me, but he can't get married after all. He asked for his ring back."

"You knew he'd soon be shipped overseas. Did you give it to him?"

Mary shook her head, bursting into tears again. She twisted her diamond ring around and around, mumbling maybe he was just scared. Paula put her arm around her shoulders.

"You tell Fuzzy there's no hurry. You'll wait for him to come back if he doesn't want to get married now."

Mary sobered and wiped her tears away. "I've already told him that. It didn't do any good. You know what I think?"

"What?"

"I think he's got a girl back home and he's trying to back out on me."

"You can't trust him."

"Oh no! I think he's too loyal. He really loves me, not her!" Mary protested.

Paula stood up and faced her. "We'll need some help to get this straightened out. If anyone can help us, it's Ma Goodwin. I happen to know that Fuzzy thinks the world of her. Do I have your permission to confide in her?"

A sudden ray of hope lighted Mary's face. "Anything you say."

And Ma Goodwin had agreed to have a talk with Cadet Fuzzy Baldwin. Now here she was in broad daylight, being served by the young man in question. She had him in tow.

Paula's attention swam back to Bonnie.

Too much was happening. How ironic that Ralph was coming home from the Pacific such a short time after Garner had gone. And only a few days before Garner left, President Roosevelt had suddenly died. Cast into shock, the people reeled with sorrow at the loss of their great leader. He was their savior through the Great Depression, their inspiration through the years of tremendous sacrifice and effort in fighting the battles around the world. He was their optimism and faith that victory was bound to come.

It was gospel that everyone remembered how they heard the sad news and just where they were at the time. Paula was at the office when the news came in. Colonel McIntyre ordered the flag lowered at half mast and he dismissed all except essential personnel for the rest of the afternoon. The date was Thursday, April 12, 1945, a date to be hallowed by every living creature fighting for freedom. Then on the 23rd, with his training completed, Garner had shipped out.

Paula's eyes filled with tears over her grieving remembrance of the gallant man who had saved his people and aided and supported the Allies with men, munitions, and his guiding wisdom.

She recalled how her parents talked about Roosevelt's bravery, a valiant fighter when infantile paralysis attacked him in mid-life. There were political enemies who spread the rumor that no one took poliomyelitis at the age of thirty-nine. It was syphillis. In a short time now, he would lose his mind and become a babbling idiot. But his staunch, though shy wife Eleanor, had stepped in and held meetings for the New York Democratic Party and made speeches and became a potent force, overcoming her shyness and saving her husband's place and the Party during those critical months of pain when he was fighting for his life.

Franklin Delano Roosevelt never gave up.

Having survived the attack, he was fortunate not to be left a complete invalid dependent on an iron lung. There was no treatment or cure for the crippling disease. The victim could only take warm baths and keep up his spirits and faith in recovery. FDR was confident he would regain the use of his legs.

Eleanor did double duty nursing Franklin and serving the Democratic Party. In this manner, a buckling synthesis was born. The aristocratic Roosevelt who suffered wrenching pain and anxiety, laid low in loss of dignity, fought through three years of tortuous days and nights to recover his strength, becoming more and more dependent upon his devoted wife, a distant cousin, another Roosevelt.

A synthesis was born of Franklin's natural bouyancy and vitality now combined with a more mature and serious personality. A synthesis was born of a more sensitive awareness of the underprivileged people's needs and of his need through the use of political power to help alleviate their condition. It was Eleanor who described these deplorable conditions, Eleanor who kept before her husband the vision of serving the people. In spite of his detractors, he ran a vigorous campaign for governor of the State of New York and won.

Paula brushed away a tear.

With a faint smile, she recalled how in 1932, she was only twelve when Roosevelt first ran for President.

She earnestly campaigned for him, talking him up at school and wearing a Roosevelt campaign button. She felt so important when he won the election. The Depression was the issue and her hero did not disappoint her. In a series of addresses, FDR explained his reform, the New Deal. He promised aid to farmers, public development of electric power, a balanced budget, and government policing of irresponsible economic power.

Roosevelt's program appealed to millions who were nominally Republicans, especially Western progressives, and that included Texas, the largest state in the union. He was elected President, then again and again. His program under the National Recovery Administration had brought the nation up from the Great Depression. His leadership within the Great Four of Great Britain, France and Russia had provided the weight in comprehensive strategy toward final victory over Germany and Japan.

President Roosevelt had died.

Now he was gone, a concept hard to accept and to realize. After a hurried search through the White House for a Bible, V.P. Harry S. Truman was sworn in as President. He said, "I felt as if the moon, the stars, and all the planets had just fallen on me."

Heartbroken, millions wept, tears streaming down their faces. In his fourth term in office, it wasn't right that their beloved FDR should die before he saw the victory he so avidly worked for and predicted.

No man could take his place. There would be no more heart warming fireside chats. Deep was their sorrow and longing for the return of their champion advocate.

Paula grieved with her fellowmen.

The rift in her recesses was deep. With Garner absent, all at once, except for her father and Burl, she was bereft of the two most important men in her life. She was still grieving for FDR when the hoped for, yet unexpected major event occurred. On May 8, Germany signed its surrender to Gen. Dwight D. Eisenhower who represented the Allies.

Everything was all mixed up.

Texas was celebrating the Centennial Anniversary of its statehood, having come into the union as its twenty-eighth state in 1845, but this was overshadowed by the war.

Now here it was June and Ralph was coming home. Where is Garner today, Paula wondered. Over Tokyo? She tried not to envy Bonnie.

Then she saw Burl Stein, his head above the crowd. In a surprising rush of unspeakable emotion, her body responded to his vigorous masculinity. She had forgotten Burl. She could paint a man like that, a real Texan, attractive in his black Stetson, white shirt and silver bolo tie. Burl was tanned and fit, his tawny coloring set off by his Sunday best.

Her gaze was still upon him when he turned his head her way. Their eyes met and they smiled at one another. Burl tipped his hat. He moved through the crowd toward her.

He must know about Garner.

Paula quickly reached into her shirred pocket, drew out a thin piece of V Mail, peeked at it, then replaced it. She repeated snatches of Garner's last letter, caressing the fine paper the while, causing a stir in her full skirt.

> ---- How are you getting along without your ever loving husband? It can't be too long now! The world will look to us and we will usher in a marvelous new age—the German rockets have fired my imagination—

His jet propulsion and going to the moon! But here was Burl. Careful! Attractions can make connections without our consent.

"What brings you out...?"

The question spoken in unison brought laughter.

"Ralph's coming home," Paula explained.

"My sort of kinfolk, my cousin's cousin, Dean Cotter, is due on the same bus."

Paula took a deep breath. "I expect you've heard that Garner's out in the Pacific."

"Yes. What do you hear from him?"

"He's been promoted to First Lieutenant."

Burl smiled his congratulations. "Japan cain't hold out much longer. We'll have a big celebration when he comes home. I'll draw and quarter my best steer and we'll have a barbecue for all our friends and neighbors from miles around. Y'hear? I'm sure he'll have lots of stories to tell."

Paula's gaze wavered and she flinched before she could control herself. Burl couldn't fathom that Garner wouldn't want to have anything to do with him. "Thanks, Burl. But I doubt if he'd like that. He'll just want to forget the war." Her eyes held the misery of long, lonely nights, private battles and debilitating uncertainty.

Burl stood contrite for being the cause of any shadow cast upon her bright spirit.

"I'm sure if anything goes wrong with Garner, you'll be notified, Paula. He'll get home all right. I still say we'll have a big celebration. In the meantime, if anything comes up and you need me, be sure to call. Anything at all. Promise?" Bending down, he peered into her face, the squint of sympathetic pain wrinkling his eyes.

Recovering, Paula promised with real enthusiasm. Burl straightened up.

"And by the way," he said, "it's time we got the mailing out on the District Court Judge election."

"But that's September!" Contrary to her objection, Paula's alert look betrayed her interest.

"Really little more'n three months away. And you know it takes a whale of educating to get the public's attention..."

"And then the proper vote," Paula broke in.

Burl grinned down at her. "You're so right! I'll give you a call in a few days."

He turned and sauntered off, leaving her feeling better, glad she had something, at least something positive and not so traumatic to look forward to.

A ten year old boy, waving his arms, whizzed into view, "It's here! The bus is coming! It says SAN ANGELO!"

A hush fell over the crowd. For a listening moment, Mother Nature herself responded. The West Texas wind suddenly died. The dust devils settled down. Then, in that ecstatic, golden lull, the sound of grinding gears overlaid by the swoosh of the pneumatic brakes of a Trailways bus was heard negotiating the sharp corners of the narrow streets.

The band struck up the lively tune, "THE EYES OF TEXAS ARE UPON YOU!"

The bus soon turned the corner and the crowd pressed forward, impatient, while it rolled into its berth. The driver nodded and grinned at the exuberant people.

Overjoyed, the band struck up the popular tune, "DEEP IN THE HEART OF TEXAS," and the crowd, in rhapsodical mood, clapped in rhythm and sang with the young people.

> The stars at night
> Are big and bright
> Clap! clap! clap! clap!
> Deep in the heart of Texas!

Webb Halsey, in army summer tans, decorated with the Purple Heart and service ribbons of the Pacific Theater, was the first down. With a big grin, he held up his fist in the V for Victory sign. A roar went up from the crowd. His old man clutched him, then eagerly examined him, heartily approving, and exclaimed, "You're looking great! Welcome home!" Friends smothered him in happy assaults and the crowd burst into song with the band once again.

> The sage in bloom
> Is like per-fume
> Clap! clap! clap! clap!
> Deep in the heart of Texas!

A tall, slim young man with a blond crew cut, came down the steps, duffle bag in hand, also in suntans, his bright blue eyes surveying the people in spirited animation.

"Dean Cotter!"

It was a squeal from his sweetheart and the crowd parted as she ran forward, followed by members of the family, Burl among them. Cotter swept his girl off her feet, giving her a solid kiss, while everyone watched, moisture filling the eyes of mothers dabbing away, and fathers grinning at one another.

Dwight Agnew was next and then Paula saw Ralph Byrnes, emerging from the doorway. Bonnie saw him, too. Ralph in navy summer whites and bell bottom trousers! It was Ralph in jaunty sailor cap, his eyes shining from a clean shaven face, teeth gleaming as white as his uniform.

His gaze roved the crowd, searching for his wife and little boy. Then he saw her! His grin widened and their eyes caught in greeting. The crowd burst into song again,

> Reminds me of
> The one I love
> Clap! clap! clap! clap!
> Deep in the heart of Texas!

Ralph came down in nimble quick-step and grabbed his pretty Bonnie, hugging and kissing her. Then he smiled down at little Douglas beside his mother and took his baby hand in his large palm.

"How are you, little one? Your Daddy's glad to see you."

The baby gazed up at him, doubtful, while the family watched, the crowd hushed. Slowly, recognition dawned on the boy's earnest face, and Douglas cried, "Daddy!"

This simple acknowledgment brought happy glances amid chuckles of relief. A look of wonder and delight covered Ralph's face and he lifted the boy, marveling at the miracle of his hefty weight and soft, baby skin. The boy looked his father over, then with curiosity satisfied, he held out his arms to his mother, and she took him. Paula had been watching the tableau with empathy and knew that Bonnie was pleased. She had taught Douglas about his father from the beginning of their lives together. Now united, the family would be happy from the start.

When all the veterans from the bus had been greeted by their families the mayor gave his formal welcome home. Then he announced a city-wide celebration to be held Saturday night with a public dance at Lake Nasworthy Park. The crowd applauded this, then grew quiet when Ma Goodwin stood to speak.

"There'll be a rip roarin' barbecue first, and every veteran and his family will be my guest. I want you all to come for good eats and fellowship and dancin'. And if any cain't come Saturday evenin', well then, you can come any time between now and Kingdom come to Ma's Cafeteria for a free dinner. I'll be lookin' for you all."

There was enthusiastic applause and a rousing cheer. Ma Goodwin resumed her seat beside the mayor.

Paula joined her mother and father who were with the Byrnes clan of cousins, aunts and uncles crowded around Bonnie and Ralph. Their hero was safely home. The long dry spell was over. There would be no gold star in the window of the Byrnes family.

※

Lake Nasworthy was the city reservoir, a treasure in the semi-desert plateau, an oasis surrounded by tall pecan trees, native mesquite, and civilized grass. The lake had made the city and the city had made the park. When Paula arrived Saturday afternoon, families and friends of returned veterans were milling about, gathered for the promised feed and dance.

Contrary to the convivial atmosphere with cold beer flowing and jokes and laughter filling the air, Paula entertained downright mean thoughts. She was ready to pull off some big lizard's tail. Only trouble was, it'd grow right back. She'd tried to persuade Mary to come with her. Sgt. Fuzzy Baldwin had given her some excuse for missing the big event, something about being Officer of the Day in the recreation hall, and Mary wouldn't come without him. That Navigator must be some sort of cad to treat Mary the way he had. He wasn't called Fuzzy for nothing! But Mary was of no help. Broken engagements were nearly as bad as divorce. Mary should at least go about as if nothing had happened and maybe the trouble would heal of itself. There were plenty of other fellows to choose from. But there she was, holed up in the apartment, crying her eyes out with a broken heart.

Paula had driven to the park early in the afternoon in order to be of assistance to Ma Goodwin. She surveyed the picnic grounds, nostalgia rising in her throat. There was the old maintenance shed off to the left and the raised dance platform already decorated with colored lightbulbs dangling all around, suspended from poles at the four corners. Women were busy covering the scattered picnic tables with rolls of white paper printed to look like red checkered tablecloths. Children were helping by setting out napkins, salt and pepper shakers, and baskets of rolls. Paula missed Garner, but reminded herself that he didn't dance. Should she stay for the dance? People might talk and she wasn't looking for much fun, anyway. She had come to see Ma.

She put a smile on her face and hurried through the picnickers. Greeting friends along the way, she moved on to the barbecue pit off to the right. A crew of six men in cowboy straw hats and large, muslim aprons with black lettering, SPARE RIBS TO SPARE, faced her. The blue smoke from dripping fat and browning meat drifted her way while the attendants turned the generous racks of beef ribs. The delicious aroma cheered her heart in spite of herself. Ma Goodwin presided over the ten foot long brazier, her face nearly as red as the glowing charcoal. She was slathering spicy, brown sauce on the meat.

"Hi, Ma! How's my Queen of the Barbecue?" Paula called.

Ma looked up and grinned. She waved the long marinating brush, her blue eyes sparkling with good humor. "Some scepter! You want to take a turn? You'd make a priceless princess!"

"No thanks!" Paula exclaimed with abhorrence, palms up in a fending gesture. "I'm already hot enough. Any news?" Ma sobered at the question. Her finely lined face seemed to shrink and she looked burdened, much older.

"I think you should fill me in. Then I'll tell you all I know," she said. She handed the sauce and brush to a young man next to her. "Take over, will you, Earl? It's time for a break. I'm gettin' too hot."

She joined Paula and they sauntered over to a clear, shady space near the trunk of a tall pecan tree, where they felt instant relief in the cool bath of a breeze in the shade. Paula spoke first.

"Mary's home, crying her eyes out. Fuzzy told her he had to be O.D. today and tonight, officer of the day in the recreation hall."

"Could be! On the other hand, he may just be laying low, avoiding her." Ma's gaze was downcast. She seemed to examine each blade of grass at her feet. Then she looked Paula in the eye. "Told him he couldn't find a finer girl than Mary and he'd be wise to make up with her, ask her forgiveness."

"What'd he say?"

"That's just it. He didn't say anything!"

"Oh!"

"I got my dander up and insisted. Why did he break off their engagement out of the blue like that for no good reason?"

"Did he seem sorry?"

"Not at all!" Exasperated at the memory, Ma wiped her forehead, reset her straw hat, and straightened up with energy. "I told him what he's doin' is unconscionable, unless he's got another girl in trouble and isn't telling anyone."

"Yeah. That could be it."

"He seemed shocked then. Said he has a girl back home and just decided he'd better break with Mary."

Paula made a wry face. "Mary feels betrayed, I can tell you!"

"He said he's crazy about her, but he loves his old girl friend, too. Asked what else could he do? He's one confused kid. I think he's glad to be going overseas and get away from all this."

"Don't feel sorry for him, Ma. He probably wanted Mary's ring to give to his other girl friend."

Ma heaved a huge sigh with her ample chest and her mouth turned grim. "Not if I can help it! I'll keep tabs on him." Then she rose to the tasks at hand. "Come on now, and help me dish up those ribs."

Paula set aside Mary's troubles with the satisfaction that she'd done all she could and Ma Goodwin would follow through. She enjoyed serving the potato salad, beef ribs, chili pinto beans, sliced tomatoes and tossed salad, seating herself at length, to taste the generous feed. By the time the tables were cleared, the sun had set and a full moon rose, its bright orange disk casting a romantic spell. Glenn Miller's "In The Mood" wafted on the evening air and young and older couples jitterbugged in high spirits. With a keen yearning,

Pauia was pulled over toward the dance area. She stopped to watch and among the whirling couples, she recognized Fuzzy Baldwin dancing with a beautiful brunette. The girl, unlike herself and many of the young women who wore bluejeans, was fancy in a white eyelet dress, trimmed with a pink ribbon sash, the full skirt floating and flaring in her stylish girations. She was a stranger to Paula.

※

Having finished their Sunday farewell dinner for Bonnie, the Roncourts rose from the dining table and repaired to the living room area. There were just the four of them, their number already diminished. Ralph and little Douglas had stayed at the Byrnes' home to finish packing for their move to Los Angeles. The fabled city was so far away, Paula mused, but Ralph had a good job at the Firestone Company and employment came first.

"I'm lucky to have had my gorgeous harem as long as I did," Floyd commented with a smile. He took his favorite seat beside the Atwater-Kent radio console. "I don't know which of you is the prettiest in your ice cream colors. All of you look good enough to eat." The women acknowledged the compliment with chuckles and side glances at one another, while Floyd gave his attention first to Esther, so fresh in her pale blue voile, then to Bonnie, who looked like an angel in cool mint, and finally to Paula, the real beauty, her face so like her mother's, only fuller, the features finer, her black hair set off by her rose linen frock.

"I'm lucky to have you for a dad," Bonnie said. "I'll miss you and Mom, and Paula." Her voice broke and she sank down on the piano bench, while her mother took a chair nearby.

Paula pulled out a flat cardboard carton from behind the open front door. "I have something for you, Bonnie." She tipped it up and an artboard slid out.

"A painting!" Bonnie exclaimed.

Paula held it up for the family to see, eager for their first reaction, and especially that of her sister's. Bonnie's lighthearted gaze swiftly changed to an awestricken mood, moisture starting in her eyes as she took in the painting.

"It's beautiful!" she gasped.

"I experimented with an ethereal scene washed in the Texas light. Do you really think it's all right?"

Her mother took the painting and held it at arms' length. "It *is* ethereal." she proclaimed. "The bridge leads off into the distance, yet the whole vision glows in whites and yellows. The mesquite trees all feathered....colors blending....lines suffused, flowing. Even the park bench in the foreground seems to exist in some heavenly place."

"This must be where old Texans pass over the bridge," Floyd joked, referring to the current popular song. Everyone laughed and Esther handed the gift back to Bonnie.

Heartened by their praise, Paula smiled. "It's the foot bridge in City Park." She was relieved that Bonnie liked it. She had tried a new technique but wasn't certain of her success. It seemed she was always doing something foolish like that at critical moments. She deplored this tendency but couldn't seem to help herself.

"It's our park," Bonnie said, "where we used to skate and ride our bikes over the bridge when we were kids. It's impressionistic.... different. I'll hang it in our new living room and remember the fun we used to have."

Paula was happy for Bonnie, but wished she didn't have to leave. The mopping up in Europe after VE Day had begun and she wondered how long it would take for Japan to capitulate. Amazingly, Bonnie and Ralph had not been required to wait for that great event. Ralph had wisely decided to return to civilian life. He was among the trickle of navy men coming home with honorable discharges for combat points earned during their years of overseas duty. Each man safely returned was another family saved. And each month Garner flew in the Pacific meant more points for him. When he had enough points, would he return home, even if the Japs had not yet surrendered? She mustn't let Mary's experience influence her to let doubts of his devotion slip in. Garner was the opposite of Fuzzy.

Paula tried to imagine Bonnie's new home and a pang of sadness overwhelmed her. "I'll miss you so!" she quavered. For a few seconds, they exchanged a tearful realization of their imminent parting. Then Paula regained her composure. "You can choose a frame for it later, when you know your color scheme."

"What color is Early Salvation Army?" Bonnie quipped.

"It must be gold," Paula responded with a laugh. The others broke into laughter, too, then Esther rose.

"Time to get to work." she said.

The three women went to Bonnie's back bedroom and were soon sorting out the baby paraphernalia and clothing that she did not want to take to California. Esther sighed as her small hands wove in and out, folding the laundered diapers on the bed.

"Babies cause a lot of hard work and never-ending care," she said. "They take your hearts, then grow up or suddenly leave. They don't remain babies very long. It only seems forever because, certainly, the impression a baby makes lasts for an eternity."

Bonnie gave her a sympathetic smile. "I know how you'll miss Dougie," she said. Esther gazed thoughtfully at her.

"What innocence! What astounding discoveries we've made together!"

Bonnie nodded, then reminded. "I'm keeping those Birdseye diapers. I hope to be using them full-time again about a year from now."

Paula shimmered with a sense of mystery mixed with desire, uncertainty and bravado churning within. She glittered, trying to sound lighthearted. "I may need them before you do!"

Bonnie chuckled at her sister's challenge. "Diapers are still scarce, so I won't part with them. But you can have some of these baby clothes. I've got too much, anyway." She set aside piles of receiving blankets, soakers, dresses, rompers and baby buntings. "There're all colors here....blue, pink and yellow...so you can have a boy or a girl."

"You mean you'd give all those baby things to me?"

Bonnie gave her sister a big hug, gazing into her eyes with deep understanding. "Of course, honey! Think of all the things you've done for me. I'd love to be of some help in giving you and Garner a start with your family."

"Thanks, Bonnie. I'll take them and put them under my bed in the apartment. They're bound to give me sweet dreams. I'm going to get pregnant one way or another, even if it's by V Mail." She flashed a grin at Bonnie, then busied herself selecting the things she wanted. "I really want a girl just like you."

Their mother laughed and said, "Better not get carried away, Paula. It's customary to have a husband for a father and I wouldn't want you to bring any babies around here for me to take care of." This admonition was nothing new to Paula. She grimaced to Bonnie behind her mother's back. Beginning at the age of fourteen, this stern admonition had become a litany. Paula could never even contemplate such a thing. She would take care of her baby herself. Bonnie gave a deep frown, shaking her head, hands on her hips, which caused Paula to go into peals of laughter.

Esther sighed. "I'll leave you two to your foolishness."

When she was gone, the two young women fell silent. Paula helped Bonnie complete her packing and the time came to say good-bye.

Bonnie gave Paula a heartfelt squeeze. "Hang tough, honey," she murmured into her ear. "I'll write, and you, too."

After Bonnie left, Paula suddenly felt let down, terribly lonely. Mary broken hearted...Garner far away in danger. She remained in the open doorway, then letting her feet take her wherever they would, she moved down along the front walk. Numb, with an ache in the pit of her stomach, her need for solace, she turned off into the side yard toward the familiar mesquite tree, its chartreuse froth unnoticed. She did not stop there to lean against it nor to take comfort in its shade dappling the ochre earth. Her feet continued their way, surely and with ease, where they had so often trod in her childhood, down to the bank of the Concho, while her mind in turmoil, had lost all sense of direction.

Halfway down the steep bank above the bend in the river, Paula collapsed at her favorite spot, unmindful of the sharp, prickly grass or the yellow dirt that could stain her rose dress. She was unaware, too, of the scent of the cool water and wild plants surrounding her in the brilliant sunlight. Bonnie had Ralph and little Douglas, while she had no one, How long, oh how long till Garner's return?

She cramped herself into a tight bundle, knees clasped to her breast, and rocked, trying to hold back the tears, eyes squeezed shut. Then she suddenly released her legs and pulled out Garner's last letter from its warm place in her bosom. Her throat quivered in dry, silent sobs as she carefully opened it with trembling fingers and began to read.

May 11, 1945

Dear Paula,

How are you getting along without your ever loving husband? Germany's surrender is sure good news! It can't be too long now! Take a good look at the floor because you're going to be staring at the ceiling for a long time.

I'm O.K. My crew and I are flying high aimed at flying straight back home when we're finished here. The world will look to us and we will usher in a marvelous new age. Our new technology will amaze even ourselves. The universe beckons to mankind. The German rockets have fired my imagination and I want to be ready.

Keep those Irish eyes smiling and your pretty chin up and I'll be home before you know it. Give my love to your folks and to Bonnie. I'm glad you have your family.

I love you, Darling,
Garner

She folded the V Mail letter again, noticing that it was becoming more and more worn at the folds. Unable to control herself any longer, she burst into tears. Agitated, fumbling in the attempt to return the letter to its hiding place, she crumpled the thin paper, crying harder, trying to smooth it out, until at length the precious words were once again pressed against her breast as if to become a physical part of her. Sobbing all the more, she hugged her legs again, head bent down, tears falling. Wracked with loneliness and longing, sorrow engulfed her in convulsive waves as she rocked and rocked, shaken by the storm.

"Garner, why did you leave me again? Don't you know I need you? Why did you ever leave again? Why? Why? Oh why?" She looked up to heaven and whispered, "I'm all alone without you." The tears rolled down her cheeks. "I need you so! I'm waiting for you!" she wailed.

Catching herself at length, she stifled her sobs, still heaving in spite of her effort to quell her weeping.

"Wherever you are or wherever you go, I'll always love you," she vowed, tense. She held her gaze at the blue sky, concentrating, listening for an answer.

None came.

Defeated, she slowly looked down again and wiped the tears off her wet hands, then smoothed them away from her face. Mesmerized in heartache, she dimly heard the quack, quack, quack of wild ducks. She stared down off to the left in the direction from which the sound came. In her agony, she was transcended to another realm, hovering far, far above, and gazed down on the river, small in the distance, retreating in its winding curves deep in the earth, dissolving in the dim mists of heaven and earth conjoined.

Then she was startled. From around the bend below, under the drooping willows, she saw three mallards, eerily silent, flying in V formation, skimming scarcely above the water. Swiftly they flew, following the wayward course of the stream, miraculously fitting themselves into its meandering pattern. She held her breath as they passed below. And they were gone!

It was a miracle! It was Garner leading his squadron, flying straight home! God had given her a sign that Garner would be coming home to her as surely as these birds were returning to their nesting places. How foolish she had been to doubt!

Paula sprang up. She paused and looked down at the river, taking time to inhale the refreshing goodness in the grasses mingled with the subtle perfume of hidden wild flowers. Everything was so alive!

Lighthearted, she turned, calm and at peace. Her step quickened on the upward path.

Chapter Thirty-Three

Ma Goodwin's office was more luxurious than her humble cafeteria. Yet it, too, was strictly utilitarian. A vintage LC typewriter, black with gold lettering, stood upon a yellow oak desk, closely flanked by a four-drawer oak filing cabinet Flowered curtains with splashes of sky-blue dressed the south window, which let in daylight over the working area, spreading through the room to reveal a stand with stacks of bookkeeping ledgers, a blue overstuffed chair, and a couple of oak chairs. The floor was covered with a linoleum rug in pleasant pattern of yellowish squares dappled with blue bonnets.

Paula had called and made an appointment to see Ma after lunch and before the evening rush hour. Intent upon her mission, she scarcely noticed the office, only glad to see her good friend.

"Come in! Come in!" Ma called, preparing to rise from her seat at the desk. Her gray hair was pinned back in a low knot and her bi-focals had slipped down on her substantial nose. She pushed them up and peered at Paula with a motherly welcome in her large blue eyes.

"Don't get up!" Paula exclaimed.

"I just want to close this door. We'll need some privacy and I get very little of that around here."

Ma Goodwin shut the door with purposeful energy. Paula pulled up a straight chair and Ma regained her seat.

Their gazes met in serious regard.

"Have you seen Fuzzy again?" Paula asked.

Ma nodded and compressed her thin mouth in disapproval. "I've also seen the girl from back home. She smelled a rat and came down here to straighten Fuzzy out."

"She must have been the one I saw dancing with him at the celebration."

"I didn't see him then, but they came in the next day. When he brought the trays back, he asked me to apologize to Mary for him. He just got mixed up, he said. He knew it was wrong. His girl came down from Indiana and she forgave him. They've made up and are going to get married."

Paula huffed a disappointed sigh. "That's what I was afraid of. A big help to Mary."

Ma shook her head. "I know. I feel sorry for Mary. She really loves him. She'll just have to get over it as best she can."

"Did you know she's still wearing his engagement ring?"

"No, but I'm not surprised." Ma picked up a red pen and examined it, rotating it between her fingers. Then she looked up at Paula again. "We've got to do something to help her. I feel awfully bad about this."

"Yes, I do, too."

They were silent for a few moments.

Then Paula murmured in her low voice, "I've got to get her to give up that diamond ring. She's got to accept what's happened."

"What about her father?" Ma asked. "He's a minister. He should be able to help."

"I don't know," Paula said slowly. "It would probably do Mary good to go home for awhile. I know her father is lonely and he'd be good for her, too."

Ma backed off from the desk. "That's settled! I think that's the thing to do, Paula. Now let's get down to business."

"You already have the brochures?"

"They're just fliers, really, and yes, the fliers and envelopes are all ready to be mailed."

"Good! "

Ma Goodwin rose and arranged the fliers and envelopes on the desk. She was a loyal Democrat and a solid precinct chairman. "We want these mailed out within two weeks," she said.

"Burl's already mentioned it to me. I'll go out and help him. How about the stamps?"

"I nearly forgot." Ma pulled out a drawer and placed several rolls of stamps on the promotional material. Then she put it all together in a large manila envelope and handed it to Paula. "There you are. But mind you, this is just the first mailing."

Paula answered with a grin. "That's politics!"

When she left Ma's office, she hoped Mary would be home. It was Saturday, and she could be at the USO. Mary wasn't there when she returned to the apartment. Paula glanced over at Garner's portrait and said softly, "Hi, Darling. You just hang in there now! I know you'll be coming back home to me and I want you to know I'm waiting for you."

She unburdened herself, putting the manila envelope and her purse up on the chest of drawers. Then she pushed open the door to the alcove bathroom, only to see Mary crouched on the stool, weeping, her face in her hands.

"Mary!"

Caught once more in her misery, Mary looked up, her face red and swollen, glance full of misery. She didn't say a word, the only sound coming from her convulsive sobbing.

"I'm sorry! I didn't know you were in here. I just got home from Ma's."

Mary jerked her head and wiped the tears away. "What did she have to say?" Her voice was dull and lifeless.

"Let's come on into the living room where we can talk. Here." Paula ran water over a washcloth and handed it to her. "Put this on your face. It'll make you feel better."

Mary did as she bade and they went into the living room, then sat down across the table from one another.

"Fuzzy asked Ma to apologize to you for him," Paula said, getting right to the point. "He's sorry. Said he got mixed up. His girl from Indiana came down and they've made up. They're going to get married."

Mary flared with anger. *"She's* forgiven him. Now he expects *me* to do the same?"

"He did break off the engagement, after all. I don't think you should be wearing his diamond ring," Paula said hastily.

"I'm certanly not going to take it out to him at the base."

"No. You don't need to do that. I can give it to Ma and she can return it to Fuzzy for you," Paula offered.

"So he can give it to his old girl friend? Not on your life! I'd rather throw it down the toilet."

Mary jumped up and before Paula could respond, she stepped into the bathroom. Fast on her heels, Paula saw her in front of the toilet, twisting off her ring.

"No! Don't do that, Mary! That ring is valuable. If you don't want to give it back to Fuzzy, you could get good money for it at the jeweler's."

Mary paused with the ring half-way off.

"I don't *want* any money or anything else from that twotiming Fuzzy Baldwin! I want to get rid of this thing once and for all."

She pulled it off her finger and Paula caught her hand just as she was in the act of throwing the ring into the toilet. "Here. I'll take it." She grabbed the ring. "I'll keep it for you until you calm down and have made up your mind about what to do with it. Why don't you talk this over with your father?"

Mary submitted, considering this new proposal, and Paula put her arm around her in a comforting embrace. She gently guided her back to the table.

But Mary was still sullen.

"You haven't seen your father for quite some time," Paula said.

Mary faced her with a remembrance in her gaze, admitting this was true. When she began to date Fuzzy, she'd forgotten everything and everyone else. She'd neglected her father.

"You know he'd love to have you come visit for awhile. He's lonely and you'd do him good. I think he'd do you a world of good, too, Mary. Why don't you go stay with him for a few days and tell him your troubles?"

"But that's all he hears all day long."

"So much the better. With such experience in these matters, he'd be able to help you more than anyone else."

Mary shrugged with a faint smile.

"And if you don't confide in him, you're shutting yourself away from your own father," Paula added. She gave Mary a meaningful look. "He's the most important man in your life."

Mary's eyes flickered back and forth with chagrin. Guilt and reluctance to bother her father with her own misery caused more anxiety. But it would be a relief to talk with her father. He was usually understanding and she hadn't really committed any great sin. "You're right, Paula. I'll do that." Her gaze swept the small apartment with disgust. "This crimpy-crampy box is getting on my nerves!"

"Yeah," Paula sympathized. "Stay as long as you like, only don't forget to come back. I don't want to lose you. I'd never find another roommate like you."

For an instant, Mary thought of Paula's own troubles with Garner flying over in the Pacific, probably over Tokyo this very minute. Again, she felt guilty over her blind self-centeredness, thinking only of herself. Paula needed her as much as her father. She perked up.

"Don't worry. I'll come back, Paula." She smiled openly, showing her buck teeth. "I've become attached to you and the yummy bakery smells every morning." She rose and went over to the chest. "Did you see this letter from Adele? It came in this afternoon's mail."

"I didn't notice." Paula took it and read with joyous exclamations of surprise. "Guess what! Adele's going to marry a millionnaire!"

"A millionnaire. Just like that?"

"Just like that. But he's older. Twenty-three years older, in fact."

"Oh!" Mary grinned with some of her old spirit. "Money isn't everything!"

❦ ✳ ❧

A few days after Mary had been gone, the crimpy-crampy box became an empty cell for Paula. She missed Mary's companionship at home and at the USO, and especially her encouragement and good common sense approach to life. Strange that she could have been taken in by such a cad as Fuzzy Baldwin. But on second thought, Mary hadn't had much experience with men and she'd fallen in love for the first time. Naturally, Fuzzy was attractive and likeable. Men like him usually were. Mary could not be blamed.

What had happened to Adele with Fred was far worse than that which Mary was going through. Losing one's husband and baby all at one stroke through deception was a life threatening blow. The more Paula thought about it, the more she realized that Adele would probably never completely get over it. She wondered if this engagement to an oil magnate was the right thing for her. Could it be true love, or was it a convenient way to get out from under her parents' domination and that awful job in the insurance office? Money was always tempting and especially to a young woman like Adele who had tasted real love only to have it end in disillusionment. It could discolor her outlook for the remainder of her life.

As Paula worked at Goodfellow and at the USO, she harbored a nagging urge to talk with Adele about this older man. Somehow, she felt responsible. Not responsible, exactly, but she wouldn't want her friend to make another drastic mistake if she could help it. Added to this concern was her own loneliness. She decided that now would be the propitious time to invite Adele to come out to San Angelo for a visit. They could stay in her apartment and take their time for heart to heart talks.

Paula called Adele and was relieved to find her in high spirits. She begged Adele to come while Mary was away and they could have the apartment to themselves. At first, Adele said she couldn't take the time off from the office, but Paula persuaded, saying she'd soon have to train someone else for the job. Then she reminded Adele that she owed her a visit, and besides, she hadn't come out for her wedding.

"I have so much to do," Adele complained. "I've got to decide where I want to go on our honeymoon, what kind of wedding to have..."

"Bring your travel brochures and I'll help you plan your itinerary. It'll be fun, Adele. I do want to see you before you get married. Who knows where that man will take you once he has you in his clutches?"

"How did you guess? He travels all the time and he says he wants me to travel with him. That's what I like about him. He includes me in everything. All right, I'll come. I'm so tickled you asked me. Can I bring Sasha?"

"Who's that?"

"She's the miniature poodle that Duane gave me on our second date."

Paula laughed. "I guess so. That is, if they'll let her on the bus."

"Oh, that's okay. I'll just put her in a basket. She's quiet and so cute. You'll just love her."

"No doubt. All right, Adele. I'll be looking forward to welcoming you and Sasha day after tomorrow. I'll meet you in my new little Willys. And I'm sure you'll just love my pet, too."

※

The San Angelo sky was pure azure blue on this warm June day of 1945, the day of Adele's homecoming visit. Paula greeted the morning with delight, breathing deeply of the fresh air, so clean and wild. It was made in heaven. Heaven come down to earth, she thought. No wonder Garner loved to fly in the wild blue. He had loved it here in Texas and must be thrilled with the 'wild blue yonder.' Far yonder over Japan! She sent him loving thoughts and dedicated herself to the sense of their spiritual union in the ether.

Now here was Adele, exuding sweetness, as was her nature. But she was more mature, more filled out and sophisticated. Her light green dress showed good taste and the color flattered her hazel eyes. Adele's soft, golden brown hair was different, falling in a shoulder length curl that accented her youthful femininity. It was swept off her high forehead, emphasizing the straight brows, which expressed a direct honesty.

Adele was an only child who had grown up being given nearly everything her heart desired. As a child she had taken piano and dance lessons, had her own pony, plenty of clothes, and a generous spending allowance. The Great Depression had not affected the Turner family as it had the Roncourts. Paula knew that Adele was spoiled, yet she had retained a soft innocence, a sweet caring for others, and it was these traits that had held the two as bosom friends. Only at times was Adele stingy. But Paula overlooked those occasions.

When Adele came down the steps of the bus holding a basket in one hand and her purse in the other, Paula gave a low chuckle.

"Here! Let me have the basket, while you attend to your weekend bag." She took the handle with a vigorous lift, causing the basket to bounce up into her face. "It's so light!" she exclaimed, laughing.

Adele threw her a look with a sly smile. "It's summertime. I didn't bring a gift of heavy foodstuffs."

Paula could not resist taking a peek inside to see the precious gift. A dark eye surrounded by curly black fur looked at her and she smiled a silent hello. It was just a puppy. This was like having a baby to care for. She wondered if that was what Duane Peterson was thinking when he gave the furry bundle to Adele. Maybe he was the man she needed, after all.

During the days that followed, the two young women took Sasha with them wherever they went, except when they visited Ma Goodwin at the cafeteria, they left her with Paula's folks. The young women didn't mind staying home with the puppy because it gave them more time to confide in one another. It had been a year and a half since they'd last been together and they had much catching up to do.

That first night, Paula eagerly questioned Adele.

"Tell me, how did you meet this Duane Peterson? Tell me all about it. After you began dating him, you didn't write very often, you know. In fact, you stopped writing altogether." She arched a brow in accusation.

"I'm sorry. I was overwhelmed at first, and I didn't want to disturb you again." Adele gave a quick shake of her head. "I didn't know how to take his attentions. At first, I couldn't believe that he was courting me. It seemed so preposterous, a man that old."

Paula's blue gaze sympathized with her. "He wasn't nearly like the boys at the USO, was he?"

"No." Adele was thoughtful.

"Well, what then? Were you attracted to him?"

"Not at first," Adele admitted. "But you see, Dad had known him for some time. He is one of my father's biggest clients. All of his casualty insurance is placed with the Turner Insurance Agency. And Dad likes him, so it was only natural that I'd look favorably upon him."

Paula nodded.

"Do you know, when he came into the office and Dad introduced us, Duane asked Dad, joking, if he could take me out to dinner. And Dad said, 'I'm not invited?'"

"What was his reply?"

"He laughed and said, 'I don't think you'd enjoy our company.'"

Paula smiled and said, "And your father said something about three's a crowd and Duane agreed with that."

Adele giggled. "And I did, too."

"I see!"

Mr. Turner had not approved of Adele's marriage to Fred and Paula understood how it had hurt her to go against her father's wishes. Here was a man of whom he did approve, and he was older, wealthy and obviously considerate of his only daughter.

"It was a whirlwind courtship," Adele said. She showed Paula her two carat diamond engagement ring, making her remember Burl's ring, which he was still holding for her. Or was he? Now she would never know. She forebore to mention that she had once had an opportunity for such a prize, with devotion and plenty of riches behind it. No need to say anything. There were no regrets on her part. Burl was a good friend and she could still work with him in politics.

"What I'd like to know is how your fiance made his money."

"Oh that! He's a graduate of Texas A. & M. and went into research after he got his Engineering degree. He invented an oil drilling tool and went into business with it. You know, he did so well, selling it here in Texas at first, that he expanded and he travels to Arabia and the Mideast. His equipment is sold wherever oil is found. It's standard."

"Wonderful! Where's he from?"

"Dallas. He's a Texas man and I think that's one reason my father likes him so well."

"No doubt." Paula sipped her lemonade. "You know, if he's as old as you say, forty-seven, he must have been married before and has children. They'd probably be grown by now."

Adele's round cheeks flushed.

Paula regretted her prying. Maybe Adele was sensitive about the fact that she was younger than the Peterson children, an awkward situation.

"No," Adele answered headlong. "He's been married twice before, but he has no children."

"Twice?"

Adele nodded and looked squarely into Paula's eyes. "He says the first one was when he was only nineteen in college. They just didn't make a match, so they both wanted a divorce. The second one was different. She was his age, but it turned out that she was a compulsive gambler. He was so tied up in his work that he couldn't be with her and watch over her all the time. As a result, she nearly ruined him. He couldn't control her at all. And she wouldn't go to a psychiatrist. She ran through his money like an oil gusher shooting off into the sky. Finally, they had nothing in common, seldom saw one another. So he gave her a good settlement and said good-bye."

Paula was silent at that.

Adele was quiet, too, then she reminded Paula with a spark of fire in her glance. "I'm divorced, too."

"Yes," Paula replied, somewhat miffed. "There are good reasons for divorce. That's no stripe against him." She thought youthful passion and haste had more to do with divorce than anything else. She asked softly, "Have you considered that when you're only forty, he'll be sixty-three?"

"I don't care. I'll enjoy him while he lives and if he dies before me, I'll have plenty of money to live on after he's gone."

"Yes, that's right. It's just that I have a friend who married a man twenty years her senior and she's very unhappy now. She'd like to go places but he just sits around the house and won't take her anywhere."

"Oh, don't worry about that," Adele exclaimed. "Duane is on the go all the time. To tell the truth, that's the only thing that bothers me. I wonder what kind of a life we'll have in our home."

"Does he dance?"

Adele laughed outloud. "Oh Paula! You and I! No, he doesn't dance!"

Paula joined in the merriment till they both got tickled and couldn't stop laughing. They rocked back and forth rollicking, uncontrollable, tears rolling down their cheeks. Bent over, they had to hold their stomachs. It was so funny! How were they ever going to manage being married to men who wouldn't take them dancing? Spend their whole lives in hard work and no dancing! It would be impossible! How was it that they'd both come up with such clods?

Sasha pranced on her hind legs, begging to be lifted up to join in the fun. This made them laugh all the harder. Adele picked the puppy up and she licked her in the face with doggy enthusiasm, wagging her tail.

Finally, they settled down and Adele became serious again. "We're not going to have any children," she said. "I don't want any and Duane doesn't either. We're going to be free to travel and live just as we want to, do whatever comes to mind. Duane is really more than a millionnaire. He has oil wells pumping oil day in and day out, besides his machinery business."

Paula nodded with approval. "I'm glad you've agreed on the way you want to live. That's so important. I expect Duane was pretty set on that after his bad experiences."

Adele laughed. "You'd better believe it!" She then put Sasha back down and said, "I'll get the travel brochures. Let's decide where I want to go on our honeymoon."

She pushed aside the curtain over the clothes closet, pulled out her bag, and set it on the bed. Then she opened the bag and brought forth a packet of folders. She spilled them on the table, spreading them out in colorful array of mountain scenes, blue-green seas and cruisers, city towers and even African animals for a safari.

"Here's one that looks like Spain," Paula said, picking up a tempting picture of a young, dark woman in bright red and black skirt dancing a fandango.

"Oh, that old one!" Adele took it and put it back in the bag. "I'm certainly not going over to Europe or anywhere off the continent of North America!"

Paula laughed. "No, I should think not! That only makes it easier to choose, doesn't it? You'll go somewhere right here in the United States. Spain will have to wait."

"Or Paris," Adele sighed. She saw one showing the Empire State Building and the Statue of Liberty. "I'd love to go to New York. But Duane's already been there so many times, I can't ask him to do that again."

"Why not? If you have your heart set on it?"

"I don't, really. What I'd like to do is go somewhere where neither of us has ever been before."

They picked up and perused the delights of New Orleans during Mardi Gras, imagining the Creole cuisine, the famous French Quarter and the fabulous parade with its jazz music. Then they considered the Grand Canyon and its breathtaking natural wonders; Washington, D.C. with all its soul stirring monuments, the Archives, the Capitol and White House, and the Smithsonian Institution and National Art Galleries; and marine fishing off the coast of Maine, all quite different from Texas. The last one was out, Adele said, because Duane was not much of a sportsman.

Paula shuffled through the folders again and found one displaying the majestic mountains and the beauty of a pristine lake unparalleled. "Lake Louise!" she exclaimed. "Here's just the thing for a honeymoon. You'll get to travel to a foreign country, be safe from the war, be among friendly people, and stay in the most beautiful place in the whole wide world. It's just perfect for your honeymoon."

Adele took it and read it, sparkling with the wonder of discovery. Those awesome mountains! Even if they never put on a ski or took a drive or swam in the lake or danced at night, here was enough inspiration to match the exultation of any pair of lovers.

She gazed at Paula with excitement. "We've found it! This is perfect! You know, I think I'll set the date for August. Duane and I would miss the awful heat of summer here and be in seventh heaven up in Canada. I'll ask him if he's ever been to Lake Louise."

"Yes, you could stay a whole month, or as long as Duane can afford to be away from his business."

"That's it!" Adele proclaimed, scooping up the brochures. "I'll be having champagne before breakfast every morning right in the most heavenly place on earth!"

An alarm sounded in Paula's psyche. Champagne before breakfast? What kind of a creature was this Duane Peterson? Most salesmen drank and some more than others. There was one thing she and Adele had not touched upon concerning this forthcoming marriage.

"By the way," she asked her. "Is Duane a Christian?"

Adele scooted the bag behind the curtain and seated herself at the table again. Suddenly serious, she met Paula's gaze.

" Yes....I suppose so. I really don't know. But he's an honest, hard working man, brilliant and ambitious, and Dad's known him for some time."

"Maybe you'd better find out. Christians are supposed to marry Christians. You remember what Saint Paul said about being unequally yoked."

"Yes, of course. But you don't have to. He also said if you find yourself unequally yoked, then bring your partner to the Lord."

Paula nodded. "That's true. But it makes life much easier if you both have the same faith. And that's basic to a good marriage."

Adele chuckled at her. "Oh, Paula! You're always wanting everything to be perfect. But things just aren't perfect. I learned that the hard way. I think I'm the luckiest girl in the world to have a wealthy gentleman like Duane Peterson fall in love with me and want to marry me and shower me with all the beautiful things money can buy."

Paula gave her a warm approval. "I'm really happy for you, honey. I feel sure Duane will be everything you want."

Chapter Thirty-Four

Paula, alone in her apartment after Adele's return to Dallas, suffered a distinct letdown. She'd been so happy with her close friend, and now she had no idea when they would ever see each other again.

One evening her loneliness was more than she could bear. The next day after work, she called her folks and said she'd like to come over. At their invitation to dinner, she drove right over, eager to help her mother cook.

They dined in the intimate setting around the kitchen table, enjoying a simple meal of whipped potatoes, carrots, green beans, round steak, and fruit-Jello salad.

Over their coffee, Floyd asked his daughter, "What do you think of Adele's intended?"

"I'm not sure, Dad. I have some misgivings. Adele thinks they'll be happy. I hope so. He has plenty of money, doesn't want any children, and neither does she. But best of all, he wants her to travel with him wherever he goes. After the war, there's no telling where all they'll go."

"Mom says he's a good deal older than Adele."

"Yes. Twenty-three years."

"Old enough to be her father," Esther remarked.

"I know," Paula murmured. Her thoughts turned to her own husband, her love, whose virile body and spirit thrilled her so. Esther and Floyd perceived the secret flash in her mind and exchanged glances. Paula had changed. She was not so desperate as she had been when Garner was flying over Germany.

Now she thought of Adele and Mary, of their agonies and broken hearts over men who had proved to be deceptive and unfaithful. Garner was quite different. She was thankful that her husband was a loyal, honorable young man of high principles and intelligence. Far off in battle, he was upholding his own precepts, his own creed, fighting the enemy to protect her and to save their country. He was a capable young man, strong in body and resolute in spirit. And he was devoted to her with a true love.

Pausing, Paula gazed into her mother's eyes. For a long, precious moment, she bathed her in wholehearted love.

"I believe in Garner with all my heart, Mother. Now I understand what you meant, how important it is for me to believe in him. He promised to come back to me and I trust he will."

Esther smiled and nodded. "Yes," she said, "like I believe in your father."

Floyd smiled at his wife, then at his daughter. "The war will soon be over."

In her mind's eye, Paula saw three mallards flying in perfect formation above the winding river, swiftly returning to their nesting place. Her smile shone with an ineffable peace.

Historical Resources

Information from the Goodfellow Air Force Base Affairs Office, Goodfellow Field, San Angelo, Texas, July 19, 1999:

> The Air Corps did not become the Air Force until 1947 after World War II. Goodfellow's beginning class of Basic Pilot Training graduated Class 41E in February 1941. Between January 1941 and August 1945, they graduated 19,654 pilots.
>
> The planes used were the North American BT-9 and Yale Voltes BT-13 Valiant. Aviation Cadets received instrument flying and night flying training. Before cadets could graduate, cadets were also required to make cross country flights.
>
> Primary training gave the fundamentals. Before 1939, the Army Air Corps trained pilots in San Antonio at Randolph and Brooks Fields. Cadets had seventy hours of instruction in Basic Training.
>
> Over extended training, 132,993 Aviation Cadets were washed out or were killed. This was forty percent of those who had entered.

Personal interview with Donald V. Birdsall, former Flight Engineer in the USAAC in the Eighth Air Force Command based at Seething Airfield in East Anglia for bombings in the B-17 Flying Fortress over Europe.

"The 1,000 Day Battle," by Britisher James Hoseason, An Illustrated account of operations in Europe of the 8th Air Force's 2nd Air Division (1942-1945), including its 448th Bomb Group and the other B-24 units based in East Anglia's Waveney Valley. Pub. Gillighan Publications.

"Experiences of Victor Lark Scovel," a cargo aircraft pilot in the China War Theater in World War II. He gives the following pay scale for the United States Air Corps servicemen:

>   Private made $21 per month;PFC, $29 per month
>   Aviation Cadets were paid $75 per month
>   2nd Lieutenants received $246 per month
>   Overseas 2nd Lieutenants in combat made $404.00, as
> Scovel was from March 1945 to February 1946.
>   The pay of $325 in 1945 becomes $2,600 a month in 1992, plus medical care and housing.

(Author's note: I give the above information because so many people have asked me about the pay, thinking WWII pilots made thousands upon thousands of dollars.)

"The Annals of America," Book 16 - "The Second World War and After" Pub. Encyclopaedia Britannica, Inc. 1968

The New Encyclopaedia Britannica, 15th Edition, 1988

"The Way We Fought," *Boston College Magazine*, Fall 1991

"Boston College Voices 1941-1946"

"Deep In The Heart Of Texas," Copyright originally held by Melody Lane Publications, Inc. 1941. Copyright now held by MCA, 2440 Sepulveda Blvd., Suite 100 - Los Angeles, California 90064.

"Harry S. Truman" by Barbara Silberdick Feinberg, Franklin Watts Library Edition 0-531-13036-3

"Biographical Sketch of Harry S. Truman," the Harry S. Truman Library, Independence, Missouri

Coleen W. Cain's passion is to examine and show the truth behind the facts. With two more novels, *Glory After The War* and *All At Once*, in a brilliant tour de force, she reveals how Paula and her peers brought about the greatest revolution in America since 1776.

Ms. Cain's journalistic assignments have taken her across the country as newspaper reporter-photographer, editor, and also in writing radio commercials. More recently, over a period of two and one-half years, she became a foreign news correspondent from Beijing, PRC, when she wrote a weekly column for the Op-Ed Page of the Bellevue, Washington *Journal American.*

She is the instructor for *Writer's Tune Up,* a critique class at the North Bellevue Community/Senior Center. She makes her home on Lake Sammamish in Issaquah, Washington.